THE KINGS OF SWING

THE KINGS OF SWING

Behind the scenes with
South Africa's golfing greats

CRAIG URQUHART

ZEBRA PRESS

Published by Zebra Press
an imprint of Random House Struik (Pty) Ltd
Company Reg. No. 1966/003153/07
Wembley Square, First Floor, Solan Road, Gardens, Cape Town, 8001
PO Box 1144, Cape Town, 8000, South Africa

www.zebrapress.co.za

First published 2013

1 3 5 7 9 10 8 6 4 2

Publication © Zebra Press 2013
Text © Craig Urquhart

Cover images front cover © Gary Player & Louis Oosthuizen:
Wessel Oosthuizen/SASPA; Sally Little: Charles Knight/Rex Features/Inpra;
Retief Goosen: The Biggerpicture/Reuters; Ernie Els: Harry How/
Getty Images/Gallo Images; golf course: Fancourt South Africa

Cover images back cover © Nick Price, Papwa Sewgolum, Charl Schwartzel
& Trevor Immelman: Wessel Oosthuizen/SASPA; Bobby Locke: Alfred Pratt

All rights reserved. No part of this publication may be reproduced,
stored in a retrieval system or transmitted, in any form or by any means,
electronic, mechanical, photocopying, recording or otherwise,
without the prior written permission of the copyright owners.

PUBLISHER: Marlene Fryer
MANAGING EDITOR: Ronel Richter-Herbert
PROOFREADER: Sean Fraser
COVER DESIGN: Sean Robertson
TEXT DESIGN: Jacques Kaiser
TYPESETTER: Monique Cleghorn/
Monique van den Berg

Set in 10.5 pt on 15.5 pt Adobe Garamond

Printed and bound by CTP Printers, Duminy Street, Parow, 7500, South Africa

ISBN: 978 1 77022 632 6 (print)
ISBN: 978 1 77022 633 3 (ePub)
ISBN: 978 1 77022 634 0 (PDF)

Contents

Foreword	vii
Acknowledgements	ix
Introduction	1

1	The Maestro	15
2	The Black Knight	64
3	Papwa	93
4	The First Lady of Swing	122
5	The Comeback Kid	139
6	The Big Easy	162
7	The Goose	201
8	The Boy Wonder	221
9	Shrek	242
10	The Machine	269
11	A South African Tiger?	291

| References | 307 |
| Index | 309 |

For Priscilla, Kieran and Shane

Foreword

When you combine the strangest sport of them all with the strangest country of them all, it makes for a riveting story. It's no secret that South Africa's golfers have notched up numerous successes in global golf. Irrespective of our racial backgrounds, the careers of this country's leading golfers have always been intertwined.

Much has been written about Gary Player and the global anti-Apartheid movement. It is well documented that when he competed at the 1974 Australian Open in Sydney, protesters ventured onto one of the putting greens in the middle of the night and wrote "Go Home, You Racist Pig" in white lime powder. But there's more to the tale. After all, I was there, and I was also targeted by Australian racists, who referred to me as "smoke".

I remember standing on the tee at a par three – 178 yards from the pin – and they were saying things like, "The smoke won't get it over the water." I stepped back to recollect myself, and then hit I a 5 iron at the flag, two feet from the hole. I turned around and said, "This smoke can play."

When I won the French Open in May 1976, I drew inspiration from a well-worn newspaper clipping I carried in my pocket throughout the tournament. It told the story of Sally Little – a giant of a lady – who earlier that month had become the first South African female to win a Major in the United States when she triumphed at the Women's International in South Carolina.

The following month, our careers were overshadowed by the tragic Soweto uprising. Who would have thought that golf could have played a role in the lives of some of the country's liberation heroes? Take Andrew

Mlangeni, for example. This caddie-turned-cadre was one of the ANC operatives arrested at Liliesleaf farm in 1963 and then sentenced to life imprisonment after being found guilty at the Rivonia Trial. He subsequently spent 26 years on Robben Island with fellow struggle heroes Nelson Mandela, Walter Sisulu and Govan Mbeki.

Around the time of the Soweto uprising, Mlangeni found a couple of golf balls in the bush, the telltale proof that the prison warders played the sport (albeit on a bleak nine-hole links). For the remainder of his incarceration, Mlangeni kept those balls hidden in his cell as a symbolic memento of the fruits of freedom. Today, he is an active MP and the proud patron of the Andrew Mlangeni Green Jacket, an annual award presented to sports personalities who have achieved and contributed immensely to sport in South Africa and its ethos of excellence and social cohesion.

There are many, many wonderful golfing stories from these shores that have never seen the light of day – until now. After all, South Africa's chequered history and this sport are intertwined, and Craig Urquhart has succeeded in reflecting this in *The Kings of Swing*.

VINCENT TSHABALALA

Acknowledgements

The morning after Louis Oosthuizen stunned thousands of spectators at Augusta – and millions of television viewers around the world – with his beautiful albatross at the 2012 Masters, it dawned on me that there was a major story that needed to be told. After all, this small-town hero from Albertinia had become yet another local golfer, under the glare of the international spotlight, to serve notice that South Africa is firmly on par with the leading golfing nations around the globe.

I asked myself how a land with so few registered golfers could become such a dominant force in global golf, capturing more Major championships than any other nation outside of the United States. I wondered why golf is this country's most successful sport in terms of international successes. A *Sunday Times* survey conducted in July 2013 revealed that, of the nation's 20 top-earning athletes, the first four places went to Ernie Els, Louis Oosthuizen, Retief Goosen and Charl Schwartzel, with a combined income of R668 million for 2012. And so, over the past few months, I have embarked on an extraordinary journey to record the many memorable moments since Bobby Locke set the golfing world alight with his unorthodox but clinical style of play.

To all the golfers, their family members, caddies, coaches and friends who cooperated with me, many thanks. I am grateful to managing editor Ronel Richter-Herbert for overseeing this project. A special mention to the following for their assistance with my research: Alfred Pratt, Sherylle Calder, Denis Hutchinson, Tracy Korsen, Barry Cohen, Rajen Sewgolum, Grant Winter, Peter Sauerman, Grant Hepburn, Sally Fraser, Rob Rotella,

THE KINGS OF SWING

Vaughn Tucker and Bob Hackett. And a big thank you to David Swanepoel, Kanthan Pillay and Marc-Andre Lang for their considerable support.

CRAIG URQUHART

Introduction

When Louis Oosthuizen shredded his opponents at the hallowed Royal and Ancient St Andrews course to win the 2010 Open Championship (on Nelson Mandela's 92nd birthday), the global media crowned him "King Louis". At that moment, the gap-toothed South African could have been forgiven for paraphrasing King Louis XIV and declaring, "*Le tigre c'est moi* (the tiger is me)." After all, he had given Woods (who limped home in 23rd place) and the rest of the world's top players a lesson in golf.

Just under two years later, the unlikeliest of global sports stars was back in the headlines. It was Masters' Sunday at Augusta – the cathedral of golf – when he hit the sweetest 4 iron of all time to score the first televised albatross of the tournament. He may have finished runner-up to Bubba Watson (thanks to an equally dramatic snap-hook in the play-off), but no matter: the boy from Mossel Bay had become the darling of the global media, which conferred on him an extension to his title: "King Louis the Second".

With his coronation complete, the 27-year-old product of the Ernie Els Foundation became the symbolic figure of a new generation of young South African golfing royalty, which stretched back more than half a century to the time when Bobby Locke, "the king of the links", began his reign and served notice that South Africa could be a force in international golf.

Following in Locke's spike marks was Gary Player (with the *nom de guerre* Black Knight), who became the incontrovertible pretender to Locke's throne, as well as a global symbol of this land of apartheid.

And just two years after Player won his final Major, Sally Little (who carries the middle name Knight) set the world of women's golf alight by winning her first Major championship.

By virtue of winning one of the four finest individual golf tournaments on the planet – the Majors – these regal ambassadors have, for the most part, served the Motherland well. Today, almost without exception, there is a South African in contention on the back nine on a Major Sunday. Between 2000 and 2012 at the Masters, for example, there were six South African runners-up.[*] During the same period, there was a South African in the top 10 at every British Open Championship.

More recently, Englishman Justin Rose, winner of the 2013 US Open, has strong ties with South Africa. He was born in Johannesburg and his cousin, Rosalind, is married to Charl Schwartzel.

Of course, other nations can – and have – laid claim to their own golfing royalty. Not least Scotland, where the game of thrones took shape all those centuries ago. This after a regiment touring mainland Europe had adopted a Belgian pastime called *chole*.

The third parliament of King James IV had decreed in 1491: "It is statute and ordained that in a place of the Realme there be used Fute-ball, Golf or uther sik unprofitable sportis contrary to the common good of the Realme and defense thereof."

One of the early devotees was David, the great nephew of Duncan, who was, incidentally, murdered by Macbeth. He ruled from 1124 to 1153 and, some 300 years later, his great-great-great-great-great-great-great-great-grandson, James II, outlawed the sport, as he feared it was luring his subjects away from archery.

---

[*] Ernie Els (2000, 2004), Retief Goosen (2002), Tim Clark (2006), Rory Sabbatini (2007), Louis Oosthuizen (2012).

INTRODUCTION

The law was repealed in 1503, and in 1513, Henry VIII's first wife, Catherine of Aragon, noted (in a letter to Cardinal Wolsey): "All his subjects be very glad, Master Almoner, I thank God, to be busy with the golf for they take it for pastime."

In 1567, Mary Queen of Scots took it up and was spotted strutting her stuff "in the fields beside Seton" just days after her husband, Lord Darnley, was strangled near Edinburgh. She is credited for using soldiers (or cadets) to assist her, laying the foundation for the role of caddies in the sport. Sadly, her career was short-lived as a result of her beheading in 1587.

Six decades later, Charles I was playing golf when he was notified that the Irish Rebellion had begun in earnest (he may have finished his round, but he, too, was put to the sword). In 1834, William IV became patron of the St Andrews Golfing Society and, in return, bestowed the title of The Royal and Ancient (R&A) Golf Club of St Andrews, a title that is likely to stick for centuries to come.

At the turn of the 20th century, King Edward VII ordered that part of his land at Windsor should be converted into a golf course. His successor, King George V, did not share the same passion ("Golf always makes me so damned angry"), but Edward VIII won several medal competitions and recorded two holes-in-one (at Royal Wimbledon and Santos in Brazil). When he abdicated in 1936, he was succeeded by George VI, and there was reason to cheer. *Golf Illustrated* acknowledged the constitutional crisis by noting that "we are fortunate in having in the new king one who has been identified with golf almost as closely as his brother and who, had he had greater opportunities for constant practice, might have been a very excellent player".

Elsewhere, other royals embraced the game with varying degrees of success.

King Christian V of Denmark was gored to death by a stag on a golf course in 1670, while King Hassan II of Morocco survived an assassination attempt on one of his own courses in 1971. Twenty years later, Prince William, second in line to the British throne, received a skull fracture after being struck by a golf club at Berkshire's Ludgrove Preparatory School. He was rushed to hospital (with the Prince and Princess of Wales in the convoy), where he received 24 stitches.

When King Baudouin of Belgium was paired with Great Britain's Ryder Cup captain Dai Rees in a pro-am tournament at Gleneagles in 1959, a newspaper headline trumpeted, "The King and Dai".

Other royal golfers included Prince Felix of Luxembourg, King Leopold of Belgium, Prince Rainier of Monaco, the Shah of Iran and Princess Asaka of Japan. Closer to home, Lawrence Buthelezi, the cousin of Zulu prince Mangosuthu Buthelezi (great-grandson of King Cetshwayo kaMpande), was the first black South African golfer to qualify for the British Open, in 1970.

And let's not forget the United States, where the game mushroomed in the 20th century, thanks largely to two of the most formidable golfers of all time, who both carried the coveted nickname of "king" (albeit at different times).

First there was Arnold Palmer, who exploded onto the scene in the 1950s, and then Jack Nicklaus, who gradually reeled him in and then protected his throne against numerous challengers as he marched towards the highest number of Majors in history.

When Nicklaus won his 18th (and last) at Augusta on a golden afternoon in 1986, he was 46 years old, his son Jackie was his caddie, and he was competing against some players who hadn't been born when he secured his first title at the same course 25 years previously. There wasn't a dry eye in the house.

And spare a thought for the age-defying Tom Watson. The "King of Scotland" won his fifth Open Championship in 1983 and, 26 years later, at the ripe old age of 59, came within a shot of doing it again at the 2009 edition of the tournament at Turnberry.

INTRODUCTION

As a child growing up in South Africa in the 1960s, I gradually became aware that I lived in a country that, despite its enormous social problems, possessed a richness and diversity that could not be duplicated elsewhere.

Where else, for example, could two of the world's most formidable leaders have found themselves on the same battlefield on the slopes of a desolate hill on the same day? And where else could one dusty street produce two Nobel laureates or, for that matter, one forgettable rural town raise two of golf's Major winners?*

Whisper it softly, but never forget – this is a land like no other. A million expats who have left these shores for safer climes will testify that life just isn't quite the same. There is, after all, no tumult or *ubuntu* in their societies.

Consider this: when my American mother (who had met my father on a blind date in Milwaukee) touched down in Johannesburg for the first time in 1954, she said the air tasted like Champagne and she knew she would never leave.

With its dramatic highs – and desperate lows – some say the beloved country is bipolar. Yay or nay, there are considerable pressures that bubble away in these climes, creating a nation that has always punched well above its weight in the international arena.

After all, the evolutionary link between the early primates and modern humanity lived here; it carried out the world's first human heart transplant; it was the first to voluntarily dismantle a nuclear weapons programme: it defied all odds by lurching away from a full-blown race war and, through its Truth and Reconciliation Commission, provided a blueprint for other nations dealing with self-inflicted trauma; it raised a legless son who outran

---

* Both Winston Churchill and Mohandas Gandhi were present at the Battle of Spionkop in January 1900. Nelson Mandela and Archbishop Desmond Tutu both lived in Vilakazi Street in Soweto, while Retief Goosen and Charl Schwartzel both lived in Polokwane (formerly Pietersburg).

able-bodied athletes; its prisoner-turned-world statesman became a moral beacon for all humankind; and it recognised the wondrous talents of a washed-up and obscure musician named Sixto Rodriguez, who surfaced in the wastelands of Detroit and morphed into an international star.

Political activist and author Olive Schreiner once offered her take on a land that is the total of escarpments, plateaus, grasslands, deserts, wetlands, subtropical forests and two oceans that converge at the southern tip of the world's brightest continent: "If nature here wishes to make a mountain, she runs a range for five hundred miles; if a plain, she levels eighty; if a rock, she tilts five hundred feet of strata on end; our skies are higher and more intensely blue; our waves are larger than others; our rivers fiercer. There is nothing measured, small nor petty in South Africa."

The 1990s are remembered for the liberation of South Africa, the 1980s for the states of emergency, which prolonged the inevitable, the 1970s for the simmering unrest that signalled the beginning of the end of the National Party government, and the 1960s as a period of full-blown segregation, when blacks, coloureds, Indians and whites lived separately and unequally – the collective products of Prime Minister Hendrik Verwoerd's mad doctrine of apartheid.

The international community may have been outraged, but South Africa was sitting on some of the biggest mineral reserves on the planet and carried significant weight. As a result, more often than not, it made its own rules.

Case in point: During the darkest days of isolation, when the United Nations had labelled apartheid a crime against humanity and (most of) the civilised world had responded by implementing sanctions and snubbing the country's sports stars, Africa's so-called Major was born. In a glittering oasis in an ancient volcanic crater in the middle of a desolate and desperately poor *bantustan* (homeland), a magnificent Gary Player–designed championship golf course was carved into the Pilanesberg mountains.

INTRODUCTION

In 1981, Sun City found a way to ride the apartheid wave and announced that it would host the richest golf tournament on the planet – the Million Dollar Challenge. The world was livid, but some of the giants of the game, including Jack Nicklaus and Lee Trevino, came to the party. It was another South African solution for a South African problem.

For a white child growing up in this splendid, surreal and scarred society, the benefits were plentiful. And this is how life was when I found myself in the early 1970s at a bustling shopping centre in the leafy suburb of Rosebank, Johannesburg.

My father drew me close and whispered, "That's one of the greatest golfers of all time." It was a Saturday morning, and Bobby Locke loomed large. At the time, my father ran an electrical engineering company in the sprawling industrial area of Germiston – the same suburb where Locke was raised.

Poised somewhere between the magnificent career that had made him a household name around the world and the tragedies that would later cloud his legacy, "the Maestro" (for this youngster) appeared to carry an air of greatness. Dressed in a check jacket, tan trousers, a cap and a tie, he clearly relished meeting and greeting well-wishers.

One career ends and another begins. Locke may have been well into the back nine of his career, but young Gary Player, educated at Johannesburg's famous King Edward VII High School (a few years after my father), had grasped the baton with impeccable timing to keep South Africa's star shining in those, the darkest of days.

The King is dead ... long live the King!

While Locke conquered Europe with his four Open championships, Player went on to conquer the world. After all, Jack Nicklaus and Arnold Palmer were the two internationally recognised giants of the game until Player muscled his way into the grouping and became part three of the triumvirate, the so-called Big Three. The great English writer Peter

Dobereiner summed up Player's contribution when he said that the South African's feats could be compared to a middleweight winning a heavyweight title fight.

In 1978, my brother and I were finishing a round of golf in the Indian Ocean resort town of Plettenberg Bay when we spotted a short white man – dressed in black – surrounded by a group of black men on a ridge high above the first fairway. For an hour or so, we enjoyed a private audience with Player and the club caddies. It was shortly after his third (and final) US Masters victory and, by virtue of his supreme successes and the volatile homeland we shared, he had become one of the most controversial sports personalities in history.

Time and again, this 1.7-metre, 68-kilogram giant unfurled his swing and swept his torso through the ball with unspeakable grace and power. There was a crack as the missile launched into life and arched onwards and upwards, riding the winds and drawing a searing white streak across the bluest African sky, and hovering for what seemed like forever before fading, falling and landing dead centre on the fairway, some 280 metres away. It was a sight to savour.

The setting may have been sun-splashed, but these were dark and dramatic days. At that time, Player was probably the most recognised South African on the planet. Nelson Mandela – 15 years into his 27 years of incarceration – was certainly the most famous or infamous, depending on which side of the fence you were on, but, because images of him were outlawed in the land of his birth, he would remain an enigma for years to come.

Locke and Player may have grown up in the same country and, for that matter, the same city, but they were, in many ways, from different worlds. Both were multiple Major winners, and both endured harrowing hardships. It was how Player handled his that separated the two men so dramatically and ensured that Player would be the patron saint of

INTRODUCTION

South African golf for decades, en route to cementing his legacy as one of the greatest sports personalities of all time.

Player's career was intertwined with that of the Durban-born Indian Papwa Sewgolum, who became a worldwide symbol of the country's hated race laws when he was forced to receive a trophy outside a "whites-only" clubhouse. The images of this great man being presented with the Natal Open trophy under leaden skies in 1963 – the year of my birth – were flashed around the world, serving notice that something had to be done to tame South Africa.

This was the imagery of isolation and injustice that Bob Dylan growled about in "Hard Rain", the searing anthem that was penned just months earlier. A year after this infamous ceremony, South Africa was barred from the Tokyo Olympics (following a proposal by India) and, within a decade, was formally expelled from the International Olympic Committee.

Nick Price, who was born in South Africa in the 1950s before moving to Rhodesia as a youngster, carried the hopes of a freshly liberated country on his shoulders, but by the time he was firmly established as the top golfer on the planet, Robert Mugabe was well on the way to wrecking Price's adopted homeland.

Inevitably, the next country in line for liberation was powerhouse South Africa, where an army of hugely talented junior golfers was cutting its teeth.

Yes, with the dark veil of apartheid lifted following the release of Nelson Mandela and the unbanning of the African National Congress, South Africa rapidly became the darling of the international community. Never again would its sporting giants have to compete in the face of global revulsion.

Those heady days, as the country steamrolled towards the first democratic elections, saw the emergence of a generation of "born free" golfers, headed by Ernie Els.

Mandela was quick to embrace these sporting heroes and, when the Big Easy won the US Open just two months after the historic April 1994 elections, the global statesman was one of the first to call. And when Els won the Open at Royal Lytham 18 years later, the man with the dreamiest swing in all of golf paid a moving tribute to Madiba. Acknowledging that he had been part of a generation of millions of South Africans who had grown up in the apartheid era, and then endured the painful transition to democracy, Els said: "I just felt he's been so important for us being where we are today as a nation and as sportspeople."

Where Els and Retief Goosen – another two-time US Open champion – led the way as torchbearers of the new South Africa, others followed seamlessly.

Let's not forget that they all cast their giant shadows during a critical juncture in this country's history. After all, South Africa had limped through numerous political and social upheavals during the 1990s and 2000s, and frequently relied on its sports personalities to unite the nation and keep the flag flying high. Despite the severity of the country's problems, successes at the Rugby World Cup (1995 and 2007) and the African Cup of Nations (1996), for example, played a key role in galvanising the country as a force to be reckoned with on the world stage and restoring national pride.

As we salute these heroes, let's not forget that the odds have been stacked against them. The United States, for example, has more golf courses – and players – than most other countries in the world combined. It hosts three of the four Major tournaments, giving its own stars – from Gene Sarazen to Tiger Woods – a distinct home-ground advantage. For foreign tour professionals, competing in the US involves a great deal of long-haul flying and other problems associated with travel.

Player, for example, may have won just half of Nicklaus's 18 Majors, but for the most part, he did so in Nicklaus's "back yard". In terms of the Champions Tour (the senior version of the Majors), Player has the most titles, with nine (one more than Nicklaus). And with 163 victories around the world, the South African has won 63 more tournaments than Nicklaus.

The Black Knight, who is the most travelled sportsman in history (25 million air kilometres under his belt), has succinctly observed that he would have won "many more" Majors if he had lived in the States (and so say all of us). He added that the US does not have some divine right to produce the best golfers in the world. "Golf is played in other countries and other countries have many great players. I'm always ready to tackle anyone in my country."

One heavyweight who took up the offer was Sam "Slammin Sammy" Snead, who visited South Africa in 1947 as the reigning Open champion and the guest of that tournament's runner-up, Bobby Locke.

For several weeks, Snead was out of his depth as Locke – the crowd favourite with "home-ground" advantage – won 12 of their 16 matches. Snead, one of the longest hitters in the game, consistently found himself closer to the pins with his approach shots, but Locke, the greatest putter of his generation, found the heart of the hole with a single putt, while the American frequently had to settle for two.

Snead returned the favour by inviting "the man from the jungle" to America, and, as a result, golf in the land of the Stars and Stripes would never be the same again. As *The New York Times* noted: "Snead conferred no favours on himself or his brother professionals when he brought Bobby Locke back to America from South Africa. For since his arrival here, the dapper little man from Johannesburg has been a thorn in the flesh of the United States stars."

And the *Washington Post* wrote of a "well-stacked South African that is 29, looks 39, plays in plus fours and may be the best golfer in the world".

I asked leading American sports psychologist Rob Rotella, who has coached most of South Africa's Major winners, what the secret is to their success. His three-part answer: "You have the weather, your golfers were playing this game long before us, and they have a deep-rooted belief in themselves."

For the most part, this book excludes the hundreds of magnificent South African golfers who have won many local and international tournaments. My yardstick – winning at least one of the quartet of annual blue-chip tournaments – is an important one, because it has elevated these golfers to an extremely select group.

Acclaimed author John Feinstein noted that while winning a Major championship does not guarantee greatness, "not winning one guarantees that you will never be considered great".

As local legend Dale Hayes reflects on his career successes, he will recall that apart from dozens of victories, he was also the youngest winner on the European Tour when he clinched the 1971 Spanish Open at the age of 18. He has also beaten several Major winners, including Nicklaus and Player. But – and here's the rub – he never won a Major. "I could win the South African Open and even the Spanish Open, but I did not believe that I had what it took to win a Major."

He is not the only one. There are many magnificent South African golfers who achieved so much locally and abroad – short of a Major.

They include: Sid Brews (winner of the French and Dutch Open and second at the British Open – all in 1934 – and winner of the SA Open eight times in four decades), Ramnath "Bambata" Boodham (the first heavyweight golfer of colour who played in The Open, in 1929), Ishmael Chowglay (played in the 1962 Open with only six clubs after pros on the Non-European tour had held a card game to raise funds to pay for his flight), Bobby Cole (1966 British Amateur champion and runner-up to Tom Watson at the 1975 Open), Vincent Tshabalala (won the 1976 French Open carrying his own clubs), Harold Henning (70 career wins), Rory Sabbatini (tied second at the 2007 Masters), Tony Johnstone (won two

INTRODUCTION

SA Opens and the Professional Golfers' Association of America (PGA) Championship at Wentworth), Tim Clark (winner of the 2010 PGA Tour Players' Championship, which is unofficially regarded as the "fifth Major", David Frost (10 US Tours wins), Gavan Levenson (won the SA Open and two European Tour events) and Hugh Baiocchi (winner of 22 international tournaments).

South Africa has also produced a number of female champions.

Maud Gibb won the British Ladies' Championship in 1908, and she is considered the founder of organised women's golf in South Africa. Alison Sheard won the 1979 British Ladies' Open. And Sally Little, who won two Majors and numerous other championships, was South Africa's biggest female sports personality in her prime.

These pioneers have laid the foundation for the generation of youngsters – male and female – who are setting their sights on golf's greatest prizes. So much so that every week, around the world, there's invariably a South African flag on the leader board.

While this study focuses on South Africa's Major winners, there are two notable exceptions – Nick Price and Papwa Sewgolum.

Price may be a national of neighbouring Zimbabwe, but he was born in Durban and spent much of his golfing career in South Africa. Sewgolum – also Durban-born – who became a worldwide symbol of the injustices of apartheid, was hugely talented. It will never be known how far he could have taken his game in a just society, but his successes – locally and abroad – indicate that, in normal circumstances, he had a Major in him.

It's no secret that the past and present golfing heroes of this country, as well as thousands of instructors and administrators, are relishing the prospect of uncovering this country's first "black diamond" – a golfer of colour who has what it takes to go all the way and become a Major winner. This book also looks at the pool of talent that is doing so much to make a breakthrough in a sport that, apart from a few rare exceptions, has been dominated by whites.

In these pages, I write of South Africa's Major winners who have put their country on the sporting map and made golf the country's strongest sport (in terms of global successes). They represent the abundance of raw talent that exists and, most of all, of their deep desire to compete with the best in this glorious 600-year-old game.

This, then, is their story.

I

The Maestro

'One six-foot putt, for my life? I'll take Bobby Locke. I've seen them all, and there was never a putter like him.' – **Gary Player**

In bars, clubs and restaurants around the world, Bobby Locke was fond of celebrating his formidable successes with plenty of beer and his much-loved ukulele – a four-stringed banjo. To his fellow competitors, he would offer the following greeting: "Tell me about your round today, master, but please start at the 18th."

In his twilight years, he would invite up to 15 people to join his Saturday-morning four-ball, leaving the starters in a tangle when they all showed up. His favourite beverages were Pabst Blue Ribbon, Tuborg, Carlsberg and Castle Lager, and his signature tune was "Please don't talk about me when I'm gone". It was a futile plea, because South Africa's "king of the links" did so much for the sport – on and off the course – and his story has never been told.

Arthur D'Arcy Locke was born in Germiston, an industrial town on the south side of Johannesburg, on 20 November 1917.

Eighty years had passed since a group of Voortrekkers had set up camp on a ridge at an altitude of 1 800 metres above sea level. Flanked by gurgling streams, they named this region Witwatersrand (ridge of white waters). Unbeknown to them, they were also living above the so-called Cradle of Humankind, an archeological treasure with some of the oldest hominid fossils, including the 2.3-million-year-old *Australopithecus africanus* (nicknamed Mrs Ples). Professor Raymond Dart, who made the discovery, announced that southern Africa was "the cradle of Man". The thought that modern humans may have originated in Africa turned the stomachs of many a European.

For the next 50 years or so, the Cape's expats enjoyed Africa at its finest: breathtaking sunrises and sunsets, rich soil, an abundance of game and, of course, the finest climate on the planet. The winters were crisp and clear and the summers hot but dry. And on most afternoons, then as it is now, spectacular summer storms cleansed the earth.

While these *boers* relished the land around and the skies above, they were blissfully unaware of what coursed through the soil and rock below. In 1886, the honeymoon was interrupted when gold was unearthed on the farm Langlaagte on the outskirts of modern-day Johannesburg in the Transvaal – or the Zuid Afrikaansche Republiek (ZAR).* George Harrison and George Walker, who made the discovery, found themselves on top of the so-called Golden Arc, an enormous former inland lake where the sand and silt contained massive deposits of gold.

The word spread and, within months, a shantytown with thousands of inhabitants – prospectors, salesmen, publicans, moonshiners, preachers, con artists, clowns and whores – had taken root.

A decade later, this shantytown had become Africa's powerhouse, the richest gold-mining area in the world and a shrine to the fearless men who crushed the earth to release its precious cargo. Thousands of foreigners – or *uitlanders* – joined the party and, for one brief, shining moment, this was the centre of the universe.

---

* Twenty years earlier, diamonds – including the 83.5-carat "Star of Africa" – were discovered on the banks of the Orange River in the northern Cape, leading to a stampede.

Johannesburg, which rose from the reefs – the deep mineshafts below matched only by the towering buildings above, became the world's only major city not located next to a natural body of water such as a large river, lake or ocean. Nevertheless, it would also become the world's biggest urban forest, with 10 million trees towering over hundreds of parks, dams and golf courses.

In 1917, when Locke was born, South Africa was fighting in World War I on the side of the Allies. But peace was on the way and, until the Great Depression just over a decade later, it was boom-time for South Africa and many of its people.

Locke was raised "by my African nurse, Esther". She had difficulty pronouncing either Arthur or D'Arcy, so she nicknamed him Bobby because of his habit of bobbing up and down in his pram. The name stuck.

The suburb the Lockes lived in was surrounded by countryside and served as one of many satellites, like Kensington and Brakpan, around the rapidly growing city of Johannesburg.

The boy's first flutter with fame came at the age of six, when a visiting British film crew spotted him swinging a club in his garden and his mother gave them permission to film him. The grainy black-and-white documentary on South Africa was later screened at the Empire Exhibition at Wembley, outside London.

Locke's love of golf was largely influenced by his father, Charles James, a Belfast-born shop proprietor who had immigrated to South Africa in 1898, just in time for the Boer-versus-Briton spat that changed the country's political landscape forever. The family lived near the Germiston golf course, where Charles, a 14-handicapper, and Bobby's mother, Olive, with an 11 handicap, were active members. At the time, the 6 524-metre, par-75 course was formidable, with long, narrow fairways, while small bunkers protected well-manicured greens.

At home, in their lounge, the Lockes played a golf game called putt-holo, which entailed putting at a box with six arches of varying sizes.

At the age of four, Bobby began showing an interest in the game, and his first club was an "old-fashioned hickory-shafted jigger", which his father cut down for him. In his autobiography, *Bobby Locke on Golf*, he recalls: "A jigger was like a short-shafted putter with about a 5 iron loft on a narrow-faced head – designed for pitch and run shots from perhaps up to 20 yards [18 metres] off the green."

The young boy spent hours in his backyard attempting to putt balls into buried tobacco tins. By the age of eight, he was playing off a 14 handicap.

Reflecting on that period in his life, he noted that he always had the services of an African caddie, "who was paid one and three pence for 18 holes and no tip necessary".

When he was nine, one of the members at the Germiston Country Club saw Locke putting with a 2 iron, and gave him an old putter with a hickory shaft and a small, upright iron head.* It was a turning point for the young golfer, and it remained in his bag for decades. At the peak of Bobby Locke's career, this "trusty rusty" became arguably the most prized (and famous) putter in the world, ranking with Bobby Jones's famous "Calamity Jane". Locke would win 38 tournaments in South Africa, 23 in Europe and 11 in the US with that putter. Peter Alliss, who had five top-10 finishes at The Open, was once given the opportunity to try it out, and described it as "beautifully balanced... It seemed to want to swing truly and it almost had a will of its own."

Despite his precocious talent, Locke had difficulty controlling his temper. He later claimed that he was influenced by a World War I veteran

---

* In the 1930s, a set of hickory-shafted clubs consisted of a driver, brassie, spoon (wood), cleek, mid-iron, mashie-niblick, jigger and putter (all clubs had names, as opposed to modern-day clubs, which are numbered).

who had suffered serious injuries and would often "fly into a rage" on the course. When Locke once missed a one-metre putt, he flung the club into a tree near the 13th green. He realised his father had witnessed the incident, "and I felt about the size of a tee-peg". Later that day his father gave him a final warning: "If you think you are going to lose your temper, count to three." It marked a turning point in the teenager's life. Was this the lesson that led to the stony-faced, mask-like self-control he exhibited throughout his career?

Indeed, in the decades that followed, his rivals remembered how his facial expression never wavered. Birdie or bogey, his demeanour was always calm and steady, which was often unnerving for opponents fighting to maintain their composure. But that was later. As a teenager and then young adult, his slight frame and nervy manner were major obstacles that impeded his progress as a sportsman.

When he was 11, the Lockes moved to Brakpan, where they joined the State Mines Golf Club. Bobby spent most afternoons practising and playing at the club. He would later pay tribute to the course green keeper Gary Roberts, saying the magnificent condition of those greens had been vital in his formative years as a golfer.

Locke's swing was mostly acquired by reading Bobby Jones instruction books and magazine articles. His other hero was Walter Hagen, who once gave him some putting tips while visiting South Africa in the mid-1930s.

At the end of 1934, Locke collected his Standard 8 (Grade 10) certificate from Benoni High School and went to work as a clerk in the finance division of the Rand Mining House in Johannesburg (with a salary of £24 per month).

But his first love was golf, and it was evident that he had a promising future.

After all, he was blessed with a very relaxed grip that prevented the arm and shoulder muscles from tensing. While he was not one of the longest hitters, he was deadly accurate with both his driving and approach shots to the green. Thanks partly to the gusty winds that often sweep across Johannesburg and other parts of South Africa, Locke focused on keeping his approach shots low and hard.

He had a relatively narrow stance, but an enormous shoulder turn that created a dramatic right-to-left ball flight – the classic hook that most golfers dread. As the "Merry Mex" Lee Trevino once observed, "You can talk to a fade, but a hook won't listen." Locke was an exception. Butch Green, a close friend who studied his style for decades, told me that Locke's theory was, when you draw the ball, the fairways become twice as wide as the straight hitter, because by approaching the fairway from the right side, you could use the whole fairway to land the ball.

But exceptional circumstances called for exceptional shots. Dennis Bruyns, the CEO of the PGA of South Africa, recalls playing against Locke in the first round of the Western Province Open at Rondebosch Golf Club in a howling southeaster. He wondered how Locke would tackle a particular par-three hole with the wind blowing right to left with his natural right-to-left ball flight and a large pine tree guarding the right-hand side of the green.

"He aimed at the right half of the green and hit a controlled slice, holding it up into the wind, and it landed gently on the green. Incredible."

Peter Alliss, who played several matches against Locke, said his short game was amazing. He marvelled at how Locke's chip shots would invariably land "limply with virtually no bounce, fire or spring".

And, of course, on the rare occasions that he missed the green, his extraordinary putting would invariably save par. Indeed, at the height of his career, he was the world authority in putting. The winning formula, according to Locke, was incredibly simple: "I have a basic rule of thumb for greens of differing pace. On a fast green, I aim to hit the ball six inches short of the actual hole; on medium-paced greens, I putt to drop the ball just over the front lip of the hole; on slow greens, I putt firmly for the back of the cup."

He would visualise many of the subtle details of contour break and surface conditions – particularly which way the grass had been cut – before taking his stance. "Everyone examines greens, but only he knows what he is looking for," noted legendary putter Ben Hogan.

Locke would inspect the line of the putt, concentrating particularly on a radius of about one metre around the hole. "This is where the ball completes its run, and what happens here is going to make or mar the putt," he noted in his memoirs. "I give very special attention to the type and length of grass and to the contours in the immediate vicinity of the hole, gradually pulling together in my mind a clear picture of overall pace."

Once this information is processed, he would "marry the picture I get of ground contour to the picture I already have of the speed of the putt, until I form a clear mind's-eye view of the ball running across the green and into the hole".

In terms of his stance, he positioned the ball further forward than most, virtually outside of the left toe, and he also kept his right foot well back, which gave the appearance that he was aiming right of the target – much like his driving. He also said he never changed his mind once he had weighed up all the factors, including the strength and line of the putt.

Putts from within 20 metres were fair game for Locke, who managed to read the greens – uphill, downhill, small breaks, big breaks, mountain-side, bent grass – and draw his hickory-shafted gooseneck putter to an inch of its maximum arc and release the blade like an arrow. The slightly hooded club-face appeared to top the ball – with the blade square – at the moment of release.

Locke used his hearing as an important tool for judging his putts. The perfect strike of a putter, he recalled, created a "pinging" sound. At that moment, he knew it had the right momentum. If, on the other hand, the sound of the contact was duller – producing more of a thud – he knew the ball had missed the sweet spot and was doomed to die before the hole. He always emphasised the importance of keeping the head down and "dead still" during the stroke. He would retain that locked angle until the ball was well on its way, and only turn to gauge its progress as it neared the cup.

Locke used his putting "hooks" to effectively approach the hole. At the same time, he always tried to stop the ball at the moment it rolled over the hole, using the front and the two sides of the cup to guide or "pour" it in.

It is a style very different from most of the modern-day players, who attack the hole and try to use the back of the cup to stop the ball. When it's good, it's in, but when it misses, there is invariably a nervy clutch-putt remaining. The dreaded three-putt was something Locke rarely had to worry about. After one very rare moment when he missed a sitter to three-putt a hole, he drained a 15-metre putt the next hole. When questioned how he could have missed such an easy putt and, minutes later, sink such a difficult one, he remarked: "The second putt wasn't any tougher; it was just longer."

Alliss said Locke believed it was crucial to create topspin the moment the putter struck the ball to ensure that its path was pure. But analysts have refuted this, saying all putts momentarily leave the ground in the split second after impact, thereby starting their journey with backspin. Either way, it worked for Locke, and if there is a scientific answer to this riddle, it may be that Locke's method of "topping" the ball countered the inevitable backspin. This kept the journey of the ball as true as possible and, while it frequently looked like it would pull up short, it continued happily on its journey.

Rob Rotella, who caddied for Locke decades ago, said his style beggared belief: "If you go by the conventional wisdom about putting mechanics, all of his techniques were wrong." And yet former US Open champion Lawson Little described Locke as "the finest putter who ever putted in America", while Sam Snead told the *USGA Golf Journal* that he once witnessed Locke floating a 26-metre putt over three ridges and, when it got about eight metres from the hole, "he started tipping his cap – the ball rolled off the last ridge, curled towards the hole, and damned if it didn't fall into the cup".

Clark Hammond, the tournament supervisor of the American Professional Golf Association, described Locke as the most accurate golfer on the planet. Lloyd Mangrum, one of Locke's 1940s' tour rivals, said, "That son of a bitch Locke was able to hole a putt over 60 feet of peanut brittle." And Ronald Norval, who wrote a biography on Locke, said that to see him at his best "[was] to see cold-blooded, classical perfection".

Gary Player said that for many years he was unable to separate Locke and Arnold Palmer in terms of their putting abilities. Palmer, Player said, was so confident and so aggressive that he was capable of holing eight or nine birdie putts a round. At the same time, Palmer was capable of three-putting two or three times a round, which Locke never did. After all, Locke rather shot at the middle of the green and then snuggled his approach putts a few centimetres from the hole. Palmer, on the other hand, always shot for the flag, with the result that it was either fantastic or it ended in tears.

American journalist Al Barkow described a 30-metre putt by Locke at the 1972 Open at Muirfield: "He wiped misty rain from his glasses with a handkerchief as he walked all the way to the cup, kept pressing his feet in a kind of never-leave-the-ground tap dance to get the speed of the green as he peered down looking for grain, finally got to the ball and gave it that same grungy stroke. He rapped the ball to within two inches of the cup. Beautiful!"

And local golf scribe Dan Retief marvelled at the pace of Locke's putts: "He seemed almost not to be holding the club and the stroke appeared to be a mishit. The ball appeared to have no momentum at all, but somehow it rolled on and on before dropping into the cup."

The putting experience then and now could not have been more different. In Locke's day, the greens were invariably so slow and/or bumpy that the putting needed to be very wristy to get the ball to the hole. With today's magnificently manicured surfaces, the challenge for the modern professional is to nudge the ball on its way with a delicate, stiff-wristed stroke.

At the peak of his career, Locke's trademark grey flannel plus fours, white buckskin shoes and stockings, linen dress shirts with a knotted tie and white Hogan caps made him one of the most recognised sports personalities on the planet. He often said that the golf course was his office, which was why he dressed for the occasion: "I am a businessman when I am playing golf, and the course is my desk."

Sports writer Norman Canale wrote of Locke's stately progress down the fairways, which "bore the gait of an ageing archbishop".

Locke won the South African Open for the first of nine times in 1935. He was just 17. When his employer, Norbert Erleigh, sent him to London in 1936, he was given the opportunity to compete at The Open, where he won the Amateur Medal. The following year, he again finished as the leading amateur at Carnoustie.

It was during his stint in London that he met Leonard Crawley, one of the leading amateurs in the world, who became an invaluable mentor for the South African. Locke also became acquainted with the legendary Harry Vardon and won the Vardon Cup. The cherry on top was securing a respectable eighth place at that year's Open Championship.

He returned to South Africa in early 1937, but was sent back to the UK shortly afterwards as part of the first-ever Springbok golf team, which included Clarence Olander, Frank Agg and Otway Hayes (Dale Hayes's father).

In January 1938, Locke, who was still an amateur, beat the legendary Sid Brews, a professional, in the Transvaal Open in Pretoria, by three shots. When a friend shook his hand and noted, "You've got the publicity, and Brews has got the money," Locke knew he had to change course. His decision to turn pro marked a significant breakthrough for the game in South Africa. Golf historian and course architect Peter Sauerman said Locke enhanced the status of the professional golfer in this country.

Locke would not regret his decision, and his first professional win came weeks later, against Henry Cotton in the Irish Open at Portmarnock. He also celebrated his 21st birthday in New Zealand that year by winning that country's Open.

With dark clouds forming over Europe, Locke completed a golf tour in the UK in August 1939 and sailed home. He arrived in Cape Town on 2 September 1939, the day before World War II began.

Locke was appointed the club professional at Maccauvlei on 1 December 1939 (he had won the SA Open at that course the previous year). However, the relationship was strained from the start and, within three months, the committee raised concerns about Locke's plans to tour the country and give a series of golfing exhibitions. It said it was strongly opposed to a tour during his period of service to the club, and it also rebuked him for giving non-members lessons on the course as opposed to a practice tee.

At a special meeting on 5 May 1940, Locke was questioned about the terms of his employment. This after he had intimated that he planned to make a "quick trip" to America to play in the US Open. It was suggested that he was attempting to use the club as "a stepping stone" to travel for his own benefit. After just eight months, Locke resigned and, on 15 October 1940, signed up for the South African Air Force, the world's second oldest air force.

While Locke's four years and 362 days of service was no doubt invaluable and valued, the extent of his sacrifice depends on which version you believe – his or the official one.

After all, he claimed 1800 flying hours in his autobiography *Bobby Locke on Golf*, significantly more than his logbook, which reflects 1162 hours. His autobiography also claims that he spent his last 12 months "in the Middle East as a bomber pilot".

"Not so," says World War II historian Alfred Pratt, who "knew and respected" Locke throughout his career: "So much so that I made the enormous mistake of aping his putting technique in my formative years, and have had to take lessons to sort myself out even now." Pratt said he took an interest in Locke's war record "because I came to realise that many claims had to be mistaken. I set about tracing various sources, going back to the 50s, and paid even greater attention to *Bobby Locke on Golf*. Areas, which I had taken unquestioned through sheer loyalty and admiration earlier, suddenly took on a new significance, and it is now quite clear that some of the mistaken claims being broadcast originate from Locke himself."

In 1993, Pratt approached researcher Colonel Graham du Toit and obtained Locke's official military files from the South African Records Office in Pretoria.

For the record, Second-Lieutenant Locke (service number 103940) worked as an instructor and staff pilot in South Africa for most of the war. From 22 December 1944, he was seconded to the Royal Air Force Training School at Aqir, Palestine, for conversion training to heavy bombers, where he qualified as a co-pilot in April 1945. After a short spell of leave, playing some golf in Cairo, he received a posting to 31 Squadron (four-engined Liberator Bombers), based in the Fogia Group of Airfields in Italy.

Locke arrived there on 11 May 1945, three days after the Allies had formally accepted the unconditional surrender of the armed forces of

Nazi Germany, signalling the end of Adolf Hitler's Third Reich. The war in Europe was effectively over. Locke then served as a co-pilot and spent the following months helping to ferry men and materials from Italy to Egypt for repatriation to South Africa. For his efforts, he received three Service Decorations (the Italy Star, the 1939–45 War Medal, and the Africa Service Medal).

Although Locke kept most of his war experiences to himself, it was evident that the experience had changed him, both physically and mentally. Pre-war, he was tall and lithe, weighing in at around 55 kilograms. He returned from North Africa as a light heavyweight, tipping the scales at 80 kilograms.

Locke later recalled that the war had given him the opportunity to refocus on his priorities: "I resolved that if I survived, I would go back to golf, put all I had into it and make sufficient money to be able to retire by the time I was 40."

Pratt said that unlike many other South African war heroes, Locke did not appear to have suffered any injuries, either physical or psychological: "His mask-like countenance was contrived as part of his self-control on the golf course and was also useful that an opponent could never tell what he was thinking or whether he was ruffled."

Almost five years after he had signed up for the war effort, Locke was a civilian again and he successfully resumed his golfing career in South Africa in 1946. He acknowledged that he had put on a great deal of weight "and something drastic had to be done".

"I cut smoking and drinking, did morning runs and a lot of hard golf practice," he said.

Before the war, Locke was friendly with Bobby Bodmer, one of the country's finest golfers, who served as a Spitfire pilot and was killed in the Western Desert in September 1941. On his return from war duty, Locke then befriended Bodmer's brother Maurice, who had also fought in the war and had been appointed as the club pro at Cape Town's Clovelly Country Club.

Retail giant Raymond Ackerman, who has had a long association with the club, told me that Maurice Bodmer gave him a 2 iron to look after before he departed for his war service. "I still had the club when he returned, but he was a very different man and the war had [had] an effect on him. Also, he suffered from arthritis and had diabetic problems. But he and Bobby [Locke] connected and remained close friends for many years."

During the war, Locke had met Port Elizabeth resident Elizabeth Hester "Lilian" le Roux while he was stationed at the Tempe Air School in Bloemfontein. The couple married in January 1942 and, three years later, had a daughter, Dianne.

Locke took up a position as club pro at the Vereeniging Country Club and set his sights on the first post-war Open.

In the pre-war years, Sid Brews had dominated South African golf and had come closest to winning the Open Championship when he finished as runner-up to Henry Cotton at St George's in Sandwich in 1934. Cotton's 283 total tied the tournament record set by Gene Sarazen two years earlier.

The 1946 edition of the championship was staged at St Andrews, the home of golf, which dates back to around 1552 and is considered to be a site of pilgrimage for golfers the world over.[*]

This windswept spit of land is a traditional links, a Scottish word derived from the old English word *hlinc*, meaning "rising ground" or "ridge", traditionally located on a coastal area of treeless sand dunes. It marks the area between fertile land and the sea that remained when the ocean receded after the last Ice Age. Author Paul Zingg defines it as an

---

[*] It is a public course, owned by the Fife District Council, and is run jointly with the Royal and Ancient Club.

"obdurate landscape, spectacularly wild and beautiful, kettled and kamed, untillable, inimitable, and irresistible".

Others suggest that there is divine intervention in the formation of a true links. St Andrews, many a time, has been described as the only course designed by the Great Architect, while the rest were merely made by man. Similarly, Ireland's breathtaking Tralee course credits God for its creation and Arnold Palmer for its design.

Alister MacKenzie, the creator of Augusta National, said the so-called golf architect simply wishes to produce the old ideas as exemplified in the old natural courses, "which were played on before overzealous committees demolished the natural undulations of fairways and greens and made the greens like lawns for croquet, tennis or anything except golf, and erected eyesores in the shape of straight lines of cop bunkers instead of emphasising the natural curves of the links".

Locke qualified easily. In near-perfect conditions, he set the course record (69) largely thanks to seven one-putt greens. But, in the second round, the weather turned and he scrambled home with a 74 in strong winds. The weather worsened further during the third round and he reached the clubhouse with a 75, three shots off the lead.

On the final day, he started three behind, but his putting let him down. He three-putted the 15th, 16th and 18th (his only three-putts of the entire tournament), effectively wrecking his chances, and he finished on 76. Sam Snead, who had entered the tournament at the last minute, made a late charge to win by four shots over Locke and Johnny Bulla.

Although Snead would never be a serious contender at The Open again, he went on to win three Masters and three US PGA championships (and finished runner-up four times at the US Open).

His Open victory set up a dream tour back in South Africa. With a guaranteed purse of $10 000, Snead agreed to play a series of exhibition matches against Locke, the runner-up.

Within the course of a year, the world had changed dramatically and a new order was rapidly taking shape. The year 1946 marked the first meeting of the United Nations General Assembly (in London), the disbanding of the League of Nations, Italy abolishing the monarchy, the launch of bikinis in Paris, the sentencing of 12 Nazi leaders to death in the Nuremberg trials, the birth of Jimmy Buffett, George W. Bush, Freddie Mercury and Donald Trump, and South Africa being placed on the agenda of the UN for the first time to answer for its treatment of its Indian population and its illegal occupation of South West Africa (now Namibia).

Also in 1946, a dynamic young lawyer named Nelson Mandela moved into a house on Vilakazi Street, Soweto ("the centrepoint of my world, the place marked with an X in my mental geography"),* from where he began to change the course of African history.

On 10 February 1947, Sam Snead arrived in a racially segregated society where the white minority enjoyed the highest standard of living on the continent and the black majority remained disadvantaged by almost every standard. Within a year, the National Party would sweep into power with a policy that would enforce the institutionalised segregation (or apartheid) of the entire population.

When Snead touched down in Johannesburg, he entered a world of LM Radio, trams, bioscopes, Herman Charles Bosman, white tennis balls, Bing Crosby, pennywhistles, *mampoer*, John Orrs, Pall Mall cigarettes, Sophiatown, the Rand Club and persimmon-wood golf clubs.

"Slammin' Sammy" was widely regarded as the best golfer in the world at the time, and a crowd favourite. American writer Jim Murray said the kind of person who would miss the opportunity of watching Snead play "would pull the shades driving past the Taj Mahal".

---

* From his autobiography, *Long Walk to Freedom*.

Snead was sandwiched between the recently retired Byron Nelson and the rising star Ben Hogan, and most agreed that The Open champion had the most perfect swing on the planet, an asset that eventually saw him notching up a record 82 PGA Tour events, including seven Majors.

Like Locke, Snead recognised the importance of money – and putting. "Keep a close count of your nickels and dimes, stay away from whisky, and never concede a putt," the folksy American was fond of saying. But on South African soil, he was no match for the homeboy, who won 12 out of their 16 matches.

The series marked a significant turning point in Locke's career.

Golf writer Henry Longhurst once noted that if you get the yips, you die with the yips, and there were times when Snead appeared to become infected by that dreaded putting disease during the tour. He conceded that he was so overwhelmed by the sight of Locke draining long putts that it impacted on his own performance. "He made me so nervous that, in one match, I missed eight putts of less than two feet," he later recalled.

Almost overnight, Locke appeared to have found the belief in himself; he now knew that he could compete on the global stage. And after licking his wounds, Snead subsequently invited Locke to register for the PGA Tour in the US.

The South African arrived in the US in April 1947, well after the golf season had kicked off. Nevertheless, he quickly found his rhythm. The first tournament was the Masters, where the Americans were anxious to see the man who had "whacked" their homeboy.

"The course was a vivid green, the people were gaudily dressed, the atmosphere bristled big-time golf," he later recalled.

Locke said he found himself "overawed", and paired with his childhood hero, Bobby Jones. The South African said he had "read and reread" Jones's 1931 autobiography detailing his Grand Slam (British Open, British Amateur, American Open and American Amateur).

Locke, who was playing with the larger American ball for the first time, said the experience was "utterly different". Nevertheless, he beat Jones and Byron Nelson in the third round and Jimmy Demaret in the final round to finish in a respectable 14th place.

Locke then raised many eyebrows in his next five tournaments, finishing first (the Carolinas Open), first (Houston Open), third (Fort Worth), first (the *Philadelphia Inquirer*) and first (Goodall Round Robin). He would later say that his 10-metre putt for birdie on the 15th against Ben Hogan at the Cedarbrook Country Club in Philadelphia was the finest of his career. The putt so unnerved Hogan that his game unravelled, and Locke went on to win by four strokes the following day.

His seven victories in the US that year set a record never achieved before (or since) by a foreign golfer. During his whirlwind tour, he pocketed $25 000, almost as much as Demaret, the leading earner, who took home $28 000. When a reporter asked Locke whether he had any difficulty adjusting to the game in the land of the Stars and Stripes, South Africa's not-so-humble export replied: "Ah yes, I very nearly lost four of the first five tournaments I played in."

For the most part, the Americans warmed to the affable South African with the cheery smile and superb manners (tipping his cap to any applause). And, significantly, the US media also took a liking to the unusual African import.

After a tournament victory in Maryland in 1947,[*] Locke was called up to give a victory speech, and he asked the band to play the tune – two verses and two choruses – of the hit "Sioux City Sue". He replaced the title with "Sue Sammy Snead" and received a standing ovation (and, shortly afterwards, got a call from the legendary Bob Hope, asking him to appear on his popular television show).

---

[*] The National Capital Open.

The *Washington Post* described Locke as "golf's new drawing card". *The New York Times* took it further by noting that Sam Snead had conferred no favours on himself or his "brother professionals" when he decided to bring Locke back to America, "for since his arrival here, the dapper little man from Johannesburg has been a thorn in the flesh of the United States stars".

During his two-and-a-half year stint in America, from 1947 to 1949, the South African secured 11 victories from 59 starts and finished runner-up on 10 occasions. In 1948, he won the Chicago Victory National by 16 strokes, which remains a PGA Tour record for margin of victory (tied with J. Douglas Edgar's win in the 1919 Canadian Open).

Locke always needed money – lots of it. "Drive for show and putt for dough," was his famous trademark. When an American professional commented about Locke's weak left-hand grip, the South African agreed, but responded by saying: "I take the cheques with my right hand."

In 1947, *Time* magazine said that at the mention of cash, Locke's "ears sharpen to a point" and "when there is money in it, Locke is willing" (so much so that he once tried to charge a reporter for an interview).

During that period in the States, Locke's game developed dramatically. He learnt to attack the pin with fairway irons and from the bunkers and developed a killer instinct – that ability to finish off an opponent the moment he shows signs of faltering.

Locke spent a great deal of time in Vermont, where he took a liking to a Canadian-born woman, Mary Fenton, who was the daughter of a local judge. She had studied at Wellesley, an upmarket college in Massachusetts and, during World War II, had served as a data analyst in the Strategic Services Department. When she met Locke, who was playing at an exhibition match in Burlington in 1947, she was employed at the Central Vermont Public Services Corporation. There was the not-so-small factor of Locke already being married, but he told Fenton to wait for him. And wait she did.

During those heady days, his course of choice was Vermont's Rutland Country Club. Bob Hackett, who has lived in the city for most of his life, recalls the day he first set eyes on the South African. "I walked around the corner [of the clubhouse] and saw a very unusual golfer. His shoes were white, his socks were white, his trousers were white, his shirt was white and his cap was white. He looked like a baker, but then it dawned on me that it was Bobby Locke."

They became good friends, and Hackett says Locke loved his golf, and "loved his beer even more".

As a teenager caddying at the club, Rob Rotella was given the opportunity of studying Locke's game while carrying his clubs. Rotella, who would become a consultant to many of the leading golfers in the world, "including most of the South African heavyweights", said it took a while to figure Locke out, not least because of his dress and demeanour. Although they identified him a mile away, Locke's plus fours, long-sleeved shirt and tie were now out of fashion. And, Rotella recalls, he was a slow starter. On most days he would only arrive at the course at around 10 a.m., hit a few wedge shots and then amble on to the tee.

Rotella said he recalled "shagging" balls for Locke and using a baseball glove for easy collection. As a crowd gathered and Locke knocked a few balls with a 7 iron, Rotella raced around the fairway, "heroically" retrieving the balls before the second bounce. But the Maestro was not amused.

He summoned Rotella, addressed him as "Master Bob", and then admonished him. "He reminded me that this was his show and not mine and that I should move into position much quicker, because the shot would invariably end up in the same place every time. He said the idea of the exercise was to make him look good."

There were no hard feelings, and Rotella recalls that Locke was a joy to watch on the course "and a lot of fun in the clubhouse afterwards".

But not everyone liked Locke, and there were rumblings within the tour ranks that he was becoming a real threat to their prize money. Organisers claimed that there was a dispute over playing commitments, and Locke did fail to pitch up and compete in tournaments he had committed to.

However, there is another school of thought – that Locke was sidelined because of growing resentment from other PGA players, who felt he was raining on their parade. Most agreed that the only player who could match him at that time was Ben Hogan. "That bastard was too good for us – we had to ban him," 1948 Masters champion Claude Harmon* told veteran South African golf commentator Denis Hutchinson. Locke fuelled the issue by taking aim at the PGA, describing its refusal to let him compete as "a lot of damned nonsense".

He then set his sights on the 1949 Open and arrived in London at the end of June. The tournament was scheduled to be played at Deal, but the course had not recovered sufficiently from the years of wartime neglect, and it was moved to Royal St George's.

A half a century earlier, William Laidlaw Purves had found himself at the top of the Clement's church tower in a town called Sandwich and observed: "By George, what a place for a golf course." Located between the Stour Estuary and the English Channel, it was founded in 1887 and named after St George, a Roman soldier who was beheaded in 303 for his religious views.

Golf writer Bernard Darwin observed that it was golf's finest coastal offering: "As nearly my idea of heaven as is to be attained on any earthly links." More recently, 2012 Open winner Darren Clarke was less complimentary, claiming there are "no real landing areas on the fairways".

---

* Harmon's son, Butch, served as the acclaimed swing coach for Tiger Woods and, later, Ernie Els.

On the eve of the tournament, Locke faced a crisis of sorts when he began spraying his putts and misjudging their length. The problem was resolved when British professional Norman Sutton, who was watching Locke on a practice green, suggested that he might be holding the putter too tightly and restricting the swing. "I immediately loosened my grip, the ball started to run beautifully, and my putting confidence returned."

Under clear skies, Locke launched his assault on Sandwich, which was playing fast because of a lengthy drought. He began magnificently, firing a 69, but followed that by a 76 after a cold front with northwesterly winds moved in. A 68 in the third round gave him a share of the lead with Harry Bradshaw and Max Faulkner.

The tournament will always be remembered for one of the most bizarre incidents in this, the strangest of all sports. Bradshaw was playing steady until the 411-metre fifth hole – he had parred the first four holes – when his tee shot sailed into the tufty semi-rough to the right of the fifth fairway. When he waded through the tangled gorse, he found his ball nestled against a broken beer bottle – a pig of a lie.

He was unsure whether he would be permitted to take a free drop – there were two conflicting rules and, in those days, there were no referees (with golf carts, rule books and two-way radios) in sight. And Bradshaw had every reason to be wary; he had been disqualified from his previous tournament for accidentally playing a competitor's ball.

Interestingly, there was a similar incident at the South African Open in 1905, when George Fotheringham was forced to play his ball, which was lodged in a ginger-ale bottle, at the Bloemfontein Golf Club.

Decades earlier, American legend Bobby Jones had observed that golf is the closest game to the game we call life: "You get bad breaks from good shots; you get good breaks from bad shots – but you have to play the ball where it lies."

The first rules of golf (penned by the Gentlemen Golfers of Leith in

1744) addressed this issue: "If a Ball be stop'd by any Person, Horse, Dog or anything else, The Ball so stop'd must be play'd where it lies."

Over the next two centuries, the rules were modified and expanded, and the issue was addressed somewhat differently. Rule #6 stated: "A ball must be played wherever it lies", but another (#11) said that with regards to the removal of obstructions, "a flag-stick, guide post, implement, vehicle, bridge, bridge planking, seat, hut, shelter or similar obstructions, may be removed...without penalty".

There was no mention of beer bottles and, in those sobering times, the common refrain was that, when in doubt, "play it as it lies". Which is what the young Irishman did. Armed with a sand wedge, he closed his eyes ever so tightly and crushed the shot with all his might. The results were mixed – he destroyed what was left of the bottle, but was only able to work his ball about 20 metres up the fairway.

The incident rattled him, and it took another two shots to reach the green, where he finally holed out in six – a very unwelcome double-bogey. He subsequently finished the round in 77 and closed the championship with 283.

Not far behind, the South African was stalking that score. At the 16th, Locke knew he needed to shoot no more than 11 on the final three holes to draw level with Bradshaw.

But a bogey at the short par three threatened to wreck his chances.

It was at that moment that he recalled a comment from an American he had befriended during the war: "Bobby, where there's life, there's hope." Harold Marting was well qualified to offer this advice. A pilot in the RAF's Eagle Squadron, he was shot down over North Africa, captured by the Italians, flown to Athens, and handed over to the Germans. He then escaped in a fishing boat and crossed the Mediterranean and, although he made it back to Africa, he spent two months recovering in hospital, during which time he penned the recommendation in a letter to Locke.

The 385-metre, par-four 17th fairway was extremely difficult to hit with all its swales (it has since been widened), but Locke fired a magnificent 6-iron approach to five metres from the pin. With 8 000 spectators surrounding the green, he sank that putt and headed for the 18th (a 403-metre, par four), where par would secure a tie and a 36-hole play-off. Again, Locke hit a superb approach that took him to the edge of the green. His 18-metre putt nestled under the flag, just 60 centimetres past the hole, which he knocked in for par and a play-off.

That night, Bradshaw's dreams no doubt centred on that beer-bottle moment, and his challenge came to an ignoble end the following day.

They began the play-off in sweet tandem, halving the first four holes, but the fifth tripped Bradshaw again when he missed a short putt. Locke took control and had a seven-shot lead after the first 18 holes, and added another five in the final round.

It may have been an anticlimax, but the result was huge. For the first time, the Open Championship was heading south of the equator. There was small consolation for Bradshaw when the R&A added a clause to Rule 11, whereby a ball could be removed from "any artificial object placed or left on the course". It was, however, too little, too late – he would never be in contention for a Major again.

While South Africa – and the rest of the world – marvelled at the new Open champion, who was now £300 richer, the American PGA put an end to the celebrations a few days later when it barred him from competing in any tournament it controlled in the US. Committee spokesman George Schneiter stated that its unanimous decision was deemed necessary "because of his failure to keep commitments at exhibitions and tournaments". It noted that Locke had on numerous occasions violated the PGA tournament regulations as well as the tournament players' agreement he had signed. It added that the sanction was necessary "to protect sponsors and to maintain the tournament schedule".

By making the announcement just days after Locke's extraordinary Open triumph, the PGA came under a great deal of criticism, particularly since Locke had just been appointed captain of the British PGA.

In defending the committee's actions, Schneiter said that "numerous complaints" had been filed against Locke, but he refused to reveal the identity of the complainants.

In the 30 months that Locke had toured in the US, he had pocketed around $60 000 in prize money alone, an absolute fortune in those days. As leading sports reporter Grantland Rice (writing in the *New York Sun*) noted: "Locke made the mistake of winning too many tournaments. He was taking away entirely too much money."

There was another twist to this saga. Locke received an invitation from the legendary Bobby Jones to compete at the 1950 Masters. In March – a month before the tournament – the PGA announced that it would remove his ban if he apologised for his failure to honour his playing commitments.

However, Locke was now in the driving seat. He had secured a deal to serve as a global ambassador for Dunlop, which meant he was no longer reliant on appearance fees.

Twenty-seven years had passed since The Open was played at Troon, a 6 020-metre, breathtaking, rugged links on Scotland's Ayrshire coast. The course that boasts the longest and shortest holes in Open Championship golf held fond memories for British fans after Arthur Havers had ended a string of American victories there in 1923.

At 3–1, Locke was the firm favourite, but he had one obstacle to overcome: over the previous 20 years, no champion had ever retained The Open title. With more than 250 entrants from around the world, it had become a truly global event.

In the qualifying round at Lochgreen, Locke shattered the course record with a 68. During the second qualifying round (at Troon), he posted a more subdued 74, to book his place with the other 92 finalists. In The Open proper, the fairways were baked hard and running fast, and Locke used his famous brassie to good effect, hitting the fairways consistently.

The greens were, in Locke's words, the finest he had ever putted on and, not surprisingly, his rusty putter was white-hot. He shot a 69 in the first round to end one shot behind Arthur Lees.

The following day, under leaden skies, Locke shot a 72. Day three's 70 put him jointly in the lead with Dai Rees and Roberto De Vicenzo.

On the final day, with a crowd of 10 000 following the drama, Fred Daly, who had won the championship three years earlier, shot a 69 and a 66 for a total of 282, leaving him level with Rees, who finished with a 72 and a 71. De Vicenzo finished one shot ahead, with Locke chasing the title and about 20 000 spectators trailing after him.

Apart from missing a 1.3-metre putt at the 12th, the South African was playing beautiful golf and, after saving par at the treacherous 17th hole, had the luxury of needing just a bogey at the par-four 18th. He parred that hole, and with a total of 279, had become the first man in history to break 280 at an Open Championship. It was the golfing equivalent of the sub-four-minute mile. In addition, he had become the first man to win consecutive Opens since Walter Hagen (1928/29) and Bobby Jones (1926/27).

And yet, not everyone was impressed. UK scribe Fred Pignon, writing for the *Daily Mail*, noted that while Locke was the best in the field, there was something "impersonal" about him: "There was no great enthusiasm about his success. It was so inevitable, so matter of fact, that he failed to arouse the crowd. He had his full share of applause, but there was something lacking – he was not the popular hero." Sour grapes, or an interesting insight into the psyche of a flawed hero?

Either way, in his post-tournament speech on the steps of the Troon clubhouse, Locke claimed his career successes had helped him turn the corner ("I was a naughty boy once, but I'm a good boy now"). He also acknowledged that the magnificent condition of the greens at Troon had complemented his putting and, for many years, he sent a Christmas card to the Troon committee with the same message: "Best wishes for this year and the future. Still the best greens in the world."

With two Majors on his résumé and plenty of prize and appearance money from the US and UK, Locke was able to purchase a cottage and apartment block in the then trendy suburb of Yeoville, bordering Hillbrow. Founded in 1890 on a ridge just north (some would say not north enough) of Johannesburg by Scottish developer Thomas Yeo Sherwell, Yeoville became a cultural melting pot with its own set of rules, particularly with regards to race-related matters.

Locke's Yalta Court was named after the Ukraine City where Churchill, Roosevelt and Stalin had signed their World War II treaty. The building on the corner of Hendon and Harley streets consisted of 18 apartments and accommodation for 14 servants in small rooms on the fourth floor. The block, which enjoyed breathtaking views of the Johannesburg skyline, was constructed during the post–World War II building boom, and Locke was able to pay for it with the winnings from his first stint in the US. There was a two-bedroomed cottage on the property, which Locke named Sandwich (after the town where he clinched his first Open victory), and he used this as his primary residence, while his parents stayed in Yalta Court for the rest of their lives.

Locke returned to the US in 1951 after his ban was lifted, where he made a strong challenge at the US Open at the Oakland Hills Country Club. The tournament was won by Ben Hogan, who secured his second straight national championship and his third US Open overall. Hogan did it by shooting 67 – the best score of the tournament – in the final round in tough conditions. He famously observed: "I'm glad I brought this course, this monster, to its knees." Runner-up Clayton Heafner shot the only other sub-70 round of the tournament with a final-round 69. Locke took the third-place honours. In the four-year period between 1947 and 1951, he also secured another third-place finish and two fourth-place finishes.

In 1952, the Open Championship returned to Royal Lytham for the first time since Bobby Jones's famous victory in 1926.

The international challenge was led by Locke, Peter Thomson, Antonio Cerda and Norman von Nida. Ireland's Fred Daly took an impressive lead with opening rounds of 67 and 69, with Locke four shots behind and Thomson a further stroke behind him.

The night before the final round (on a Saturday, back then), Locke made the most of the occasion by entertaining guests with his ukulele and a singalong at a Blackpool pub, about 10 kilometres from the course. At 7.45 a.m. – one hour before he was due to tee off – he strolled to a private home near the hotel to get his clubs, which were locked in a car that was locked in the garage.

When he discovered that the garage door was bolted, he rushed off to try to track down the home owner, who was not around at the time. "I found a milk-delivery man, enquired where the garage owner was and was told he would be arriving at about nine o' clock and that he lived 15 minutes away," Locke recalled in his book, *My Golfing Life*.

Locke jumped on the cart, gave the milkman 10 shillings and instructed him to drive to the owner's other house.

Locke arrived at the course just in time to walk on to the first tee "with no time for a few loosening swings". Despite feeling "really strung up", the South African settled down to business quickly and holed a nine-metre birdie putt at the first.

The crowd grew to 10 000, and Locke was cautioned for slow play. With a strong westerly wind, the course was in a mean mood and Daly faltered badly, giving Locke and Thomson a shot at the title. Locke shot a superb 74 and 73 (two rounds were played on the final day) to overhaul Daly. Locke's winning total was 287, one shot ahead of Thomson, who ended at 289. Locke had joined Harry Vardon and James Braid as the only group of golfers who had won The Open three times in four years. Soon afterwards, he was honoured when a wax statue of his likeness was unveiled at Madame Tussauds.

Despite his heady successes, the travelling took its toll, and his wife Lilian carried the unenviable title of the "world's best-known golf widow" in the media. Shortly before the Johannesburg Magistrate's Court granted her a divorce on the grounds of "desertion" in 1952, she expressed her frustration in a media interview: "It's very lonely with Bobby away so often. It's been like this for the last eight years." The court granted her custody of their only child, Dianne, who was just seven at the time. (Locke reportedly never saw his daughter again, and Lilian, who severed all contact with Locke's family, later remarried.)

The 1957 Open was scheduled to be played at Scotland's Muirfield, but was switched to St Andrews at the 11th hour after Egypt's Colonel Nasser nationalised the Suez Canal Company, which led to an invasion by Britain and France and the subsequent loss of oil supplies and the introduction of petrol rationing. Because of Muirfield's remote location, it was decided that St Andrews would be a much more viable location, as it was connected to all the major centres by railway.

The chunky Locke arrived at St Andrews bruised because he had failed to make the cut the previous year, and there was now also the not-so-small matter that a contender for his throne had surfaced in Johannesburg, of all places. Uneasy lies the head that wears the crown, warned Shakespeare, and young Gary Player was turning heads everywhere. By the mid-1950s, he was somewhere in between the kid who could play a little and Locke's likely successor as South Africa's global superstar.

Peter Thomson, who had won the second of his three-in-a-row titles over the Old Course just two years earlier, was the favourite and was again in contention. After three rounds he was tied second with Eric Brown, three shots behind Locke, who had completed his morning round in 68. This was the first championship in which the leaders went out last, but they were still playing the two final rounds in one day.

It was only at the 16th hole in the final round that Locke learnt that Thomson, his closest competitor, had finished on 282. Pars on the final three holes would give him the championship. Spurred on by thousands of spectators and hordes of reporters and photographers, Locke parred the 16th and 17th and, at the last, found himself just 118 metres from the pin with his piercing drive.

His approach – an 8 iron – floated in from the right (as usual), pitched onto the ample bosom of the soft and receptive green, and settled just 60 centimetres from the cup. His ball was directly in the line of playing partner Bruce Crampton, whose challenge had faded, and Locke marked it and moved the marker two putter-heads off the line. All in order, until the champion-elect, clearly distracted by the seething excitement, replaced his ball in front of the marker – and not in its original spot, two putter-heads away. He missed the putt, but made sure with the second and took a bow, relishing the fact that he had become the first person since Walter Hagen in 1929 to win The Open four times.

At the prize-giving ceremony, he serenaded the crowd with a song, blissfully unaware that trouble was brewing. After all, on the 18th green, which serves as the High Altar of the spiritual Mecca of the game, the most famous course of them all, beneath the grey stone clubhouse that doubles as the sport's headquarters and ancestral home, a flip-wedge away from the intersection of Golf Place and Links Road, under the gaze of St Andrew, the patron saint of golf and where, incidentally, the rules and regulations of the game are penned, Locke had violated Rule 20-7c. And, for the first time, all the drama was being broadcast live on television.*

You couldn't make this up.

Someone – it is unclear whether it was a spectator or one of his challengers – had notified the rules officials and television footage confirmed the glaring error. The golfer who stood to gain the most was Peter Thomson, who would be the champion if Locke was disqualified.

Would Locke be censured? Could he lose his title? Stranger things have happened in this, the most fickle of all sports.

In 1968, for example, Argentina's Roberto De Vicenzo, the winner of the 1967 Open Championship, would enter the final round of the Masters two strokes behind the leader, Gary Player. The reigning Open champion fired a seven-under 65 to finish at 277 through four rounds, forcing an 18-hole play-off with Bob Goalby the next day. Or so he thought. On the 17th hole, De Vicenzo made a birdie three, but playing partner Tommy Aaron, who was keeping his opponent's scorecard, recorded it as a four.

With all the hysteria and the green jacket within reach, De Vicenzo signed the incorrect scorecard, meaning he had to take the higher score at that hole.†

That gave him a 66 rather than the 65 he actually shot, and gave the Masters title to Goalby. "What a stupid I am," was his memorable reaction. Fellow professional Jimmy Demaret observed that 25 million television viewers had witnessed the 17th-hole birdie "and I think that would hold up in court".

As four-time Major winner Ray Floyd once noted, "They call it golf because all the other four-letter words were taken." Forty years later, the

---

* The Open was filmed from 1955, but only the highlights were broadcast.
† According to the rules of the game, "no alteration may be made on a card after the competitor has returned it to the Committee. If the competitor returns a score for any hole lower than actually played, he shall be disqualified. A score higher than actually played must stand as returned."

hurt was still evident when De Vicenzo was interviewed by *Golf Digest* magazine: "For me, the [1968] Masters hasn't ended. Technically, the ending was legal. But there is something missing. The winner hasn't yet emerged. It lacks an ending. Someday, maybe in another place, it will be decided."

South African/Rhodesian star Denis Watson was left to rue the couple of seconds that may have cost him a US Open title at Oakland Hills, Michigan. It was 1985, and Watson missed the chance to force a play-off, having incurred a two-stroke penalty earlier in the tournament incurred on the 8th hole in the first round, after he had waited longer than the permitted 10 seconds for a six-metre putt, which sat trembling on the lip of the hole. The ball did (eventually) drop, but the birdie was disallowed and the penalty strokes added.*

Incidentally, the United States Golf Association (USGA) and R&A, the sports-governing bodies, have since amended the penalty for this rules infraction to just a single stroke. It was a career-altering error for Watson, though, who never found himself in contention at a Major again.

And defending Open champion Tom Lehman was probably unaware of the Locke saga when he committed the identical error at the 1997 tournament at Royal Troon. On the second hole, in the second round, Vijay Singh asked him to move his ball marker, as it was on his line. He then forgot to return his marker to the original place before putting. He only realised his mistake on the next tee, but by then it was too late and he received a two-shot penalty.†

---

* Watson had violated Rule 16-1h of the game, which allows a golfer "enough time to reach the hole without undue delay and an additional ten seconds to determine whether the ball is at rest. If by then the ball has not fallen into the hole, it is deemed to be at rest."

† Golfers are expected to call penalties on themselves, a practice that is virtually unheard of in lesser codes, and anyone who spots a rule infringement can report it and have official action taken.

More recently, Tiger Woods received a reprieve from disqualification at the 2013 Masters due to Rule 26, which is rarely invoked. The two-shot penalty was incurred after a television viewer alerted course officials about the drop Woods took on the 15th hole during the second round. After his approach shot cruelly struck the flagstick and found the water, Woods dropped a couple of yards behind the spot where he hit his first approach. By his own admission, he had violated the "as near as possible" portion of dropping at the original spot where the ball was hit.

A strange game indeed.

Would Locke's foolish error on the greatest stage of them all sabotage his greatest triumph? The incident sparked a million debates, and the Royal and Ancient committee members scrambled to deal with this unprecedented incident. No doubt, they would have reminded themselves that in 1897, the Royal and Ancient Golf Club was assigned the responsibility of framing and maintaining the rules of the sport.

A violation in today's game would result in a two-stroke penalty in stroke play, with the additional requirement of correcting the error in the case of a serious breach. But in 1957, instead of a two-stroke penalty, the rules only allowed for a player to be disqualified. After a great deal of debating, the committee used its authority to waive or modify a penalty of disqualification in exceptional individual cases.

Eight days later, it ruled that "with his three-shot lead and no advantage having been gained, the equity and spirit of the game dictated that [he] should not be disqualified".

Once the dust had settled, the following letter was written to the multiple champion:

> You will have already heard from the secretary of the Royal and Ancient Golf Club that the championship committee intends to take no action with regard to the incident on the last green, which

appears in the television film of the Open. Your winning score remains at 279. A penalty may, in exceptional cases, be waived if the committee considers such action warranted. This committee considers that when a competitor has three feet for the Open Championship from two feet, and then commits a technical error which brings him no possible advantage, exceptional circumstances then exist and the decision should be given, accordingly in equity and the spirit of the game.

It was a fitting decision, and although Locke was haunted by his blunder (and outraged at Thomson, as he was convinced he had tried to get him disqualified through low-grade trickery), he was later elected as an honorary member of the Royal and Ancient Club at St Andrews.

While seven others have won The Open four times or more, Locke's four victories in nine years at The Open remains unmatched. Nevertheless, young Australian Peter Thomson secured a hat-trick of victories from 1954 to 1956, and would add another two to become a member of a very select group who has won five times or more. Locke was 40 when he clinched his fourth and final Open Championship, and his long international journey was nearing its end. His record shows that he secured 11 PGA Tour titles, 23 European Tour titles and 38 South African tour titles.

With Locke's international career drawing to a close, he kept his promise to Mary Fenton, the feisty, fun-loving woman he had met in Vermont a decade earlier. Their wedding took place in Surrey in 1958 with just 20 guests present, and the newlyweds embarked on a golfing honeymoon around the UK.

Two years later, in February 1960 – the year of the Sharpeville massacre – their only child, Carolyn, was born in Cape Town. But the couple's finest moment coincided with their biggest setback. Two days after the seven-pound baby was delivered, Locke and his lifelong friend Maurice

Bodmer* drove from the Clovelly Country Club to visit mother and child at the St Joseph's Sanatorium in Pinelands.

At a railway crossing in Retreat, the flashing lights at the intersection alerted them to the approaching 8.53 p.m. train from Southfield.

A half-century had passed since South Africa's first serious vehicle accident had occurred, on a railway line in Maitland a few kilometres away. On 1 October 1903, Charles Garlick and two passengers had found themselves stuck on the track in Garlick's 1.5-horsepower Darracq car, with a Johannesburg express train bearing down on it. All three were injured in the collision, but made complete recoveries.

Locke stopped while the train passed – from right to left – and, moments later, attempted to cross the line. However, a second train, unsighted because of the first, was travelling in the opposite direction – from Cape Town to Muizenberg. Neither Bodmer nor Locke knew what was happening as the train crushed the rear of their car. The impact was dramatic, and the vehicle was thrown some 30 metres away.

The yellowing photograph in my hands shows the rear of the mangled wreckage of the Vauxhall Cresta at the scene the following morning. The chassis is clearly bent, and both the left-side door and the boot are completely mangled. Two khaki-clad policemen and a nurse are among the onlookers.

A Clovelly member who inspected the wreckage the following day told me "there were heavy bloodstains in dried streams down the boot lid and into the boot compartment".

---

* Bodmer had joined Clovelly as the club pro in 1935 and the pair were responsible for probably the most famous game at the course. In 1947, they teamed up to challenge Sam Snead and Australian Norman von Nida in an exhibition match that the South Africans won.

Bodmer, with head and rib injuries, was trapped in the passenger seat, while Locke, propelled by the centrifugal force, was thrown through the rear-view window and onto the boot. He was lying in shock with a crushed eye socket as witnesses ran towards the vehicle. By the time paramedics arrived at the scene, the legend was unconscious. Shortly afterwards, he was stabilised and ferried to Cape Town's Groote Schuur Hospital (where a team of 30 surgeons, doctors and nurses would carry out the world's first human heart transplant later that decade). Well into the night, Dr Brian Myers, the duty doctor, and his team monitored both victims.

Back at the scene of the accident, it emerged that two of Locke's golf clubs – a 5 iron and his famous putter – were missing. Former Springbok tennis player and close friend Leon Norgarb was at his side when he regained consciousness the following day, and he said Locke asked where his putter was. Nobody knew. Had the clubs been thrown from the damaged vehicle or had a bystander stolen them?

A family friend reportedly contacted the *Cape Times*, offering a £10 reward for the return of both clubs and, when there were no takers, later upped it to a more "substantial reward". There was a happy ending a few days later when an Elsies River resident came forward to say he had found a couple of clubs, including the famous putter, in the veld on the side of the road near the car wreck.

Butch Green and his father Hendry – lifelong friends of Locke – were among the first to visit him in hospital

"His face was so swollen, we did not even recognise him. His right eye was seriously damaged, and when the swelling came down it was obvious this champion would never be the same golfer again," Green told me.

As Locke regained his senses and slowly began recovering, he would have recalled the similar fate of another giant. Nine-time Major winner Ben Hogan had been a major influence on the young Locke, who said one of the highlights of his career was sinking an 11-metre putt in a PGA tournament in Philadelphia in 1947, which so unnerved the American that Locke left him for dead.

Like Locke, Hogan's career was interrupted in its prime by World War II (he served as a utility pilot with the rank of sergeant from 1942 to 1945). In 1946 he won the US PGA and, two years later, won it again, along with the US Open. However, in February the following year, Hogan and his wife, Valerie, survived a head-on collision with a Greyhound bus on a foggy morning near Van Horn, Texas. Hogan threw himself across Valerie at the moment of impact to protect her and would have been killed had he not done so, as the steering column punctured the driver's seat.

This accident left the 36-year-old hospitalised with a double fracture of the pelvis, a broken collarbone and left-ankle fracture, and blood clots that would affect him for the rest of his life. Two months later, Hogan was discharged, with doctors predicting that he would probably not play competitive golf again. But within a year he had returned to the PGA Tour and would go on to win six more Majors, to tie with Gary Player's tally of nine.

Long before his accident, Hogan had offered the following advice to anyone who would listen: "As you walk down the fairway of life, you must smell the roses, for you only get to play one round."

An ocean away and a decade later, Locke and Bodmer were on the mend. Their injuries were not life-threatening, and they were discharged a couple of days after the accident. However, the doctors were worried that Locke may have suffered from partial paralysis, and his vision was definitely damaged. In addition, he experienced painful migraines and a violent temper. Weeks later he began playing golf again, but this one-time colossus would never be the same again. South Africa's "Maestro" had started the back nine of his life and a truly momentous career was effectively over.

According to former Clovelly member Alfred Pratt, "Locke's behaviour changed greatly after the accident. His previous occasional irrational actions, outbursts and more-or-less tolerable eccentricities became far more extraordinary and predictable after 1960. That dreadful bang on the head did more than impair his vision and end his career."

The tragedy marked the start of a series of legal battles. Although it was unclear whether alcohol had played a role in the accident, the South African Railways & Harbours (SAR&H) indicated that it planned to sue Locke. A full inquiry was launched, but it appears that a Clovelly Country Club member, who was affiliated with Gelb & Gelb Solicitors, got the state to drop the case. Locke had claimed that he thought it was a single railway track and, when he saw the first train pass, the crossing lights stopped flashing, so he drove off. However, SAR&H proved that the lights and signals were working and must have been flashing for the second train as well as the first.

For Locke, the 1970s were marked by a series of highs and lows – on and off the course. Rather than scaring him straight, the train accident seemed to alter Locke's outlook on life. The decade began with him facing drunk-driving charges after being involved in a relatively minor traffic accident in Vereeniging. Under cross-examination, Locke stated that he was only a moderate drinker, but occasionally had a bit more to drink than he should, for example when he won an important tournament.

Asked what effects alcohol had on him, he replied that it did not affect him badly, and he knew when he had enough, "as a smile comes along". Although the district surgeon testified that Locke had admitted that he had consumed between eight and 10 beers on the evening of the crash, the case was thrown out because his blood samples had been mislaid.

In July 1972, Locke was inducted into the American Golf Hall of Fame in Foxburg, Pennsylvania. After the ceremony, he returned to Vermont and won the Vermont Open, his last US victory, at age 55. A year later, back in South Africa, he recorded his 18th hole-in-one in a mid-week four-ball at the Crown Mines course.

In 1976, Locke's achievements, which included 81 tournament victories, were recognised by the Royal and Ancient Golf Club when he was named an honorary member. The following year, he was elected to the World Golf Hall of Fame, becoming only the second member after Gary Player who did not come from either the US or the UK.

On 23 October 1978, Locke was involved in a dispute with a labourer, which highlighted his volatile temper. He told the Johannesburg Magistrate's Court that the part-time employee, "Big Boy" Ndlovu, had been instructed to carry out some maintenance work on his Yeoville apartment block. The work wasn't done properly, Locke claimed, and an argument ensued.

Ndlovu said when he demanded his R220 wages, Locke had over-reacted: "I walked away from him and, as I walked down the stairs, I heard the sound of a gun and I felt a pain in my right back shoulder."

Locke's response: "He was about to turn when I fired a shot. He was obviously coming back to make a contest. I am a golf professional and I didn't want to damage my hands."

Ndlovu lived to tell his tale and Locke was found guilty of discharging his .32 Smith & Wesson snub-nosed pistol. He was fined R120 (or 60 days) and received a three-month jail term, suspended for three years. In addition, his firearm licence was suspended for six months.

It was a bitter humiliation for a man who had become a whisper of the legend who had captured the imagination of millions. In Johannesburg's upmarket northern suburbs, where the chattering classes dine and whine, there were rumblings about the number of times "a pickled" Locke had to be driven home from the city's golf clubs.

Locke told his old American friend Bob Hackett that his dearest wish was to retire to Vermont, where he had courted Mary all those years ago, but he was unable to get his money out of South Africa because of the strict exchange-control regulations. His earnings may have been handsome but, with hindsight, his investments had evidently been poor. And, of course, he had played in an era before huge purses and sponsorships were on offer.

During (and after) his illustrious professional career, he spent much of his time at two of Johannesburg's most famous courses – Observatory and Parkview.

The Observatory Golf Club was a convenient "watering hole", within walking distance of Locke's Yeoville home. Today, the clubhouse boasts a shrine of his memorabilia, including several trophies.

Further north, in the safer northern suburbs, Locke spent much of his time playing – and socialising – at Parkview. Fittingly, the club was founded in 1916 – a year before his birth – in the wake of the biggest gold rush in history. This immaculate parklands course became an oasis for the well-heeled suburban set and, over the decades, retained its charm.

Locke won both the SA Amateur and the SA Open championships at Parkview in 1935, and he was a member of the club for most of his life. He played his final round at the course on 8 March 1987 and, as per normal, was the star of the show at the evening prize-giving ceremony.

Late that night, he was hospitalised with meningitis, an inflammation of the membranes covering the brain and spinal cord. The following day, he breathed his last.

His funeral was held at St Mary's Anglican Cathedral[*] in Johannesburg, a fitting venue that had been consecrated in 1929, just 12 years after his birth. It also served as the venue for his first marriage, in 1942.

---

[*] The church is famous for its strong ties to the anti-apartheid struggle and, in the 1950s, it was one of the few non-racial churches in downtown Johannesburg. Its Anglican worshippers included Helen Joseph, while Beyers Naudé preached there (security policemen apparently attended his services to keep an eye on him). In the 1970s and 1980s, when Archbishop Desmond Tutu was dean of the church, struggle services were held there, and the venue housed the body of ANC stalwart Oliver Tambo before his burial in Benoni in 1993.

Under its famous pipe organ, mourners heard how the Maestro had put South Africa on the map. Some of South Africa's finest golfers, including Fulton Allem, Teddy Webber and John Bland, were there that day. Former professional Denis Hutchinson, who was a pall-bearer – "he was a heavy bugger" – told me that Locke had died at 69 "because he was determined not to break 70" (the true worth of older golfers is often gauged by their ability to shoot their age). Hutchinson, who is an internationally acclaimed golf commentator and an honorary life president of the PGA of South Africa, played numerous matches against Locke. He added: "I've always said he was the greatest player of all time."

A bridge at the 13th hole under the chestnut and jacaranda trees pays homage to Parkview's most famous son, and an annual tournament is held in his honour.

With Locke at peace and no doubt inspecting the great green in the sky, Mary and Carolyn moved into one of the third-floor apartments at Yalta Court in Yeoville and, in the early 1990s, changed the name of the building to Bobby Locke Place (after receiving council approval). Sandwich, the quaint cottage (with a heart-shaped swimming pool) was retained as a trophy room for all the golfing memorabilia Locke had accumulated around the world.

In the heady days of post-apartheid South Africa, Johannesburg underwent a cataclysmic transformation. The relaxing of the Group Areas Act in the 1980s had started the flow of rural poor to the cities. Squatter camps started taking shape on the fringes of the city, while established urban suburbs like Hillbrow and Locke's neighbouring Yeoville became a melting pot of cultures. eGoli, or the City of Gold, had become a lair for prostitutes, drug dealers and other criminals.

While Mary and Carolyn may have embraced the liberation of South Africa, they soon found their entire wealth invested in an ageing apartment block in a decaying suburb.

South Africa's first democratic elections in 1994 coincided with enormous social upheavals. The underbelly of urban areas – Johannesburg in particular – was fast becoming a magnet for millions of impoverished citizens from neighbouring countries. The apartheid-era military machine had destabilised most of the countries (Namibia, Angola, Lesotho, Swaziland, Botswana, Zimbabwe and Mozambique) in the region, and it would take decades for them to start recovering.

In the dizzy post-apartheid days, Yeoville become an ideological melting pot of different cultures, attracting giants like Barbara Hogan, Johnny Clegg, Albie Sachs and Joe Slovo, along with countless immigrants from around the continent and the rest of the world. In the shadows of the once-splendid Bobby Locke Place, Yeoville's underworld was heaving. At the time, I was a reporter on a Johannesburg newspaper, and on several occasions I accompanied police and members of the narcotics bureau on raids in Yeoville's vibrant Rockey Street. As the crime levels surged, property prices tumbled.

One of the more colourful characters doing the rounds in Yeoville at this time was Gary Beuthin, Johannesburg's most notorious bouncer. He was big, bad and, in the words of one judge who gave him a seven-year jail term (for knocking the stuffing out of a Hell's Angels heavyweight with a baseball bat) "ugly enough to know better".

In and out of jail since his teens, this thug-about-town plied his trade with the notorious Bouncer Gang. He was jailed for three years for his role in the murder of gay nightclub owner Lourens Snyman in 1984, but that paled in comparison with his kidnapping of Carolyn Locke's best friend, Jill Reeves.

For 12 days in May 1992, the nation was on edge as Beuthin went on a cocaine- and alcohol-fuelled binge, with his girlfriend, Reeves, in his custody. The drama ended when bouncer-turned-pastor Ray McCauley eventually persuaded Beuthin to surrender to the police. But the damage was done; the socialite had been so badly assaulted that she was unable to talk for days. When eventually she was back on her feet, she drove to the Kruger National Park, where she parked her car in the middle of nowhere and took her own life. Beuthin may have received a 25-year jail term for the kidnapping of Reeves, but it was small consolation for Carolyn, who had lost a soul mate.

It was during this period that Locke's daughter, who played keyboard for a pop group called Image, found comfort in the arms of Mike Paledi, a Diepkloof, Soweto, resident she'd met at a party. At an "unofficial wedding" at the plush Sandton Sun hotel, she told journalists she had found her "angel". The headline in the *Sowetan* trumpeted, "Locke'd in love", but the relationship didn't last, and Carolyn moved back into flat No. 33 with her mother.

In 1993, Mary and Carolyn were invited to attend the British Open at Royal St George's as guests of the R&A. They were accompanied by businessman Ron Boon, who had arranged for a series of events to be held around South Africa in 1985 to celebrate the 50th anniversary of Locke winning the double: the SA Amateur and the SA Open.

"At that time," Boon said, "Bobby gave me the putter that he had won his four British Open titles with, along with a signed photograph of the Parkview Golf Club that had formed part of those celebrations."

After the 1993 Open, Locke's remaining memorabilia was auctioned at Sotheby's in London on 9 July. The memorabilia included one of his spare putters that Mary and Carolyn claimed was the one he had used to win his British Open titles.

When Boon found out, he reminded Carolyn about her father's gift to him. "Her response was that they were in need of the money and nobody would ever know that it was a replica putter that was auctioned," he said.

Locke's four Open Championship winning medals, several trophies and other memorabilia were sold by Christie's in London for £178 000. The highest price paid was £24 150 for Locke's first Open medal, won at Royal St George's in 1949.

Carolyn, who attended the auction with her mother, defended the decision to release these treasures: "We didn't have to sell the items, but since I don't have any children, we decided it was best to put them up for sale to interested people around world."

Before his death, Locke had requested that his famous putter should be given to a friend, Colin Taitz, who decided to have it auctioned. The auction notice described it as Locke's "Magic Wand", measuring "32 7/8 inches from endcap to hosel with hosel to base an additional four inches". It said the blade was stamped with Locke's accustomed putter manufacturer Slazenger (Gradidge model) on the sole, and had had lead added to the back to get it to his exact specs.

It said the handle consisted of three distinct wrappings – a "made-in-England" leather grip attached to a red leather grip, which was "completed" with black tape. The putter was accompanied by a one-page letter from Mary Locke, confirming that it was "our dear Bobby's putter".

The club may have been a distant forerunner of today's hideously priced, perfectly weighted putters that come in all shapes and sizes, but it was extremely difficult to gauge its value.

When the club didn't sell, the auctioneers alerted US memorabilia collector Steve Pyles. The Ocala, Florida, resident told me that although he had heard of Locke, he'd had no idea how valuable that putter was.

"They seemed to think this was a special club with good provenance, so I bought it and set it aside until recently, when I saw Bobby's British Open medal sell for around $80 000... I started reading about him, and it was then I discovered that he was known to be the greatest putter that ever played the game."

Jimmy McKenzie, a former senior general manager at Barclays (now FNB), was recipient of one of Locke's putters. He was responsible for hosting the Barclays Classic tournament at Sun City in 1987. "The plan on the opening day was for Locke and Sam Snead to tee off, but Snead pulled out at the last minute when his brother died. After Locke's death, Mary and Carolyn came to see me, on a few occasions, for some financial advice and at the last meeting that I saw her, she presented me with the putter that I still have."

And Jack Plummer, who was a senior golf administrator for many years, also received a putter from Locke. Both McKenzie and Plummer donated their putters to the Southern Africa Golf Hall of Fame.

Gauging the value of Locke's original gooseneck putter – and the rest of his memorabilia – depends on who you talk to. Florida-based memorabilia collector Richard Metz puts the value of the club "somewhere between a couple of bucks and priceless".

"You would pick up a similar club for $10 in a thrift store, but that one's got the Locke factor. The reality is, you really can't put a price on it – everyone will view it differently."

For decades, Metz ran a store in the Rockefeller Center in New York, where he sold golf memorabilia, including old clubs. One "business-as-usual day" in the 1970s was enhanced when South Africa's biggest golfing ambassador, with Mary in tow, walked into the store.

"It was a big deal. He was larger than life, and we immediately connected."

Metz said he closed the doors and, "for the next four hours or so", was regaled by the Maestro's stories, "particularly regarding his duels with Snead and Hogan ... He held court and I was in awe. He was a gregarious individual ... a very interesting man."

Locke gave Metz two of his prized clubs – a 19-centimetre Gradidge and a 7 iron – which had served him so well over the years. When Metz learnt of Locke's death, he travelled to Johannesburg to comfort Mary and Carolyn.

"There was something about her [Carolyn]. I'm not sure if it was drugs or alcohol, but something was wrong. She was very emotional."

Metz visited Bobby Locke Place, the couple's Yeoville apartment and the cottage where all Locke's prized possessions were stored. During his stay in Johannesburg, he bought a bouquet of flowers, which he placed on Locke's grave.

Despite the sale of Locke's memorabilia, Mary and Carolyn were still burdened by the hugely undervalued apartment block, which, like much of their suburb, was becoming increasingly rundown. Residents in the area said they very rarely ventured out of their third-floor apartment.

On 23 September 2000, family friend Tracy Korsen enjoyed Sunday lunch with 80-year-old Mary and 40-year-old Carolyn at Bennigan's restaurant in Bedfordview. She told me there was nothing untoward about the occasion, except "Mary was a bit sour and Carolyn was quite serious and earnest".

Later that evening, Elias Nhlapo, the watchman at Bobby Locke Place, checked on the couple before they bolted the door to their apartment, changed into their nightgowns, drank in the breathtaking view of the Johannesburg skyline, consumed half a bottle of Champagne and a fistful of sleeping pills, and climbed into bed together.

When the domestic worker, Miriam Magorosi, was unable to unlock the door the following morning, she alerted Nhlapo, who sensed that something was wrong and ran to the nearby police station. After the door was broken down, their bodies were discovered.

Korsen, who rushed to the scene, said Carolyn was holding Mary, who had one eye wide open, "almost like she may have changed her mind. Looking back, there had to be a bad ending with Carolyn – she was off the wall and living very fast. I'm just surprised Mary went the same way."

Korsen, who'd attended St Andrew's school in Bedfordview with Carolyn and their mutual friend Jill Reeves, said Carolyn had always "lived in Bobby's shadow, to her detriment".

A family friend, Sheila Featherstone, said mother and daughter had left a clause in their will asking that if they died before their spaniel Charlie, he should be euthanised and his ashes scattered over their graves at West Park Cemetery. However, there was no room for Carolyn's coffin, so she was cremated and her ashes were scattered – along with Charlie's – over the graves of her parents.

Six years after their deaths, there was another tragedy at Bobby Locke Place, when the Batswana pilot of a Piper Cherokee 140, en route from Lanseria to Rand Airport, was caught in a severe thunderstorm and his aircraft plunged into the building. He was killed instantly.

Cape Town's Clovelly Country Club was one of the champion's favourite hunting grounds during – and after – his professional career. Located between Fish Hoek and Kalk Bay on the Cape Peninsula, it is tucked into the fynbos-draped mountains facing the Indian Ocean, with the Atlantic Ocean behind. The dune-lined course is one of the finest in the land. When the southeaster whips in off the False Bay coastline and up into the valley, its par-five 9th hole is one of the most challenging in the country. But today, apart from the gentle rushing of the waves in the distance and the occasional cry of seagulls, it is calm and peaceful.

Twenty-five years after Locke's death, Barry Cohen's mind wanders back to the day when he first saw the champion pacing the fairways and greens below us. It was at the 1964 Western Province Open Championship and, gauging by the surging crowds, the 12-year-old knew he was witnessing something out of the ordinary.

When Locke, clad in his powder-blue cardigan, drew his two-wood brassie from his bag, a murmur ran through the gallery: "Bobby is using the driver." He never wore a glove, preferring to blow spit onto his left hand to improve his grip. And when he pressed his tee into the ground and placed his Dunlop 65 series four (his ball of choice, because it served as a reminder of his four Open wins), the crowd fell quiet. When his drive soared up – and over – the trees on the right-hand side of each and every fairway, there was a collective gasp. And when it corrected itself and carved towards the target – almost always the fairway – the cheers of the spectators rose in unison.

Cohen recalls that when the Maestro putted, he was cocooned in concentration: "There was something surreal about the whole exercise. He inspected the putt from every angle. He looked at the cup, the lie of the grass, the slope of the green, and then knelt behind the ball while weighing it all up. And he had this funny habit of flicking the putter around in his wrist while inspecting the line."

The four-time Major champion may have finished fourth that day (behind Retief Waltman, Gary Player and Harold Henning), but Cohen knew he had found his calling. Days later, he traded a set of pram wheels (intended for the construction of a go-kart) for a set of wooden-shafted clubs.

One of the glories of golf is that a wide-eyed youngster – or, for that matter, an ageing hacker – can stand and, thanks to the handicap system, compete on the same hallowed ground as the giants of the game. It is a bond between the king and the subject that no other sport can offer. And so it was with Cohen.

Locke, who spent up to three months a year at Clovelly, took the boy under his wing. And Cohen, who went on to become an outstanding amateur and a prominent golf administrator, returned the favour in 2009, when he inducted Locke into the Golf Hall of Fame. In his speech, he recalled how the champion's joviality belied a steely determination and concentration: "He would tell me never to talk to him while he was playing a competitive round. After his round, he would give me his golf balls from his bag, and there would not be a scratch on them, such was the crispness with which he hit the ball."

Cohen told me that Locke's contribution to the sport was massive.

"In his prime, he was huge. He was a major ambassador for the game and for the country... much like Ernie [Els] is now."

Today, the bar at Clovelly is named after Locke and his prized ukulele is framed and mounted on the wall at the club, a reminder of glorious days (and intimate nights). Cohen remembers that there were many an evening when he would wait outside the bar for his lift home with one of the most famous chauffeurs in the world. And, irrespective of the weather, there was always a warm glow inside the clubhouse as Locke strummed away, on his instrument of choice, with his signature tune, "Please don't talk about me when I'm gone."

2

The Black Knight

"Player, golf's Little Big Man, is of course a phenomenon. He rants about his religion, his dedication and the searing nature of difficulties he has mastered. But there is no doubt about his place in the deity of the game."
– James Lawton

When Gary Player, Arnold Palmer and Dow Finsterwald were all square coming off the 18th green at the 1962 Masters, the young South African had to dig deep – very deep – just to be able to show up for the play-off the following day. With shafts of soft light streaming through the Georgia pines, the contest was proving to be as dramatic as the setting. But it was also proving to be too much for the foreigner, who found sanctuary back in his room.

Sleep did not come easily that night, and he experienced some kind of mental block about the decider. "I just didn't want to go," he later recalled. His friend, George Blumberg, was tasked with transporting him from their rented house through the traffic and huge crowds to 2604 Washington Road and down Magnolia Lane – flanked on either side by those majestic 60 magnolia trees – which lead to the clubhouse.

Player felt the sweat roll down his forehead and his hands were trembling as he waded through the crowds. He only had time to hit a few long irons at the driving range and a few putts on the dewy practice green before being ushered to the first tee and his date with destiny.

On both sides of the fairway – from tee to green – were thousands of excited supporters, the majority members of the famous "Arnie's Army". But, with or without the crowds, no sport is as solitary as this one. In his book *Down the Fairway*, Bobby Jones (one of the founders of Augusta) noted that, in golf, "the player is all alone with his God".

And American golfer Hale Irwin observed that this is the most isolated sport of them all: "You're completely alone with every conceivable opportunity to defeat yourself. Golf brings out your assets and liabilities as a person. The longer you play, the more certain you are that a man's performance is the outward manifestation of who, in his heart, he really thinks he is."

Seven-time Major winner Sam Snead once noted: "Of all the hazards, fear is the worst."

The deeply religious Player used his ball to press the tee into the ground, stepped back and peered down the aisle of the cathedral, flanked by the giant pines. This was his world. And then there was silence; pure and perfect silence. In the moments that followed, he was overcome with that sense of calm that true champions experience when they are in the zone. In golf, it's the moment when the athlete's entire world is focused on a 45.9-gram, dimpled ball that will reflect – in its speed, rhythm, trajectory and distance – his or her very being at that moment.

The South African had learnt at an early age that pure talent can only take one so far and that the mind must take over and lead the body into that realm of perfection. And years of mental training, meditation and self-hypnosis had taught him that the mind can be trained to uphold the nerves. That spiritual awakening on the course would leave the young man drenched in adrenalin and sharply focused.

Golf historian Pat Ruddy once observed that just as the breeze fits itself to the shape of the sea and the shape of the land, a golfer's mind must fit into the land shapes, flow with the winds and rejoice in the craggy mental terrain that lies between the first and 18th green and, yes, between games throughout life. After all, Ruddy noted, life is a mere continuation of golf.

Prominent sports psychologist Dr Rob Rotella says the challenge of the first hole at Augusta is that the sand traps and pine trees frame the fairway. "Obviously, a player wants to avoid each of them," he observes in his book, *Golf Is Not a Game of Perfect*. "But a player who stands on that tee, fighting nerves already, and thinks about where he doesn't want to hit it, only multiplies his chances of hitting it badly. He needs to use his practice rounds to learn where the hazards are and establish the right target for his drive – fade or draw, long or short. Then, when he steps onto the tee in competition, he must think only of that target."

And so it was with this player, as a sense of calm washed over his mind and body. He straddled over the ball, swung wide and long, and crushed his drive en route to an opening birdie.[*]

Born in Lyndhurst outside Johannesburg on 1 November 1935, Gary was the youngest of Harry and Muriel Player's three children. There were two significant issues that had a profound impact on Gary's life during his formative years – the death of his mother when he was eight, and his lack of height, which resulted in him being ridiculed at school. There is some irony in the fact that his two siblings – Ian and Wilma – had similar physical attributes to their father, a tall man, while Gary took after his relatively short mother.

Gary's father was appointed mine manager at the Robinson Deep and Crown mines and the family moved to Booysens, one of the city's rougher pockets, sandwiched between the drab mine dunes that symbolise South Africa's mineral wealth and the world's youngest city.

---

[*] Palmer won his third Masters title in the tournament's first three-way play-off. He defeated Player, who was the defending champion, and Finsterwald in the play-off.

In a 2002 *Golf Digest* interview, Player said that his father told him that "men died like flies in those mines. I went to visit him one day, and when he came off the skip – the elevator that lowered them into the mine – he immediately sat down. He took off his boot and poured water out of it onto the ground. I asked him where the water came from, and he said, 'Son, that's perspiration. It's hot as hell down there.'"

Player recalls tying a rope from a branch on an old pear tree in the back garden and spending countless hours building up his calloused hands, and the muscles in his arms, shoulders, back and stomach. The family moved out of the house in 1947 and, about 15 years later, when the adult Gary made a sentimental trip back to the old house as a world-famous sportsman, he spotted the same rope hanging from the tree. "I cut it down and took it with me. My hands were not those of a boy. They were more wrinkled, but they hadn't forgotten," he recalled.

His mother battled with cancer, and she had several operations that merely delayed the inevitable. When she succumbed to the disease, brother Ian was in Italy with the South African Armoured Brigade and, long before he received a telegram with the news that any child would dread, he said he knew his mother had died.

Years later, Player said he learnt the most valuable lesson about life – and golf – through that tragedy: "It had happened, and there was nothing I could do to change it. The ball just had to be played as it lay. There was no point in protesting about bad luck or cursing misfortune or demanding why it had happened to me. The only task was to make the best of what was left and to get on with it."

The event also triggered his remarkable *joie de vivre* and an undertaking that he had to settle some "unfathomable debt", and he didn't want to waste any time making the most of his own life. "I am an animal when it comes to achievement and wanting success. There is never enough success for me," he wrote in his 1991 autobiography, *Grand Slam Golf.*

He told sports writer Norman Canale that the sense of emptiness made him cry in his sleep. "All my adult life I've had the same dream over and over again. And I always wake up in tears. In my dream I see my dear mother. I'm trying to tell her what I have achieved, but she cannot hear me. I just wish she could have seen me become a world champion, but she never saw me hit a golf ball."

After Player had won the SA Open at Cape Town's Mowbray Golf Club in 1975, Canale saw a stranger hand him a photograph and the champion broke down in tears. It was an old box-camera snapshot of his mother, father and himself on a train before departing on holiday to Scottburgh on the coast. "I was so choked up that I never thought to ask the man his name or where he got the picture," Player told Canale.

In an interview with *The Telegraph* in 2008, Player reflected on that period in his life: "My father was working in the gold mine. My mother was dead. My brother was at the War. I suffered as a youngster, like a dog. You know what, I am very grateful for it. That is why I became a champion."

Player vividly remembers sitting on benches in the darkness of the bitterly cold Highveld winter mornings waiting for the trams – and buses – that would ferry him across the city to school. He often arrived home late in the afternoon, but before his sister or father had arrived from work, and he would have to wait in the dark for them.

This was the hard side of Johannesburg. But even though the family lived on "the lower side of the tracks", Player was fortunate to attend the prestigious King Edward VII High School on the northern side of the city.

Spurred on by the ridicule he suffered because of his size, he went the extra mile with all the sports he competed in. He won honours in rugby, cricket, athletics, swimming and diving, captained the first team in soccer and won the trophy for the best all-round athlete in school.

THE BLACK KNIGHT

And, of course, there was the not-so-small matter of golf. His father, a two-handicap, left-handed golfer, took him to play a round at the age of 14, and he parred three of the first nine holes. Recognising his talent, his father took out a loan to purchase a set of clubs, and the teenager became a regular feature at the Virginia Park golf course. Jock Verwey was the well-known golf professional at the club, and Player spent countless hours playing golf at the course with Jock's daughter Vivienne and son Bob.

Player was only 14 when he had a terrifying near-death experience. During a break at high school, he dived head first into a compost heap – mostly grass and dead leaves – next to one of the fields. The landing wasn't as soft as he'd expected, and he was knocked unconscious, suffering a broken neck. He was rushed to hospital, stabilised and fitted with a neck brace. The doctors expressed concern that he might not walk again, but three months later the brace came off and he resumed his training with a lot of gratitude and a sense of urgency.

He spent a great deal of time practising on rugby fields near his home, striking the ball through the giant posts from different angles. By the age of 16, he was a scratch golfer and a serious student of the great Ben Hogan.

When Player was growing up, television was unheard of in South Africa. However, foreign movies were extremely popular and one of these, an American cowboy offering called *Have Gun – Will Travel*, left a lasting impression on the teenager. The main character, named Paladin, was a gentleman of the West who dressed in black and used a calling card inscribed with a chess knight. The image stuck. Player started wearing black and adopted the nickname "the Black Knight"[*] throughout much of his career as a golfer as well as for his brand and corporate identity.

---

[*] In 2004, the SABC launched its 100 Greatest South Africans contest and featured billboards with Player as "the Black Knight" and Desmond Tutu as "the Black Bishop", and calling on the public to choose.

The teenager was telling anyone who would listen that he would be the top golfer in the world and, at the age of 17, he signed up as a professional. Despite the protests of his father, who had promised his mother on her deathbed that her youngest son would go to university, Gary set his sights on a career in golf. He became a coach at Virginia Park (earning £29 a month) and began dating club professional Jock Verwey's daughter Vivienne.

These were exciting times for the young Player — on and off the course — but there were concerns about his seriously flawed swing. At the time, he had a classic hooker's grip, with four knuckles of the left hand showing, while his backswing was way too vertical. These were issues that would prevent him from making any real breakthroughs in his game. However, under Verwey's guidance, his game improved steadily.

A fitness fanatic, Gary spent many hours practising from sand traps, with the result that he became one of the greatest bunker players of all time. "The harder I practise, the luckier I get," became his famous refrain. This personal motto had its origins in a bunker at a Texas practice green in 1958, when a local resident saw Player hole his shot and offered him $50 if he could repeat the feat. Player complied, and the man upped the stake to $100. Once again, Player nailed the shot. As the exasperated stranger peeled off the notes, he remarked: "Son, I've never seen anyone so lucky in my life."

Player won his first tournament — the East Rand Open in Benoni — in 1955, and when he walked off the 18th green and saw his 1.9-metre father "crying like a puppy", he knew he had found his calling.

The teenager then set his sights on Europe.

Thanks to the bank-overdraft facility his father had secured — and a few donations from the members of the Killarney Golf Club, where Player was spending much of his time — he winged his way to England in

1955 with £200 in his pocket, an unquenchable spirit, a hunger in his belly and a heart full of hope.

En route, he beat Harold "the Horse" Henning in the Egyptian Match Play Championship, earning £300 in prize money. He then entered The Open, at St Andrews, and slept on the West Sands beach off the Firth of Forth (where *Chariots of Fire* was filmed) because he was so short on cash and couldn't get a cheap room.

When he teed off at the first, his drive veered out of bounds, struck a fence and kicked back onto the fairway. The starter commented: "You must be a hell of a chipper and putter, because you can't hit the ball worth a damn."

Over the next few months, Player shared a digs in London with Henning and a group of other South Africans, including Brian Wilkes and Doug Evans. On his return to South Africa, he defended his East Rand Open title, won his first South African Open, and won the Dunlop and Ampol tournaments in Australia.

In August 1956, he proposed to Vivienne, and they were married the following year – after he had won the Australian PGA title, as well as the Coffs Harbour and Transvaal Open tournaments.

Their first child, Jennifer, was born in 1959, and they went on to have four more children – Marc, Wayne, Michele and Theresa – in quick succession, with a *laatlammetjie*, Amanda, born in 1973. Player's travelling took its toll – he missed the birth of three of his children, and he has always saluted Vivienne for raising the children single-handedly.

His first victory on the US PGA Tour came at the Kentucky Derby Open in 1959, and he secured a second-place showing in the US Open (with a $5 000 pay-out). This was followed by the successful defence of his Coffs Harbour title, his first Australian Open win, and victories in the Natal Open and Ampol tournament.

These successes were coming fast and furious, but they paled in comparison to his performance at The Open in 1959, just two years after Bobby Locke had won his fourth (and final) Open Championship.

Player had arrived at the salt-scrubbed Muirfield 10 days before the tournament and was struck by the unforgiving wasteland and the size of this "beast". "There it was, laid out along the shore of the Firth of Forth, 6 217 metres through and across the sand hills, a hard wind running from west to east, big sandstone clubhouse, the primal-named Greywalls Hotel just behind, some dykes, everything vigorous, virile, hard, lean, masculine, muscular. Very Scottish. Not a sympathetic place."*

To add to his concerns, he was prevented from playing the course because he was not a member, and the course officials said they were preparing for the championship. It took a phone call to the president of the PGA, John Moore-Brabazon, to rectify the situation, and Player was allowed just one round a day.

On the opening day, the course bared its teeth as the winds off the Firth of Forth became a shrieking gale. Player made a shaky start to the tournament, opening with a 75, which left him seven shots off the lead.

But at the end of the second-last day, he told a friend, Pat Mathews, that he knew he was going to win it. They were prescient words, and Player would later attribute this confidence to "a deep and very real inner conviction". His third-round 70 saw him make up four shots on the field, placing him eight shots behind Fred Bullock, the professional from the Prestwick St Ninians Club.

On the closing day, the South African had an aggressive and impressive front nine, shooting 34. He then scored a birdie at the 10th, the 12th, the 13th and the 16th, putting him within reach of a magical 66.

---

* Extract from Player's *Grand Slam Golf*.

THE BLACK KNIGHT

At the 17th, he left his approach putt four metres short, disturbed by clicking cameras and crowd movement. Spectator Tom Brown, who witnessed the drama, recalls how Player dealt with the situation: "I beg you – I'm playing for my life here. I ask you from the bottom of my heart not to move." He sank the putt to secure par.

At the 18th, Player made a hash of the 390-metre par four. He gave his drive a decent lick, but the ball caught a left-side bunker. He hit a weak 6 iron from the trap, rolling the ball about 90 metres up the lumpy fairway. Using the same club, he fired directly at the pin, but he flubbed the shot and the ball came to a rest at the bottom of the cavernous green. From there, it was a nervy three-putt – the third a desperate scramble from 50 centimetres as the ball quivered in the fresh wind before the hole swallowed it.

In that moment of despair, Player recalled how Sam Snead had once thrown away a US Open with a botched eight and had never won the tournament again.

Player was physically and emotionally drained and, with a hungry pack now in hot pursuit, he needed to get away from the scene of the wreckage. Years later, he would observe that it is "easy to win gracefully, but a lot harder to lose well". Back at his North Berwick hotel, he had a cold bath. Fellow South African Harold Henning kept calling with updates from the course, and it slowly dawned on them that this championship was becoming too close to call.

As the fear faded from his face, Player returned to the clubhouse to watch the drama unfold on television on the second floor. It came down to Belgian Flory von Donck and Fred Bullock (a journeyman pro from Prestwick St Ninians, with his daughter Sandra as caddie) each needing birdies on the 18th to level with the shaken South African.

Bullock blew it with a 74, while Von Dock had driven into the same bunker as Player. He was left with a 12-metre putt to tie the championship, but he missed, and his 73 left Player the victor (and £1 000 richer). It's called an ugly win, but a win it was, and Player must take the credit for becoming only the fourth golfer in history to improve his score with every round (75, 71, 70 and 68) and, at 23, the youngest winner since Willie Auchterlonie in 1893.

Back at the hotel a few hours later, the young man received a hero's welcome. The South African flag was unfurled, the hotel band played "Sarie Marais", and the world was in awe of the latest golfing sensation.

Player then set his sights on the United States and Augusta.

However, adjusting to the conditions in the US took a great deal of time. He found that the courses were, for the most part, wide open, with lush fairways filtering towards exquisite greens. As a result, the American professionals frequently fired directly at the pin, comfortable in the knowledge that a well-struck ball would bite and come to a stop within a few feet of its pitch mark.

Player found the American bunkers "severe" and strategically placed to invite players to try to clear them. In South Africa and Europe, it was a different ball game altogether – golfers would invariably focus on striking the ball with a great deal of accuracy to ensure that it would negotiate the bunkers and roll onto the green before losing its momentum.

In *Grand Slam Golf*, Player observed: "Our game is that much more conservative, theirs is that much more aggressive. That is why the Americans really are the best players in the world, judged by almost any standards. They don't know more about the mechanics or the technique of swinging, and hitting the ball. They don't have any magic, any exclusive insight into the game. But their golf courses in the main lend themselves to aggressive play, and they are products of an aggressive way of life."

At his first Masters in 1957, Player made the halfway cut, but finished last on the final day. By 1960, he had finished eighth and set himself the target of winning in 1961, the year that the Union of South Africa broke from the monarchy and became a republic.

When he arrived at Augusta in 1961, Player had a strong feeling that he was going to win. Three rounds of near-perfect golf set him up for a final-day showdown with Arnold Palmer.

Palmer, the defending Masters champion, had been the leading money winner the previous year. By now, the American – with the backing of his army of supporters – struck the fear of God into most opponents with his breathtaking and aggressive style of golf. Palmer had won three of his first eight tournaments that year, while Player was then at the top of the PGA Tour's money list.

And so it was fitting that they would go head to head on the final day. Palmer had led through all four rounds the previous year, and his opening score of 68 in 1961 kept him at the top of the leader board. He would keep that lead well into his third round of the tournament, when Player swept past to secure a four-stroke lead. Sunday's play was rained out and, despite the agonising delay, the South African was once again overcome with a premonition that he would win.

He opened the final day's play with two birdies and made the turn at −2. But Arnie's Army was on the march, with Palmer making one of his dramatic charges. By the turn, the American had a one-shot lead. The tournament was then decided by the back bunker on the 18th green, which caught both men.

Player splashed his ball out to about two metres from the pin, "and somehow pulled my ragged nerve-endings together and holed the putt". Palmer, with his slender one-shot lead, caught his bunker shot thin, and the ball flew over the Bermuda green, through the crowd and down a slope. He pitched back up to the green, but the ball scurried five metres past the pin. He missed the putt, and his double-bogey saw Player becoming the first non-American to win the Masters since it had been restructured and renamed in 1939. Incidentally, it would take another 19 years before another foreign-born player – Seve Ballesteros – would again win the tournament.

After missing the cut at the 1962 Open at Royal Troon in Scotland, Player winged his way back to the US to compete at the PGA Championship at Aronimink in Philadelphia. It was the first of five times in the 1960s that these two Majors were played in consecutive weeks in July (apart from 1971, when the PGA was played in late February). The PGA Championship would move permanently to Augusta in 1969.

Aronimink was designed by acclaimed course architect Donald Ross in 1928, and a bronze plaque near the first tee records his impressions when he visited the course in 1948 for the first time in 20 years (he died months later): "I intended to make this my masterpiece, but not until today did I realize that I built better than I knew." Tournament director Bryn Mawr claimed that the PGA Championship, with 7500 bleacher seats, television monitors for spectators and 40 acres of parking, would be the most modern golfing event ever.

Player arrived at Aronimink the day after his failed Open campaign, and long before most of the other 169 competitors. For four days, he awoke before dawn and made his way to the course. He used empty milk bottles as targets on the green (the holes hadn't been cut yet) and he headed back to his hotel only after dark.

By Wednesday's pro-am, he had the course figured, even though this was his first visit. Contrast that with Jack "Fat" Nicklaus, who reportedly ate three breakfasts that morning, while the chain-smoking Arnold Palmer had flown directly from Troon after winning his second consecutive Open Championship.

Not surprisingly, the South African (there were only four foreigners competing) found himself in contention throughout. On the final day, he had built up a four-shot lead, but when Bob Goalby, his closest pursuer, birdied 14 and 16, the lead was trimmed to one, with one hole remaining.

THE BLACK KNIGHT

On the final hole of the tournament, Player fanned his drive into the trees on the right-hand side of the fairway. However, he hit a magnificent recovery shot with his 3 wood, reaching the green and coming to rest about nine metres from the hole. Two putts from there saw him beat the American by a single shot to secure his third Major. Player finished the tournament scoring rounds of 72, 67, 69 and 70 for a two-under-par 278. He celebrated with a tall glass of milk.

It was a particularly significant feat because, while the next generation of South African golfers would conquer the Masters and both Open championships time and again, only Nick Price would add his name to the Wanamaker Trophy that century. The PGA celebrated the 50th anniversary of Player's victory with a special exhibit at the 94th PGA Championship at Kiawah Island in South Carolina in 2012.

These were happy days for Mark McCormack, who managed Player, Palmer and Jack Nicklaus. McCormack's International Management Group (IMG) grew into a major international corporation, branching off into other sports as well.

With Palmer winning the Masters and Open in 1962 and Nicklaus winning the PGA, the title "The Big Three" – golf's all-powerful cartel – was born. Between 1960 and 1966, this trio of golfers won every Masters tournament. While Player was unable to hit the ball as far as these gorillas (he was just 1.7 metres tall and 68 kilograms at his peak), he made up for it with other aspects of his game (and mind). Long before golfers recognised the importance of exercise and nutrition, Player became a pioneer for working out. No doubt his mental prowess also played a significant role in his career successes. ("The softest thing about Gary was his teeth," golf commentator Denis Hutchinson told me.)

Player's career was always associated with Nicklaus and Palmer and, at the peak of their powers, thanks to their engaging on-course personas, there was always a healthy tension between them. They were largely responsible for the sport's global surge in popularity. Off the course, they enjoyed a binding friendship and remain close to this day.

At the time, Player viewed the Open as the greatest golf tournament in the US. With narrow fairways, slippery greens and deep, gnarly rough, the stated aim of the USGA is to provide a brutal challenge and to protect par. With around 5 000 players entering – through local and regional qualifiers – each year, foreign players seldom made a lasting impression. It had been 45 years since Ted Ray's win in 1920 (the only other non-American, Harry Vardon, won in 1900).

In preparation for the 1965 edition of the tournament, at the Bellerive Country Club in Missouri, Player went through an arduous training regime, ensuring that his mind and body were up for the challenge. By this stage, he was squatting 150 kilograms and focusing on core, leg and forearm strength exercises.

He made notes and drew sketches of the course – bunkers, water hazards, trees and the rough – and studied these in his hotel room at night. "Every day I went down to the practice tee, where they had a scoreboard with all the past Open champions' names on it, and I stood there and visualised my name etched on it."

He also wrote a list of "dos and don'ts" and strictly adhered to them for a 10-day period leading up to the event. These included driving (cars) slowly, shaving and bathing slowly, avoiding newspapers, sugar and white bread, and any fats. In this state of self-hypnosis, Player believed he underwent a minor personality change and once again experienced some sort of revelation – "that positive, powerful feeling, indeed certainty, that I was going to win the championship".

At 6 575 metres, the course was a monster – the longest of all US Open courses, with magnificent greens guarded by enormous bunkers and water hazards. Player started confidently with an opening round of 70, two behind Australian Ken Nagle.

A second-round 70 saw him one shot ahead of Nagle, and a third-round 71 gave him a three-shot advantage for the final day. However, at the long par-three 16th, Player rushed his shot and his ball plugged in the greenside bunker. The subsequent double-bogey saw Nagle cutting the lead to one and, with a birdie on the 17th, squaring the championship with one hole to play.

That's the way it ended, but in the 18-hole play-off the following day, a female spectator needed stitches in her scalp after being struck by a wayward drive from Nagle. Player, meanwhile, streaked ahead to hold a five-shot lead over the first eight holes, and he went on to win by three shots – his first Major victory in a play-off. In an interesting twist, Player returned his winner's cheque to USGA director Joe Dey with the request that it be used for cancer research and to fund junior golf development.

The 29-year-old South African had become only the third golfer – after Gene Sarazen and Ben Hogan – to achieve golf's Holy Grail, the Grand Slam. To this day, he remains the only foreigner to have done so, and only Jack Nicklaus and Tiger Woods have achieved this feat since.

The 1968 Open was the fourth to be played over the links at Carnoustie, the scene of Ben Hogan's historic win in 1953. Thanks to the construction of bridges over the Forth and Tay rivers, the venue had become considerably more accessible, and grandstands had to be erected to accommodate the swelling crowds.

As the longest (6 631 metres) and most northerly course on the Open circuit, it squats along Carnoustie Bay and the North Sea, often bearing the brunt of gale-force winds and with a reputation as the toughest. Player noted that there was nothing charming about the place: "It is a bleak course in a bleak town."

Of course, that could be said about many courses and towns in Scotland. The late Earl Woods – Tiger's father – took it further when he said: "Scotland sucks, as far as I'm concerned. It has the sorriest weather. People had better be happy that Scots live there instead of the soul brothers. The game of golf would never have been invented."

But Scots have always viewed it differently, as their famous saying infers: "Nae wind, nae rain, nae golf." And popular television commentator Peter Alliss once observed: "One of the good things about rain in Scotland is that most of it ends up as Scotch."

Wet and windy conditions marked the opening round, and although Player struggled with his long game, he managed to score 74, two behind joint leaders Brian Barnes and Michael Bonallack. The second round belonged to Billy Casper, who shot 68 to go four strokes into the lead, with Player and Nicklaus close behind.

In the third round, the weather deteriorated again, but Player had another steady performance, finishing with a total of 216, just two off the lead, which was still held by Casper.

For the first time, a cut after 54 holes was initiated, which reduced the final day's field from 80 to 45. While Casper faded fast (shooting a 78), Player made his charge, taking the lead at the sixth hole. At the 441-metre par-five 14th, which Player described as a "sheer green beast", he decided to try to carry the infamous "Spectacles" bunkers, which are located about 64 metres short of the green. It's a risk-reward shot that all too often ends in tears.

"I had to lean sideways to see the top of the flag," Player later recalled.

With a 3 wood, he drilled the shot with every ounce of his body. For the first 40 or 50 metres the ball barely lifted off the ground, but then acquired the gift of lift and rode the winds, soaring up towards the green and landing just centimetres from the cup. With steely focus, Player holed the putt (it was his second eagle at the hole in consecutive days) for a two-shot lead.

Playing partner Jack Nicklaus mounted a strong challenge at the death. By the 17th, there were still two shots separating him and Player. Nicklaus struck a searing drive down the 17th, but failed to get the birdie he needed, while Player hit an 18-metre putt from the fringe of the green that stopped 15 centimetres from the hole to save par. At the 18th, Player put his approach shot into ugly rough on the right, while Nicklaus's second shot ended in the right-hand bunker next to the green.

Nicklaus needed to hole out from the bunker to have any chance to tie, but he chunked his effort and it was not to be. Player was down in two to gain his second Open title. With a total of 289, he finished one over par, with Nicklaus and New Zealander Bob Charles two shots behind in joint second place. The course, which succumbed to only two scores under par the entire week and saw a winning score of one over par, had lived up to its fierce reputation.

By now Player was one of the most recognised sports personalities on the planet and as a white (and very successful) South African, he became a magnet for the anti-apartheid movement, which was gaining momentum – particularly in the US. Certainly, this period of Player's career coincided with some of the most monumental political developments in South Africa – including the Sharpeville massacre.

In Australia in 1974, protesters ventured onto one of the putting greens in the middle of the night and wrote, "Go Home, You Racist Pig", in white lime powder.

Player frequently received death threats in the US, and the FBI closely monitored and travelled with him on American soil to ensure that he wasn't harmed.

At the 1969 PGA Championship at the NCR Country Club in Dayton, Ohio, protesters hounded him throughout the tournament, seriously affecting his concentration. On the Saturday, Player was paired with Jack Nicklaus, and they were both in contention for the lead. Hundreds of policemen were monitoring the situation. At the fourth tee, Player was addressing his ball when a programme was thrown from the gallery, landing at his feet. From then on, every time Player addressed a drive, chip or putt, he was expecting to be distracted.

When they made the turn and walked towards the 10th tee, someone in the crowd called Player's name. When he turned, a cup full of ice cubes was thrown in his face. The demonstrator was hauled away by security – one of 11 arrests that day – but the damage was done. Moments later, a civil rights activist charged at Nicklaus, who raised his putter as a deterrent. Both players were now genuinely concerned about their safety. Four holes later, Player was about to putt when a golf ball was tossed onto the green and across his path.

It got worse, as Player recalled in an interview with *Forbes* magazine: "They were charging me on the greens when I was about to putt, and screaming as I took the putter back. I had police protection escorting me around the golf course, even when I had to go to the bathroom and had lunch at the clubhouse. It was difficult for me to be viewed as an apartheid supporter when I was not, and was actually trying to find ways to bring my country together, not split it apart."

He told *Golf* magazine, in an article published in 2009, that the threat was serious. "They said they would kill me. I had policemen guarding me. It cost me seven strokes." At the end of the day, he managed to take his game to new highs – Nicklaus said it was the finest round of golf he had ever witnessed – and yet the South African lost by one shot to Ray Floyd. Player would look back on this farce as the tournament that cost him a magical 10th Major.

In his book *To Be the Best*, he said he became an easy and obvious target for abuse, criticism – and sometimes much worse: "I could not step off a plane without being held answerable for the apartheid system, and all my protestations about sport and politics not mixing were brushed aside, I was regarded as a spokesman for apartheid – or at least the one tangible target its opponents could easily attack."

THE BLACK KNIGHT

When he returned to the US in 1970, he was continuously protected by armed guards while he was playing and received 24-hour police protection off the course. Nevertheless, he still wondered whether someone would carry out the numerous death threats he received. The Black Panthers, a radical African American group, agitated against Player's continued presence in the US and successfully ensured that Ernest Nipper, Player's black caddie for more than a decade, threw in the towel.

But through the fog of that era, Player strode on, and the image of the small man, dressed in black, dominated the popular imagination around the world.

At the 1972 PGA Championship at the Oakland Hills Country Club in Michigan, Player hit one of the greatest shots of all time to secure his sixth Major. After shooting a spectacular round of 67 at Oakland Hills en route to winning the 1951 US Open, Ben Hogan had remarked that he had tamed "the monster". Few have ever been as fortunate.

With 10 players within two shots of each other and in the lead on the final nine holes, Player found himself in tangled rough on the right-hand side of the 16th fairway. He had bogeyed the previous two holes and, with a slender one-shot lead, the championship was showing signs of slipping away. Between his ball and the pin were a large willow tree and a stream guarding the green.

As he walked up to his ball, surveyed the damage and began contemplating what club to use, he noticed an old (and familiar) divot. It turned out to be the same divot "with a strange shape" he had made four days earlier during a practice round. And it served as a timely reminder of how to deal with the same situation – with a Major now on the line.

During that practice round, Player had fired at the pin with an 8 iron, to very good effect. Back live, and the conditions were slightly different. The grass had more moisture now, and he knew it would be more of a "flyer" in current circumstances. So he selected a 9 iron, and the moment he struck it, the trajectory was perfect. As it began its descent, the ball tracked the pin and stopped a metre from the hole. That birdie saw off the challenge from Tommy Aaron and Jim Jamieson, who finished two shots behind.

Player went into the 1974 Open at Royal Lytham and St Annes with two Open championships (Muirfield in 1959 and Carnoustie in 1968) under his belt, and with the first black caddie – Alfred "Rabbit" Dyer – in the tournament's history. "I stick out here like a fly in buttermilk," Dyer reportedly observed.

Then, like now, Lytham was a course like no other, located on the smallest piece of property of any links course in the Open rotation, and the only course that does not offer a glimpse of the water. A railway runs along the right side of the outward nine, with homes surrounding the rest of the property. In the distance – and out of sight of the golfers – is the Irish Sea.

And then there are the bunkers, great big holes all over the course, providing the biggest minefield in any Major anywhere. And, over the years, the course officials have shown no signs of letting up. Today, there are more than 200 bunkers around the course, including 17 on the closing hole. There is nothing genteel or gentle about the place.

In the build-up to the tournament, Player spent much of his practice time escaping from the sand traps. He also decided to keep his driver in the bag and to rely on his trusty 1 iron to keep the ball low and long.

Difficult weather conditions turned the seaside Lancashire town north of Liverpool into a significant challenge. But that suited Player to a tee. During the course of his career, whenever he heard his competitors grumbling about adverse weather conditions, he knew he had the upper hand: "I told myself that I loved playing in the wind and rain and went out and played with a positive mindset." Interestingly, Tom Watson, who secured five Open championships, and nearly a sixth at the age of 59, shared

Player's sentiments. "Wind and rain are great challenges. They separate the real golfers. Let the seas pound against the shore, let the rain pour," he once observed.

The tournament would be remembered for the mandatory use of a larger, 4.3-centimetre ball for the first time in the championship and ugly cheating allegations involving the South African. Opening rounds of 69 and 68 in blustery winds saw Player ease ahead with a five-shot lead over the field, headed by Peter Oosterhuis, with Jack Nicklaus trailing by nine strokes.

With the difficult weather conditions continuing into the third day, Player's performance dipped slightly and he carded a 75. Oosterhuis shot a 73 to close the gap to three, while Nicklaus was the big mover of the day, shooting a 70 to stay in contention.

In the final round, Player fired three birdies and an eagle in the opening seven holes and, in his own words, said he putted like Houdini.

As he marched onto the tee at the 17th, he had a six-shot lead. "I turned to my caddie, Rabbit, and asked: 'What do we need to do here?' He told me: 'Laddie, Ray Charles could win from here. You could go seven-seven and still win the Open.'"

But acclaimed golf writer Michael McDonnell saw it differently. He once titled an article on Royal Lytham "Where No One Escapes", saying, "It is one of the most exhaustive examinations in championship golf, with unquestionably the most gruelling finishing stretch of five holes lying in wait to ambush both hope and ambition." Indeed, the 14th to the 18th, which are all par fours, have been referred to as "Murder Mile".

And so it was when Player's 6-iron approach to the 17th found deep rough.

In his book *To Be the Best*, he recalled: "As we walked towards the green, I wondered whether we would ever find the ball. The first thing I did was to ask an official to put the watch on me to observe the five-minute rule. I was in full view of the cameras. Imagine winning the Open and then somebody claiming I'd gone seven seconds over my allotted time.

"It is a unique aspect of golf that anybody anywhere who spots a rule infringement during play can report it and have official action taken. It was a frantic search in which I even got down on my hands and knees looking for the ball. I asked everybody around me to join in the hunt, but it still seemed like a hopeless task. There was barely a minute of time left when a marshal found the ball."

But the ball was buried in a thick, tangled mass of grass, so deeply that Player was only able to hack it forward about two metres. A bogey took him to the 18th, where, again, he made a hash of his approach shot. The ball came to a rest so close to the clubhouse behind the green that the marshals ruled the structure was an integral part of the course and Player was not entitled to a free drop. He subsequently used the back of his putter and a left-handed stroke to put the ball three metres short of the hole.

Two putts from there gave him a 282, four shots clear of Oosterhuis, with Nicklaus a further stroke behind. He had led throughout the tournament and was the only player to finish under par.

With this triumph, Player shared with Harry Vardon the distinction of claiming the title in three separate decades. But no sooner had the cheering died down than the rumours began surfacing that all was not as it had seemed back at the 17th. The allegation was that the ball he had played was not the one he had hit into the rough, and, even more damningly, that his caddie, Rabbit Dyer, may have placed an identical ball there during the search.

To be sure, this would be a cardinal crime in this, the most sacred of all sports, but Player lashed out at his detractors. As Michael Murphy noted in *Golf in the Kingdom*, "the best players come to love golf so much, they hate to see it violated in any way".

Incidentally, it was not the only time the Black Knight was accused of cheating. In a high-stakes, televised Skins Game in Arizona in 1983, multiple Major winner Tom Watson accused Player of having moved a growing leaf from behind his ball to improve the lie. Both Jack Nicklaus and Arnold Palmer said that they had not witnessed anything untoward. Player hit back, saying it was unacceptable of Watson to make the allegation at the end of the tournament, after he had left the course.*

In addition, Player noted that Watson had won two Majors in 1977, using clubs that did not conform to the rules. "I would hate to have won two World championships – the Open and the Masters – knowing I had used illegally grooved clubs." Watson's curt reply? "It would degrade the championship if I were to get involved in a debate with the little man."

The tournament officials ruled in Player's favour.

The next wave of controversy to envelop him occurred off the course. In 1975, an organisation named the Committee for Fairness in Sport was launched to counter pressure groups that were successfully highlighting the horrors of apartheid around the world. The chairperson of the committee was highly controversial businessman Louis Luyt, and shortly afterwards, Player and Wilf Isaacs, a cricket star, were appointed as its directors.

One of Player's tasks – as the most famous sportsman in the country – was to woo the movers and shakers of American industry. With government funds, some of the giants of corporate America were invited on an all-expenses-paid trip to South Africa "to see the other side of the story".

---

* In 1991, Sherwood Forest Golf Club member John Buckingham instituted legal proceedings against two fellow members – Reginald Dove and Graham Rusk – who accused him of moving his ball to create a more favourable lie. A jury of seven women and one man determined that the allegation was not entirely unjustified and that Buckingham had not been libelled. In terms of the current rules, a penalty can't be imposed once a tournament is over unless the player knows he had broken a rule.

When a group of investigative journalists revealed that Luyt had spearheaded the launch of a pro-government newspaper, *The Citizen*, with taxpayers' funds, it sparked an outcry. Like the Committee for Fairness in Sport, it was a shadowy initiative aimed at prolonging the status quo – the fool's paradise that was apartheid South Africa. The investigation led to government agent Eschel Rhoodie, who had targeted – and snared – two of the most famous white South Africans, Player and surgeon Chris Barnard. While Barnard had pursued a different path in life – medicine – he had shot to international stardom when he successfully carried out the world's first heart transplant in the late 1960s.

Rhoodie, one of the fall guys in the scandal, highlighted the role of Player and Barnard in his tell-all book, *The Real Information Scandal*: "From time to time we were fortunate enough to get the willing co-operation of two great South Africans, Gary Player and Chris Barnard ... In the United States, Gary Player was known to just about every second person because of his famous victories. Between 1975 and 1978, when we were struggling to prevent American investors taking their money out of South Africa, Player played a most important role."

Like Player, Barnard was young, dynamic and easy on the eye. He wined and dined with kings, queens, presidents and other prominent celebrities. And yet, despite his successes in the operating theatre, he was a deeply flawed individual. The notorious Information Scandal, which had snared Player, eventually led to the downfall of the Minister of Information Connie Mulder and Prime Minister John Vorster. "It seemed harmless enough and nothing more than a public relations exercise," Player later recalled. "I had done nothing of which to be ashamed, but perhaps the shock waves of my marginal involvement revealed the scale of the secret strategy."

When I approached Player about this chapter in his career, he bristled at any suggestion that he had willingly endorsed this initiative, saying he had been "duped". He also strongly denied that he had made a R5 000 donation to the committee, and says that while his participation was "perhaps naive", he should not have been implicated in the scandal.

Around this time, Player purchased a retreat far from the madness that was part and parcel of his high-profile international career. About 25 kilometres from Colesberg, in the Karoo semi-desert, he built an oasis that he still calls home. The nearest train station is called Agterlang, and freight trains clatter through the night en route to the industrial centres. His house is nestled against a rocky mountain range that provides some shelter from the freezing winds that whip through in winter. His 8 000-hectare stud farm sits above some of the purest spring water in the country and is home to numerous thoroughbred horses.

Apart from a nine-hole golf course, there is an enormous round stone table used for the inevitably large family gatherings, and a natural swimming pool. While Player also has a home on Jupiter Island, Florida, as well as a jointly owned home (with Jack Nicklaus) at Leopard Creek bordering the Kruger National Park, he finds peace and solitude here in the heart of his homeland.

In 1978, Player won the last of his regular tour Majors – his third US Masters title – at the grand old age of 42. Trailing American Hubert Green by seven shots going into the final round, Player reeled off seven birdies over the last 10 holes and fired a spectacular 30 on the back nine to card a final round of 64. He would later describe that back nine as the finest of his entire career.

Three of his pursuers – Tom Watson, Rod Funseth and, of course, Green – had a chance to catch Player and force a play-off. But Watson saw his 3.6-metre birdie putt die at the death, while Funseth's six-metre putt had the length but never broke, and ended centimetres to the right of the hole.

More than a half-hour after Player had signed his card, Green put his approach 80 centimetres from the hole and prepared for the most important putt of his career. With one Major under his belt – the previous year's US Open – he was accustomed to the cauldron of championship golf. However, the thought of a play-off was surely knocking around his head, because he had lost 17 of them.

Green examined the putt from all angles, and addressed the ball before his concentration was broken by the hushed tones of CBS commentator Jim Kelly in the radio booth beside the green. Green backed off and glared at Kelly before resuming his stance. At the moment of impact, the putter blade opened – ever so slightly – and the ball missed to the right.

It remains probably the greatest Sunday rally at the Masters, and while it was Player's last victory at Augusta, he would compete at the famed course for three more decades.*

On 10 April 2009, Player played for the last time at the Masters, for a record 52nd time. He was the last of the so-called Big Three (Nicklaus, Player and Palmer) to retire from this tournament, a testament to his longevity.

Through no fault of his own, the peak of Player's career coincided with the darkest days of apartheid, and it was therefore inevitable that he would be a red flag for the global anti-apartheid movement.

Player acknowledges that, like millions of white South Africans, he was brainwashed into accepting a political system that was, unanimously, unacceptable; so much so that the United Nations labelled the apartheid system a "crime against humanity". During those dark and dizzy days, particularly in the 1970s, Pretoria was building nuclear weapons, invading its neighbouring states, gunning down men, women and children in the townships, and crying foul when the world took notice.

The reality is that Player was the best available scapegoat for a genera-

---

* In gusty winds at the 1998 Masters, Player became the oldest golfer ever to make the cut, breaking the 25-year-old record set by Sam Snead.

tion of Americans trying to come to grips with their own country's sordid history in matters relating to race relations. Augusta, for example, has come under an enormous deal of criticism over its race (and gender) policies. For decades, all caddies had to be black – Player drew from this pool, using Ernest Nipper on numerous occasions.

Club founder Clifford Roberts once reportedly said: "As long as I'm alive, all the golfers will be white and all the caddies will be black." Until 1990, blacks were denied membership, and the first women – former US Secretary of State Condoleezza Rice and businesswoman Darla Moore – were only admitted in 2012 (after President Barack Obama waded into the debate). For many years, Augusta defended its membership policies, using the tried (and not so trusted) global exclusive club argument that they are "private".

The fractious debate over Player's role as an international star during the apartheid era will never simmer down. Widely excoriated for failing to speak out against the system, he did experience a revelation of sorts.

"My views began to change, particularly as I travelled around the world. The injustice was so obvious and the implications quite chilling. I am now quite convinced that I have played a significant role in trying to eradicate apartheid in South African sport. It was a terrible system," he said.

Whatever his faults, Player – like millions of other white South Africans – reformed his attitude and thinking and embraced the liberation of the country.

His 18-year relationship with caddie Alfred "Rabbit" Dyer often came under the spotlight. It was one of the special bonds in golfer-caddie folklore. They travelled the world together and, in South Africa, Dyer stayed at Player's home, despite the fact that the apartheid-era authorities frowned upon it.

Player also enjoyed a warm relationship with South Africa's first democratically elected leader, Nelson Mandela. Shortly after his release from prison in 1990, Mandela saluted Player for the role he'd played in improving the lives of millions of South Africans. "You have not received the recognition you deserve," he said.

In an interview with *Playboy* magazine, Player said that he has peace within himself that he has always done his best for his country. He added that claims that he did not play a big enough role in challenging apartheid "often hurt me most deeply, because it [was] so untrue".

Player's immense accomplishments have filled many books and, with nine Majors under his belt, he is likely to remain his country's primary golfing pride for many years to come.

Here are a few of his other notable achievements:

On the Senior PGA Tour, he won 18 times from 1985 to 1995. He won the South African Open 13 times and the Australian Open a record seven times (Nicklaus, with six wins, and Australian Greg Norman, with five, come closest to this). He secured five wins in the World Match Play Championships, and he is the only golfer to win The Open in three different decades.

In 2000, he was voted Sportsman of the Century in South Africa. He was inducted into the World Golf Hall of Fame in 1974. The Player Foundation, established in the 1980s, has raised more than $50 million for needy children on six continents. Having covered at least 25 million kilometres in the air, he is the most travelled sports personality of all time... and, of course, most of this was done on commercial airlines, unlike many of today's leading players, who have their own jets. He has spent most of his life living in hotels and motels (and more than a year of his life at Augusta, Georgia). Oh, and he still found time to do 1 000 sit-ups a day well into his seventies.

If Sinatra did it his way, Player did it the hard way.[*]

---

[*] In July 2013, Player became the oldest athlete (at the age of 77) to pose naked for ESPN's *Body Issue*.

3

Papwa

"I have an idea that it will be only a matter of time now before a Major title falls to the world's greatest cross-handed golfer — Sewsunker Sewgolum."
— Herbert Warren Wind

The young boy clawed his way through the tangled bushes that ran alongside the Umgeni River. Its waters snaked towards the Indian Ocean — nearby, he knew, because of the droning of the rolling surf. The air was thick and heavy as it always is deep in summer, and the tropical fragrances of Durban's colourful foliage were magical.

Above and around him, the chattering of vervet monkeys served notice that he was being watched. Barefoot and naked, save for a dhal, he moved as swiftly as the thick overgrowth would allow. And then he saw the light streaming through a gap in the bushes. He edged closer and observed what appeared to be an enormous field. There was movement — a group of European men carrying large bags and sticks.

They would talk among themselves and then stand over small white balls. He watched these missiles streaking through the air before disappearing into bushes, sandpits and ponds. The men were persistent, though, and time and again they would find themselves back on that giant lawn. Their target, it seemed, was an elevated mound with the flattest (and greenest) surface this wide-eyed youngster had ever seen. On that stage, the men continued with this, the strangest of rituals. A flag was lifted out of the ground and, one by one, the balls were guided into a hole.

Young Sewsunker Sewgolum had witnessed the most unique sport on the planet, a game that had its origins on the windswept plains of the Royal and Ancient Golf Club of St Andrews. It may have been a world away for the poor, illiterate child, but one day he, too, would strut his stuff on those hallowed links. After what seemed like an eternity, the boy walked back along the banks of the river where his ashes would one day wash into the ocean.

Sewgolum's great-grandparents were among the thousands of indentured labourers who had sailed south from Madras and Calcutta to a new land that offered hope and prosperity. The first group, which arrived on board the *Truro* goods ship in 1860, had secured a three-year contract paying 30 shillings a month to cut sugar cane. Over the next 50 years, more than 150 000 Indian labourers would arrive in Natal, and most decided to stay after finishing their contracts. They also paved the way for an influx of wealthier Indians – predominantly from Gujarat state – who were established traders and businessmen.

Sewgolum was born in Durban on 12 December 1928, the fourth of six children. His nickname, Papwa, was derived from the Indian term meaning "darling child". His father, who cut lawns for the Durban municipality, spent much of his recreational time playing football for a local Indian team. Sewgolum would frequently return to the Beachwood Golf Club, about a kilometre away, and watch members of this whites-only institution at play.

The year after his birth, 1929, saw the opening of South Africa's first golf club for "non-Europeans". The Durban Indian Golf Club, a nine-hole goat track located at the Indian Recreation Grounds in Currie Fountain, became an institution overnight.

When Papwa related his experience of witnessing the game of golf, his father took him back into the bushes, where they selected a suitable branch from a guava tree and whittled it into the shape of a putter. Unusual perhaps, but Gary Player, Sam Snead and Chi Chi Rodriguez all started with clubs carved from branches (with the latter using crushed cans as balls). And European giant Seve Ballesteros's first weapon was the discarded blade of a 7 iron that he had glued to a stick.

Sewgolum's putter became an instrument of much joy. He levelled the dirt in his back garden, inserted an empty tin can into the ground and spent many hours putting towards it from every position imaginable. Despite being right-handed, the boy felt most comfortable holding the club with his left hand below the right, the most unorthodox grip imaginable.

In addition, his hands were separated with no overlapping or interlocking fingers to assist the wrist to work in unison. Because the grip hindered a natural swing and forced him to bend his left arm on his back swing, he compensated by turning his hips much earlier during his downswing in order to generate enough club-head speed. "I believe a man should swing a club the best way he knows how," he told *Golf Digest* in 1964.

Sewgolum might have been drawn to the rarest of grips, but he was not alone. Johannesburg-born Vincent Tshabalala, who won the European Tour's French Open in 1976, also played his full shots cross-handed. Today, a World Cross-Handed Tournament is still held annually. This unorthodox reverse-grip style has also become increasingly popular with golfers trying to control putting or chipping yips. It helps to lock the forearms and encourages the shoulders to move the arms in unison.

When the boy was eight years old, the glint of a club that had been left in the rough at the Beachwood Golf Club caught his eye, and his father used a hacksaw to cut the shaft to a suitable size. On weekends, the young boy would accompany his father on fishing expeditions on the beaches north of Durban, where he spent hours hitting "bunker shots".

He attended the Sir Kumar Reddy Indian School until Standard 2 (Grade 4), but following the death of his father in 1938, the family was beset with another tragedy when his mother, Parvathy, lost her eyesight, when Papwa was just 13. Sewgolum's formal education came to an end when he was forced to find work.

His love of golf saw him return to the Beachwood course, where he was able to secure part-time employment as a caddie, earning less than 2 shillings per round (excluding tips). Nevertheless, the experience was invaluable, and for the next 14 years he learnt the art of reading a golf course. Although it was an all-white institution, caddies were allowed to compete at the club championship, where Papwa made the quarter-finals in 1939, at the tender age of 11.

As a teenager, he began shooting sub-par rounds as well as several unofficial 62s – well below the course record of 64. There is a subspecies of the mighty albatross – a hole-in-one on a par four – and Sewgolum achieved this once at Beachwood's 16th hole. Analysts said he was able to draw on his deep spirituality as a practising Hindu to release any physical and psychological tension in his body – on and off the course.

In 1946, the year Papwa made his first big break as a golfer, the Indian government requested that the discriminatory treatment of Indians in South Africa be included on the agenda of the very first session of the General Assembly. This after the government of General Jan Smuts, in the face of outrage by its Indian population and the strongest protests from the Indian government, enacted the notorious Asiatic Land Tenure and Indian Representation Act, the so-called Ghetto Act. This legislation sought to give Indians limited political representation and defined the areas where they could live, trade and own land.

India demonstrated its outrage by imposing trade sanctions and withdrawing its High Commissioner. The largely Durban-based Indian community, with the blessings of Mahatma Gandhi, launched a passive resistance struggle over the next two years. Smuts addressed the UN Assembly in 1946 to defend the country's policies, arguing that the UN was not the correct forum in which to discuss the matter. The global body rejected his argument and, with a requisite two-thirds majority, called on Pretoria to bring its treatment of its Indian population in conformity with the basic principles of the UN Charter. South Africa ignored the order.

Back in Durban, Sewgolum secured his first tournament win – the Natal Indian Open – at Curries Fountain with borrowed clubs (and shoes).

In 1950, he married Suminthra at a low-key wedding. They were both 22. Like the union of his parents, it was an arranged marriage in the Hindu tradition. The couple would have five children: Dinesh, Rajen, Sewnarain, Romilla and Deepraj.

Papwa's break came one afternoon in 1957, when he was caddying for heavyweight businessman Graham Wulff and two of his colleagues, Jack Lowe and Edmund Anderson. Another Beachwood member, David Andrews, made up the four-ball and, at the fifth hole, the volatile Andrews hit a weak drive and asked the barefoot caddie for advice on the club selection for his second shot. With 146 metres remaining and playing into the lightest of breezes, Sewgolum drew a 6 iron from the bag and handed it to him. The shot was fair, but well short, and Andrews questioned the young caddie's selection.

With tempers frayed, Sewgolum placed the bag on the ground and turned and walked away. Wulff, who regarded Sewgolum as "very timid and respectful", was silenced by the reaction, while Andrews called him back and handed him the same club. After an awkward silence, there was stifled laughter as Sewgolum – with that astonishing stance – addressed the ball. But the swing was wide and wonderful and the ball soared towards the green before landing softly, less than a metre from the hole. Andrews and the rest of the four-ball were suitably impressed, particularly when the caddie added that he was a scratch golfer and had secured a string of victories in local non-white tournaments.

At the time, Wulff was well on his way to becoming a giant in the international cosmetics industry. His most successful invention, Oil of Olay cream, is one of the top skin-care retail brands in the world, accounting for around $3 billion of Procter & Gamble's annual revenue.

The couple subsequently played together, alone, and the Danish national believed that his caddie – despite that bizarre upside-down grip – could go far: "He was very supple, coiled like a snake, and he hit the ball with tremendous power." Wulff employed Sewgolum to place caps on the bottles of the cream products at the Durban factory, which gave him a steady income and, more importantly, the afternoons off to work on his game.

Wulff also met Sewgolum's family, who was living in one of Durban's ruined slums in the same shack where the breadwinner was raised. Wulff bought Sewgolum "a decent set of clubs" and his family a comfortable, single-storey house nearby. However, it appears that Papwa's deeply superstitious wife, Suminthra, vetoed any ideas of relocation, and an exasperated Wulff was forced to sell the property.

By the late 1950s, the National Party government was battling to deal with the complex race issue, and the groundswell of antagonism from other countries added to the pressures it was facing at home. The sweeping race laws that defined – and deeply divided – South African society at the time posed a challenge for sports administrators throughout the country. Who could compete with (or against) whom? Or who could watch what (and where?) were all burning issues for a government that had so badly lost its way.

In golf, the absurdity was evident, with some of the biggest tournaments, like the South African Open or the Natal Open, implying that they were indeed "open" in every sense of the word, just like the US Open. In these strange days, the word "open" meant open to white South Africans.

Interestingly, in 1958, after Wulff's business partner Jack Lowe spent a year in Australia, they came up with the idea of getting Sewgolum to tour there. Wulff arranged for a film to be made of Sewgolum demonstrating his reverse grip with Athlone professional Phil Retsina. "It was sent to Australia, and shown to the appropriate authorities, but they would not grant him a visa to go there. Although the Australians criticised our country, they do not encourage dark skins in theirs," Wulff said at the time.

Nevertheless, following Lowe's return, their cosmetics business was booming and Wulff needed to fly to England to set up a European leg of his operation. It was then that he and Lowe came up with an extraordinary idea: enter Sewgolum in Europe's lucrative Open Championship.*

In 1959, Sewgolum's entry for the Open Championship at Muirfield was accepted but, as Wulff recalled, that was the easy part: "He had no papers whatsoever, so we had to guess a date of birth for him, get him a passport, and teach him to write his name simply by copying one I had written out for him."

And there was the not so small matter that he had never set foot outside of Durban.

A keen pilot, Wulff was a member of the Aero Club of South Africa, and was chairman of the Durban Wings Club. His business successes enabled him to purchase a single-engine Piper Comanche 250 ZS-CKH four-seater aircraft, which had a retractable undercarriage and was capable of flying up to 1000 kilometres at a time.

"A good friend of mine, Wolfie du Plooy, who was an airline captain with Rhodesian Airways and had recently flown a light aircraft to Europe from Durban, gave me a lot of good tips, and I planned the trip very carefully before setting off," Wulff recalled years later. "As the Comanche did

---

* Another Durban-born Indian, Ramnath Boodhan, had paved the way three decades earlier when he competed (with little success) at the tournament.

not have an autopilot, I would have to fly and navigate myself, so I planned to fly only in the mornings, leaving the afternoons free to do business where possible and some sightseeing."

On 27 May 1959, the golfer's friends and family arrived at Durban's Stamford Hill aerodrome to bid farewell to their hero, who wore a blazer and the official tie of the Durban Indian Golf Club. His wallet was stuffed with banknotes from well-wishers at the club. The aircraft carrying Wulff, his second wife Mavis and Papwa peeled away from Durban, banked over the Indian Ocean and headed for the first hurdle – customs control in Johannesburg.

Fast-forward nearly half a century and I am leafing through the late Wulff's yellowing photo album and unpublished memoirs with his daughter, Sally Fraser. She's recounted her father's extraordinary friendship with Sewgolum ("we never saw colour") and, of course, that adventure of a lifetime. "For years we heard different accounts of this trip, and it's still unbelievable. They visited some incredible places and had some narrow escapes," she said.

From Johannesburg, the trio flew to Beira, Mozambique's second largest town, which is located on the banks of the Pungue River and above the beaches of the Indian Ocean in Sofala Province. They stayed at the Grand Hotel, which was just five years old at the time and was being billed as the "pride of Africa". Although widely regarded as the most spectacular hotel on the continent, its owners failed to secure a casino licence and the venue was never profitable. During the Mozambican Civil War from 1977 to 1992, it served as a refugee camp and is now occupied by thousands of squatters who use the swimming pool to wash their linen.

Wulff recalled how he visited his passenger in his luxurious hotel room: "Papwa had a huge double bed to himself, and when I went to see him, he was chipping balls across it."

And dinner that evening was also an eye-opener: "He was quite bewildered with everything, especially meals, and did not know why we each had three knives and forks to use."

Next stop was Dar es Salaam, Tanzania's biggest and richest city, where they stayed at another beachfront hotel. They then headed north over Kenya, dipping and soaring through the valleys, over the Ngorongoro Crater and the plains with the biggest herds of animals on the planet, and past the thrilling, snow-capped peak of Kilimanjaro (Africa's highest). Said Wulff: "The whole flight was a tremendous thrill, especially as it was at a comparatively low altitude level, and we were at the best advantage, as we were able to see all the features along the route."

After spending a night in Nairobi, it was west to Entebbe on the Lake Victoria peninsula for a further fuel stop. There were further stops at Juba, a river port on the banks of the Nile in Southern Sudan. They then flew 1 200 kilometres northeast to the capital Khartoum at the confluence of the White Nile, flowing north from Lake Victoria, and the Blue Nile, flowing west from Ethiopia. The next leg of the journey took them over the mighty Sahara Desert, the world's third largest.

Fraser said her father often let his wife fly the plane when they were at cruising altitude so that he could take a nap. "One afternoon he woke up because of the turbulence over the desert, and saw that they were surrounded by storm clouds. He took over the controls and dropped the plane quickly. After a while, he spotted the Nile and followed that into Cairo."

They landed in the largest city in the Arab world, where they spent a week taking in the pyramids and viewing the recently discovered gold statue of Tutankhamun, the boy king of Egypt, at the city's museum.

The final leg of this epic journey through Africa took them to Benghazi and then Tripoli in Libya (where Muammar Gaddafi was a teenager living in a family tent near Sirte, where he would meet his end in 2011).

THE KINGS OF SWING

Eighteen years before the trio's whirlwind visit, most of South Africa's 2nd Infantry Division had faced the onslaught of German General Erwin Rommel's tanks and Stukas at Tobruk and Benghazi.* The fortified port cities were vital for the Allies to ensure the defence of Egypt and the Suez Canal. Despite suffering enormous losses, the Allies regrouped and, at the end of 1942, secured a key breakthrough with victory at El Alamein. By May 1943, the entire North African region had been cleared of German and Italian troops.

After crossing the Mediterranean, the party of three had further refuelling stops in Tunis and Rome before heading to London, the cultural centre of the world. They had navigated their way across Africa and Europe and yet, as Wulff recalled, they couldn't find Gatwick Airport.

"I crossed the coastline at what I thought was Brighton after flying north from France over the Channel. We should have been at Gatwick in nine minutes. There are no real landmarks in that area, with numerous towns, railway lines, roads and the rivers all looking the same. I could not spot the airport, and then found we were approaching London, so I called 'mayday' on the emergency frequency, and the RAF station answered.

"Suddenly I saw a huge aerodrome below, and as my fuel was running low, I decided to land and radioed Gatwick accordingly. The aerodrome turned out to be the famous fighter base Biggin Hill, and we received a wonderful reception. After taking on some fuel, we went on to Gatwick, only some five minutes' flying time away. There, again, we had a super reception by air traffic control, customs and immigration, and then we caught the train to Victoria Station."

The post–World War II reconstruction effort was in full swing, and record numbers of imports and exports and tourists were passing through the city.

---

* About 160 000 South African volunteers (of all races) had served in East Africa, the Western Desert and Italy.

First stop was a branch of Barclays Bank, where Wulff discovered that the manager was from East London (that's South Africa's East London). "He was a keen golfer, and as I had brought Papwa over to compete in the British Open, he was extremely interested and we got on famously."

Their accommodation at 30 Craven Road, near Paddington Station, was basic (£7 per week), but there was plenty of colour in the form of a brothel directly across the road.

Wulff then flew his "bewildered" passenger to Edinburgh and made arrangements for him to practise golf at Gullane, North Berwick and Muirfield, where the British Open was to be held. One of the highlights of the week building up to the Open was that he was able to practise with Gary Player, who, Wulff said, "took a liking" to Sewgolum.

Player (who was joint favourite, along with Peter Thomson, to win the tournament) was beaten twice by Sewgolum in their practice rounds, but when the tournament proper rolled around, it was an altogether different story.

In the qualifying rounds, Sewgolum shot a 147 to (just) qualify for the main championship, along with 59 others. He then scored 79 and 73 (152), failing by four shots to make the cut for the final two rounds. Player went on to win the tournament, his first Major victory.

Wulff conceded that it must have been "a tremendous strain" on Sewgolum's nerves, but, at the same time, he believed the experience had been invaluable and that it would surely be a launch pad for other victories. The South African–born Indian was subsequently entered for the French and German Opens and, while he performed "reasonably well", it was at the Dutch Open at the Haagsche Golf and Country Club in The Hague where he made his mark.

Perhaps Player's ice-cool display at that year's Open had had an effect on him, because he displayed nerves of steel in the opening round, to lead with a 67. This was followed by an impressive 69 and, with a three-shot lead over Dutch champion Gerard de Wit, the Durbanite was in the driving seat. Following the final day's 36-hole contest, Sewgolum held a slender two-shot lead over De Wit, with one hole to play. Then, for the first time, he stumbled. He bombed his drive into the rough on the left-hand side of the fairway, while De Wit's effort was crisp and straight.

With 220 metres left to the hole, Sewgolum fired a 3 wood long and left onto an adjacent fairway behind a row of trees, which blocked his path to the green. With the wind shifting constantly, he changed his clubs repeatedly. He settled on a pitching wedge – wide open – and cleared the trees, but found rough again. His fourth shot landed safely on the green, leaving him with a 1.5-metre putt for the championship. His stroke was perfect, and the ball disappeared down the throat. Sewgolum (67, 69, 74, 73 – 283) had become the first golfer of colour to win a national tournament in Europe and the third South African after Sid Brews (1934 and 1935) and Bobby Locke (1939) to win that particular tournament.

Back in South Africa, news of the triumph was met with wild celebrations – particularly in Durban's Indian community.

In the documentary film *Papwa – The Lost Dream of a South African Golfing Legend*, his wife, Suminthra, recalled that "there were huge crowds lining the streets" to see their hero. From the National Party government, however, there was a steely silence as it tried to fathom the significance of the feat. *The Leader* magazine noted that the racial barriers the nationalist government had implemented in sport were backfiring badly: "Papwa's success in the home country of the original Voortrekker, the birthplace of Dr Verwoerd, makes the embarrassment even more unbearable for the apostles of apartheid."

And the *Golden City Post* noted the irony in that Sewgolum's own government didn't recognise him as a full South African, and that "back home, the winner of the Dutch Open wouldn't be allowed to take part in a white tournament except in a menial capacity".

Sewgolum received a hero's welcome when he returned to the port city. The streets were a splash of colour with thousands of saris, the air was thick with the fragrances of incense and spices, and the cheers of the crowds mixed with the exotic tunes of another continent.

The *Daily News* described his breathless arrival as follows: "The plan was that the tired sportsman should return home as soon as the aircraft touched down. But this was not to be. A cavalcade of cars and buses followed his car after he had been chaired shoulder-high from the tarmac airstrip. At Clairwood, the motor convoy was mobbed by residents. Many onlookers clung to his car, stood on the sides and even held on to the roof as it crawled along."

For white South Africans who were relishing the successes of Bobby Locke and Gary Player at home and abroad, Sewgolum, with that upside-down grip, remained something of an enigma. However, for the hundreds of thousands of Indians (South Africa has the largest population of Indians outside of India), he was a giant, a home-grown sporting hero who was capable of berating the best – at home and abroad. Like Tiger Woods decades later, he was responsible for taking what was almost exclusively a whites-only sport to a much bigger audience.

Nevertheless, once the euphoria died down, the Dutch Open champion found himself back at the Olay factory placing caps on the endless line of bottles. The fact that he was barred from competing in "white" tournaments meant that the victories he continued to notch up didn't pay the bills.

Funding remained a problem, and Louis Nelson, who was now managing the rising star, set up the Sewgolum Trust Fund with the aim of raising funds for international travel. The target of £1 000 was reached within a few months, and Sewgolum was able to make his second trip to Europe. He played in a number of tournaments in England, securing a fifth place in the Yorkshire *Evening News* tournament, and he also qualified for the Open Championship at St Andrews. However, it proved to be a repeat of the previous year, as he was unable to make the cut for the final two rounds.

Nevertheless, at the Dutch Open Championship at Eindhoven, he successfully defended his title with scores of 69, 71, 71, 69 (280), a three-shot victory over fellow South African Denis Hutchinson (72, 71, 70, 70). This double triumph once again shifted the spotlight onto his troubled homeland. Within a few months, the Sharpeville massacre, on 21 March 1960, which left 69 unarmed protestors dead, served notice that there were serious problems with the country's race laws, and the international antagonism towards the apartheid regime continued to gather momentum.

When the Natal Golf Union received Sewgolum's application to compete in the whites-only Natal Golf Open Championship in 1960, it became a political hot potato. The issue was referred to the South African Golf Union (SAGU) – the country's governing body – but the request was turned down on the grounds that the entry of non-Europeans into national and provisional championships "would be a departure from customs and traditions". The issue was also addressed in England when Dennis Brutus of the South African Sports Association backed Sewgolum, and called Labour Party MP Fenner Brockway to urge the British Professional Golfers' Association to reprimand SAGU.

Sewgolum then applied to compete in the South African Open in March 1961, and SAGU approached the government for authorisation. In terms of the Group Areas Act – one of the cornerstones of apartheid – different "races" were required to live in separate areas. Nevertheless, there was a loophole in the law that was open to interpretation. If, for example, a golf tournament that permitted all races was held in a so-called whites-only area, then "non-whites" would be permitted to compete – with restrictions.

On the eve of Dr Hendrik Verwoerd's departure to a Commonwealth Prime Ministers' Conference, where Pretoria's membership was on the agenda, the government backed down and a permit was granted (by F.W. de Klerk, the then Minister of the Interior). The next hurdle was to circumvent the Group Areas Act by securing a permit enabling Sewgolum to travel from Natal to East London in the Eastern Cape, where the tournament would be staged. This was granted, and he arrived at the club, where he was not permitted to use the change rooms (in terms of the petty apartheid laws).

Shortly before teeing off, he gashed a finger in his car door (he used the vehicle as his change room) and had to be treated by a doctor. He failed to mount any challenge during the tournament and finished 16th.

In his biography *From Pariah to Legend*, Chris Nicholson notes that the issue of obtaining a permit for every tournament affected Sewgolum's game and left him emotionally exhausted. Even when permission was granted, it often came through at the very last minute, and he was not always in the best state of mind to participate in the event.

Sewgolum's problems were compounded with a personal tragedy when he lost his youngest son after a short illness in November 1962. After a lengthy break from the game, he won the Natal Non-European tournament yet again, with a record five-under-par 67.

He successfully defended his title the following year, and became a three-time winner of the event in 1963.

The 1963 Natal Open at the Durban Country Club was the tournament that would put Sewgolum on the map for various reasons. The course, which opened in 1922, has always had the elements of a classic parklands course, combined with a seaside links. It was also a venue that was a microcosm of the ills of apartheid society in Natal. Like many other exclusive clubs around the country, it selected its members on the basis of race and religion, so, at various times, other ethnic groups, like Afrikaners or Jews, were excluded.

The "whites-only" club attracted some of the most affluent and successful businessmen and other personalities of the time. And, like so many upmarket institutions in the vicinity of the tourism Mecca of the time – Durban's famed Golden Mile, they were served by Indian staff. Indian doormen would welcome them at the entrance, Indian chauffeurs would park their cars, and Indian waiters would take their food and drinks orders. On the course, of course, Indians were largely restricted to carrying golf bags.

It was in the maw of this surreal situation that Sewgolum found himself at the 1963 edition of the Natal Open. With the car park chock-a-block with horse-drawn carts and dilapidated cars, Sewgolum was the crowd favourite. He opened with a lacklustre 73, but a 70 on the second day saw him tied with Barry Franklin, just a shot behind the leader, Cobie le Grange.

On the final day, with squalls of rain passing through, Sewgolum kept his game on track and found himself on the par-four 18th needing just a par to beat Bobby Verwey (Gary Player's brother-in-law) and Denis Hutchinson. He laced a solid drive that caught the wind and ended up deep on the right-hand side, below the fairway and the green. He then fired a full pitching wedge to the edge of the green and two-putted from there.

It was one of the most extraordinary achievements in South African sport. Sewgolum was hoisted onto the shoulders of his adoring followers – a new icon for any person of colour in this land of apartheid.

What followed went down as one of the most shameful incidents in South Africa's sporting history. As the rain swept across the course, the laws of the land kicked in and the white competitors, their supporters and the club members made their way to the clubhouse. Sewgolum, who was surrounded by hordes of supporters who were clamouring to touch, hug and hold him, made his way back to the car park, where he changed into dry gear.

A temporary structure had been erected on the terrace, where Sewgolum received his trophy and a cheque for $1120. The camera flashes highlighted the moisture – rain, sweat and tears – on his face. An official history of the club recalls the moment: "A fierce wind blew and the sky was black... Then down came the rain in pounding torrents."

The local and international media devoured the story. Images of the prize-giving were flashed around the world and played a significant role in cementing the sporting boycott against South Africa. "In any normal land, the treatment of this fine player would be considered an insult to him and an acute embarrassment to everyone else," said the defiant *Rand Daily Mail* the day after the event. The headline of the *Post* newspaper screamed: "The Glory and the Shame". The *Daily News*: "South Africa is a land of perpetual mid-summer ideological madness". And London's *Daily Mirror* smirked: "Here's a story to warm the cockles of your heart – that is, if you are a bigoted, prejudiced and vicious racialist." Incidentally, South Africa's state broadcaster, the SABC, had cancelled its live commentary of the tournament at the last minute and failed to broadcast the result.

Allan Henning, who won the SA Open in 1963 and who played against Sewgolum on many occasions, told me that he shudders when he thinks of the damage that moment caused. "It was an absolute crime. I could cry about it."

But was there more to this story? "Absolutely, but nobody will ever get it right." When pressed, Henning says there is a bigger picture. "The guy was a phenomenon and he had a massive support base. When he played in Durban, the place would swarm with his supporters. It was an unbelievable experience."

Henning suggests that one possible reason for the snub is that the clubhouse couldn't accommodate all his supporters.

Either way, the incident had further highlighted Sewgolum's potential and, at the same time, marked a new low point in the failed experiment of racial segregation. The issue was addressed in parliament when Helen Suzman, the lone parliamentary representative of the opposition Progressive Party, noted: "Papwa receiving his trophy in the rain will do more to establish our image abroad than all the glossy pamphlets issued by the State Information Department."

The Minister of Information, Frank Waring, conceded that the incident had caused the country considerable harm, but he blamed opposition parties and the media for fuelling the flames.

Sewgolum's characteristic low-key response to the saga was: "There would have been no fuss if it hadn't rained."

After the 1963 Dutch Open, Sewgolum selected Fred Paul, an insurance salesman with the Southern Life Assurance Company, to manage his affairs. Paul realised very quickly that he was associating himself with the most controversial sportsman in the country at the time, who was under the watchful eye of state security operatives.

In November 1963, Sewgolum won the Grand Prix tournament – with a mixed-race field – at the Royal Durban Course. Once again, he received his trophy in the rain, but the situation was somewhat defused when the runners-up also received theirs outside. A few days later, he was informed that his application to play in the 1964 South African Open had been accepted – along with that of Ismail Chowglay. The tournament in Bloemfontein presented fresh challenges for the two players of colour and the National Party government.

In terms of the laws of the Free State province at the time, Indians were not permitted to spend more than 24 hours at a time inside its borders. As a result, the two Indian golfers were forced to commute from Kimberley every day. At the tournament, they were provided with a standing-room tent, pitched a few metres from the clubhouse, in which to change. Allan Henning won the tournament, with Gary Player, Sewgolum and New Zealand star Bob Charles finishing joint third, three shots behind.

The following year, Sewgolum was allowed to compete in the Natal Open again, and this time he would face the country's most decorated golfer. Gary Player was at the peak of his career and either loved or loathed around the world. And yet there was enormous speculation about how he would fare against Sewgolum.

Certainly, the duel had all the ingredients of a world-title boxing match. In one corner the Black Knight, a 1.7-metre giant of a man who had three Majors under his belt; in the other an illiterate former caddie who had won at home and abroad, despite some seemingly insurmountable obstacles. The smart money was on the white guy.

The stakes got even higher when Sewgolum returned to his vehicle in the car park before the tournament and reportedly found a dead Indian mynah bird placed under one of the windscreen wipers. He tried to block the image out his mind and focus on the task at hand.

For three days, Player and Sewgolum were neck and neck as their support bases swelled and became increasingly vocal and animated. On the final day, Sewgolum drove off the first tee two shots behind Player but, by the 18th, held a two-shot lead. By then, thousands of people were lining both sides of the fairway. Sewgolum's drive faded too far right and tumbled down a slope, far below the green. His wedge shot flew into a greenside bunker, and it took three more shots to end his agony with a bogey five.

Player, who had found the green in regulation, was faced with a three-metre putt to force a play-off. The path of the putt was straight and true but, at the death, it wobbled slightly and lipped the cup. Sewgolum had stared down his challenger and had become the finest golfer in all of South Africa (for that day, at least). Player, to his credit, saluted his opponent and noted that he had chipped "like a man from Mars".

Days after this magnificent feat, the National Party government saw it necessary to further restrict "non-white" audiences from attending certain sporting events (this would effectively block Sewgolum's army of supporters from attending the SA Professional Golfers' Association Championship later that year). Prime Minister Hendrik Verwoerd then took matters even further by warning New Zealand that they would not be allowed to tour South Africa with mixed-race Maoris in their squad. The world took notice, and a number of new boycotts were implemented.

In 1965, Sewgolum came within a whisker of winning the South African Open, losing out to Retief Waltman by a single shot. The apartheid-era sports authorities again set their sights on him when he applied for a permit to play in the Natal Open in 1966 as the defending champion.

His rejection letter stated that the permit allowing "Mr Sewsunker Sewgolum (Indian) to occupy the Royal Durban Golf Club is refused". No reasons were given, but a few days later the decision was reversed. This time, it was Player's turn to win the event (with Sewgolum in second place), and it was now evident that any efforts to compete in predominantly white tournaments was an exercise in futility. Sewgolum learnt that the Security Branch, which had been monitoring his movements for some time, had a thick file on him.

While preparing to compete in the Western Province Open in Cape Town, rat-faced security police hauled him out of bed in the dead of night while he was staying at the home of prominent activist Sissy Gool. They warned him that he had become an embarrassment to the South African government. Shortly afterwards, Sewgolum and Paul drove to Port Elizabeth for the General Motors Open. The organisers had arranged a caravan for the two on the course but, when darkness set in, they felt alone and uncomfortable. They checked into a non-white hotel in the city, and when they returned the following morning, they said the caravan reeked of gas. An apprentice came to inspect the leak and discovered that the pipe had been cut.

On 6 September 1966, South Africa was rocked to its core with the assassination of the so-called architect of apartheid, Prime Minister Hendrik Verwoerd. Moments after taking his seat in the House of Assembly, he was attacked by a knife-wielding parliamentary messenger,* who managed to stab him four times before being apprehended.

Verwoerd was replaced by Balthazar Johannes Vorster, who oversaw the abolition of the coloured voters' roll, the escalation of South Africa's border wars, and further alienation for Sewgolum and other sportspeople of colour.

Sewgolum had become a severe embarrassment for the National Party government, which was facing growing international scrutiny, particularly in the wake of the 1960 Sharpeville massacre. However, instead of easing its race laws, it was determined not to give in to the growing pressure.

Sewgolum was subsequently denied permission to compete in a number of events. The government, which had decreed that mixed sport would not be permitted, lashed out at the global community, but the country was almost completely isolated during the 1970s and 1980s.

When Sewgolum was barred from competing in the Transvaal Open, it effectively prevented him from competing at the lucrative Major championships overseas. He took his plea to Vorster:

> This humble letter is designed to bring to your notice the many difficulties I am faced with in order to play in the South African Golf Circuit... I am proud to be South African and I shall always remain loyal to my country. This banning order preventing me from playing

---

* The assailant was later identified as Dimitri Tsafendas, the illegitimate son of a Mozambican mother and a Greek father. He was declared mentally unfit to stand trial.

golf for a living will indeed cripple me financially. And, as a result, my family will be destitute. In this hour of crisis, I can only appeal to you to consider my plight and the plight of my family. I close this letter with the fervent prayer that my pleading will not go in vain.

He received no response.

Papwa then accepted an invitation to compete at a tournament in Calcutta. He had become a household name in India, and there was a great deal of interest in the treatment he had endured as an Indian in a country with a "white" government. And, of course, many wondered aloud how this land at the southern tip of Africa had produced a champion golfer when India, with a population of more than 610 million at the time, had failed to do so.

Large crowds followed Papwa around, and although he only managed a sixth place in the tournament, he made many friends. He then signed up to compete in tournaments in Dallas, Houston, New Orleans, Oklahoma City, Wentworth, Dublin and Toronto. But he was homesick, and when he came down with food poisoning during the Houston Open, he threw in the towel and returned to South Africa.

After receiving extensive medical treatment, he returned to the UK for the 1967 Open Championship. The venue was Royal Liverpool (Hoylake), and he breezed through the qualifying stages, but failed to make any headway in the championship proper. He also lost the Dutch Open by a single shot to Donald Swaelens's 273, and was fifth in the French Open with a score of 281.

Soon afterwards, the UN General Assembly called on all its member states to suspend sporting ties with South Africa. In England, the Halt All Racist Tours (HART), which was headed by South African–born activist Peter Hain, began baring its teeth and, in 1969, it severely disrupted a rugby tour of the UK by an all-white South African team.

Sewgolum's last Open was at St Andrews in 1970, where he shot a record-breaking 64 in the qualifying tournament. However, he shot 72 and 78 in the tournament itself, to miss the cut by one.

A decision was taken that Sewgolum would not return to the UK and Europe in 1971 but, at the end of that year, he travelled to Australia with Gary Player, who also helped fund that trip.

In 1972, the South African government – clearly smarting from the hostile reaction by governments and organisations around the world against its race policies – introduced a new policy allowing top black golfers to play in a few leading tournaments, including the South African Open. Ironically, the first player of colour to win the Open was Vijay Singh, an Indo-Fijian of Hindu background, who triumphed at Glendower in 1997 and went on to become the top-ranked golfer in the world in 2004 and 2005.

Heavy with sorrow, Sewgolum had become a shadow of his former self, and alcohol had numbed his killer instinct and shaken his steady resolve.

Nevertheless, he returned to the UK in 1976 and competed in the Kerrygold Tournament at Waterville in Ireland. His final tournament was the 1977 Natal Open for "non-whites". He won it for the 20th time in 22 starts.

By then, he was ready to concede that his career was effectively over. In an interview with sportswriter Norman Canale in 1978, Sewgolum noted that while it was heartwarming that golfers of all races were beginning to mix freely, "it's come too late for me".

Canale observed: "Sadly, Papwa, the shuttlecock of sports apartheid for so many years and the man who did all the front-running in the movement for mixed golf, was now too old to savour the honours out there on the fairway."

Contrast that to Gary Player, who won his ninth – and final – Major championship, the US Masters at Augusta, that year. While it marked the end of an incredible chapter in Player's life, a new one was opening. Over the next three decades he would win a further nine Majors – this time on the lucrative seniors' Champions Tour, for professional golfers over the age of 50 – and focus on golf-course design and other business ventures.

Washed up and wounded and shorn of purpose, Sewgolum began to throw in the towel. His weight ballooned and, coupled with excessive drinking (he was sponsored by Gilbey's Gin) and smoking, his health deteriorated quickly. Vapid and frustrated, he spent much of his time reflecting on his remarkable career and, no doubt, wondering what might have been.

When Wulff reflected on Papwa's rags-to-riches and back-to-rags story, he was clearly exasperated: "He never learnt to better himself and he spent the money he made on keeping his family going. If he had stayed under our guidance, we would have arranged for him to have royalties on clothing, shoes and sporting equipment bearing his name. With his publicity and fame and the fact that he was a hero in the eyes of the Indian community, they would have sold well."

On the evening of 4 July 1978, Sewgolum began complaining of chest pains at his Riverside home. He spent the evening in bed, but didn't sleep well. The following morning, shortly after brushing his teeth, the 49-year-old suffered a massive heart attack. Within minutes, he was dead.

Although his family was desperately poor, the community came together to provide a decent burial. The body was bathed, anointed with a mixture of water and sandalwood, and daubed with turmeric powder and water. It was then garbed in new cloth, and flowers, incense and rose water decorated the coffin. An enormous cavalcade snaked its way from the family home to the Clare Estate Crematorium.

When the open coffin was removed from the hearse, it was carried through a tunnel of friends and family who held golf clubs in the air to form a symbolic arch. While his son Deepraj chanted the Hindu prayer commanding his father's spirit to be reincarnated, Graham Wulff looked on pensively. Their unlikely journey together was now over. What it was and what it could have been. The funeral pyre was lit and the flames consumed what was left of this Durban giant. The ashes were collected and Sewgolum's sons released them into the Umgeni River, where they washed into the Indian Ocean.*

Thirty-five years after his death, I'm standing on a tee-box with his son Rajen and grandson Nisharlan, and staring down at one of the finest settings on any golf course, anywhere. It is the signature 17th hole at Ernie Els's Oubaai links course on the Garden Route. The par-three green is guarded by four large bunkers and is framed by the blue-grey waters of the Indian Ocean, which slap onto the cliffs far below.

A gleaming-white $45 000 Mercedes-Benz C200 – the trophy for a hole-in-one that day – squats alongside the tee-box. There is light cloud cover, the wind is gentle and westerly, and the pin lies 144 metres away, below, towards the back, left side of the green and guarded by the front, left bunker.

Rajen, a scratch golfer, selects a club and addresses his ball. The resemblance to his father, in almost every way, is uncanny. The 50-year-old is lean, handsome and wears his moustache well. Like his father, he is right-handed and, like his father, he is most comfortable holding the club with his left hand below the right. His stance is wide, he leans into the stroke and hits an easy 6 iron. From the moment of impact, its flight is pure. The ball soars to the right over the bunkers and fades left towards the flag before landing, pin high, about 15 metres from the cup on the lightning-fast green.

---

* In terms of Hindu tradition, within 10 days the soul of the deceased is believed to have acquired a new body, and the consequences of the last life, its rewards and punishments, are unfolded.

It slowly begins to track the hole and, for a moment, threatens to release and gain momentum before it dies a respectable 10 metres away.

I follow with a full 7 iron, and our shots are similar. Mine, too, starts out right before easing left, but the ball catches the slope on the right-hand side of the green and dribbles into the first bunker.

Next up is Nisharlan, a PGA-accredited professional at Durban's Windsor Golf Course. He selects an 8 iron and, yet again, the green is attacked from the right with a well-controlled fade. His ball lands softly, a couple of metres from his father's, and although I put my bunker shot between theirs, he drains his nine-metre putt for birdie and the hole.

During the course of the day, we attempted to unpack Papwa's incredible career. Rajen, who was 16 at the time of his father's death, has spent much of his adulthood nurturing his father's legacy, and he bristles at published claims that he died in a shebeen. ("It was at home…I was at his side when he died.") He is adamant that the circumstances "Dad" found himself in were the direct cause of his death.

"Yes, he smoked, but everyone did back then. And yes, he drank, but there were underlying factors. A year after he won the Natal Open [in 1965], he was banned. That happened when he was in his prime as a sportsman and it hit him hard. Golf was his trade and he didn't have anything to fall back on. He was emotionally and physically crippled. Alcohol was an escape," he says with his voice trailing off.

When Rajen reflects on his father and his legacy, he sums it up by saying "there is no anger".

"My father was never bitter despite all the things that happened to him. He was very humble on and off the course and he always controlled his temper. He was a good man."

We reflect on that infamous Natal Open prize-giving ceremony – one of those bizarre "only in South Africa moments" that thrust Sewgolum and the rest of the country's sports stars into the glare of the international spotlight. And we agree that it marked a significant turning point in South Africa's relationship with the civilised world.

After all, in 1964, South Africa was barred from the Tokyo Olympics following India's proposal. Eight years later, it was formally expelled from the International Olympic Committee, and South African sport remained in the spotlight for all the wrong reasons and a target for the rapidly growing global anti-apartheid movement.

In 1967, South African–born "coloured" cricketer Basil D'Oliveira found himself plying his trade with Worcester and at the centre of an international storm when he was selected to play for England against his former homeland. There was an outcry in the British House of Commons when Pretoria ruled that "teams comprising whites and non-whites" could not be allowed to compete in South Africa. The tour was called off, and South African cricket (which was enjoying a golden era at that time) found itself isolated.

Two years later, Dawie de Villiers led his Springbok rugby team to the UK, where they faced the full wrath of the anti-apartheid movement. An attempted hijacking of the touring bus by protestors saw the vehicle veering out of control in central London and ploughing into stationary cars. Torchlight parades were held outside the visitors' hotel and smoke bombs hurled onto the field.

Attempts by the authorities to soften the race laws for soccer had mixed results and, in 1974, tensions peaked when Kaizer Chiefs met Hellenic in the final of the "non-racial" Chevrolet Cup. A riot broke out at the Rand Stadium and referee Jack Taylor, who had blown the whistle at the recent Germany-versus-Holland World Cup final, was powerless to stop a pitch invasion. Two years later, Soweto erupted in flames and the revolution began in earnest.

In 1981, a Springbok rugby tour plunged New Zealand into its biggest ever political crisis with full-blown riots tearing the country apart and a deciding Test match marred by activists dropping flares and flour bombs from a light aircraft into the stadium.

When South African golfer Jeff Hawkes, while competing in the Scandinavian Open in 1982, reportedly said, "Negroes are like children," and "You can't teach people to drive before they can ride a bicycle," it went down like a lead balloon. Shortly afterwards, the Netherlands (where Sewgolum had enjoyed his greatest international triumphs) barred South African golfers from competing at the Dutch Open at Zandvoort.

In 1984, a barefoot Bloemfontein teenager named Zola Budd beat the sports boycott by competing in the 1984 Los Angeles Games under British colours. In the 3 000-metre women's final, race favourite Mary Decker got tangled in Budd's legs and was unable to finish. Budd continued to lead the race for a while, but the chorus of boos and whistling crushed her spirit and she finished far back in the field. Ironically, Budd's running career effectively ended when she was found guilty by the IAAF of competing in South Africa.

In 1985, the French government banned its Renault Ligier team from racing at Johannesburg's Kyalami racetrack, which had hosted the Formula One flagship event for many years and had to be mothballed for international competition.

For the rest of that decade, South Africa, in the grip of a state of emergency, increasingly isolated and bruised, began limping towards liberation and the dawn of Archbishop Desmond Tutu's Rainbow Nation.

Twenty years after Sewgolum's death, Enuga Reddy, the former director of the United Nations Centre Against Apartheid, spoke of the significance of Sewgolum's infamous prize-giving ceremony, saying, "It greatly helped the boycott of apartheid sport," and, as a result, played an important role in the liberation of the country.

In 2004, Sewgolum was posthumously awarded the Order of Ikhamanga, South Africa's highest honour for achievement in the performing arts and sport. President Thabo Mbeki's citation read: "Sewgolum had the crowning experience of winning the Natal Open and then suffering the humiliation of receiving his award in the rain outside the clubhouse, because the Group Areas Act did not permit him to receive it inside."

Today, a golf course in Durban is named after him. The Papwa Sewgolum Golf Course is an 18-hole flat woodland course situated in the suburb of Reservoir Hills. And, across the hills, towards the ocean, another course has attempted to find peace with itself. At the Durban Country Club, where the most infamous prize-giving ceremony in South African history had taken place, a plaque is now fixed to the clubhouse facing the 18th green. Its citation recognises Sewgolum for being the first person of colour to win a professional golf tournament in South Africa, and it salutes "the talent of this self-taught legend of the game".

A good man, a great golfer and a beacon for all of South Africa, Papwa Sewgolum may not have won a Major, but the role he played in levelling the courses in this deeply fractured land can never be underestimated.

4
The First Lady of Swing

"Hit it with your arse." – **Percy Little**

Soon after South Africa's Sally Knight Little set the golfing world alight with her first tour victory – thanks to one of the finest killer blows in championship history – her homeland ignited and the revolution began in earnest.

On the afternoon of 9 May 1976, global golf's new female hero scored a famous birdie to win the inaugural Women's International in South Carolina by a single stroke.

Just five weeks later, on the morning of 16 June 1976, thousands of seething Soweto students marched from their schools to the Orlando Stadium to protest against the National Party government's policies. Shots were fired and 13-year-old Hector Pieterson (and many others) died. It marked the beginning of the end of white minority rule and the flames, as Peter Gabriel predicted, grew higher and higher.

Images of the riots spread around the world, not least in the United States, where there was no shortage of racial tension and where the Black Power movement was fast gaining momentum.

Not surprisingly, high-profile South Africans plying their trade in the land of liberty were soft targets. Of course, it was nothing new for battle-hardened heavyweights like Gary Player, who had been a symbol of his homeland for many years, but for this up-and-coming female star, it was a bitter pill to swallow.

Nearly 40 years later, Little's journey has gone full circle and she's sharing her experiences with me in Cape Town's affluent suburb of Mouille Point, where she grew up and first made her mark. Like Little, this area has experienced significant upheavals and, like her, it has weathered the storms and emerged looking magnificent.

On the far side (just) of 60, her eyes are blue and clear, her skin is radiant and she still looks every inch a lean and lithe athlete. Mouille Point is bathed in dramatic light – and darkness – as the sun repeatedly tries to break through menacing winter clouds. Behind us, a wedge away, the gorgeous Metropolitan golf course is framed by Signal Hill. In front of us, the Atlantic Ocean shimmers as ships and yachts slide past and waves slap gently against the breakwater, which was built by slaves in the 18th century.

Across the bay lies Robben Island. During the apartheid era, when its prison housed Nelson Mandela and many of the country's future liberation heroes, Mouille Point was classified as a whites-only area. That meant that its beaches, parks and, of course, golf club were off-limits to the vast majority of the population.

The suburb's original golf club, which was established in 1895, was used to stable thousands of horses during the Anglo-Boer War (1899 to 1902). After that, it flourished and enjoyed a reputation for its manicured fairways and pristine setting. With the liberation of the country in 1994, Mouille Point also went through a revolution of sorts. Like many other residential areas near the country's urban centres, there was an influx of prostitutes, drug dealers and other criminals.

In the late 1990s, trendy restaurants in the neighbouring areas of Sea Point, Camps Bay and the V&A Waterfront – the country's most popular tourist attraction – were targeted by a shadowy terror group. There were many casualties.

But the residents in these Atlantic seaboard suburbs fought back and won. Today, this cosmopolitan area is viewed as a model of urban rejuvenation and it commands some of the highest property prices on the continent.

When the "new" South Africa was given the rights to host the 2010 FIFA World Cup – global football's showpiece event – the organisation's heavyweights scoured Cape Town for the most spectacular site for a 68 000-seater stadium capable of hosting one of the tournament's semi-finals. They identified it slap-bang in the middle of the golf course where Little had learnt her trade decades earlier. To say that the decision divided the club, the community and the city is an understatement, but there it stands, white, loud and, most of the time, empty.

In return, area residents were rewarded with a magnificent new urban park and a golf course that snakes its way around the venue and boasts the finest greens in the province.

When she reflects on the "early years", Little is well aware that she had a privileged upbringing in this breathtaking setting. She was born on 12 October 1951, and, by the age of 10, was a keen golfer. She secured an apprentice membership at the Metropolitan Golf Club thanks largely to her flamboyant father Percy, whose frequent advice to any golfer within earshot was "hit it with your arse".

"He took pride in all aspects of my game, to the point of being over-analytical about it," she says. "Most of all, he helped me develop a solid, positive attitude."

Little (Junior) took it all in and her game improved dramatically during those formative years. Back then, girls and golf were not a popular mix and the young teen found herself sneaking away to get her fix. Today, she credits her late father for building her swing. "He warned me to steer clear of [instruction] books because they might complicate it."

A pupil at the Ellerslie High School in Sea Point, Little had begun to turn heads with her golfing talent when she had a life-altering setback at the age of 15. Her boyfriend – with her on the back of his motorbike – slid into a car in Camps Bay, a few kilometres away. They weren't wearing helmets and Little bore the brunt of the impact when she mangled her right femur "and lost half my ear". After being admitted to Groote Schuur Hospital, she was in traction for 15 weeks and was required to wear a caliper for six months.

Despite making an almost full recovery, her right leg was the "weak link in my armour" for much of her glittering career, and she underwent several knee operations. Her cartilage has been completely removed and, today, under the guidance of orthopaedic surgeon (and legendary former Springbok scrumhalf Divan Serfontein) she is determined to avoid having knee-replacement surgery. "The alternative is hyaluronic acid injections. It creates a padding in the joint of the knee and reduces the pain levels."

When the teenager's caliper was removed she resumed training, but was restricted to chipping and putting "and that's when I really got the golf bug".

"Gary [Player] had watched me play before the accident and sent me a get-well telegram when he heard about it. That meant a lot to me, and it was a major incentive for me to compete at the highest level."

In 1967, when she was just 15 years old, the Capetonian was picked for the Western Province team and won the Women's Western Province Championship in the same year. Two years later, she represented the Western Province Males team in an interprovincial, where she played off the championship tees and matched giants like Dale Hayes.

She also won the Transvaal Stroke Play Championship on three occasions, the Natal Match Play in 1969, and the Rand Match Play in 1969 and 1970.

By the age of 17, Little was the Metropolitan Golf Club's most famous export, having clinched more than a dozen national and regional amateur titles.

Her provincial career was intertwined with several other formidable female youngsters, most notably Alison Sheard and Gillian Tebbutt. Sheard won the South African Open Title on nine occasions, as well as the Spanish Open and Welsh Classic and, in 1976, attained the ladies' course record at St Andrews in Scotland, which she held for 16 years. In 1979, she also won the Ladies' British Open at Southport and Ainsdale, taking the title by three strokes from Mickey Walker. Tebbutt, who won her first Western Province Match Play Championship in 1972 at the age of 18, would go on to win it 15 times, along with the South African Match Play title (on five occasions), the Hong Kong Open Amateur Championship three years in succession, and her club championship (Rondebosch) 36 times. She also played in two World Amateur Team Championships (Vancouver and Malaysia), and was the coach of the South African team at the World Championship in Germany in 2000.[*]

But Little was, almost always, a metre ahead of the chasing pack. In 1971, after shooting the lowest individual score at the World Amateur Team Championship in Madrid and clinching the South African Match Play and Stroke Play titles, the young Springbok was voted South African Sportsperson of the Year. It was time to turn pro.

A bigger stage beckoned, and Little set her sights on the United States, where the game had mushroomed, thanks largely to the exploits of Jack Nicklaus, Arnold Palmer and, of course, Gary Player. When she touched down in New York in 1970, America was still the unchallenged giant of the capitalist world and an exciting cultural melting pot.

That year Richard Nixon was president, the rock band Aerosmith

---

[*] Sheard and Tebbutt were inducted into the Southern Africa Golf Hall of Fame in 2010.

formed, a Boeing 747 made its first commercial passenger trip to London, the US invaded Cambodia, Billy Casper won the Masters, the US *Apollo 18* and the USSR's *Soyuz 19* linked up in space, students protesting at Ohio's Kent Place University were gunned down, *Sports Illustrated* magazine cost 15 cents, and the Beatles released *Let It Be* and then disbanded.

Young Sally Little, America's exciting new import, was making waves with her unbridled enthusiasm and striking style of play. She used her entire body, coiled within a lithe and lanky frame, to manufacture an aesthetic and fluid swing. And it wasn't just Little's large game that turned heads. Under the headline "LPGA's Swinging Beauty", the *St Petersburg Times* described her as "well-built with a Hollywood face framed by long brown hair, falling below her shoulders".

Let's pause for a moment and consider the soap-opera world of ladies' professional golf that Little had joined. Their game had taken shape back in the 1930s, when female golfers were hired by sporting goods companies to travel around the country and host clinics and exhibitions. They attracted considerable interest, and it was decided to arrange a series of contests (with $100 war bonds as the prize money). The Women's Professional Golf Association – the precursor to the LPGA[*] – was formed in 1944 to serve their interests, and it is the oldest female professional sports organisation in the US.

Its blueprint was the men's tour, which had been flourishing since 1917 and, from the start, the women's umbrella body has always played catch-up.

In Little's day, the LPGA women were operating in a man's world. At most LPGA tournaments, the women temporarily took over the more spacious men's locker rooms (with pot plants or banners used to cover the

---

[*] The LPGA was founded in 1960 by 13 female players. Although it is primarily based in the United States, it has also hosted tournaments in Canada, Mexico, Singapore and the UK.

urinals). Corporate sponsors leaned heavily in favour of the men's tour and were more influenced by the LPGA's so-called celebrities, like Nancy Lopez, than in the standard of their play. The television coverage of the men's tour was also significantly greater. But there were signs of hope.

By the mid-1970s, when Little began to find her feet, the leading players were taking home around $150 000 a year – more than the total purses of all the LPGA tournaments 20 years earlier.

At her first Ladies' Professional Golf Association (LPGA) tournament in Winchester, Virginia, Little earned a pay cheque of $44, "and I knew it could only get better" (it did, and she pocketed a total of $1 670 for the season).

"Back in South Africa, I used to think I was the greatest. It took me some time to accept the fact that, in America, I am just a terribly tiny fish in a very large pond," she was quoted as saying in Mark McCormack's book, *The World of Professional Golf.*

Little said that she was unaccustomed to the determination of the American tour pros and said it didn't suit her. "When I started pounding balls like them [at the practice range], it didn't do me any good. In fact, it was detrimental to my game."

When Gary Player had first arrived in the US in the early 1960s, he found the conditions very different to South Africa. After all, the fairways were wider, softer and longer than the "tight and fast" offerings throughout most of South Africa. Little concurs: "It's much, much longer and you really have to *hit* the ball."

On top of that, there was the not-so-small matter that she was missing her friends and family back home. "I gave myself 12 months and told myself that if I hadn't made it, I would head back home." But she would get caught up in the moment and it would take longer – much longer – for her to find her feet and secure her first tour win. She required knee surgery before the 1973 season, which affected her game, but the following year she returned with a bang and had her most successful season to date in terms of prize money.

However, life in the fast lane, fuelled by fast food and partying, took its toll, and her weight mushroomed. At one stage, she topped the scales at 72 kilograms and began realising that it was hurting her prospects. She said her weight problem had seriously endangered her professional career. "I was just plain fat, but I never realised it until I went home to South Africa, where my mother took one look at me and nearly had a heart attack."

She booked herself into a Cape Town health spa, where she adjusted her diet significantly and, as the kilograms dropped off, her energy levels soared and the putts began dropping.

Despite nursing a wrist injury, Little came within a whisker of winning the US Open Championship for women in 1975. After sharing the lead after the third round, a final-day 79 derailed her campaign. Her first big break came at the $70 000 inaugural Women's International (Ladies' Masters) at Moss Creek Plantation on Hilton Head Island in South Carolina in 1976. The event was modelled on the Masters, with a mixture of the leading professionals and amateurs. It was even originally named "The Ladies' Masters" until Clifford Roberts, the co-founder of Augusta National, got wind of it and warned that there would only ever be one Masters. Sandwiched between thick forests and swampy alligator-rich marshes, the course is nicknamed "Devil's Elbow".

The previous week, Little had a forgettable performance at a warm-up tournament in Augusta, "and I realised that all the [negative] media comments about my game were getting to me. I was determined to relax that weekend, to take it easy and enjoy myself. And it worked – from start to finish."

With opening rounds of 71 and 69, she climbed through the field of 71, which included Mickey Wright, the greatest female golfer of all time, with 82 victories behind her. But Little's track record showed that she still had a long, long way to go. "I've led tournaments before, then done some really stupid things," she told reporters that night.

The early favourite was Savannah, Georgia, native Hollis Stacy, who opened with a pair of 72s, but two front-nine double-bogeys on the Saturday wrecked her campaign. Despite recording three bogeys, at the 13th, 15th and 17th, Little bounced back with a three-metre birdie putt at the 18th to sign off for a three-round total of 211, five under par and sole possession of the lead. Hot on her heels was Australia's Jan Stephenson, while Americans Judy Rankin, Debbie Massey and Murle Breer were tied in third place.

On the final day, Little lost her lead to Stephenson at the 13th, fought back to tie at the following hole, regained the lead at the 15th, before three-putting the 17th for a bogey. Under pastel skies, the Australian, who posted another 70, sat back to see if the South African could notch up a par at the last to secure a tie and a play-off.

With everything to play for, Little clattered her drive into the rough, leaving the ball above her feet for the second shot. Because the greens were extremely fast that day, she knew she had to just clear the bunker to the left of the green to attack the flag. She muscled into the shot that arched towards the pin from the moment of impact, but the ball caught the lip of the bunker and dropped in.

Her third shot was about 70 feet from the pin, and she later recalled that her knees were shaking: "I had to get it up and down from there … it was a big, big challenge." She selected her 56-degree Wilson wedge, climbed into the bunker, dug her feet in and splashed the ball onto the green. It bounced once, twice, rolled towards the open-mouthed spectators and, all the while, tracked the pin. When it dived in, South Africa's little giant leapt into the air to celebrate one of the finest shots ever seen on the tour. Game over. Even Stephenson, who had been savaged by that blow, joined in the applause.

"What a blast!" was the *Golf World* headline, which described the feat as "a mighty Little explosion". The drought was over. South Africa's most famous female export had finally quietened her critics about her mental strength under pressure.

"As a kid, I always fantasised about my first big win and how I would achieve it. This was better than anything I had ever dreamt about." The LPGA agreed, and a plaque at that hole records this feat ("Sally Little holed out from this bunker to win the 1976 Women's International"). With birdies on three of the last five holes, her 71, 69, 71, 70 – 281 saw South Africa laying claim to its first Women's Major winner. The great Gary Player, who was momentarily out of the spotlight, overshadowed by Little's success, joined the rest of the nation in saluting its latest sporting icon.

As Little said, "I had many, many chances over the years, but had folded when it really mattered. This marked a big breakthrough for me. You have to learn to win."

That heady victory opened the floodgates, as she went on to win 14 more professional titles in all, 12 of them between 1979 and 1982, when she finished third on the money list with $228 000.

Her second tour victory came in March 1978 at the expense of dynamic rookie Nancy Lopez at the Honda Civic Classic (following a play-off). That year, Lopez marked her debut by igniting the tour with a series of victories. She was being tipped as the natural successor to the great Mickey Wright and, like Little, her youthful good looks brought some shine to a tour that was deep in the shadows of women's tennis, where Martina Navratilova, Chris Evert and Billie-Jean King were hogging the headlines. The Mexican-American shrugged back her Honda Classic setback to win a record nine tournaments that year.

The Colgate Women's PGA European Championship at Sunningdale in August 1978 demonstrated how Little had matured. Although she finished runner-up to Lopez, three-time Open Champion Heny Cotton was one of the first to congratulate the South African when she walked off the 18th green. SA Golf Union official Judy Henderson, who witnessed the duel that day, said Little was completely comfortable in the limelight.

"I had the feeling that she was quite the crowd favourite, and the galleries [that] followed her seemed to bear this out. She is every inch the professional golfer, but warm and friendly with everyone."

Her performance at the 1978 US Open soon afterwards turned many a head when she shot a career-low 65 "by sinking every putt I looked at". Little went on to win two more tournaments that year – the Barth Classic in August and the Columbia Savings Classic the following month.

A year later, Little and Lopez would do it all over again at the Bent Tree Classic when Little breezed through armour-piercing rain on the final day to shoot a five under 67 (10-under total), leaving Lopez two shots behind.

Under the headline "Sally Little for President", golf scribe Jim Achenbach said it was unfortunate that she wasn't old enough and hadn't been born in the land of the Stars and Stripes (two of the requirements for that poisoned chalice). He noted that Little had recorded six straight one-putt greens. "Call it one-putt-itis. Call it birdie fever. Whatever, the 27-year-old native of South Africa came face-to-face with immense pressure and responded brilliantly."

The 1980 LPGA Championship – the first Major of the year was played at the Kings Island Grizzly course in Mason, Ohio – and Little was in contention from the start. With a three-round total of 212, she was in the mix with the previous year's winner Donna Caponi Young, two-time US Open champion JoAnne Carner and, most notably, Jane Blalock, who found fame with 27 LPGA Tour wins – and infamy for a rules violation that ended up in court.[*]

---

[*] After the second round of the Bluegrass Invitational in Louisville, Kentucky, in 1972,

Little's final-day campaign got off to a spluttering start when her drive found a bunker at the 1st and she carded a bogey. Only at the 165-yard, par-three 5th did she steady her campaign with a searing 6 iron into stiff wind, which landed three feet from the pin for a tap-in. At the par-five 9th, she received a reprieve when her 3-wood second shot found a pond guarding the green but skipped out, and she was able to salvage par. She followed that with a 20-foot birdie putt at the 10th to take a three-shot lead, but then scored bogeys on the next two holes.

The stakes were sky high at the 16th, a tricky 80-yard par three guarded by a lake and swirling winds. The 1.76-metre South African hit a strong left-to-right fade that took the ball out over the water and into the teeth of the wind, which deposited it three metres from the pin, where she secured par.

On that home stretch, she hit four of the last six greens in regulation and romped home in 73, for a total of 285 and the only player south of par that weekend. Blalock was three shots behind. Little, who was $22 000 richer, said the victory had given her confidence an enormous boost "and I'm ready for whatever lies ahead".

She would go on to win three times in 1981: the Elizabeth Arden Classic; the Olympia Gold Classic; and the CPC Women's International, where she defeated Kathy Whitworth in a sudden-death play-off. However, her

---

she was disqualified for signing an incorrect scorecard, after it was ruled that she did not mark her ball properly on the 17th green and then failed to take a two-stroke penalty for the infraction. The LPGA executive board subsequently suspended her for a year following claims that players had signed a petition arguing that probation, a fine and disqualification from the Louisville tournament was not enough punishment. She took the LPGA Tour to court and won the case (and $4 500 in damages). Those damages were tripled in March 1975, and the LPGA was ordered to pay her hefty legal fees ($95 000).

season was derailed with a bizarre injury she picked up while leading the Lady Light Tournament in New York in July. She lifted her golf bag in a hotel lobby and felt "something go" in her back. Although she played on through the pain, she had to withdraw, in tears, halfway through the final round. A chiropractor said the injury to her spine was related to the motorcycle accident she'd had as a teenager.

In 1982 – Little's golden year – she secured four tour victories, plus two runners-up and three thirds. The most significant victory that year was the $310 000 Nabisco Dinah Shore because, a year later, it was elevated to Major Championship status.

The stretch of desert called Rancho Mirage is not for the faint-hearted. The streets are named after stand-up comics, and banjos and handguns are the weapons of choice. In the build-up to the event, Little was firing on all cylinders, with four top-10 finishes, including victory at the Olympia Gold Classic near Los Angeles.

At the 6 255-yard Mission Hills Country Club course, Little kept American Hollis Stacy in her sights. Thursday's driving rain and gusty winds were replaced by perfect conditions on the Friday, when Stacy carded a 65 to hold a three-shot lead. A 71 on the Saturday saw her increase her lead to five, but on the Sunday, Little carded four birdies on the front nine and began to reel her in.

At the 12th, the lead switched hands and Little – one hole behind – went on to shoot the lights out and card another four on the back nine to shoot 64 – 10 under par. Throughout the round, her approach shots nestled under the flag and a steady putter finished the job. "I was playing at a level that I reach sometimes," she later said. It was the best round of her life (76, 67, 71, 64 – 278), and Stacy, who limped home three shots behind, acknowledged that she had spent much of *her* round watching Little's "ass bending over to pick her ball out of the hole".

That year was memorable for two other reasons; Little's father died, in March, and she secured her US citizenship.

Not surprisingly, that got tongues wagging in South Africa, which was, by 1982, half-ruined and fast running out of friends. When Gary Player, who had made a point of keeping South Africa as his base, took a swipe at Little, it hurt. It still does. Explaining this significant decision, she said she had become a target for anti-apartheid activists "and it was a massive problem".

"Pepsi, which sponsored a tournament in Atlanta, threatened to pull out when they heard I was playing; I received death threats; I was barred from entering Japan and they sent me back [to the US] on the next plane. The same thing happened in Mexico. I was looking over my shoulder everywhere."

In that heady period between the Soweto uprising and the liberation of the land in 1994, South Africa had become reviled around the world. And stars like Little, because of their international prominence, bore the brunt of this.

"Unlike Gary, by 1982 America had been my home for many years. That was where I lived, where my career was," she said. "It was not about a political viewpoint; it was about making the most of my career."

No sooner had the Florida-based Little settled into her new role as an American citizen than she began suffering from a serious stomach ailment. She was diagnosed with endometriosis, a gynecological medical condition in which cells from the lining of the uterus appear and flourish outside the uterine cavity.

"I was told that I had six months to fix it or I would be in serious trouble." She switched to a "100 per cent holistic diet" in which she eliminated sugars and meat "and focused on the good stuff like carrot juice". That and four operations over the next three years saw her gradually regaining her health.

She would subsequently throw her weight behind the Susan G. Komen Foundation, the largest non-profit breast cancer organisation in the world, serving as its global ambassador.

In 1984, her best finish was a second place at the Potamkin Cadillac Classic and, the following year, she tied for fourth at the du Maurier Classic (which saw her become the LPGA's 12th dollar millionaire).

In 1986, Little came close to a third Major, losing an 18-hole play-off to Jane Geddes at the 1986 US Women's Open. While the following season was largely uneventful (her best finish was tied 14th at the Keystone Open), she was back to her best at the 1988 British Championship, where she came within a whisker of winning her second Major, at Nottinghamshire's Lindrick Golf Club.

In a dramatic sudden-death play-off for the title, Australian Corinne Dibnah sealed the deal with an 8-iron approach shot to six feet at the second extra hole, which set up a birdie and the title. Defending champion Alison Nicholas put up a brave defence of her title, finishing one shot behind.

Little's final LPGA victory came at the 1988 du Maurier Ltd Classic, which was sponsored by du Maurier Ltd (an associate of Imperial Tobacco Ltd and one of the four Major tournaments on the Tour). The tournament was staged at the Vancouver Golf Club in suburban Coquitlam. Little, who eased into the lead in the second round, seemed in control on the final day until two bogeys opened the door for big-hitting Brit Laura Davies, who had won the US Open the previous year.

At the 18th, Little hit a long drive down the middle, while Davies fired into a row of trees on the right-hand side. Little found the green, but Davies hit the shot of her life to get her ball back into play. It found a greenside bunker, and Davies then "stiffed" her bunker shot to two feet from the pin. Little stepped up and glided her eight-metre putt into the hole for a round of 71, a 72-hole total of 279 and a one-shot victory.

It was her first tournament victory in six seasons and the 14th of her career.

Little was subsequently awarded the 1989 Ben Hogan Award from the Golf Writers' Association of America. The award salutes golfers who have fought back from serious illness or injury.

The rest of the decade was, for the most part, forgettable (her best finish was tied 18th at the 1989 Jamaica Classic). That trend continued into the new decade and for the rest of her professional career. Her last full season of play was 2000, when she was recognised during the LPGA's 50th anniversary as one of the LPGA's top 50 players and teachers.

In 2005, 28 years after she had settled in the US, Little returned to South Africa, saying that "the passion I have for my homeland became a powerful calling". But her journey was not over, and she harboured a dream of ploughing her considerable experience back into the sport, particularly at junior level.

It was, of course, an entirely different society from the one she had left all those years ago. The ostracised nation that had limped from one crisis to another during Little's self-imposed exile had become a giant among nations, with the sun shining brightly on its impressive liberation. Its sports stars, no longer shackled by race legislation, took the world by storm, not least in golf, where Ernie Els and Retief Goosen were ranked in the top five in the world, with an army of talented male – and female – juniors rising through the ranks.

A year after her return, Little's motherland won the 2006 Women's World Amateur Team title in Cape Town, with Nike-backed Ashleigh Simon looking like the most likely successor for her crown. And several of her compatriots were plying their trade on the Ladies' European Tour, including Stacy Bregman, Lee-Anne Pace, Morgana Robbertze, Tandi Cuningham and Laurette Maritz. This progress was rewarded, and the

South African Women's Open returned after a two-year absence in 2012, co-sanctioned by the Ladies' European Tour.

The challenge, for Little, was to identify and nurture young black female golfers "and give them [a] chance". She subsequently established the Sally Little Charitable Trust, which channels corporate sponsorships to create job opportunities for young black women to teach the game in rural areas. The grassroots campaign received government approval after Little addressed parliament.

In 2005, Little was honoured with a Lifetime Achievement Award for her efforts as a player, coach and supporter of South Africa's development programme. And in 2009, she was inducted into the Southern Africa Golf Hall of Fame.

As Little reflects on her extraordinary career, she takes considerable pride in the fact that she played a pivotal role in putting South Africa's women golfers in the global spotlight. Her journey is by no means over, but she also takes comfort from the fact that the sport was good to her. "Remember, the game is much bigger than any individual, so nurture it," is her parting advice.

5

The Comeback Kid

"For all his kindness and gentility, Nick Price is as driven as anyone in the game." — **John Feinstein**

The Soweto riots coincided with the collapse of white minority rule in South Africa's northern neighbour, Rhodesia, and by 1978 Prime Minister Ian Smith – who had once vowed that there would not be black rule in his country for a thousand years – recognised that the game was up. With his regime near the brink of collapse, he signed an accord with three black leaders, led by Bishop Abel Muzorewa, who offered safeguards for white civilians. As a result, elections followed in April 1979. The United African National Council (UANC) party won a majority, Muzorewa became prime minister and the country's name was changed to Zimbabwe.

In December 1979, delegations from the British and Rhodesian governments and the Patriotic Front signed the Lancaster House Agreement, ending the civil war. In fresh elections in February 1980, Robert Mugabe and his Zimbabwe African National Union (ZANU) party won a landslide victory.

"If yesterday you hated me, today you cannot avoid the love that binds you to me and me to you," said Mugabe as the world watched in awe.

The continent's second last white colony had fallen, and the international spotlight now shifted to South Africa, which was fast becoming the pariah of the international community.

For Nick Price, both countries would mould his upbringing and shape his golfing career, one that would ultimately see him ranked as the top golfer on the planet.

His British-born parents – Raymond and Wendy – were pioneers, and their respective journeys took them to Asia, where they met and married. They both served as volunteers in the Indian Army during World War II (he was a major in the infantry, she a lieutenant in the nursing corps). Their first son, Kit, was born in 1946.

When the India-Pakistan clashes broke out in 1947, the young family boarded a mail ship with the aim of settling in Sudan. But it was not to be.

From 1898, the United Kingdom and Egypt had administered all of present-day Sudan as the Anglo-Egyptian Sudan, but northern and southern Sudan were administered as separate provinces. In 1943, the British began preparing the north for self-government but, three years later, in 1946, they reversed this policy and decided to integrate north and south Sudan under one government. The South Sudanese authorities were informed at the Juba Conference of 1947 that they would in future be governed by a common administrative authority with the north. Tensions soared, and the owners of the mail ship gave Port Sudan a swerve and headed for safer climes.

During the war years, South Africa had provided crucial ports – particularly in Durban and Cape Town – which served troops travelling from Europe to Burma and the Pacific Islands. And thousands of visitors drew hope from the immortally magnificent Perla Gibson – the so-called Woman in White – who spent countless hours at the end of Durban's long breakwater serenading them with favourites such as "Wish Me Luck as You Wave Me Goodbye". When the Prices' vessel docked in Durban, Gibson was long gone, but the setting was still surreal.

Soon afterwards, Price bumped into an old British friend who had moved to South Africa after the war. This, then, was a land of extraordinary promise. Price set up a clothing manufacturing business and the couple had two more sons – Tim in 1950 and Nick in 1957.

In 1961, the family packed up and headed to Rhodesia, South Africa's northern neighbour. Nick was just four at the time, and although his memories of this period are "very vague", he does recall the "black Plymouth with tail fins" his father owned and the fact that his parents were "dead against apartheid".

At the time, Rhodesia was the so-called "breadbasket of Africa" and, reportedly, the safest country in the world. Nevertheless, like South Africa, the political system was fatally flawed and, for the white minority government, unsustainable. Although the Bush War or Second *Chimurenga* ("rebellion" in Shona) was still a decade away, insurgents from ZANLA, the military wing of ZANU, and ZIPRA, the military wing of the Zimbabwe African People's Union (ZAPU), had begun agitating against the Rhodesian goverrnment.

But for the young Nick Price and his siblings, who were growing up in one of the most beautiful countries in the world, such issues were far from their minds. Reflecting on his upbringing, Price is aware that he experienced something out of the ordinary.

His large hands, powerful forearms and broad shoulders serve notice that he remains a formidable athlete despite the fact that his glory days continue to fade. His face is well tanned and the twang on his tongue – he has been based in Florida for many years – belie the fact that African blood courses through his veins and he's grounded in African values. When he draws you into his world, he is engaging, formidable and, as all will agree, immensely likeable.

America's 2012 Ryder Cup captain Davis Love III said there is a consensus among professional golfers that Price is the "nicest guy around": "He is the same every day. He says 'hello' to everyone. He's just a genuinely nice, friendly guy."

Price says he is content with what life has served him and he reflects on his childhood with pleasure.

"It was a wonderful time. There wasn't any money, but we got by just fine. It was a simple and healthy lifestyle, and sport was just about everything in our lives," he recalls.

Apart from participating in rugby, cricket, soccer, tennis, volleyball and hockey, the Price brothers also spent hours hitting plastic golf balls into cans that had been buried in the garden.

Their father was a keen sportsman and, in Nick's words, "a huge supporter of us".

"Because of the military background, he was a real disciplinarian. What he passed on to my brothers, they passed on to me," he said.

As the clouds began forming over the small, landlocked state, the eight-year-old was aware "that something was brewing. It was 1965 and Independence had been declared and we kind of knew that the country was in trouble, but we didn't really know what it meant."

His brother Kit bought a collection of second-hand clubs from a local second-hand dealer. It was a mix of old clubs, "and not one of them matched". And there was another twist – the future champion was left-handed. So, for years, he was only able to play cross-handed – much like Papwa Sewgolum. Once he had managed to switch his grip to the normal left-hand-on-top, Nick became a natural, striking the ball with almost every stroke imaginable.

As a teenager, he attended the Prince Edward School in Salisbury, where he captained the golf team.

During this period, Rhodesia's tobacco industry was huge, generating more than half of the country's foreign currency. Despite international sanctions following the Unilateral Declaration of Independence, a heavyweight cartel smuggled the product out to world markets disguised as South African or Portuguese products. While the country's economy depended so much on tobacco revenues, many of its people were slaves to the product. Raymond Price was one of them, and when Nick Price was just 10, his father died from lung cancer. Despite this, the three brothers also took up the habit, and Nick would battle for years to quit.

I addressed this issue and told him that, like my own father, it's a struggle I also went through (years ago).

"I was in a situation where 80 per cent of the people smoked – it was that kind of environment." Price says the effort to quit continues, but "it's just something I'm not particularly good at". He adds that he's always been conscious of the stigma attached to the habit and avoided smoking around children, particularly during tournaments, when he was seen as a role model.

In 1973, at the age of 16, Price was convinced that he was going to become a successful professional golfer and, as a result, made the decision to switch to the larger American golf balls that were used on the PGA tour.

A year later, he won the Optimist Junior World Championships at Torrey Pines in San Diego.

Price spent six months of the next year (1975) playing in amateur events in South Africa and Europe. However, the political climate was heating up, and Price was recruited to do 18 months' mandatory service in the Rhodesian Air Force. By then, guerillas had put the economy under siege, while the government had virtually abandoned efforts to defend its borders and was now trying to save the key economic and industrial hubs. Large parts of the countryside were no-go areas.

While Price was trained as a radio operator, he was spared the full-flown destruction that so many of his friends endured. On the upside, the rigours of military life – the 4.15 a.m. wake-up calls, inspections and the enormous sacrifices – instilled a sense of discipline that augured well when he began competing against the best golfers on the planet.

The war years were, in a sense, the best of times and the worst of times. For these young men, the fact that their lives were on the line meant that they lived their lives to the full. Price said there was a sense of fatalism, because "you never knew when your time was up".

"Yes, we drank hard and the parties were fantastic. When there is death all around you, you tend to drink for your friends who never made it and, of course, to celebrate your own life."

Decades later, the battle-hardened Price says those war years are still etched in his memory.

"It was a horrible situation. My friends today, my whole age group, we still reflect on some of our old mates – the guys who didn't make it. We wonder where they would be today... what they would have done with their lives."

This was the creed that millions of white youngsters lived by in the dying days of white rule in the southern parts of Africa.

After he completed his service, Price joined the South African and European tours as a 21-year-old professional in 1978. Understandably, it was a major adjustment, and he battled to adapt to the weather. With few notable performances it became an expensive exercise, and Price had enough cash to fund only two more tournaments before he would have to head back to Rhodesia – and a desperately uncertain future. Fortunately, his game came together in the nick of time and he secured fourth- and third-place finishes and a temporary reprieve.

After finishing 11th on the European Tour Order of Merit in 1980 (and scoring his first big win at the Swiss Open), his game went off the boil the following season and he returned to Africa to play the South African Tour.

In those days, the sporting connections between South Africa and its northern neighbour were blurred, with several prominent sportsmen plying their trade in both countries and striking gold overseas. Bruce Grobbelaar, who also fought in the Bush War, was goalkeeper for Durban City before enjoying a lucrative career at Liverpool. And golfer Denis Watson, who was born in Salisbury (now Harare), was Rhodesian Sportsman of the Year in 1975, but went on to represent South Africa in the World Series of Golf in 1980 and 1982.

In January 1982, Price began receiving lessons from childhood friend David Leadbetter, who had emigrated to Florida in the US and was widely regarded as one of the top teaching professionals in the country. When "Lead" showed Price a videotape of his swing, he was horrified. It was, to put it bluntly, all over the place, with up to five different swings. Basically, his swing plane was too steep and his backswing had too many moving parts. The result was that he struck the ball very erratically.

With eight weeks of intensive coaching, Leadbetter laid the foundations for what would become one of the most clinical swings on the circuit. Price began striking the ball quickly and sharply. The club did what it had to do – and nothing more. The result was a measured, sharp and clean strike.

Price could also manipulate the flight and trajectory of the ball better than anyone in the world at one stage. So, while the power-hitters like Seve Ballesteros, Vijay Singh, and the thirsty and tortured John Daly were ripping their drives, Price was finding the fairways. In addition, his short game was special, his deadly putting making a huge difference.

When he was at the peak of his career – a decade or so later – Price told leading golf consultant Rob Rotella that he felt so confident when he stepped up to a straight putt that he almost felt as if he were cheating.

Just six months after Price had been coached by Leadbetter, he arrived at Troon – the "Royal" prefix was bestowed on the occasion of the club's centenary in 1978 – confident that he was going to play well.

This was the oldest Major championship in the world (the first was staged in Prestwick in Scotland) and its relevance continues to grow.

Let's pause for a moment and put this setting in perspective.

In the shadows of an ancient castle, where local hero Robert the Bruce was born in 1837, lies this brutal and breathtaking links course. Founded in 1878 on the Ayrshire coastline, it is perched on a muscular hill on the coast of the outer Firth of Clyde in southwestern Scotland.

Troon was perfect for Price's game. After all, there were very few driving holes and it was more suited to 3 woods and low irons off the tees.

Against the backdrop of the flags of all the competing nations and the cry of the bagpipes, Price stepped onto the first tee to launch his Open career.

In Norman Dabell's book, *One Hand on the Claret Jug*, Price recalls how overwhelming the moment was: "I remember walking down the fairway with Chip [Beck] – it was his first Open as well – and we kind of looked at each other, drinking in the aura, the feel. It was the feeling of returning to the home of golf, playing in the national championship of the home of golf. People had been playing golf on these grounds for hundreds of years, and here we were, part of it. It was simply a remarkable feeling, a feeling of almost overwhelming gratitude for having the opportunity to be there."

And Price did not disappoint. His opening two 69s saw him five shots behind 22-year-old American Bobby Clampett, with Bernhard Langer, Des Smyth, Tom Watson and Sandy Lyle also in contention. Price, as the underdog, was poised to pounce.

On the Saturday, in windier conditions, Clampett, who had a ruinous triple bogey at the 6th, and further dropped shots at the 10th, 11th, 13th and 15th, saw the championship starting to slip away from him. A late rally saw him back in the clubhouse with a nervous one-shot lead over Price, two ahead of Lyle and Smyth, and three ahead of Watson.

Watson, incidentally, had put Turnberry on the map in 1977, when his "duel in the sun" with Jack Nicklaus had thrilled the golfing world. Neck and neck for most of the round, the two Americans had played out of their skins and, when Nicklaus sank a 32-metre putt, Watson was left with a 50-centimetre putt for the title. The noise was so great that Nicklaus had to appeal for calm, and Watson made no mistake.

On the final day of the 1982 edition, Price roared out of the blocks, scratching birdies on the first two holes to take an early lead. A bogey on the 9th saw him taking the turn one shot behind Watson. He then played the best three holes of the championship. He birdied the 10th and the 11th, where his eagle putt lipped out, as well as the 12th. The Claret Jug was in his sights as be entered the final stretch.

But there was trouble ahead. Troon's motto is *Tam Arte Quam Marte* ("As much by skill as by strength"), and it would take all the skill to master the home stretch. Price bogeyed the 13th, but steadied himself with a par at the following hole.

At the 15th, however, the fickleness of the game was demonstrated yet again when Price drove into the rough, but he then slashed a magnificent 4-iron approach shot. The ball arrowed towards the green but, as it descended, clipped a ridge and leapt into a bunker (he later said that he hadn't been aware of a bunker there). He scrambled back onto the fairway, but his fourth shot was weak and he needed two putts from six metres for a double-bogey (his only double-bogey for the championship).

After parring the 16th, Price's 2 iron at the 203-metre, par-three 17th came up short. He hit a weak chip shot and then missed the par putt.

Watson, who was already in the clubhouse after carding a 70, was the new leader.

Knowing that he needed a birdie at the last hole to tie with the American, Price found another gear and went for broke. He put his approach to eight metres, but the putt broke left of the hole and pulled up short. He had lost by a single shot to Watson, who was sincere and sympathetic in his victory speech: "I have to feel for [Price], because I've been in that position before and I think the man will shine again – there's no question about it."

In the post-tournament interview, Price put on a brave face: "I blew this one, but I'll know enough not to blow another one. I'm going to dream about this and have nightmares, but I don't expect to be depressed after placing second in the world's greatest championship."

Time would tell whether he would come back from such depths, but he later acknowledged that it had been a vital stepping stone to his later career successes.

In 1983, Price joined the PGA Tour full time and showed great promise, winning the World Series of Golf that year by four strokes over Jack Nicklaus. After that victory, it would take another eight years before he would win again on the PGA Tour, even though he showed plenty of promise.

The 1986 Masters will be remembered for generations to come for Nicklaus's extraordinary win, but Price set the pace with an opening round of 63, a course record at Augusta at the time. "I think [course architect] Bobby Jones held up his hand from somewhere and said: 'That's enough, boy,'" Price observed.

The 1988 Open returned to Royal Lytham and St Annes for the first time since Seve Ballesteros had scored an emphatic victory there in 1979. However, the hugely talented Spaniard had been misfiring for some time and had not won a Major since the 1984 Open.

Nick Faldo was defending his title, and Price, who had one US Tour title and three European Tour successes behind him, was playing Lytham for the first time. He tamed the billowing breeze off the Lancashire coast – parring the first seven holes, birdying the 8th, and parring the next three before dropping a shot at the 12th. Another birdie at the 16th gave him a one-under 70 and a share of fourth place.

On the Friday, Price matched Seve Ballesteros's first-round 67 – thanks partly to an eagle 10-metre putt on the 6th – to take a one-shot lead over the Spaniard. Going into the rain-delayed final round (the first time it was played on a Monday), Price had a two-shot lead over Ballesteros and Faldo, courtesy of a third-round 69.

Craig Stadler, Andy Bean, Bob Tway, Sandy Lyle and Fred Couples were all in contention. Faldo was the first to blink when he three-putted on the 7th, while Price and Ballesteros both eagled that hole. The rest of the field faded behind them. When Ballesteros rolled in a six-metre birdie putt on the 9th, he and Price were all square. At the 11th, Ballesteros got another, but then relinquished it with a bogey at the 12th. Another Ballesteros bogey at the 14th presented Price with a gap he failed to take when he matched the Spaniard's dropped shot. All square again.

Ballesteros took a one-shot lead at the 16th, thanks to a magnificent 9-iron approach, which left him with a tap-in. At the 17th, Price couldn't afford to slip further and, despite pushing his drive into the rough, managed to scramble for par. With a left-to-right cross wind blowing and thousands of spectators lining the 18th fairway, Price stood alongside one of the greatest players in history, trailing by a single shot. They both unleashed their drives towards the final green. Price split the fairway with his, while his opponent narrowly missed a pot bunker some 237 metres away on the right-hand side.

Price then pulled his approach nine metres left of the pin, while Ballesteros found a dip left of the green. Ballesteros hit an exquisite chip shot – perfect height, pace and angle. It neared the hole but, at the death, just stayed out. Price for birdie and the championship. But his ball dived past the pin, leaving him with a tricky return putt, which he also missed. Again, the dream was all over for Price, and the popular Spaniard tapped in for a memorable 65 and his third Open championship.

The sages say a golfer has to lose an Open before winning one. Price had overemphasised that point by missing out twice. As CBS commentator Bob Schieffer once observed, "There is a Golf God, a bunch of them in fact, and they are a crafty, nasty lot." Tom Watson, who won five Open championships, also noted: "If you want to increase your success rate, double your failure rate."

And yet, Price wasn't too hard on himself: "I'm not feeling down. If I had played badly, I might be. But when you are beaten by somebody, especially the way he played, you bow out gracefully. It was such a thrill to play this standard of golf."

When asked to explain his nationality, Price told reporters: "I was born in South Africa, raised in Rhodesia, I have a British passport and I live in the US. You pick one."

In the late 1980s, he went to see prominent sports psychologist Rob Rotella. He had two Major failures under his belt, six years had passed since he last won a tournament, and there was the not-so-small matter that he was now on the dark side of 30 and, seemingly, a fading force in the game.

Price told Rotella that his thought patterns during a round depended on how the opening holes went. If he was on song, he sang his way through the round. If, however, he faltered early on, he would become increasingly erratic as he tried to "fix" the problem. Price, Rotella, observed, was letting the events control the way he thought rather than taking control off his thoughts and using them to influence events.

On the plus side, Price had the incredible ability of retaining a target in his mind. Once he had picked it out, he could look back at his ball and the target was still in his mind, locked and ready to be hit. Rotella's advice was that Price would have to learn to decide — before the round starts — how he would think and then train his mind not to deviate from that thought pattern.

Price acknowledged that Rotella had an uncanny knack of being able to turn the most complicated situation into a simple one. It marked a

Golfing legends from years gone by. From left to right: Bobby Locke with Herman Barron, Byron Nelson and Sam Snead at the Goodall Round Robin golf tournament at the Wykagyl Country Club in New Rochelle, N.Y., in May 1949

Bobby Locke wins the 1952 British Open. He would win it four times

Gary Player wins his first Major – The Open at Muirfield, July 1959

Papwa Sewgolum, whose injured finger hampered his chances in the 1961 SA Open

Sally Little sinks a one-foot putt for par on the 1st hole in a sudden-death play-off with Nancy Lopez, who bogeyed, to win the LPGA Kathryn Crosbie Classic at Rancho Bernardo Golf Club, San Diego, in March 1978

AP Photo/Lennox McLendon/PictureNET

Tom Watson hands over the green jacket to Gary Player after he won the Masters in April 1978. The victory made Player a three-time winner of the event, and it would be his last Major

Nick Price with his Open trophy at Turnberry, July 1994

Ernie Els's caddie, Ricci Roberts, congratulates him after he won the 1994 US Open

Nicolas Asfouri/AFP/Gallo Images

Retief Goosen with his US Open trophy at Shinnecock Hills, N.Y., June 2004

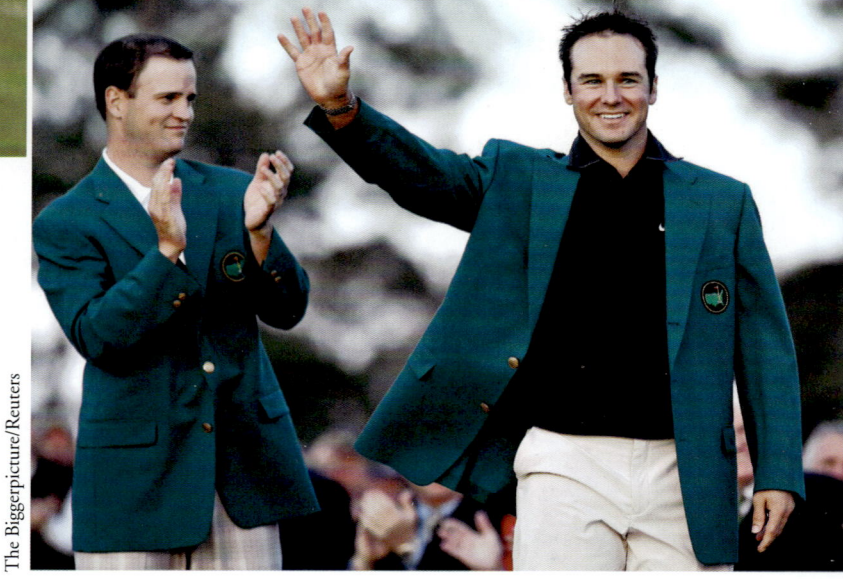

A beaming Trevor Immelman in the green jacket at the 2008 Masters at Augusta, Georgia. Behind him is the former champion, Zach Johnson

Louis Oosthuizen proudly holds The Open trophy in 2010

Kyodo via AP Images/PictureNET

Streeter Lecka/Getty Images/Gallo Images

And after making his historic albatross at the US Masters in 2012

Former champion Phil Mickelson congratulates Charl Schwartzel on winning the 2011 Masters

What a comeback! A proud Ernie Els celebrates his remarkable victory at the 2012 Open at Royal Lytham and St Annes

turning point, and his big break finally came in 1991, when he won two PGA events, the Byron Nelson Classic and the Canadian Open.

The dramatic turnaround also coincided with Price securing the services of Squeaky Medlin, a low-key but dedicated caddie. In his book *Lifemanship*, British author Stephen Potter addressed the importance of the caddie/golfer relationship: "Make friends with your caddie and the game will make friends with you." It was advice that Price took to heart, and the pair enjoyed an extraordinary six-year journey together. Price described Medlin as diligent, conscientious, honest, humble, low-key and, of course, damn good on the bag.

Price, who had come within three strokes of winning two Major championships, finally struck gold at the 1992 PGA Championship, the Major that is known as "Glory's Last Shot". The tournament is traditionally played in mid- to late August and, as a result, is associated with high summer and hot and humid conditions.

The 74th edition of the tournament was held at the Bellerive Country Club in St Louis, Missouri. At 6 536 metres, with its Zoyzia grass fairways framed by thick bluegrass rough, it was a monster. With moderate temperatures on the opening day, Price fired a 71 to tie with Ian Baker-Finch, Greg Norman and Hale Irwin, four shots behind Gene Sauers. A 69 on the second day saw Price tied seventh. Despite a nervy start at the third round, where he lost two shots, he bounced back quickly with four birdies in a row (nine through 13). Another birdie at the 17th saw him two shots behind Sauers, who finished with a 70.

When he birdied the 4th, to go eight under par, Sauers had the championship within his grasp, but he then began to unravel. Three putts at the 5th and a dropped shot at the short 6th hole saw Price draw level. The 35-year-old would go on to fire 10 straight pars in the final round. Jeff Maggert and John Cook were now his only real competitors, but birdie putts on the par-three 16th and par-five 17th kept Price in the driving seat.

On the 18th, Price, holding a two-shot lead, pulled his drive into the left rough, but he hit a spectacular 5-iron recovery shot to the back of the green. He parred the hole, Cook bogeyed it and Africa had its first Major winner in more than a decade.

This victory opened the floodgates and, over the next two years, Price would win 16 of the 54 tournaments he played in worldwide. As *The New York Times* noted, he had transformed his game from good to great and had entered "a special sweet spot in time where the complex becomes simple and where the most difficult game to subdue somehow becomes easy".

Price was hitting the ball almost 10 metres further off the tee than two years previously, and his accuracy hadn't been sacrificed in the process. From 1991 to 1993, he went from 28th on the PGA Tour in greens hit in regulation to sixth.

Having won the final Major of 1993 and then the big curtain-raiser of the next season – the Players' Championship – Price arrived at Augusta as a hot favourite. However, he misfired through the opening rounds and was never in contention.

The Open Championship at Turnberry in 1994 afforded him an opportunity to make amends for his narrow loss to Watson in 1982 at the same course. His form at the two previous Majors that year (tied 35th at the Masters and missing the cut at the US Open, where Ernie Els won in a play-off) did not augur well. But, nevertheless, he had won eight tournaments in the US since that PGA Championship and, along with Greg Norman and Nick Faldo, was now established as one of the three top golfers in the world.

He also had one of the most respected caddies in his camp. Jeff "Squeaky" Medlin may have had a high-pitched voice, but he would be a pillar of strength that weekend. "When I'm on the practice range, Squeaky is my eyes. He checks my aim and alignment, and that keeps me on target," Price said at the time.

There were major concerns about the course, which had borne the brunt of a dry and cold spring, but late rains and plenty of sunshine saw it take shape beautifully ahead of the tournament.

In the final practice round, the heroes of the 1977 championship – Jack Nicklaus and Tom Watson – were paired against Price and Greg Norman, and they left the youngsters for dead.

On the opening day, fresh winds were followed by steady rain as New Zealander Greg Turner posted the lowest opening round (65). American Mark Brookes beat that by one the following day, but Tom Watson was the second-round leader after shooting 68 and 65. One behind were Swede Jesper Parnevik and American Brad Faxon, with Price a further shot behind. Gary Player, who was playing in his 40th consecutive Open, missed the cut, along with Nicklaus and Lee Trevino.

On the Saturday, Fuzzy Zoeller fired a 64 to tie with Brad Faxon at the top on 201. Price and Tom Watson, who shot a 69 and 67 respectively, were a shot behind, and they were followed by Parnevik and Ronan Rafferty on 202.

And so, with one round to play, six players were within a shot of each other, and Price noted, "There is so much experience [at the top] of the leader board." Watson, who was eyeing a sixth Open title, wished aloud that the final day would see wet and wild weather. But it was not to be, and he would pay the price. In pleasant conditions – sunshine and a light northeasterly wind – Turnberry was in a generous mood that Sunday.

At the turn, five players – Zoeller, Rafferty, Price, Feherty and Parnevik – were all tied at eight under. Price, whose two birdies had been cancelled by a pair of bogeys in the front nine – was spraying many of his shots, and he looked to be the obvious casualty.

In the home stretch, Parnevik was the first to make a move. After a string of pars, he birdied the 11th, 12th and 13th, but Zoeller and Price stayed in sight with birdies at the 11th and 12th respectively. Parnevik's first stumble came at the 15th when he missed the green and bogeyed. He cancelled this with a birdie at the next.

When Price reached the 16th tee, under the backdrop of the magnificent granite island of Ailsa Craig in the outer Firth of Clyde, he was two shots behind. And then a roar that funnelled away from the 17th green served notice that Parnevik and his deadly putter had birdied the hole to take a three-shot lead going into the last.

The smart money was on the son of Sweden's most famous comedian, Bo Parnevik, but, as we have seen so often, the final hole of any Major is a dangerous place to be. And so it was with Parnevik, who has always stood out because of the upturned brim on his cap.

While Price birdied the 16th with a brave four-metre putt, Parnevik made a crucial mistake – he decided not to look at the leader board when he tackled the 18th. Had he done so, he would have seen that he could afford to hit a 4 iron into the fat of the green, instead of a five to attack the pin, tucked in menacingly at the front of the bunker-guarded stage.

Back at the par-five 17th, Price's drive was solid and, after discussing his approach with Medlin, he selected a 4 iron and landed the approach to about 15 metres from the pin. When they addressed the putt, they believed an eagle was necessary to secure a play-off.

The putt from the left rear of the green was nasty, with a slight break, so the main challenge was to ensure that it reached the crest of a ridge between himself and the hole. Price set his sights on a spot – a patch of discoloured grass the size of a one-pound coin – at the top of the ridge. He returned his head to address the ball and, with that spot – the immediate target – fixed in his mind, released the club for the most important putt of his life.

The stroke was firm and true, and the ball angled along the spine of the slope, and over its target. It then turned and began heading towards Medlin, the pin and the hole. The pace seemed perfect, and it rolled gently on and on. About a metre from the cup, it struck a spike mark and, for a moment, veered ever so slightly, but regained its course. There was a will-it-won't-it moment as it struck the corner of the cup, danced for a second, and dived in for one of golf's most spectacular single blows. Eagle three.

It was probably the single greatest shot of Price's magnificent career and ranked right up there with Bobby Jones's 13-metre screamer at the 18th, which decided the 1930 US Open at Interlachen, Jack Nicklaus's 12-metre putt at the 16th that clinched the Masters in 1975, or Hale Irwin's 13-metre cracker at the last at the 1991 US Open at Medinah, forcing the play-off, which he won.

At the 18th, Parnevik found himself 140 metres out, and he under-clubbed his approach. The ball hit the bank and sank deep into the grass below the green. His recovery stopped two metres from the pin, but he missed that putt. Bogey.

"When I walked off the green and saw that I had held a two-stroke lead, I was crushed because I should have looked at the leader board," he later recalled. Over two dramatic holes, there had been a three-shot turn, and Price now held a one-shot lead going into the 18th.

Unlike Parnevik, minutes earlier, Price glided his approach into the centre of a generous green, leaving 10 metres for two putts and glory. The first putt lagged to one metre from the cup, the second dropped gently. His 268 was just one shot shy of the championship record that Greg Norman had shot at Sandwich a year earlier. There were tears of joy and tears of sorrow. Price hugged Medlin, his wife Sue and then, moments later, the most prized trophy in all of golf.

"In 1982, I had my left hand on this trophy. In 1988, I had my right hand on the trophy. Now I finally have it in both hands," he said.

Price and his group, joined by Turnberry captain Charles Jack, partied long into that breathtaking balmy Scottish night. Towards 11 p.m., with the streaks of light fading over the western horizon, Tom Watson (tugging on a cigar) and Jack Nicklaus were spotted chipping and putting on a par-three course at the Turnberry Hotel, where they were all staying.

After a short but blissful sleep, Price arrived at the Prestwick Airport the following morning to find a note from Greg Norman taped to the door of his Lockhead Jetstar 731 aircraft (which the Australian had previously owned). "Two years in a row this plane has carried the claret jug home. Congratulations. Well played," wrote Norman, who had finished a respectable joint 11th.

First stop was Norfolk, where his mother Wendy now lived, just a few miles away from her eldest son, Kit. One of Nick's closest supporters, she had been unable to attend the Open because she was being treated for stomach cancer. Emotional? "Yes, hard to describe, but it was very emotional in a very happy way," Price said. Incidentally, at the time of writing, Wendy was 90, in good health and still living in the same town.

Just three weeks later, Price competed at the PGA Championship at the 6249-metre Southern Hills in Tulsa, Oklahoma. With 151 players competing, the early movers were Tom Watson, US Open champion Ernie Els, Ian Woosnam, Phil Mickelson, Colin Montgomerie, Fred Couples and Price. At the end of the day, which was played in near-perfect conditions, Price and Montgomerie shared the lead with 67s, one ahead of Mickelson, Els, Couples and Woosnam. Price surged ahead on day two, taking his total to 132, five ahead of Corey Pavin, Ben Crenshaw and Jay Haas. The cut fell at 145, and the casualties included Jack Nicklaus, Jesper Parnevik, Seve Ballesteros and Arnold Palmer.

On the third day, temperatures soared well into the 90s, and hundreds of spectators were treated for heat-related problems. Price marched on, and despite carding a couple of bogeys, ended with a 70, keeping him three shots ahead of Jay Haas, with Corey Pavin and Phil Mickelson a further shot behind.

The final day dawned with the temperature dramatically cooler. Greg Norman, who had crept into fifth place, five shots off the lead, was fast out of the blocks that Sunday, scoring consecutive birdies on the opening two holes.

But Price held his ground and birdied both the 3rd and the 4th. Norman's charge then faded, and there were no other late challengers.

Price played the first nine in 32 and, although he was erratic over the closing nine holes, firing three birdies, three bogeys and three pars, he shot a 67 and kept Pavin and Mickelson out of reach. The championship was his for the second time.

"To lead every round of any Major championship – or any tournament, for that matter – is very difficult, because you go to sleep thinking about all sorts of things. Had I not won, there would have been a big question mark about my character. I would have been very depressed," he said in the post-tournament press conference.

He had become the first golfer since Walter Hagen in 1924 to win the Open and PGA championships in the same year and, apart from Mark O'Meara and Nick Faldo, the only player to win two Majors in a single year in the 1990s. He had also delivered the *coup de grâce* to American golf by ensuring that, for the first time in history, an American would not hold one of the four Majors. Apart from Price's PGA and Open wins, José Mariá Olazábal had clinched the Masters, while Ernie Els had won his first Major with the US Open.

By now, Price had established himself as the best player in the world. On the PGA, he led the tour in scoring average (just under 69 strokes per round), topped the PGA Tour money list in 1993 and 1994, setting a new earnings record each time, and spent 43 weeks at number one in the Official World Golf Ranking.

He was the first to concede that he was on top of the world: "I'm playing golf for the pure enjoyment of it now. I'm just a very content person right now, but I still have the desire to compete. I don't ever want to lose that."

But, as quickly as Price's career had soared, it began dipping. Looming large was a young American who was about to change the face of golf – and sport – forever. Tiger Woods turned professional in 1996 and, by April 1997, had already won his first Major, the 1997 Masters. Woods first reached the number-one position in the world rankings in June 1997. There was a double-whammy as well. Sweeping changes to golf equipment caught Price off guard. After all, he had grown up without titanium heads, graphite shafts, perimeter-weighted irons, loft wedges or belly putters. Almost overnight, he was playing catch-up with a new generation of V8 golfers – and longer courses to match.

Price conceded that he lost his rhythm when he attempted to hit the ball further. And as Ernie Els would discover when his putting lost its shape, it's almost impossible to get it back.

Price recalls that from 1930 to 1996, the ball averaged a 30-centimetre-per-year increase in distance: "Twenty metres in 66 years is manageable but, from 1995 to 2003, it increased the same amount."

In 1932, O.B. Keeler, writing in *The American Golfer* magazine, had observed that "with our marvelous modern development of clubs, stepped up ten yards at a step, and a lively ball that travels so far, we have lost a little something in golf".

Price also noted that the head of a driver in his prime had a sweet spot about the size of a pea. It was now bigger than the ball. "The art of driving the ball is swinging the club through an arc of 20-plus feet [six metres] and returning it to that point. That's what made great drivers, and that's where you would find cracks in a guy's swing. Especially under pressure," he said.

After 1994, he won just three more times on the US Tour, four more on the Sunshine Tour and three Zimbabwe Opens. So, not surprisingly, he turned to the Champions Tour in 2007 for his next paycheck. He concedes that his run in the 1990s, when he had peaked, had left him drained "and a bit burnt out".

"I had it for 18 months... signing 3 000 autographs a day. I was starting to resent people wanting things from me," he said.

If anything symbolises the end of Price's purple patch, it was the death of Squeaky in 1997. After all, this unlikely duo had set the golfing world alight with a unique brand of clinical golf, and they represented an era when really nice guys finished first.

In an interesting twist, Medlin would go on to notch up one more Major than Price – thanks to Price.

At the 1991 PGA Championship, the triple-Major champion withdrew at the last minute due to the impending birth of his first child, Gregory. John "grip it and rip it" Daly, who had missed 11 cuts in 23 starts preceding that week in Carmel, Indiana, was included in the field at the last minute. Medlin and the hard-drinking, heavy-smoking Californian met that Thursday morning – and it was a match made in heaven. Playing partner Billy Andrade recalled "Bombs Away" Daly's not-too-technical strategy on the opening day: "Where do I hit it, Squeaky?" Andrade said Daly was like a blind man with a guide dog, but their partnership worked, and he ended that day with an impressive 69.

When Sue Price gave birth the following day, the slightly unhinged Daly (who once confessed that he'd started drinking four years after he started playing golf, "and I started playing golf when I was four") took control of the tournament with a 67, and he never relinquished his lead.

It was a fitting finale for Medlin, a former bricklayer who had seen the world and served two of the greatest players of all time. He was diagnosed with chronic myelogenous leukemia in 1996, and the last time he would carry Price's bag was at the Sarazen World Open in Georgia in November that year.

On 16 June 1997, Medlin succumbed to the disease at his home in Columbus, Ohio.

At that weekend's Buick Classic at Westchester, players and fellow caddies, who had shown their support during his illness by wearing green ribbons, wore black armbands, while the flags at the club were flown at half-mast throughout the tournament.

"Squeak was a huge part of my success – I will always miss him," said Price at the funeral.

And Ernie Els, who had propelled to the top of the world golf rankings that weekend after successfully defending his title at the Buick Classic (just two weeks after his second US Open win), said: "It's unfair to see him go like that. He was such an honest, dear man – you couldn't help but like the guy."

It was even more emotional for cancer survivor Paul Azinger, who had briefly topped the leader board earlier in the tournament. Three weeks previously, Azinger had visited Medlin, who was ravaged by the disease and no longer able to swallow, walk or talk: "I think he was at peace, and he's better off now," the 1993 PGA champion said.

In 1997, Price watched playing partner Tiger Woods crush a 300-metre drive at the Tournament Players Club at Las Colinas near Dallas. A spectator in the gallery shouted: "I did that in my dreams last night!" Price replied: "So did I." It was time to step aside or be steamrollered by the sport's latest and greatest phenomenon.

Over the course of his spectacular career, Price's wins included 18 PGA Tour championships (and 28 other professional tournaments around the world). In the process, he earned in excess of $20 million.

In 2003, he was inducted into the World Golf Hall of Fame, which offered the following citation: "If there was ever a golfer who took the road less travelled, it is Nick Price. His was an intricate puzzle, but when all the pieces were finally in place, Price at his peak played at a level rarely reached in the history of the game."

Although Price continues to play professionally, he has expanded into golf-course design with his own company. He lives in Hobe Sound, Florida, with his wife Sue and three children.

In 2012, he was limited to just eight tournament starts after rupturing two tendons in his left elbow. He underwent surgery to the joint early in 2013.

His contribution to the sport was recognised with his appointment as captain of the International team for the 2013 President's Cup.

6

The Big Easy

"There's no player alive that's had their heart ripped out and played their best golf and taken more swings at Tiger and not knocked him out than Ernie." — **Claude Harmon III**

There was a jarring moment on the 18th hole – day four – of the 2000 US Open at Pebble Beach as front-runners Ernie Els and Tiger Woods wrapped up their rounds. The tournament had been out of the ordinary for two reasons: the defending champion was dead, and the sport's new global superstar – in four days of explosive golf – had obliterated any contenders to his throne.

Three-time Major winner Payne Stewart was killed in a plane crash on 25 October 1999, just four months after his US Open victory at Pinehurst. At the time of his death, I was a news editor at a Cape Town newspaper. A wire alert came in late at night, reporting that an aircraft carrying "a US Open champion" – his family had yet to be informed – was missing. I wondered aloud whether it might be Els (who had won the tournament in 1994 and 1997). We held the presses into the early hours of the following morning and, as the tragedy played itself out, replaced the lead report. Stewart died when the cabin of the Lear jet in which he was travelling from Orlando to Dallas for the Tour Championship depressurised.

It emerged that the pilots had not responded to a call to change radio frequencies and the aircraft, flying on autopilot and veering off-course, was observed by several US Air Force F-16 fighter aircraft as it continued its wayward journey over the southern and Midwestern US. It eventually ran out of fuel and plunged into a field in South Dakota.

Before his death, Stewart had acknowledged that Woods had single-handedly transformed the sport: "Tiger is the greatest thing that's happened to the Tour in a long time. He has brought incredible attention to golf at a time of year when football and the World Series always take precedence. Everything I've heard about him seems to be true."

Umm, er... more about that later.

Ahead of the 2000 US Open tournament, many of the players gathered along the 18th fairway on the Monterey Peninsula to pay tribute to the three-time Major winner by simultaneously driving balls into the Pacific Ocean as the waves slapped the rocks (Woods skipped the ceremony and, instead, played a practice round).

And then it was down to business.

On the final hole of the Open, South Africa's finest golfer since Gary Player was in the home stretch of the championship he had won twice before. Tied in second place, his silky swing had produced the goods over the past four days – three over par and level with Spanish Ryder Cup player Ángel Jiménez. In a different time, or in a different place, they would be going head to head. But there was the not-so-small matter of Woods, the young star who had revolutionised the sport with his unbelievable style of attacking, aggressive golf.

After winning his first Major in 1997, the ultracompetitive Woods had made a number of sweeping changes to his swing. The results were mixed, and for most of 1998 and early 1999, he didn't feature. However, once his new formula kicked in – towards the end of 1999 – the world witnessed the most extraordinary domination of the sport by any individual in history. Indeed, Woods clocked up five out of six Majors, including four in a row.

Els joined the rest of us who looked on in awe.

The 18th tee-box juts into the Pacific Ocean and the fairway hugs the sea. As this pair set off towards the green that day, the contrast couldn't have been greater. Tiger, burning bright with that final-day blood-red shirt and the demeanour of a gladiator, held a 15-shot lead while he contemplated his next move. As the American stalked his ball with the summit of Mount Nicklaus (and those 18 Majors) now well within sight,[*] the South African was hurting. The Big Easy looked like he had the weight of the world on his shoulders. The 1.91-metre gentle giant later conceded that there were times when he walked onto the first tee with Woods and he felt as if he were climbing into the ring with one of the Klitschko brothers. It was no contest.

Golf, as Mark Twain once famously observed, is "a good walk spoiled". And so it was with Els (and Jiménez) that day. As the sun began dipping over the Pacific Ocean, Woods was purring with pride after carding a massive 12-under 272 – the only player south of par for the tournament.

Els paid tribute to the new number one and retired to the change room to lick his wounds and wonder what his once (brilliantly bright) future now had in store.[†]

That weekend, Woods either set or broke nine US Open records, and *Sports Illustrated* described it as "the greatest performance in golf history". His total score tied with that of Jack Nicklaus (1980) and Lee Janzen (1993) for the lowest total ever. He broke the record for the largest margin of victory (15 shots) in the tournament – a record that had stood since 1862 – and also in any Major championship. He had also played the last 18 holes without a bogey, didn't three-putt throughout the tournament and bogeyed

---

[*] Nicklaus missed the cut in this, his 44th and final, US Open.
[†] Els had finished runner-up to Vijay Singh in the Masters two months earlier and he would finish runner-up to Woods – again – at St Andrews the following month.

just six holes all week. It was Woods's third Major championship win and his first US Open win.

In addition, it was also the first step to his so-called "Tiger Slam". He went on to win the 2000 Open and 2000 PGA Championship, and then the 2001 Masters, becoming the first golfer ever to hold all four Major trophies simultaneously, a feat that has never been achieved before and, in all probability, will never happen again.

"Tiger has raised the bar," said Tom Watson, who had won his only US Open at the same venue in 1982, "and it seems that he's the only guy who can jump over that bar."

In a way, these outrageous accomplishments were nothing less than Woods deserved, and yet, something didn't add up.

Theodore Ernest Els was born on 17 October 1969 in Kempton Park, east of Johannesburg. At the time, his father Neels was juggling his personal and professional life with varying degrees of success. As the eldest of seven children, he had been thrown in at the deep end at the age of 18 when his father, riddled with cancer, handed him his transport business – and the responsibility of helping to raise the rest of the children. Soon afterwards, the youngest child – a four-year-old boy – was run over outside their home, and Neels's mother, stricken with grief, died at the age of 50.

Ernie Vermaak, Neels's father-in-law, then introduced him to golf at a local driving range, and he never looked back.

Fifty-six days after Ernie's birth – on 12 December – Neels had his last alcoholic drink and vowed to God that he would never touch alcohol again. "And he gave me something back. He gave me Ernie," Neels told journalist Tom Callahan years later.

This significant sacrifice was rewarded, over and over, not least at the World Match Play tournament in 1994, when Els was beginning to make his charge in the global arena. After narrowly beating his childhood hero

Seve Ballesteros following a 35-hole thriller at the tournament, the Spanish giant approached an emotional Neels in the change room and described his son as "very special". Ricci Roberts, who was on Els's bag that day, backs this up, saying Ballesteros told him that Els was the best golfer he had ever seen.

Els spent much of his childhood at Dellville Primary playing rugby, cricket, tennis, and, from the age of eight, golf.

In the mid-1970s, South Africans were adapting to the culture of television for the first time. The National Party government had viewed television as a threat to the Afrikaner culture. Former Prime Minister Hendrik Verwoerd had compared it with atomic bombs and poison gas, claiming "they are modern things, but that does not mean they are desirable". He warned that the government "had to watch for any dangers to the people, both spiritual and physical". And so, viewing time ran to less than 40 hours a week, divided, of course, between English and Afrikaans, with the national anthem closing down the evening's drivel.

Nevertheless, on the evening of 9 April 1978, flickering screens across this troubled land reflected Gary Player winning the last of his regular tour Majors – his third US Masters title at the grand old age of 42. Trailing Hubert Green by seven shots going into the final round, the old warhorse birdied seven of the last 10 holes and shot 30 on the back nine to card a final round of 64. Els recalls watching the drama unfold in the family room, "and I don't know who leapt up higher, me or my dad, when he made that putt on 18 to win".

Els won the Eastern Transvaal Junior Tennis Championships at age 13. He spent several happy years accompanying – and caddying for – his father at the Kempton Park Country Club. A product of the Jan de Klerk High School, he had talent to burn and he soon overtook his father (and older brother, Dirk). By the age of 14, this lanky teenager with the laziest of swings was a scratch-handicap golfer.

In 1984, his stratospheric talent saw him win the Junior World Golf Championship in San Diego in the 13-to-14 age group. Interestingly, an equally likeable young American with a big and easy left-handed swing finished runner-up. Twenty years later, Phil Mickelson would settle the score when he went head to head with Els in one of the most thrilling duels in the back nine on the final Sunday at Augusta.

Els was awarded his Junior Springbok colours in 1984 and, in 1986, at the age of 16, won the SA Boys and SA Amateur championships (breaking Bobby Locke's 51-year record as the youngest winner). The following year, the laid-back teenager won the South African Amateur Championship (aged 17), becoming the youngest ever winner of that event and breaking the record, which had been held by Gary Player. He received the State President Sports Award in 1987 and, in 1988, his full Springbok colours.

In 1989, the spiky-haired blond got his first taste of real links golf when he competed as an amateur in The Open at Royal Troon. "It was love at first sight, you might say. I just found the whole experience very natural to my game – I could see the shots easily in my mind's eye and playing shots in the wind felt almost like second nature. You have to hit it solid on a links course, and that's always been a strong feature of my game."

Els's decision to turn professional after The Open coincided with dramatic changes in South Africa's political landscape. After President P.W. Botha suffered a stroke and was sidelined by his cabinet, F.W. de Klerk took the reins in 1989 as the nation's last white ruler.

De Klerk recognised that the game was up and realised that a negotiated settlement with the African National Congress (ANC) and other liberation movements was inevitable. In February 1990, less than a year after assuming office, he announced the unbanning of all political parties and the release of political prisoners, including Nelson Mandela. For the first time in our history, South Africa would be free.

Within four years, democratic elections would be held, and Mandela and his ANC would sweep into power. But an uneasy, troubled journey still lay ahead. A violent power struggle erupted – fuelled by a third-party, government-sponsored force – and thousands would die before the polling stations opened.

Nevertheless, there were signs of hope as South Africa slowly found its feet again, and the country's acceptance into the international sports arena provided a great deal of optimism for the future. During those halcyon days, there was also a great deal of excitement over how South African sports people – isolated for so long – would perform on the world stage.

In the early 1990s, a new breed of sports personalities emerged. These rainbow warriors, the likes of Lucas Radebe (soccer), Penny Heyns (swimming), Josiah Thugwane (running) and, of course, Els, were members of a born-free brigade. And they gave all of South Africa a reason to hope.

Springbok captain Francois Pienaar, who celebrated the country's 1995 Rugby World Cup triumph with Nelson Mandela and the rest of the planet (apart from an obscure cluster of islands in the southwestern Pacific Ocean), captured the mood of the moment when he observed: "Something special was happening in our country. It was not normal. It was not expected."

For the young Ernie Els, who had a reputation for playing gracefully and partying hard, life was good.

While competing on the Sunshine Tour in the early 1990s, he had a near-death experience in the landlocked kingdom of Swaziland. En route to the Swaziland Open in Mbabane, and shortly after crossing the border from South Africa in heavy mist, the Nissan Els and his friend, Nico van Rensburg, was travelling in collided with a tractor. Van Rensburg recalled that the collision happened a moment after Els had put on his seatbelt. Van Rensburg was trapped in the wreckage, but Els, who struck his head on the windscreen, was able to pull him free from the wreckage. Moments later, another car ploughed into theirs. During that period, Els limped away from other car wrecks as well, and earned a reputation for living life in the fast lane.

Despite this, in 1992 Els became only the third South African (after Bobby Locke and Gary Player) to win the triple-crown: the SA Open, the SA Masters and the SA PGA.

This launched his international career and secured him a spot at The Open, where he lit up Muirfield by opening with a 66, eventually finishing in a very respectable fifth place. The following year, he won his first tournament outside of South Africa, at the Dunlop Phoenix in Japan, leaving heavyweights Jumbo Ozaki, Tommy Nakajima, Fred Couples, Vijay Singh and Barry Lane scrambling for second place.

Els kicked off 1994 with his first victory on the PGA European Tour, at the Dubai Desert Classic, which included a course-record 61 in the opening round. He also finished eighth at the Masters, beginning a long love-hate relationship with America's most famous course.

Just weeks after South Africa had stunned the world by holding its peaceful democratic elections and inaugurating Nelson Mandela as the country's first black president, Els found himself in contention at the 1994 US Open at the Oakmont Country Club, in the foothills of the Allegheny Mountains near Pittsburgh, Pennsylvania. But like that historic poll in his homeland, he faced a formidable challenge.

Earlier that year, José María Olazábal had won the US Masters, the sixth foreign winner in seven years (Fred Couples, in 1992, was the only exception), and there were growing concerns that America's own national championship, the US Open, faced a similar foreign threat.

When the course was completed in 1903, Oakmont was regarded as the toughest in the US. The 6351-metre course has hosted more combined

USGA and PGA championships than any other course in the US, including eight US Opens, five US Amateurs, three PGA championships and two US Women's Opens. It remains one of the most difficult courses in the country, with 210 deep bunkers, hard and slick greens that slope away from the player (Dave Hill six-putted the 5th at the 1962 US Open), and tight fairways requiring accurate driving. In addition, that weekend the temperatures soared to around 100 °F (37.7 °C).

The opening two rounds were memorable for Arnold Palmer's valiant effort to make the cut in this, his 40th – and final – US Open. He limped home amid thunderous applause and, despite missing the cut by 11 strokes, gave a tearful and moving departure speech, saying "it's been 40 years of work, fun and enjoyment".

On day three, the lanky young South African, 40 years younger than Palmer and oozing panache and confidence, was turning heads with his big and easy swing. The gentle giant shot a 66 in that round to rise from tied seventh to lead by two. Although he had missed five fairways, he still hit 16 greens in regulation and scored a 30 on the first nine, matching the Open record.

The final-day tussle was between Els, Colin Montgomerie and Loren Roberts, and Els came agonisingly close to throwing it away at the 17th. With Roberts already on the final hole and Montgomerie in the clubhouse, the South African hooked his drive behind a grandstand, with the ball lying deep in a wooded tract. However, a local rule was in force, allowing him to move his ball 14 metres closer to the hole. While television commentator Bob Rosburg spluttered about the injustice of it all, Els took full advantage of his break to bump a sumptuous chip up the fairway to within two metres of the hole.

At that stage, Els was unaware that Roberts was going through a minor meltdown on the 18th green. Facing a 1.2-metre par putt – uphill with a slight right-to-left break – he choked. "I had trouble taking the putter back," he later recalled. The blade of his putter opened on impact and the ball never threatened the hole.

Els then made a schoolboy error when he neglected to check the scoreboard, and he was unaware that Roberts had carded a 279 – the same score as Montgomerie. When he arrived at the 18th tee, he thought he needed a birdie for the championship, so, instead of gliding a 3 wood or long iron down the fairway, he took his driver out and "tried to smash the living stuffing out of it". The result wasn't pretty, and the ball finally came to rest near the 15th tee.

As he contemplated a Ballesteros-type freak shot to the green, caddie Ricci Roberts saw the scoreboard and realised that Roberts had blown his chances. Els chipped back onto the fairway, hit his approach to within 13 metres, and took two putts for a bogey five and a place in the play-off.

In the 18-hole play-off the following day, Els picked up where he left off, pulling his opening drive into the rough behind a motorised crane carrying a television camera. Tournament referee Trey Holland mistakenly ruled that the crane was immovable and granted Els line-of-sight relief and a free drop. It was the second major controversial break for the relieved youngster, who may have bogeyed that hole but knew that the punishment could have been far worse. The second hole saw Els scoring a triple-bogey, but there was the small consolation that Montgomerie and Roberts were also misfiring.

Montgomerie, the bridesmaid, the perennial near-winner who was widely regarded to be the best player never to have won a Major (that's BPNTHWAM for the business card), was the first casualty after shooting six over par in the opening nine.

Roberts had a narrow one-stroke lead over Els on the 16th, but he bogeyed that hole. They both birdied the 17th and parred the 18th to finish all square and force a sudden death. After halving the first extra hole, they headed to the 11th, where Roberts found heavy rough. Els found the green with his second and, after Roberts's par-putt lipped out, Els two-putted for the championship. He had become the first foreign-born golfer since Australia's David Graham in 1981 to capture America's championship.

In the wake of Els's victory, Curtis Strange, who had missed the play-off by a single shot, described Els as the "next god", while *Sports Illustrated* observed: "Who else but a god could win a US Open after playing most of his approach shots out of wheat fields, leaving his brain at the hotel and starting a Monday play-off bogey, triple-bogey?" And yet, the magazine conceded, as crooked as Els had hit the ball, as seldom as you could see his shoes as he stood in the rough, he would never quite go away.

A global television audience of many millions had witnessed South Africa's graceful and gracious favourite son take the title. Afterwards, Els told reporters, "I dug very deep today and brought it out. Whenever I had a putt that I had to make, I made that putt."

Archbishop Desmond Tutu's Rainbow Nation – just two months old – had a new sporting icon. Els was humbled by the reaction and moved to tears when he was handed a phone and the voice on the other end was that of Mandela, saluting his accomplishment.

The following year, Els came desperately close to securing his second Major, at the PGA Championship at the Riviera Country Club in Los Angeles, before throwing it away at the death. The easy-going South African held a three-shot lead – a tournament record of 197 going into the final round – before psyching himself out of the race and finishing third, two shots behind winner Steve Elkington.

The loss haunted him for years, particularly as he realised that he had talked himself out of the championship: "All I thought the whole day was the word 'lose' instead of 'win, win, win'. I played conservatively, and I lost.

I began thinking about not losing instead of winning, and that mindset, I think, cost me the PGA."

Despite this setback, he was still voted European Tour Golfer of the Year, becoming the first non-European to hold the title.

Over the next three years, Els won twice in the US, twice in Europe and twice in South Africa, including an individual triumph in the 1996 World Cup of Golf.

In 1997, Els and Montgomerie would do it all again at the US Open – this time played at Congressional. The club, which is located near Washington, D.C.'s Capital Beltway, was established in 1921. When US Open entries closed in May, a record 7 013 players had signed up for a shot at the tournament, exceeding the previous mark, set at the 1992 Open at Pebble Beach, by more than 800.

Els was considered one of the favourites, as he had a string of PGA Tour victories under his belt and strong finishes in the Majors, including a tie for fifth in the 1996 US Open at Oakland Hills, outside Detroit. Nevertheless, he had only one top-10 finish so far in 1997, and had missed the cut at the Kemper Open in nearby Potomac, Maryland, which preceded the US Open.

While Tiger Woods had won the Masters by 12 strokes in April, he would not feature at Congressional. Rather, it was the 27-year-old Els who was back to his best, holing critical putts in the rain-delayed third round. Els played five holes in three under with three consecutive birdies, starting at the 15th. It got him right back into the championship, which was threatening to slip away, while playing partner Montgomerie (in the penultimate group) knew that his chances of securing at least one Major were starting to fade.

On the final day, the caravan of leaders – Els, Montgomerie, Tom Lehman and Jeff Maggert – rolled into the turn on that wild and wonderful Sunday afternoon with everything to play for.

Els made a charge at the 10th with a chip-in birdie on the par four from the front of the green, which lifted him into a tie for the lead.

With US President Bill Clinton (and daughter Chelsea) in the stands at the 16th, Lehman and Maggert made matching bogeys, while Els and Montgomerie teed up at the 438-metre, par-four 17th hole.

Els later told me that his drive at the 17th had been one of the most defining shots of his career. Needing two pars to win, he hit a majestic drive at the downhill, 438-metre dogleg, and then "the best 5 iron of my life" from 195 metres to five metres, and two-putted from there. Montgomerie, after missing the green, chipped to two metres and then missed the putt.

At the 18th, Els was in the driving seat with a one-shot lead. Lehman – one hole behind – faltered when his approach to the 17th struck a bank to the left of the green and trickled into the water for a ruinous bogey. At the 18th (a par three), Els played with a safe 5 iron to 10 metres and two putts, the second a nervy 1.5-metre putt. Montgomerie then missed an eight-metre putt that would have forced another play-off, three years after Oakmont. Game, set and match to Els.

The South African had maintained a cool head despite the close, red-hot finish, parring the final five holes for a one-under 69 and a four-under total of 276.

Lehman, who had held a two-shot lead going into the final round, was gutted (it was the third year in a row he had led after 54 holes only to see the national title elude him), while Montgomerie, who finished second by just a shot, retreated in tears. Jeff Maggert was fourth at 281, having played the last four holes in four over par.

Under the towering six-level Mediterranean-style clubhouse, Els had become the first foreign player since Scotland's Alex Smith (1906 and 1910) to win the US Open twice. He expressed his gratitude at securing two massive titles at such a young age: "The first one was out of the blue. This one seems so much more."

But by 2000, Els was a worried man. Just three years had separated his first two Major victories – in 1994 and 1997 – but these hadn't opened the floodgates as most had expected. In 2000, Els always seemed to be the runner-up. In three of the Majors (the Masters, the US Open and The Open Championship) he finished second, and he recorded another seven second-place finishes in other tournaments around the world.

But it got worse. In 2001, he failed to win a US PGA Tour event for the first time since 1994 (but recorded a further nine second-place finishes).

In 2002 he managed to stop the bleeding with a win at the Heineken Classic at the Royal Melbourne Golf Club. He then defeated Tiger Woods to lift the Genuity Championship title before setting his sights on The Open Championship.

Woods and Els were the two favourites at Muirfield, but the American suffered a near collapse when the weather turned (the wind never blows in the same direction at this venue). "It's like turning up to hear Pavarotti sing and finding out he has laryngitis," was how whimsical television commentator Peter Alliss summed up Woods's third-round implosion when he shot an 81. It ended his 2002 Grand Slam bid and launched his longest winless streak in the Majors.

A front nine of 29 on the Friday and a back nine of 32 on the Saturday put Els in contention. While the weather had behaved on the opening two days, it was brutal (the Scots would say "adverse") on the Saturday. Woods spent much of the day trying to hack out of the knee-high rough, his Grand Slam hopes now in tatters. Colin Montgomerie, who may have been dreading the thought of another play-off with Els, also suffered an inglorious collapse, shooting an 84, 20 strokes worse than his offering of the day before. Els's 72 kept him on top of the leader board – five under and two shots ahead of Denmark's Soren Hansen.

On the Sunday, at the short 13th, Els produced the shot of the tournament when he escaped a wicked bunker lie to salvage par. In a similar situation at the following hole, he wasn't so fortunate in a sand trap and dropped a shot. At the 16th he missed the green and, instead of playing for a bogey four, he tried a tricky flop-shot, which backfired when he hit it thin, and he had to settle for a double-bogey.

But the champion in Els came to the fore at the next hole, when he hit a beautiful drive, approach and putt on the par-four 17th for a precious birdie. And by managing to par the 18th, he secured a four-hole play-off against Thomas Levet, Steve Elkington and Stuart Appleby.

The R&A ruled that the play-off would consist of two-balls – Levet and Elkington, and Els and Appleby – over four holes: the 1st, the 16th, the 17th and the 18th.

Elkington bogeyed the 1st, birdied the 17th and bogeyed the 18th to end his campaign. Appleby found himself in the same boat when he bogeyed the 16th, birdied the 17th and bogeyed the 18th. Levet scored a birdie on the 1st, a par on the 17th and a bogey on the 18th to remain level with Els, who had recorded four straight pars. In normal circumstances, they would have been within shouting distance of the clubhouse but, at that moment, the tension – and noise – was unbelievable.

The Frenchman (who suffers from severe vertigo) said the crowd was so loud that he couldn't hear his caddie, who was standing just a couple of metres away. Back at the 18th, Levet stuck to the game plan he had maintained throughout the tournament on that hole – a long drive down the right-hand side of the fairway (where the rough is very forgiving), and then a short-iron to the middle of the green for a birdie chance. But, for the first time that week, the ball veered low and left and found a bunker.

Els played an iron to the middle of the fairway, leaving a long approach to the green. The following shot was the product of a nervous swing, and there was that familiar gasp when the ball found the greenside bunker with a lie that Levet described as "awful". But Els climbed into the trap, dug himself in, waggled his wedge and spun the loosest, loveliest flop-shot to within one metre from the pin. It was a putt for history, and he guided the ball home.

"It's hard to describe how it felt when the putt went in. At first, it's a relief. Just a huge, huge relief that you've done it."

His wife Liezl, whom he married in 1998 and who was heavily pregnant with their second child, and their daughter Samantha were there to celebrate his crowning achievement.

For the next year, Els and the Claret Jug were inseparable; it travelled all over the world with him. When the time came to return the prized trophy, Els said he gave it an extra clean because of all the different beverages it had held.

Els's son, Ben, was born in October shortly after Ernie won the World Match Play Championships-CA Championship at Wentworth, a short distance from their family home.

Els won several times in 2004 on both tours, including impressive wins at Memorial, the WGC-American Express Championship and his sixth World Match Play Championship (a new record). But there were also some bitter disappointments. After all, Phil Mickelson's first Major victory came at the expense of Els, after the American sank a five-metre, final-hole birdie putt at the Masters.

The Sunday afternoon back-nine duel saw two of the greatest golfers of all time at their very best in one of the most exciting finishes ever at Augusta as they traded birdies and eagles back and forth. It was the closest Els had come to getting the Augusta monkey off his back, but the American's maverick, unorthodox style of play finally won the day ("Watching him play golf is like watching a drunk chasing a balloon near the edge of a cliff," popular television commentator David Feherty once observed).

At Shinnecock Hills, Els was two shots off Retief Goosen's lead at the start of the final round of the US Open when a double-bogey at the 1st effectively ended his challenge (he finished ninth).

Nevertheless, Els was the bookmakers' favourite at The Open at Royal Troon.

With a third-place finish at the Scottish Open at Loch Lomond the previous week, Els was in good shape. So much so that an unidentified punter placed a £62 000 bet on him. Els aced the 112-metre 8th hole with a wedge (his second in a Major), but cancelled that out with a double-bogey at the 17th to finish at 69, two under (in 13th place). Another 69 on day two kept him within three shots of the lead.

On the Saturday, American Todd Hamilton made a charge with an impressive 67, which gave him a one-shot lead over Els. And not far behind was Levet, whom Els had pipped in that play-off two-years previously; Mickelson, who had dashed Els's Masters hopes so cruelly; and friend and countryman Retief Goosen, who had left him for dead in the final round of the US Open.

On the Sunday, Els was joint leader at the turn when he double-bogeyed the 10th.

At the following hole – a 448-metre par four – he seemed to kill off what remained of his chances when he clattered his drive deep into gorse, the low, brambling shrub common to Scottish courses and wasteland. But, miraculously, his ball was nestled on a branch about 60 centimetres off the ground. A baseball strike took it back to safety, and a solid approach and four-metre putt salvaged par.

At the 18th, Els had a birdie putt for the championship, but the ball scraped past the hole. In the play-off, Hamilton and Els parred the 1st and 2nd holes, but Els dropped a shot at the par-three 17th. At the 18th, Hamilton had a spectacular bump-and-run approach to the pin, leaving it just 60 centimentres away, with Els needing to birdie a spine-tingling three-metre putt. But the putter went cold and the ball stayed out. Hamilton, a one-Major wonder who grew up playing on a nine-hole course in Oquawka, Illinois, had beaten the South African fair and square.

At the fourth – and final – Major of the year, the PGA Championship, Els finished fourth after a three-putt on the 72nd hole cost him a place in the play-off. It was another bitter disappointment. After all, 2004 had seen Els finishing in the top 10 of all four Majors, including second-place finishes at both the Masters and the Open. (But as Gary Player often notes, "Only your wife and your dog remember your second-place finishes.")

While Nicklaus, Palmer and Player had made up the Big Three in the 1960s and 1970s, a new grouping was beginning to take shape.

In September 2004, Vijay Singh overtook Woods in the Official World Golf Rankings, breaking the American's record streak of 264 weeks in the top spot. Woods rebounded in 2005, winning six official PGA Tour money events to reclaim the top spot in July, after swapping it back and forth with Singh over the first half of the year. Nevertheless, his crown was under siege.

Between 2004 and the start of 2007, nine Majors were won between Woods, Singh, Els, Goosen and Mickelson. They became known as the Big Five, and often had head-to-head duels between each other. During this period, Woods insisted on using his tried-and-trusted True Temper Dynamic Gold steel-shafted clubs and smaller steel club-heads, which promoted accuracy over distance. The problem was that his competitors were using larger club-heads and graphite shafts, which made them significantly longer.

In July 2005, there would be another twist (literally) in Els's roller-coaster career when he ruptured the ligaments in his left knee while sailing with his family in the Mediterranean. It would cost him several months of the 2005 season.

Nevertheless, he won the 2006 SA Open and, at the start of the 2007 season, he laid out a three-year battle plan "to totally rededicate myself to the game" and secure the number-one position he had previously held.

But it was not to be. For much of the year, he was misfiring. When he missed the cut by two strokes at the 2007 Masters, Els ended a spectacular, tour-leading consecutive-cut streak on both the PGA and European tours. On the PGA Tour, this run had begun at the 2004 Players Championship (46 events), and on the European Tour at the 2000 Johnnie Walker Classic (82 events).

In April 2008, Els officially announced that he was switching swing coaches from David Leadbetter, who had trained him since 1990, to Butch Harmon, who has revamped the golf swings of many established pros, including Tiger Woods.

Around this time, acclaimed mind coach Jos Vanstiphout said he regarded Els as "a spoilt brat", "cocky" and "a waste of a God-given talent". For the Belgian, the challenge was to get the South African to agree with him so that they could work together to improve his game. Vanstiphout (who calls himself "Jos the Boss") recalled the time he approached Els on the putting green at Royal Lytham in 2009 and allowed himself to offer his opinion.

"He was standing over a putt of a few metres and I said, 'You will hole this,' and he ignored me and holed it. With the next, I said again, 'You will hole this,' and he did. But then, with the third, I said, 'You will miss it,' and he ignored me and he missed it. And then, when he looked up at me in surprise, I told him that he is the greatest underachiever I have ever seen."

Els was taken aback and reportedly said us much ("You can't talk to me like that"). Added Vanstiphout: "He also used some words that you don't want to put in your book."

Els dismissed the Belgian and resumed his struggle with the putter. The altercation may have slipped from his mind but for the fact that Vanstiphout and his mind-doctoring was widely credited for Retief Goosen's surge in form several years earlier, resulting in him winning his first Major, the 2001 US Open.

A few minutes later, Els's caddie Ricci Roberts approached Vanstiphout. Roberts, says Vanstiphout, "used to call me the 'poisoned little Belgian dwarf'. He said, 'My boss wants to talk to you.'"

Vantstiphout recalls that he stood "no higher than Ernie's shoulders, and he could have knocked me down with one slap".

"I might be short, but I am honest and I told him so. And I told him I don't care if he is Gary Player, Tiger Woods or the Queen of Sheba."

They would talk and work together with varying results (Els would fire him twice in one week). Nevertheless, there were signs of hope when Els found himself in contention at the 2010 US Open at Pebble Beach – a decade after that crushing defeat by Tiger Woods. Paired with eventual winner Graeme McDowell in the final round, Els scored three birdies in his first six holes, but then dropped four shots in three holes during the turn. A wayward drive at the 10th effectively ended his campaign, and he wound up in third place (and stormed off the course without addressing the media). It marked a new low in his downward spiral, and he later conceded: "I was gone."

In 2011, Els dropped out of the top 50 in the Official World Golf Rankings for the first time since 1993, and the following year, he failed to qualify for the Masters.

When, for the first time in 18 years, Els did not receive a special invite to compete at Augusta, he felt a great deal of resentment because he had been such a popular ambassador for the sport. The committee rubbed salt in the wound by offering a special invite to rising Japanese star Ryo Ishikawa despite the fact that he hadn't achieved anything outside of his homeland (it was viewed in some quarters as a purely commercial decision to boost television audiences in Japan).*

---

* There are 19 exemption categories for the tournament, which include past champions and players who finished in the top 16 places of the tournament the year before. In

Either way, the world's 12th best player at the end of 2010 had plummeted to No. 68 a year later. And the jibes hurt. The underlying theme – as Els saw it – was that there was a consensus that he was washed up and should consider quitting. He conceded that his confidence had taken a big hit "and, without confidence, the putts just don't drop".

"I was coasting everything up to the hole and I wasn't giving it a scare," he said.

The Big Easy was in big trouble and had become a soft target for the likes of former tour pro David Feherty. Commenting at the 2012 Tavistock Cup, the American remarked that Els looked like he was "putting with a rattlesnake". Els's displeasure with himself, his situation and the former Ryder Cup star was evident: "If you're going to take the piss out of me, fine, but don't do it with a microphone in your hand and in front of the whole world. People were laughing at me and making jokes about me and really hitting me low, saying I'm done and I should hang it up."

To be fair, the inexhaustible Feherty is usually the first to take the piss out of himself. Reflecting on his role in the 1991 Ryder Cup team that narrowly lost the War by the Shore at Kiawah Island, he said that he was "shaking like a pregnant nun" when he stood over his first putt (he beat Payne Stewart in the singles).

With Els's troublesome putter misfiring in recent years and fed up with his inconsistency on the greens, he finally switched to a belly putter, the device *du jour* for many of the game's elderly statesmen. Broom handle or belly putters, which were pioneered by European Ryder Cup captain Sam Torrence and other yip-prone heavyweights in the late 1980s, are tucked beneath the chin or against the chest or belly. Because they create

---

addition, the top 30 players on the PGA Tour's money list, the top eight (and ties) in the US Open, along with the top four at the previous year's US Open and PGA Championship, crack the nod.

a pendulum effect, they affect different nerves and muscles. Although only three players before 2001 had won PGA Tour events using a long putter, their popularity surged that decade.

Ironically, a decade earlier (as the highest-ranking golfer on the planet), Els had called for belly and long putters to be banned. He famously observed that "nerves and the skill of putting are part of the game". He also took a swing at countryman Trevor Immelman, who had used a belly putter to win the 2004 Deutsche Bank-SAP Open in Heidelberg, saying it amounted to cheating.

But with his nerves shot and his putter cold, Els changed his tune and quipped that he was "happy to cheat as long as it [was] legal".

The dip in his form since his third Major victory had coincided with a personal challenge that Els and his wife Liezl were trying to come to terms with. The couple had gradually noticed that their only son, Ben, a beautiful boy with the bluest of eyes, was different. And, like most couples facing additional challenges, they were not always sure how to deal with it. Autism affects information processing in the brain by altering how nerve cells and their synapses connect and organise, but there are different schools of thought on the disorder.

The first public intimation came in 2008, when Els started to display an "Autism Speaks" logo on his golf bag. When questioned, he acknowledged that his son was autistic (like 1 in 88 American children) and that he was ready to support the cause.

"We suspected for a few years that something was not quite right. There's a process that every kid goes through. Crawl at nine months, walk at 12 months, and then start talking, and so on. With Ben, we started thinking: 'Why is he not crawling? Why is he not walking? Why is he not looking me in the eye?' Things like that. We soon discovered he was quite severely touched by autism. Like any family will tell you, it's not easy. And it's a change of life, a change of priorities. You've got to be ready for it. And it's happening more often. I never knew about it, never thought about it, until it's in your lap."

Els acknowledged that autism "hits families hard" and pledged to spend the rest of his life helping others in the same situation.

It took a great deal of soul-searching for Els to deal with his anger at the situation but, once he had done so, he and Liezl threw themselves at the problem. There was a gradual shifting of priorities, and they subsequently established the Els for Autism Foundation in 2009 with the goal of funding an Autism Centre of Excellence, the first of its kind in the world. The centre will incorporate all the services a child with autism needs, including cutting-edge education, therapy and research. Through its planned digital learning programme, it will have a worldwide reach, helping autistic children and their families who are unable to travel to the United States.

The inaugural Els for Autism Pro Am attracted several heavyweights, including Jack Nicklaus, Greg Norman, Gary Player and Luke Donald, and raised more than $700 000 for the cause.

Ben's condition was the main reason the couple relocated from Wentworth to West Palm Beach in Florida, where he was able to receive more intensive therapy. "He understands everything we say and is particularly in tune with our emotions; it's almost like a sixth sense. And thank God he's got such a nice nature. He's a very friendly, very happy, very shy kid, and the more loving attention he gets and the smiles that he sees, the better."

Els, who has been in the international spotlight for much of his life, concedes that while he – and Liezl – are private people, he also recognises that his talent as a golfer has given him a magnificent opportunity to raise funds and awareness for the causes of autism and its possible treatment.

And, perhaps most importantly, he loves his son like every father should. He describes Ben as the most loving person he has ever known, with a great sense of humour and an easy disposition, "and we don't want him any other way".

In March 2013, his foundation announced plans to construct a $30-million "epicentre for autism research, transition and treatment" in the Limestone Creek area near Jupiter, Florida. It aims to be the first charter school in the county for children with autism to offer education from first grade through high school, followed by transition to adulthood.

With his dip in form on the course, Els started spending more and more time at the gym and began watching his diet. One evening shortly after the 2012 US Open, while having dinner and enjoying a glass of wine with his long-time caddie and friend Ricci Roberts, Els announced that he had had enough of alcohol and planned to take a break from it. For someone who had in the past joked that his private jet often carried more alcohol than fuel, it was a brave pledge, but he stuck to it.

There was deep significance in his decision. After all, when he was just 56 days old, his father had "changed the cycle" after years of heavy drinking.

Els attributed much of his renewed confidence to Sherylle Calder, a sports scientist and performance coach who had worked with the Springbok rugby and hockey teams. They had first met a decade earlier, when Els had been one of the best putters in the world and "I didn't need any advice".

Calder, who was employed by the Springbok rugby team when they won the 2007 World Cup, has a simple motto: "See better, judge better, execute better, play better and score better."

Her offices at the Sports Science Institute in Newlands, Cape Town, and the Stellenbosch Academy of Sport, resemble shrines to the who's who of global sports. Autographed photos adorn the walls, and she clearly relishes the hope she has provided for many frayed sports stars.

She was introduced to Els by leading South African businessman Johann Rupert – a mutual friend – who had been alarmed by the Big

Easy's loss of form, at the Volvo Golf Champions at Fancourt early in 2012. Calder said she could see Els was battling.

"The immediate issue was to win his trust," she told me. "He had that look that [said] he had tried everything and why would I make a difference?"

Their first session confirmed the worst – the world's former number one was a basket case with his putting. "His eyes were all over the place and his thought pattern was clearly out of sync." Els would later concede that his mind was so cluttered that he couldn't think properly. His set-up was "gone", his eyes were moving, and the calm and collected Big Easy was nowhere to found.

Els admitted that it had got so bad that he was standing over five-metre putts worrying about the 50-centimetre putt he invariably would be left to deal with. And, as any golfer will confirm, stroking a putt in doubt is deadly. After all, when the mind twitches, the body twitches, the hands twitch and, of course, the putter twitches.

Contrast this to Nick Price, in his prime, who said that he was nailing his putts with such frequency that the only niggles in his mind were that he might be cheating. And compare this to the legendary Ben Hogan, who spoke of his battle with "the jerks", which left him "petrified" standing over a one-metre putt. "I have no concept of where it's going ... I'm embarrassed about getting out there in front of a lot of people. I might hit one of them," the nine-time Major champion (tied with Gary Player) confessed in 1964.

In his book *Golf Is Not a Game of Perfect*, Rob Rotella says there is no neurological basis for poor putting. Indeed, nothing about the physical ageing process dictates that a golfer cannot putt as well at 60 as he did at 20. Rotella says that players of Els's calibre accumulate baggage along the way, and therein lies the problem: "Maybe playing for years with Major championships on the line inevitably produces memories of missed putts in crucial situations. After a while, those memories become so burdensome that the golfer can't keep them out of his mind as he stands on the green. Then he loses the instinct to look at the hole, look at the ball, let the putt go, and know that it's going in."

And yet, Calder recalls, there where were signs of hope. "When we moved on to his short game, chipping off the edge of the green, I saw something special, something beautiful about his style."

Calder, a former elite athlete, firmly believed that Els possessed a "superior" talent, and she told him so. "Just know you are a master golfer," she kept telling him. When Els expressed surprise at her belief in him, she realised just how bruised he was. They both agreed that his self-esteem was very low.

Every tour pro knows that a practice putting green at a professional golf tournament is like a boxing ring at a title fight. When the heavyweights like Woods, Rory McIlroy and Adam Scott mingle with the hungry journeymen and all their aides (caddies, agents, sponsors, and swing and mind coaches), anything goes. And dagger eyes and forked tongues are part and parcel of this soap-opera world. It may seem light-hearted and cloaked in humour, but they often niggle each other, trying to out-psyche each other and, of course, there are often casualties.

Part of Els's training included using a computer program called *Eye-Gym*, which is designed to strengthen hand-eye coordination and improve the memory.

"It is a research-based software training program that has proven to simulate how you use your vision and execute your skills and decision-making on the field of play," Calder explained to me. I asked her to elaborate. "It also simulates and trains the ability to make effective decisions under pressure – in essence, it accelerates your performance and gives you an edge. I work on visual motor performance – how accurately you use the information you see and put it into your hands to respond. Every time your eyes move, they take in new information, which you need to process. So, you obviously want to avoid that when you putt."

One of the exercises consists of balls of different shapes and colours floating across the screen with the objective of reacting – by hitting the space bar – only when a particular shape or colour comes into view.

"If you don't concentrate, you can't do these exercises, and the same applies to putting – it takes a great deal of concentration to ensure that you strike the ball crisply."

She added that one of the beauties of the online program is that she is able to monitor the amount of time Els spends in training and, of course, assess his results, irrespective of where in the world he is.

Their sessions included a 10-day intensive camp in the US, after which Els noticed a significant improvement in his PGA Tour putting statistics. But the first real sign that Els was well on the mend came at the 2012 US Open at the Olympic Club in San Francisco. While Graeme McDowell, Jim Furyk and Webb Simpson exchanged the leadership, Els boxed an enormous eagle putt to move into a share of second place. However, a couple of soft mistakes saw him dropping shots on two of the last three holes.

"I feel that where I was last year and where I am now, it's a huge change," he said after finishing in ninth place, three shots behind Simpson. "I really felt like my old self. I'm contending now. I feel I have a chance, and if I eliminate those mistakes, I could win one of these things again. So I got the belief back."

Calder said Els's positive assessment of his campaign was a remarkably constructive change from Pebble Beach in 2010, when he stormed off following a similar back-nine mini-meltdown.

"Els is again a prime threat at a Major, especially at the British Open, where despite missing the cut the past two years, he has an exemplary record," she predicted.

With Ricci Roberts back on the bag (for years he has shared this duty with former Canadian ice-hockey star Dan Quinn), Els sent him from his Halifax home to inspect Lytham three weeks before The Open. Following days of torrential rain, the course was drenched, with large puddles in its famous bunkers.

Nevertheless, as the construction workers erected the scaffolding, Roberts set to work with a laser to measure the distances and contours (the new yardage charts had not yet been printed) and, when he reported back to Els, told him it was playing long. Els, whose past record there was second (1996) and third (2001), was, understandably, salivating.

"I wasn't going to shout about it, but I liked my chances. I genuinely felt like something special might happen," Els said.

And so, 18 years after winning the first of his three Majors and a full decade since he had won the third, a new-look Ernie Els winged his way from London to Royal Lytham on the economy carrier easyJet. No, money wasn't an issue (the ticket cost him £150, including the clubs). Rather he had recently sold his private jet and hadn't yet decided on the upgrade – either a Gulfstream IV or V (decisions, decisions!).

Peering down at Emerald Isle (or "Mud Island", as the formidable contingent of UK-based South African expats prefer), Els ruminated on the years he and his touring mates used to fly out from Heathrow on a Tuesday morning and return on a Sunday night, when they'd invariably group together in the old smoking section at the back of the aircraft. On the Monday, they would wake up with sore heads and, a day later, do it all over again.

No doubt, he also reflected on his first Open campaign at Lytham – 16 years previously. After making an explosive late run that saw him reining in Tom Lehman, Els was waiting to see if the American, who held a two-shot lead at the 18th, would stumble at the death. Sitting next to him was a 20-year-old amateur named Tiger Woods, who asked his advice on whether he should turn professional. And he recalled the double-whammy that followed (Lehman closed the deal and Woods did turn professional).

Els may have been ranked 40th in the world and a 45–1 outsider for the 2012 edition of the tournament, but his performance so far that year, including that late charge at the US Open, showed that he was well on the road to recovering his form.

Yet again, the spotlight was on Tiger Woods, who entered the tournament as firm favourite, even though four years had passed since he had previously won a Major (the 2008 US Open).

Three days of solid golf in near-perfect conditions saw Els cocooned in concentration and blessed with the graceful, flowing swing of old. And yet, as Gary Player has noted, beautiful swings don't win Majors; it's the putting that matters.

Lytham is famous for its heavy rough and firm greens, a course where golfers will be rewarded for keeping the ball on its narrow fairways. And, for the most part, that's exactly what Els was doing.

On the Sunday, brisk winds whipped off the Irish Sea, making those treacherous pothole bunkers – all 205 of them – even more formidable. Since 1974, Scotsman Ivor Robson has been the starter at the Open Championship. At 2.10 p.m. that Sunday, he announced: "Ladies and gentlemen, this is game number 40. On the tee, Ernie Els."

Adam Scott, who had won eight times on both the US and European tours, began the day with a four-shot lead. However, his opening three holes – bogey-birdie-bogey – indicated that his ship was yawing from side to side and he might have difficulty steadying it as he chased his first Major victory.

There was an interesting twist to the Woods/Scott duel, because the Australian's caddie, Steve Williams, had served in both camps before he had a highly publicised fall-out with Woods (calling him "a black arsehole"). During his glory days with Woods, Williams was the highest paid New

Zealand sportsman thanks to the 10 per cent of Tiger's winnings he took home. Incidentally, both Woods and Williams have had high-profile run-ins with Mickelson. Williams was once quoted calling Mickelson "a prick" and commenting on his "tits". The jibes hurt, particularly since Mickelson has defended his protruding breasts, saying he carries "subcutaneous fat" and "there's nothing I can do about it".

But back to The Open: Woods, who had a largely forgettable final day, finished joint third (with US countryman Brandt Snedeker) after a closing 73, which included his first triple-bogey in a Major for nine years and three successive bogeys on the back nine.

Six shots behind when the day began, Els matched Adam Scott on the first nine (36) despite scoring a bogey at the 9th. That setback, as he later recalled, "almost [got] me in a different mindset".

But, he immediately gathered himself and later recalled: "I felt good. I wasn't ahead, I wasn't far behind. I was in the moment, for once. I just felt that a golf course is such that if you doubt it, it's going to bite you. There are too many bunkers, too much trouble, and a bit of breeze."

With birdies at the 10th, 12th and 14th, Els improved to six-under par for the tournament – alone in second place – and he was walking tall with the bounce back in his stride. At the 16th, he pushed his drive but then threaded the ball through the bunkers, only to narrowly miss the par putt.

Caddie Ricci Roberts had one eye on his boss, the other on the scoreboard and, at that stage, thought they were playing for second place.

Scott appeared to have the championship in the bag at the 14th, when he scored a birdie to take a four-shot lead over Els.

But the home stretch at Lytham – the final four par-four holes have been referred to as "Murder Mile", as the world No. 13 was about to find out – would prove too much. Scott stumbled at the next with a bogey, and then missed a one-metre putt at the 16th.

And herein lies the twist in this tale. Like Els, Scott had also struggled with his putting and, again like Els, he'd switched to a body-anchored putter. The Australian's Scotty Cameron Studio Select Kombi with a broom-handle shaft had helped improve his game dramatically and, along with a magnificent long game, had placed him in the driving seat that Sunday. But, with the end in sight, his putter turned on him.

Playing partner Graeme McDowell said that the missed putt at the 16th was "huge". With a 6 iron from 160 metres into the par-four 17th, Scott's ball flew left and nestled in the rough. McDowell noted that he had "half of England right of that pin, and he missed it left".

Els, two holes in front of Scott, was wrapping up his campaign in impressive style.

His long legs, broad shoulders and powerful forearms have always promised something special, and it was no different at that moment on the 18th tee at Lytham. With a choice between laying up at the greenside bunkers or trying to carry them, Els selected his Callaway FT-9 driver and unleashed all of his genius.

Bernard Darwin, a golf essayist (and grandson of famous naturalist Charles Darwin), once described the "certain drowsy beauty" of Bobby Jones's swing. It would have been every bit as apt to depict the effortless, flowing, fluid swing Els creates with a huge shoulder turn (belying the fact that his club-head usually hits the ball at more than 200 km/h).[*]

And so it was on that last day when Els teed off and, with gentle and devastating effect, the ball arrowed towards the last bunker with a fade and landed pin-high between the green and the grandstand.

---

[*] The current regulations mandated by the R&A and the USGA state that the maximum velocity of the ball may not exceed 76 metres per second (274 km/h) under test conditions.

With those large, soft hands, Els then feathered his approach to five metres away from the pin. And then, with his head dead still and eyes ever so quiet, he sank that putt for a 68.

When he plucked the ball from the hole, he celebrated like a champion and flicked it into the crowd. At that moment, it seemed, it didn't seem to matter whether he had won the thing. No, this was far sweeter. The big man was in a good space again.

Sherylle Calder, who was witnessing the drama unfold in the crowd at the 18th, saw the tournament change course within a few minutes. Her bags were already backed, as she was planning to fly to Canada with Els immediately after the round for another tournament, "but this changed everything".

She elbowed her way through the crowd to Els, who knew he had secured second place – nobody could catch him. They began to prepare for a possible play-off. "At that moment, I knew that Ernie would win [a play-off] with his eyes closed – he looked invincible," she said.

Els's final-hole birdie was greeted with rapture, and when the roar tunnelled down the 18th fairway, Scott knew he was in deep, deep trouble. A one-shot lead with two holes to play, and his nerves were shot to pieces. After finding the greenside rough at the 17th, the 32-year-old Australian scored another bogey.

As he stared down the 18th fairway with its notorious undulations (pockmarked with 17 cavernous bunkers, all capable of sucking in a golf ball), he had a look of bewilderment.

He was faced with a choice of whether to lay up short of the fairway bunkers or clear them. But, in that heady moment, the Australian took the one club that was likely to reach it and just as unlikely to clear it – the 3 wood.

Any connoisseur of Open links courses will advise any golfer not to tease the bunkers. Aye, avoid them at all costs, because looks are deceptive and the ground around is invariably hard and slopes towards them, sucking the ball in like a magnet.

Ahead of the 1969 Open at Lytham, Peter Thomson noted that there was a 30-metre square of fairway about 200 metres out from the last tee, and "I've been thinking about that piece of fairway for nearly a year because on July 12 at about 4.30 p.m., I may have to hit a shot under awful pressure".

Charles Price, who (briefly) held the lead at the 1964 Open, said the challenge is to balance pressure with grace. "So what did I do? I just did what comes naturally. I vomited." And Seve Ballesteros, addressing Lytham's narrow fairways, once observed: "Everyone misses them, not just me."

"It's lost," said Gary Player, who was watching Scott in anguish: "He's gone with an iron all week – you either lay it up, or you go. The 3 wood is in the bunker zone, and that's a certain hazard. I said, 'Under this pressure, he's going in that bunker.'"

Player blamed Williams, Scott's caddie, for the decision to use that club at the 18th. "If I were him, I would have gone with a driver. It's got a beautiful swing and is so long that it can carry that bunker."

With all Scott's frustrations from the near meltdown funnelled into his booming drive, the ball dived into a bunker. With his second shot, Scott pitched out and then put his approach just over two metres from the cup. With his hit-and-hope posture, he then missed the putt left of the cup, his knees buckling under the weight of the world. It was one of the biggest meltdowns in Open history, a nightmare of Scott's own making.

Els was quick to console his old friend and President's Cup teammate following the gut-wrenching collapse: "I told him that I've been there many times, and you've just got to bounce back quickly. Don't let this thing linger. So yeah, I feel for him. But thankfully he's young enough.

He's 32 years old. He's got the next 10 years [to] win more [Majors] than I've won."

Scott, who had wept openly as a 15-year-old schoolboy in Queensland at countryman Greg Norman's infamous collapse at the 1996 Masters, had, to use a stock phrase, become the biggest choker in golf. Fellow Australian Geoff Ogilvy tweeted: "I am happy for Ernie, but I feel sick right now."

The victor and loser would text each other on several occasions over the next few days as Scott battled to come to terms with the biggest meltdown of his career. "Double, double, triple and trouble; Lytham reduced them all to rubble. All that is, except Ernie Els, who has his own scrapbook full of woe to throw on the pile," was how golf scribe Jim Moriarty viewed Scott's meltdown. But just nine months later (and two years after sharing second at the Masters), Scott would win his first Major title in commanding fashion at Augusta.

Els, who was $1 405 890 richer (in prize money alone), saluted his caddie and long-time mentor Ricci Roberts. It was their 58th win (including all four Majors), but it had not always been plain sailing. They have, as Roberts is quick to point out, been through as many divorces as Elizabeth Taylor and Richard Burton, and his job is about as secure as that of a Chelsea Football Club manager.

Els had become the first Open winner to make up six shots on the field since Padraig Harrington's smash-and-grab victory over Sergio García at Carnoustie in 2008. And, like Bobby Locke, he had won a fourth Major. But, unlike Locke, he had done it on both sides of the pond. He had also become one of only six golfers to win both The Open and the US Open twice.

Starter Ivor Robson, who had introduced Els earlier in the day, announced the triumph: "And the champion golfer of the year, with a score of 273 ... Ernie Els!"

Ever the diplomat, Els spent much of his acceptance speech saluting Nelson Mandela and reflecting on how, when he became post-apartheid South Africa's first Major winner at the US Open in 1994, Mandela had called to congratulate him.

In his gracious post-match assessment, Els also paid tribute to his only son, saying he had made a lot of his clutch putts that day with Ben in mind. "He loves it when I hit golf balls. I know he was watching today and I was trying to keep him [watching] because he gets really excited. You guys should see him. He's a wonderful boy now, a bright boy. We're going to have a lot of fun."

Els had become the second successive 42-year-old to win the championship following the equally popular Darren Clarke, and he had taken South Africa into fourth place in the all-time Open list with 10 wins, behind Scotland and the US (both 41), and England (22).

He had also joined an elite group of 27 golfers to have achieved four Majors or more, and had become only the sixth player to win the US Open and Open Championship twice (along with Jack Nicklaus, Tiger Woods, Walter Hagen, Bobby Jones and Lee Trevino).

Along with the European Ryder Cup team, which had fought back to beat the United States in the so-called "Miracle of Medinah", Els was nominated for the 2013 Laureus World Comeback of the Year Award thanks to his Open triumph.[*]

Els had become the third golfer in just 12 months to win a Major[†] using a long putter, and more than a quarter of the field that weekend had also made the switch (which wasn't lost on the guardians of the game).

---

[*] The Dominican Republic's Felix Sanchez won the award after winning the Olympic 400-metre hurdles gold medal in London eight years after he won it for the first time in Athens in 2004.

[†] The others were at the 2011 PGA Championship (Keegan Bradley) and the 2012 US Open (Web Simpson) while Adam Scott added the Masters in 2013.

The morning after Els's triumph, Peter Dawson, the chief executive of the R&A, which establishes the rules of golf (along with the USGA), indicated that these putters had become a burning issue. Soon afterwards, both organisations announced that they would outlaw the anchored strokes with the next official revision of the rules in January 2016.

As the big South African enters the twilight of his career, he leaves behind a conflicting legacy. Nevertheless, with more than 60 professional career victories to his name, including three Major championships, two World Golf championships and a record seven World Match Play titles, he will be remembered as one of the giants of the game. He has triumphed in tournaments all over the world – in South Africa, Europe, the US, Asia, the Far East, the Middle East and Australasia, and was inducted into the World Golf Hall of Fame in 2011 and the Southern Africa Golf Hall of Fame in 2009.

However, this is all a fraction of what it could have been. Like Greg Norman, who exploded onto the scene but didn't quite fulfil his potential, Els will be left to rue a number of missed opportunities.

Like Els, Norman was big, brave and blond, and a magnificent striker of the ball. He spent 331 weeks as the world's top player in the 1980s and 1990s, winning 85 international tournaments, including two Majors. But there should have been more. Many more.

While Norman finished runner-up in all four Majors (the 1984 US Open, the 1987 Masters, the 1989 Open and the 1993 PGA), Els has finished runner-up in six Majors, all too often left for dead by the man with the red shirt who lifted trophies in seven of the 11 Majors between August 1999 and June 2002. Els finished runner-up to Woods on seven occasions – more than any other golfer.

Those who find themselves closest to the glare of glory are usually those who get the most burnt. And so it was with South Africa's greatest golfer since Gary Player.

In 2006, when Woods was asked whether Mickelson was his biggest rival, he replied that Els was "the person I've gone head to head against the most". In a Fox Sports column on Woods in 2009, golf writer Robert Lusetich observed: "He's a rivals' serial killer. Ernie Els, let's face it, is a shell of the player he once was and, in a quiet moment, he'd probably admit that losing over and over to Woods in the early part of this decade took its toll."

Woods's former swing coach, Hank Heney, said that while he was often overwhelmed by the greatness of his student, he regarded him as one of the most complicated individuals he has ever met. In his bestselling book *The Big Miss*, Heney says that although he had worked with hundreds of top golfers, Woods was in a class of his own and he couldn't believe his skills.

He said Woods had developed a variety of tactics to keep people from getting too close to him, and as their own relationship deteriorated, Heney noticed warning signs that Woods was dangerously distracted. Although Heney tried desperately hard to figure Woods out, at the same time Woods was trying just as hard to prevent him from doing so.

Contrast this to Els, the easy-going, warm and affable giant, who never yearned for the gym. Was Els ever a threat to Woods? The answer is, "probably". For starters, Woods never appeared to warm to Els. On a practice green before heading out with Els to play the third round of The Open at Hoylake in 2006, Woods was overheard to coldly remark about the South African: "If I can break this big guy's heart just one more time, maybe he'll go away and stay away." For the record, they both shot 71 that day, but Woods, displaying his trademark menace, closed with an impressive 67 to become the first man to bag back-to-back Opens since Tom Watson in 1982 and 1983.

Searching for clues in the styles of these two athletes becomes an exercise in futility. They couldn't be more different, after all.

Compare Els (1.92 metres), with that broad stance, the rolling shoulders, that impossibly wide swing and arc, and timing that belies his enormous strength, to Woods. At his peak in 2000/01, Woods probably had the most explosive swing in the history of the game, as he seemed to attack the ball at every given opportunity. Butch Harmon said the rest of the field was clearly afraid of him.

However, that swing came at a price. Flaws in his technique complicated his swing and, along with a series of niggling – and serious – injuries, he began adopting "smoke and mirrors" to address the flaws. Woods has carried an injured left knee since his daredevil childhood. When doctors removed a cyst from the joint in 1994, they discovered significant scar tissue from very old injuries. One of the tricks of his trade, in his prime, was to snap that left knee to its fullest possible extension at the moment of impact to add an extra 20 metres or so to his drives.

Despite helping to resurrect Woods's career after a disastrous 2003, Heney believes that his client clearly missed the opportunity to reach his full potential.

However, the reality is that Els's misses were even greater – through no fault of his own. If it's any consolation, there have been plenty of other magnificent pros who have been left wondering, in the wake of Tiger mania, what could have been.

Phil Mickelson is probably the most notable of these, and he readily acknowledges it. In 2007 he noted that even if he managed to maintain his high standards for the rest of his career, "I still won't get to where Tiger is right now." The solution, Mickelson offered, was not to compare himself with Woods. And this set Mickelson free and enabled him to put everything – including his other interests, family and friends – into perspective.

As the shadows begin to lengthen for the big South African, many believe he's still got a Major (or two) to add to those he's already bagged.

Either way, he has been a magnificent ambassador both on and off the course, and has ploughed a great deal of his wealth back into the game in South Africa.

7

The Goose

"The black mamba will strike. Nobody knows who Retief Goosen is. It will be a sneak attack. Nobody will see it coming."
— Jos Vanstiphout

In *Search of Burningbush* is a fictional account of a middle-aged American's quest to find the ultimate Scottish links course. Ravaged by a brittle-bone disease and years of chain smoking, Don gets dangerously close to finding it during a spectacular storm. As great bolts of lightning illuminate the sky, he reveals what he considers to be a dream death: "Struck by lightning on a golf course. That's perfect. For a second, you've got all the energy of the universe in your brain, and then you just sink into the course."

For Bobby Jones, the first Grand Slam winner, the experience was a lot less perfect. In 1929, during a practice round at East Lake, Augusta, he was caught in a violent thunderstorm. As he scrambled to safety, the clubhouse chimney was hit, spraying shrapnel everywhere. "A jagged edge ripped my shirt and put a scratch about six inches long on my right shoulder," he recalled.

In the blockbuster movie *Caddyshack*, Bishop Pickering (Henry Wilcoxon) is playing a round of golf in a thunderstorm when he declares: "The good Lord would never disrupt the best game of my life." Moments later he is struck by lightning and his caddie, Carl Spackler (Bill Murray), slinks away.

And Lee Trevino was hit by lightning at the 1975 Western Open in Illinois. The six-time Major winner lived to offer the following advice: "If you are caught on a golf course during a storm, hold up a 1 iron. Not even God can hit a 1 iron."

Half a world away, and a few years later, 15-year-old Retief Goosen was also caught in a storm on a golf course. There was the throaty rumble of thunder, an explosive crack and, for what seemed like eternity, a deafening silence as he lay shredded by the strike.

Goosen was born on 3 February 1969, the youngest of three brothers by six years. The trio spent much of their childhood playing golf at the local 18-hole parklands course, which was established in the late 1800s.

Their town had been founded in 1886, by Andries Potgieter, who named it Pietersburg in honour of Boer hero Petrus Joubert. At the turn of the 19th century, the British built a concentration camp in the town to house almost 4 000 Boer women and children.

While there was nothing particularly exciting or notable about the town, it was an important agricultural hub and a bastion of Afrikanerdom during the apartheid era.

The Goosen family led a simple and proud middle-class life. Retief's father Theo was a successful businessman and a strict disciplinarian, while his mother, Annetjie, was devoted to all three of her sons.

Retief's older brother, Francois, who became a scratch player as a junior, said they started chipping and putting with table-tennis balls and, even then, Retief was able to manipulate the balls with backspin, fading and hooking.

Theo recalls how his youngest was particularly fond of the game and spent hours hitting balls in the backyard or at the local course: "He would ride there with his golf bag strapped to his back."

On a sweltering hot day in January 1985, the day that a lightning bolt would shape Retief's destiny, Theo had also been planning to play a round of golf, but cancelled at the last minute because of the inclement weather.

Later that afternoon, the searing heat eased as the thunderclouds rolled in and released their load. Goosen and his playing partner, Henri Potgieter, were walking past a pine tree when it was hit. The bolt knocked Potgieter backwards and found Goosen's steel-shafted clubs in the bag slung over his back. The hair at the back of his head was burnt off and his shoes disintegrated. His watch-strap melted as he crumpled to the ground in a pile.

When Potgieter finally managed to sit up, he saw his playing partner lying deathly still, flat on his back. Their golf bags were nowhere to be seen.

Potgieter recounted the incident in an interview with *Golf World*: "His tongue was down his throat and his eyes [had rolled] backwards, and he was breathing weird. He had no clothes on; they'd been burnt from his body. I remember picking up his spectacles. I didn't know what to do. It looked like he was dead. I was screaming for help. Fortunately, there were guys teeing off on the 12th hole. They came running towards us. From then on, I can't remember much. They picked him up and put him in a car."

When a neighbour ran over to Theo's house shouting that Retief had been seriously injured, they rushed to the course and expected the worse. "He was in a bad way. It was touch-and-go – we didn't know if he would make it," his father said. Twenty minutes later, when they were in a car on the way to hospital, the teenager slowly regained consciousness, "and we had hope". In addition to the burns, the strike had burst one of his eardrums.

Goosen spent six days in hospital recovering, but, just two weeks later, he was back on the course.

When I told Theo that my own brother had been struck by lightning on a golf course (and lived to tell the tale), he flinched. He's clearly relived his ordeal many times over the years. "By the grace of the good Lord, we were spared," he said. He is adamant that his son's survival was a sign from God that he, in turn, would leave a mark.

It's probably a blessing that the softly spoken champion has no recollection of the incident, but when he fully regained his composure and balance many weeks later, a scar on his wrist and a slight deafness in one ear would remain as permanent reminders of what might have been. How that moment changed his life will never be known, but anyone who has been targeted by an act of God – good or bad – will surely never be the same again.

Excluding incidental catastrophes and disasters, lightning causes more deaths – around 24 000 – than any other natural event or phenomenon around the world. While about 240 000 people survive lightning strikes each year, survivors frequently suffer neurological after-effects, including brain damage, cardiovascular problems, seizures, depression and other personality disorders.

Dr Ryan Blumenthal, an expert on karaunomedicine (the study of lightning and its effects on humans and animals) at the University of Pretoria, says there are six different mechanisms by which lightning injures a person: directly, touch potential, side flash, step potential, upward streamers and the so-called electro-blast effect.

Because it appears that a tree was hit a millisecond before Goosen, he was affected by a side flash, where a proportion of the energy was "dumped" on the object that was first struck, "and one would expect to find less severe injuries than one would expect in direct strikes".

Whether the near-tragedy affected Goosen's psyche is unclear, but there was a dark, moody side to the teenager that occasionally sought an outlet. Goosen concedes that he was often "bad-tempered" on the course and, on one occasion, broke three clubs in a round. When his father warned him that he would pay to replace them, he learnt to keep his temper in check.

Some of Goosen's playing partners described him as a steely, determined individual who would one day be nicknamed "the Iceman" because of his cool demeanour.

The Telegraph once observed that "he can be so vague that you wonder if Pietersburg stands on the river Lethe". And vague doesn't begin to describe Angela Jones, his media agent at IMG World in London, who seemed perplexed as to why I would want to interview her client (I gave up after 10 months of trying).

Belgian sports psychologist Jos Vanstiphout, who worked with Goosen at the peak of his game, told me that his client never mentioned the incident. "But by knowing his mama and papa and his family, I started to understand the guy and I heard about the lightning [strike], but he never spoke about it. He gave the impression that it's no big deal."

When Goosen had recovered and his golf training commenced, one of Theo's teaching aids included a wooden structure that framed his son's body and prevented him from lifting his head at the moment of impact (during his purple patch in the new millennium, he had one of the steadiest heads in golf).

The teenager also studied Ben Hogan's *Fundamentals of Golf* and Jack Nicklaus's *Golf My Way*. Raised in an Afrikaans home, he was unable to read in English, but he spent hours studying the photographs and illustrations and practising in front of a mirror.

In the late 1980s, the political temperature in South Africa was sky high as the country lurched from one crisis to another, and a state of emergency was enforced to keep a lid on the bubbling cauldron.

As a white South African, Goosen was required to serve in the military, and he reported for his basic training at Voortrekkerhoogte in 1988. After his three-month basic training, he was able to use his talent as a golfer to escape the grind of military service and spent much of his time (like Ernie Els) playing golf. Within two years, P.W. Botha had been ousted as the country's leader and the progressive F.W. de Klerk, who replaced him, began implementing the sweeping changes that would lead to the country's first democratic elections.

Slightly under 1.8 metres tall but physically ripped, Goosen won 30 amateur titles and was crowned South African Amateur champion in 1990. He turned professional the same year.

Playing on the Sunshine Tour, he recorded his first pro victory in 1991, when he captured the Iscor Newcastle Open. The following year, he won the Spoornet Classic, the Bushveld Classic and the Highveld Classic.

In 1992, he won the European Tour's Qualifying School, as well as four titles on the European Tour International Schedule. In 1993, he finished second in the Dubai Desert Classic, sixth in the Irish Open, and tied 10th in both the English Open and the Volvo Masters to finish the year in 44th position on the Order of Merit.

In 1993, he met Tracy Pottick, the owner of a promotions staffing company at the Ryder Cup at The Belfry. She had just come out of a bad relationship and was understandably reluctant to begin dating again, despite Goosen's good looks and gentle charm.

Nevertheless, she became the light he needed, but old habits die hard and he continued to let negative thoughts – particularly those relating to his infuriating trade – enter his mind. Pottick warned him that she would leave him if he didn't undergo a radical mind shift.

On the course, Goosen's results were mixed. During the mid- to late 1990s, he made his mark on the European Tour. In 1994, he improved five places on the Order of Merit but, within a year, had dropped to 95th in the standings.

Matters improved in 1996, when he won the Slaley Hall Northumberland Challenge, and also secured top-five finishes in the Peugeot Open de France and the Deutsche Bank Open TPC of Europe. He ended the year in 25th place on the Order of Merit.

The next 12 months were even better (victory in the Peugeot Open de France, second in the Compaq European Open, third in the Gulfstream Loch Lomond World Invitational, fourth in the Alfred Dunhill SA PGA, sixth in the South African Open, and 10th at the Open Championship at Royal Troon) and saw him finish seventh on the Order of Merit.

It was during this period that he embarked on a journey of self-discovery to help improve his mind and body both on and off the course. As part of the process, in 1999 he turned to acclaimed Belgian sports psychologist Jos Vanstiphout to address his negative mindset.

The son of a miner and the youngest of 10 children, Vanstiphout had enjoyed a chequered career as a pop singer, salesman and then self-taught "mental coach", inspired by Californian guru Tim Gallwey, who wrote *The Inner Game of Golf*. He picked up his first golf club at the age of 40 and, within 14 months, had reduced his handicap to 11. What fascinated him was the mental barrier, that voice in his head that constantly taunted him and crippled his progress.

He spent two years on the European Tour plying his trade before he made a cent, but he earned a reputation for being an invaluable mind coach.

When Goosen came knocking, Vanstiphout already had a number of heavyweights on his books, including Ireland's Darren Clarke, Padraig Harrington and Paul McGinley, Denmark's Thomas Bjorn, Spain's Sergio García and New Zealand's Michael Campbell.

While Goosen had initially dismissed Vanstiphout and other "brain mechanics" plying their trade on the circuit, his determination to keep the woman of his dreams motivated him to undergo some psychosurgery.

While Goosen conceded that he used to be way too negative on the course and "tended to drag too many bad things along", Vanstiphout said he immediately recognised the golfer's huge potential.

Vanstiphout's reprogramming of the golfer's subconscious involved striving for pure relaxation through yoga and hypnotism in order to purge the mind of negative thoughts and, into that vacuum, inserting the right messages. This included making personal tapes – about 10 minutes long – to reinforce "all the positive things". Vanstiphout believed that the biggest hurdle between Goosen and global success was countryman Ernie Els, who cast a giant shadow with his seemingly effortless successes. And yet, there was plenty of hope.

"The black mamba will strike," the Belgian said in reference to the deadly South African snake. "Nobody knows who Retief Goosen is. It will be a sneak attack. Nobody will see it coming."

And so it was when the new millennium rolled around and Goosen began hitting his stride. In 2001, he struck gold despite two of the most nerve-wracking moments of his life, which happened within two months of each other.

The first occurred on 28 April 2001, when Goosen stood at the altar of the 800-year-old St Mildred's Anglican Church in Tenterden, Kent, facing the woman he had met eight years earlier. She said, "I do," after which they wined and dined the night away at the Leeds Castle that, incidentally, had been home to six queens. After the ceremony, Goosen reportedly said: "If I can do this, I can do anything."

Except, perhaps, sink a sitter to win the US Open.

At the 101st edition of the tournament at the Southern Hills Country Club in Oklahoma, the newly-wed was in contention from the start despite the fact that he had never mounted a serious challenge at any tournament on American soil. While the South African had won four PGA European Tour events and had finished in the top 10 in two British Opens, he had never made it into the top 10 of an American event.

By the Sunday, Goosen, who was ranked 44th in the world at the time, was involved in a seesaw contest with Americans Stewart Cink and Mark Brooks. The triumvirate had left Ernie Els, Phil Mickelson, Nick Price and Tiger Woods in their wake. Woods, with the so-called Tiger Slam under his belt, had been the big drawcard, with crowds of around 35 000 attending each day. However, his challenge faded and he finished joint 12th.

Cink and Goosen, playing together, arrived at the final hole tied, one shot ahead of Brooks, former winner of the PGA Championship and the sole Major Championship title holder among the three leaders.

Goosen's crisp second shot at the 393-metre par four landed in the middle of the green, but Cink's approach went over the back. His chip left him four metres short and, when Goosen lagged to within 60 centimetres, Cink knew he had to sink the putt. But the ball just missed on the high side, leaving him a 60-centimetre putt for bogey. It was game over for the 28-year-old, who botched the return putt as well to card a double-bogey and a 277 finish, one shot behind Brooks, in third.

With Cink's meltdown etched on his mind, Goosen stepped forward to face the biggest moment of his life (apart from that lightning strike and his wedding). The green was slippery and he failed to scare the hole. The ball leaked past and stopped 50 centimetres away, leaving a nervy, white-knuckle putt for the championship. And, as every golfer knows, a 50-centimetre putt is as important as a 50-metre approach shot. There is a comedy in this, noted American author John Updike, "and a certain unfairness even, which makes golf an even apter mirror of reality".

Sir Walter Simpson addressed moments like this in *The Art of Golf*: "When a putter is waiting his turn to hole out a putt of one or two feet in length, on which the match hangs at the last hole, it is of vital importance that he think of nothing. At this supreme moment he ought to fill his mind with vacancy. He must not even allow himself the consolation of religion."

Easier said than done.

The last time a championship contender had been in a similar situation was at the 1970 Open Championship at St Andrews, when Doug Sanders needed two putts on the 18th for the title. Leading Jack Nicklaus by one, he stood over a downhill left-to-right putt (the kind that is often followed by an uphill right-to-left putt) and appeared to freeze. As playing partner Lee Trevino appealed to the spectators to be quiet, Sanders suddenly bent down to remove a blade of grass off the ball and, without stepping back and regrouping, hurriedly pushed his putt past the hole. He would later confess that his mind had been occupied with how he would be celebrating his victory.

It is rumoured that Sanders spent the entire evening staring at the stars and ruing that miss and, of course, Nicklaus finished him off in the play-off the following day. From time to time, Sanders (who finished second in four Majors but never won one) is quoted as saying that he occasionally goes a whole five minutes without thinking about it. And yet, as multiple Open champion Tom Watson once observed, many players who have never choked have never been in the position to do so, "so go easy on them".

As the crowd gasped, Goosen addressed the ball again but, at the moment of impact, the putter blade faltered and twitched ever so slightly, and the ball barely glanced at the hole as it scurried past the right lip and stopped even further away than the previous effort.

The quiet South African now had to knock in the third putt just to secure a play-off.

The great Walter Hagen once observed: "If you three-putt on the first green, they'll never remember it. But if you three-putt the 18th, they'll never forget it."

Half a world (and eight time zones) away, Goosen's father Theo was watching the flickering drama unfold on television late at night at the family home in South Africa. Like day four of every US Open, it falls on Father's Day, fuelling the emotions.

"I couldn't sit – obviously – and I couldn't stand either because my knees were shaking so badly," he recalled.

The young South African was facing the biggest Major meltdown since Jean Van de Velde's final-hole calamities at the 1999 Open at Carnoustie (needing a double-bogey to win, the Frenchman sprayed a driver onto the adjacent 17th fairway, hit an iron into the rough, where it struck a grandstand, sent his chip shot into a water hazard, took a drop, cleared the burn but landed in a greenside bunker, splashed out and landed two metres from the pin, then sank the putt to force a play-off, which he lost).

Facing the longest putt of his life, Goosen tried to steady himself. With nerves of steel, he wrapped his fingers around his putter (named Tracy, after his wife), drew his fingers, hands, wrists, arms and shoulders back and forward, and through the ball. Mercifully, with the dying roll, it disappeared.

His total of four-under 284 (66, 70, 69, 71) tied him with Brooks. The irony of ironies was that it was the South African's magnificent putting that had taken him so far in the tournament.

Under the headline "Yawn of a new era", *The Telegraph* reported that Goosen, Brooks and Cink had produced a display of putting on the 18th green that was reminiscent of a family outing at a crazy golf course, "concluding with Goosen winning this year's Jean Van de Velde award for the most hapless final-hole short-circuit in a Major championship". And it added that Goosen's famous lightning strike was the closest he had ever come to being associated with electricity ("Goosen is laid-back on a golf course to the point of making Ernie Els look [like] a nervous wreck").

Television commentator Johnny Miller described Goosen's meltdown as "the worst three-putt in the history of golf". *Guardian* reporter David Davies concurred: "It was possibly the most calamitous loss of nerve ever seen in a Major championship. Never was a shorter, easier putt for a Major championship missed."

Would the 32-year-old South African have to live out the rest of his life knowing that he had come so close?

Despite nearly throwing it away at the death, Goosen at least had a lifeline with an 18-hole play-off the following day.

After he returned to his hotel room, Vanstiphout joined him and immediately realised that there was still some hope when he asked Goosen if he could come up with anything positive from the round he had just played. Goosen's response – "Now I know that I can beat them all" – marked a seismic shift from the player of old who would have beaten himself up over the near collapse.

They went through a damage-control exercise to reprogramme his subconscious. The mind coach said his challenge was to get Goosen to look at the "big picture" – the entire tournament, where he had outplayed the best golfers in the world – rather than that momentary lapse at the last.

Ernie Els, who had made the cut but finished tied 66th, told reporters that he would be sending Goosen a note of encouragement, "but I'll be writing it in Afrikaans so you bastards won't know what it says" (this was the first 18-hole US Open play-off since 1994, when Els defeated Colin Montgomerie and Loren Roberts).

Nevertheless, the 40-year-old Texan was the clear favourite, having played in 47 Majors (and winning the 1996 PGA Championship). Goosen, on the other hand, had just 16 Majors behind him. When he awoke that Monday morning after a "pleasant" nine-hour sleep, he knew that he still had a 50 per cent chance of closing the deal.

Despite a sluggish start, he made a charge at the par-three 6th hole with a magnificent approach shot that left a 1.8-metre putt, which he sank for a birdie.

At the following hole, the American drove into the trees and made bogey.

Drenched in sweat, Brooks began wilting in the 90-degree heat. He recorded another bogey at the 9th, while Goosen drained a slippery five-metre putt for a birdie three.

At the turn, the Goose was flying. He held a three-shot lead, which he increased to five when they respectively birdied and bogeyed the 10th.

Clearly, all was forgiven between Goosen and the putter named Tracy, as he one-putted eight of the first 10 greens. With a five-shot cushion, he could afford to play conservatively, and he simply matched Brooks shot for shot for the next four holes.

At the 15th and 16th the American had realistic birdie opportunities, but he saw his first effort, from two metres at the 15th, spin round the hole and stay above ground, before his three-metre effort at the 16th slid past the left edge of the cup. These misses effectively sealed his fate. A birdie at the 17th was too little, too late, even though Goosen also had a late wobble with a bogey on the same hole.

At the 18th hole, with a three-stroke lead, Goosen again failed to seal the deal painlessly. Brooks hit his second shot into a bunker, while Goosen left his second shot just short of the green. The South African putted up the hill with his third shot, and the ball stopped six metres from the hole. Then, after Brooks hit a solid bunker shot to one metre, Goosen putted to within two metres, then sank his final putt for bogey and the championship.

Goosen, with his two-shot victory, had followed Gary Player (1965) and Ernie Els (1994 and 1997) onto the US Open roll of honour and had become one of only five foreign players to win the tournament since the end of World War II. And, significantly, he gets the credit for ending Tiger Woods's "Tiger Slam" run of four consecutive Major championships.

Goosen, who had risen from 83rd in the world when he met Vanstiphout to third, publicly saluted his mind coach but, in true fashion, also down-played the enormity of his recovery.

"I felt like I needed to win this today somehow, from what happened yesterday. But it's just a game. It's not a life-or-death situation. There are a lot of people out there worse off than me. I wasn't going to look at it like if I don't win, it's the end of the world."

An interesting take from someone who had stared death in the face...

Goosen had long been regarded as the poor cousin of Ernie Els, who, despite being eight months younger, had won two US Opens and been a top-three finisher in all four Major championships. But this triumph at Oakland Hills had gone a long, long way to closing that gap. Goosen was $900 000 wealthier and now known as the "New Easy". Later that year, the two South African giants teamed up to win the World Cup of Golf for their homeland.

Goosen completed his second wire-to-wire victory of the year at the Scottish Open at Loch Lomond. He finished the year with three wins, 11 top-10 finishes and the European Tour Order of Merit. He followed it up with another in 2002, and he also became the first non-European to win the Order of Merit.

His big breakthrough in the US saw him competing more regularly on the PGA Tour in 2002. He raised eyebrows with the length of his driving, which was almost as long as that of the mighty (but vulnerable) John Daly. Goosen won the BellSouth Classic, and finished runner-up in both the US Masters and the WGC-American Express Championship. Despite spending more time in the US, he also topped the PGA European Tour's Order of Merit for a second time after capturing the Johnnie Walker Classic and tying for second in the Smurfit European Open and Dunhill Championship.

In 2003, he won the Trophée Lancôme, was a runner-up in the Carlsberg Malaysian Open, came third in the Deutsche Bank-SAP Open TPC of Europe, and fourth in the Johnnie Walker Classic. Across the Atlantic, he added another American title to his list of successes when he won the Chrysler Championship, placed second in the International, was third in the Tour Championship and the BellSouth Classic, and fourth in the Mercedes Championship.

Goosen and Els's successes on the international stage helped South Africa secure the rights to host the 2003 President's Cup, at Fancourt.

With Gary Player captaining the Internationals and Jack Nicklaus in charge of the US, the contest ended in a thrilling tie after the sun set on the challenge between Els and Woods.

The 2004 US Open at Shinnecock Hills will be remembered for the brutal playing conditions that left most of the field exasperated. It is one of the few links courses in the US and is located at the eastern end of Long Island, where the terrain is not too dissimilar to the coastline along the great UK links courses.

By the end of day four – with steaming heat, dried-out greens and difficult pin placements – a row had broken out between the USGA and the club, and, as a result, the tournament would be pulled out of the greater New York area for a full decade. USGA executive director Mike Davis said that well-executed shots were compromised because of the rock-hard greens and his organisation was determined to prevent a repeat at future tournaments.

For the first time since 1963, no player shot under par during the final round. Some of the lightning-fast greens were so baked that course officials were watering them during the final round just to keep them playable. Goosen began the final day with a two-stroke lead over Phil Mickelson, while Els, who was in third place, faltered at the end, posting a 10-over-par 80.

Playing in the group in front of Goosen, Mickelson had a roller-coaster performance on the back nine. A bogey at the 12th dropped him three strokes behind, but he slammed home a six-metre putt for birdie at the following hole.

Goosen then made a hash of the 13th by missing first the fairway and then the green. Bogey and lead down to one. At the 15th, Mickelson hit his approach to two metres from the hole and sank the putt for a birdie and a tie of the lead. He did it again at the 495-metre, par-five 16th to take a one-stroke lead. Goosen was tracking the crowd favourite's progress by the extent of the cheering, but he drew deep on his inner reserves.

He knew from the gallery's reaction that Mickelson was making a move but, with grit and class, he matched the American with a 3.6-metre putt for birdie at the 16th. All square again.

Mickelson was the first to blink at the par-three, 163-metre 17th. After hitting a 6-iron tee shot into the left bunker, "Lefty" managed to get it out, but the ball scurried over the green, charged two metres past the hole, and left him a tricky downhill putt for par. Mickelson barely touched the ball, which – fuelled by a gusty wind – veered left of the hole, finally stopping one metre below the cup. He missed that as well, to score a double-bogey.

When Goosen reached the 18th green with a two-stroke lead, the horror of 2001, when he three-putted from four metres at the death, must have crept into his mind. Nevertheless, he was determined not to give the American another crack at the championship, and he closed the deal with two putts for par.

The South African and his blistering putter – he had 11 one-putt greens on the Sunday and 31 for the championship – finished with a one-over-par 71 for a four-under total of 276. It was widely acknowledged to be one of the greatest clutch-putting performances in the history of the Majors.

The result was a bitter blow for Mickelson – despite winning the Masters earlier in the year, it was his third second-place finish at the Open (he'd lost by one stroke to Payne Stewart in 1999 and by three strokes to Tiger Woods in 2002). Afterwards, Mickelson took a swipe at the course officials, saying that despite playing some of the best golf of his life that day, he had failed to shoot par.

In fact, Sunday's final-round scoring average was 78.7 – the highest final-round score at the Open since 1972 at Pebble Beach. Robert Allenby was the only player to shoot par (70), while Goosen's one-over-par 71 put him at four under for the tournament – two shots ahead of Mickelson, who was the only other player who finished under par.

Soon afterwards, Goosen experienced an avulsion fracture of his pelvis after falling off a jet ski and was forced to miss August's PGA Championship. Nevertheless, he had another particularly sweet victory at the Tour Championship in November 2004, coming from four strokes behind on the final round with a six-under-par 64 to win by four strokes over Tiger Woods. It was his second Tour win of the season and it secured him a career-high sixth-place finish on the 2004 money list (he would remain in the top 10 in the world rankings for 250 weeks).

The year 2004 is also remembered as the start of the "Big Five era", a period when Goosen joined friend and counterpart Ernie Els, Tiger Woods, Vijay Singh and Phil Mickelson as the heavyweights in the game. They alternated in the top five of the Official World Golf Rankings, and Woods was even toppled by Singh, who became the best golfer in the world for a while. Between 2004 and 2007, nine Majors were won between these five players.

In 2005, the Goose was again in the driving seat at the Open, and came close to capturing a third US Open title. Leading by three strokes after three rounds at the Pinehurst number-two course, he had a near collapse on the Sunday, dropping six shots in the first nine holes and five more after the turn to shoot 81 and finish in 11th place. It was his worst finish in a Major in 2005 (he finished tied third at the Masters, tied fifth at the Open Championship and tied sixth at the PGA Championship).

Nevertheless, that same year he won the Linde German Masters in Europe, the International in the US and the VW Masters in China. He finished second in the Johnnie Walker Classic and third in the WGC Accenture Match Play Championship. His earnings for that year alone were $3.4 million.

But the following year he would fail to win on US soil for the first time since 2001, although he had four top-five finishes, including a second place at the Players' Championship and a third place at the US Masters. He also won the South African Airways Open, was runner-up at the BMW International Open and, in China, successfully defended his VW Masters title.

The 2007 season brought Goosen a victory in the Abu Dhabi Championship, while he finished as the runner-up in the US Masters, but a series of injuries – niggling and otherwise – was affecting his game. He was receiving treatment for his back, legs, toes and eyes, and, because he was in his forties – the twilight years for most professional golfers, the injuries took longer to heal.

Like the other senior statesmen on tour, there was also the small matter of him competing with youngsters who were driving the ball much further. Despite the dramatic changes in equipment and technology over the two decades that Goosen had been a professional, his driving was now significantly shorter.

In 2008, he won the Asian Tour's Islander Johor Open, finished second in the WGC-CA Championship and came fourth in the WGC-Bridgestone International.

Goosen found his winning form in the US again in 2009, when he captured the Transitions Championship. He also finished second in the RBC Canadian Open after a play-off, third in the AT&T Pebble Beach National Pro-Am, and tied for fifth in the Open Championship. On the European Tour, he took third place in the BMW International Open and finished sixth in both the South African Open and the Barclays Scottish Open.

Goosen credited Gary Player for inspiring him to dedicate himself to a new diet and fitness regime, which helped take him to 22 in the world rankings, his highest position since November 2007.

Goosen's glory decade ended on a sour note with a number of injuries, including a broken toe courtesy of a mishap with a chair, a broken finger thanks to a stair railing, and a fracture of another toe while he was scrambling to move his boat into a garage with a hurricane approaching. A decade earlier, he had broken his left arm while skiing, and since then had been unable to completely straighten it on the downswing.

In August 2012, his ongoing chronic back problems required surgery after a year of mixed results on tour (his best finishes on the US PGA Tour were two tied-10th places at the US Open and the Canadian Open). Surgeons repaired a disintegrated disc and installed a titanium-and-rubber replacement (increasing his height by about eight millimetres).*

Goosen has residences in his home town of Polokwane, Ascot in England, where his children attend school, and Orlando, Florida.

Much of his time is now devoted to the Retief Goosen Charitable Foundation, which was established to promote, increase awareness and raise money for charities, primarily in South Africa.

With career winnings of more than $27 million – and more than 40 professional wins under his belt – Goosen has established himself as one of the most successful golfers in history and one of South Africa's finest sporting ambassadors.

Goosen's mid-life aches and pains pale in comparison to what his former sports psychologist Jos Vanstiphout has been through. On 20 December 2011, he fell off a four-metre ladder while hanging Christmas lights outside his apartment in Houthalen, Belgium. He was in a coma for four months and hospitalised for 14 months.

"Nine out of 10 [patients] would not have made it," he recalls. "When you have spent days and weeks and months counting the seconds, the minutes and the hours, it is a very big relief to be able to walk again."

---

* He was forced to withdraw from the 2013 US Open because of back problems.

And yet, like his former client who had a near-death experience, Vanstiphout deflects the issue elsewhere: "I live in the present, not the past."

8

The Boy Wonder

"His swing is absolutely the closest that I have seen to Ben Hogan, and I've always thought that Ben Hogan was the best striker of the ball from tee to green." – **Gary Player**

Within the space of 10 dizzy days, Trevor Immelman experienced the greatest high – and deepest low – of his young life. One moment he was soaring like an albatross, riding the winds with the world far below. The next, he was lying on the ground, wracked in pain and fighting to breathe.

In December 2007, the young pro had reached a new milestone in his career by winning the Nedbank Golf Challenge at Sun City, leaving some of the finest golfers on the planet – including Luke Donald and Adam Scott – in his wake.

Fast-forward to Pearl Valley, Paarl, a few days later. Immelman is living the dream as the star attraction at the SAA Open, but it was not the nerves that were attacking his respiratory system. He withdrew from the tournament and, days later, received a chilling diagnosis: the CT scan had identified a tumour "the size of a golf ball" lodged in his diaphragm.

Immelman was born in Cape Town on 16 December 1979, a date steeped in South African history.[*] His father, Johan, was the former commissioner of the Sunshine Tour, and his love of the game was passed down

---

[*] On 16 December 1838, 470 Voortrekkers killed 3000 Zulu warriors in Natal. Until 1994, its anniversary was marked as the Day of the Covenant.

to his two sons, Trevor and Mark. Trevor began hitting balls at the age of five and spent much of his childhood at the Somerset West Golf Club.

He told me he was "very blessed" to have grown up in such a carefree environment with so many public courses (and a putting green in his garden).

After school his mother would drop him off at one of the golf courses and his father would collect him on the way home from the office. "And the next day, we would do it all over again." The weekends were made up of competitions, and Immelman, in his own words, became "a very good junior".

He also excelled at athletics, tennis, cricket and rugby, but golf had a particular pull. "I was very focused on the sport, in love with the game. And I was constantly having competitions with myself, trying to hit the ball further... trying to hit it straighter... trying every shot imaginable."

Like the great Gary Player, he told anyone who would listen that he was going to cut it as a tour professional.

At the age of five, Immelman met Player for the first time and would spend years emulating the legend. And, 21 years later, Player would return the favour by making Immelman one of his captain's choices in the President's Cup. By then, Player had recognised that Immelman's swing was a work of art, "almost as pure and sound", and as good, as Ben Hogan's.

Even though he is left-handed, like his brother, Immelman has always been a right-handed golfer – the opposite of Phil Mickelson, who is right-handed off the course.

At the age of six, Immelman won an under-10 tournament in the United States and, on 23 April 1988, at the age of eight years and four months, became the youngest South African to score a hole-in-one.[*]

---

[*] Tim Clark, who won the 2010 PGA Tour Players' Championship, had held the record at eight years and seven months when he recorded his first ace at Umkomaas in 1984.

In the years between, Immelman spent countless hours pounding balls at the driving ranges and courses in the area. Former caddie Deon Brown, who joined the boy at the Somerset West Golf Club most Mondays, said: "He was already one step ahead of all the other juniors in the area." Brown recalls how the boy, aged just 11, had the course figured out, except for the par-five 12th, where a water hazard was so imperfectly placed that it invariably played havoc with his second shot.

Immelman had faced this challenge once too often when he removed his 3 wood from the bag and drilled his second shot at the cart bridge over the hazard. It was a direct hit, and the ball bounced off the concrete and landed perfectly on the other side of the fairway. When Brown and Morgan Raubenheimer – the other playing partner that day – raised their eyebrows in unison, Immelman dropped a second ball and repeated the feat.

Brown, incidentally, became a provincial player "thanks to Trevor", and still regards him as "a very good friend".

Not surprisingly, by the age of 12 Immelman was a scratch golfer, and at 14 had represented South Africa at an international tournament. In 1995, he beat Bubba Watson in the finals of the Rolex Junior Classic in the US. The following year, he won the Maxfli PGA Junior Championship, and went on to finish as runner-up in the Junior World Championship, the British Amateur and the New Zealand Amateur. He was ranked as the second best junior golfer in America, despite being a foreigner. He then won the South African Amateur Championship at the age of 17.

In 1997, he began training at the David Leadbetter Golf Academy in Orlando, Florida, where he quickly earned a reputation for going the extra mile. He spent hundreds of hours interacting with other top golfers and studying video clips of their swings.

Not everyone was enamoured with Immelman's on-course etiquette. At the SA Amateur at Cape Town's Westlake course, the 19-year-old had tongues wagging in the opening round when he marched off the greens before his playing partners had finished their holes. My former colleague

Dale Granger, who covered the tournament, said some interpreted Immelman's actions as discourtesy in the extreme. "Immelman, a teenager being touted as South Africa's next golfing megastar, will travel a tough road once he turns professional unless he can refine an attitude being increasingly interpreted as unsporting on and off the course," wrote Granger.

Mercifully, Immelman did refine his attitude, unlike his big, brash countryman Rory Sabbatini, who sparked an outcry during the final round of the 2005 Booz Allen when he became so fed up with Ben Crane's slow play that he marched ahead of his playing partner at the 17th green, with commentator Paul Azinger describing his behaviour as "psycho" (the Durbanite later apologised for his behaviour).

Sabbatini, who tied for second in the 2007 Masters (he briefly led in the final round), also stirred the pot following the Wachovia Championship that year when, after leading the field by one stroke and then giving up five strokes to Tiger Woods to lose the tournament, proclaimed that the American was "more beatable than ever". Woods's succinct response was: "Everyone knows how Rory is." Not surprisingly, in a subsequent *GQ* poll of PGA Tour pros, Sabbatini topped the list of partners they least wanted to play with.

Observed *Golf Digest*: "Sabbatini's eyes are narrowed and set close on a broad face, and his jaw muscles are either working a wad of Nicorette or a lower lip with chew. A poor shot or missed putt routinely elicits a glower that looks as if it could easily advance to a trembling, exploding head."

A headline in *The New York Times* said: "Sabbatini's Goal Is to Win Tournaments, Not Friends".

And yet there is another side to this University of Arizona graduate, three-time all-American.* Others speak of his generosity and sense of humour.

---

* An All-America team is an honorary team from any American college sport composed of outstanding amateur players.

THE BOY WONDER

But back to Immelman: in 1998, he won the US Amateur Public Links at Torrey Pines, the famous US Open venue, which earned him a spot at the 1999 Masters, where he made the cut. Shortly afterwards, the young Springbok turned professional.

But it was not all glory. Constant travelling, small purses and adverse weather tested his character, but he saw it through.

The Somerset West prodigy's first win as a professional came in the Kenyan Open in 2000. Soon afterwards, he beat Ernie Els, another childhood hero, to win the Vodacom Players' Championship in Cape Town. Immelman had confirmed his champion credentials, but he was aware that he was following in the footsteps of giants.

In 2001, he became a full member of the European Tour and notched up several wins. The next year saw a series of near misses but, in 2003, he captured his maiden European Tour title, the South African Open, after beating Tim Clark in a play-off in his backyard at Erinvale. He also won the Dimension Data Pro-Am and the World Cup of Golf for South Africa in partnership with Rory Sabbatini.

Immelman married his childhood sweetheart, Carminita, in December 2003, and, by doing so, broke many a heart. Blessed with *GQ* looks (and piercing green eyes), outstanding course management, impeccable manners (he refers to Gary Player as "Mr Player"), a pleasant disposition (he uses the word "humbled" when addressing his successes) and fabulous wealth (career earnings of around $16 million), Immelman has only ever had eyes for the girl he met when they were both 14 at Somerset West's Hottentots-Holland High School.

In 2004, Immelman became the first golfer to successfully defend the South African Open title since Player in the 1970s, and he also won the Tournament Players' Championship of Europe in Germany.

Immelman began spending more time on the PGA Tour after receiving a two-year PGA Tour exemption on account of his selection for the

International Team at the President's Cup. With this feather in his cap, he departed for the US to collect his green card – and a date at Augusta. Within a few months, he won his first PGA Tour event at the Cialis Western Open, a result that moved him into the top 15 in the international golf rankings.

At the 2005 Masters, he also posted his first top-five finish at a Major.

Immelman withdrew from the 2006 Open Championship to be present at the birth of his first child. Nevertheless, he secured two second-place finishes that year, and beat Tiger Woods on the back nine at the Western Open in Chicago to win his first PGA Tour title, climbing to a career high of 13 in the world. He also finished that year in the top 10 of the PGA Tour money list and was named Rookie of the Year. At the time, *SA Golfers Yearbook* noted that "he has a Major title within sight and it would be a rash gambler, indeed, who would bet against Trevor Immelman adding his name, in the not-too-distant future, to the pantheon of players whose names have been etched on golf's Major trophies".

He also began working with legendary swing coach David Leadbetter, who, as we have seen, played a pivotal role in guiding Nick Price towards his three Majors in the 1990s. The swing coach helped Immelman shallow out the angle of his swing to create more loft and less spin.

At the 2007 Nedbank Golf Challenge,* Immelman received a late invite after Sergio García withdrew. The Capetonian had been just shy of his second birthday when Sol Kerzner, Sun City's grand architect (with the blessings of the apartheid-era authorities) responded to global sanctions by staging the first "Million Dollar" challenge, the world's richest golf tournament. With the birth of democracy, the tournament gained more credibility and almost all of the world's top golfers paid a visit to the challenging Gary Player Country Club.

---

* Nedbank became the title sponsor of the Million Dollar Challenge in 1994.

Ahead of the 2007 edition of the event, Immelman was competing in the Far East at the Hong Kong Open, the HSBC Challenge and the World Cup of Golf (with Retief Goosen as his teammate). During the second week of that tour, he picked up a nasty cough that persisted despite him completing a course of antibiotics.

When he flew to Sun City, with Goosen, he saw another doctor and was given the all-clear to compete against some of the finest golfers on the planet. Immelman went on to survive a jittery closing run of three successive bogeys ("I choked worse than I ever have") to win the tournament by one stroke from Justin Rose.

"It was a dream of mine to win that title, because I had watched so many Million Dollar tournaments as a young boy growing up in the 1980s and 1990s," he said at the media briefing.

With his $1.2-million cheque – endorsed by Nedbank CEO Tom Boardman – Immelman was living the dream when he winged his way back to Cape Town as one of the wealthiest 27-year-olds in the land.

But all that counted for precious little when, just a few days later, the pain returned to his chest.

A stone's throw from his birthplace, Immelman was the star attraction at the SAA Open at Pearl Valley in the Cape Winelands. At the second hole on the Jack Nicklaus–designed course, his breathing became shallower and shallower, and he knew he was in serious trouble. The pain medication did little to alleviate his discomfort, "and my chest was so painful that I had to put my head between my knees just to breathe".

After withdrawing from the tournament, a medical examination by family doctor Johan Herbst identified symptoms of pleurisy, an inflammation of the lining of the lungs that leads to chest pains. But an X-ray of his chest identified a mass on his ribcage. A subsequent CT scan then identified the lesion on the inside of the chest wall.

"It was big and it had to come out," said anaesthetist André Phillips, who prepared the golf star for surgery at the Vergelegen Medi-Clinic in Somerset West.

Back at Pearl Valley, history was being made without Immelman. Forty-two-year-old South African James Kingston won the Open by a single shot over England's Oliver Wilson for his first win on the European Tour. He received his trophy with tears running down his cheeks.

At that moment, Trevor Immelman was fighting a different kind of emotion.

He had every reason to be worried. In 1999, shortly after joining the Tour, he had experienced his first brush with death when he was admitted to hospital with meningitis and faced the very real prospect that he might never play again. There were concerns that the disease had spread to his brain, and Immelman had to draw on all his resources to deal with the crisis.

The illness had claimed the lives of two of Africa's greatest golfers, Zimbabwean Lewis Chitengwa and Bobby Locke. Chitengwa, who beat Tiger Woods at the Orange Bowl Junior Invitational in 1992 and then became the first non-white golfer to win the SA Amateur the following year, succumbed to the illness during the Telus Edmonton Open in Canada in 2001. He was just 26.

And earlier, in 2007, long before the tumour was discovered, Immelman had lost 25 pounds from a stomach parasite and spent months regaining his weight and form.

Five days after withdrawing from the Open, one of the world's brightest young golfers was wheeled into theatre where Phillips, cardiac surgeon Wynand "Spanner" van Zyl, a surgical assistant, a scrub sister and two nurses began the procedure.

Everything went according to plan – until his back was opened up, "and the growth was nowhere to be seen". They double-checked the X-ray and then realised that the tumour wasn't attached to the chest. Rather, it was connected to a stalk that was attached to the diaphragm, which enabled it to move around.

Ninety minutes later the lesion had been removed and, for the next two days, the fallen hero lay "whacked on medication" as his family waited for the doctors to present their verdict. The mass was identified as a benign calcified fibrosis tumour, and Immelman was given the all-clear.

Understandably, it was a life-changing experience, and he resolved to make the most of every moment, "because it can all be taken away so fast".

An 18-centimetre scar from the operation would serve as a permanent reminder of how different this story could have ended. When Trevor's brother Mark, a respected US-based college golf trainer, visited him in hospital, they decided that he would become his coach.

They set goals and Trevor worked on his swing, grip and stance. However, it took a full three months before he could swing a club properly again.

As a result of his subsequent rehabilitation, Immelman missed the first eight weeks of the 2008 PGA Tour season. After that, there was a gradual return to form, but the pain lingered and he was terrified of re-injuring himself. "I was particularly worried about big swings in rough that was too thick."

Four months after the operation, his form began to return and he decided to compete at Augusta. The 2008 season started ominously, with four missed cuts in seven stroke-play events on the PGA Tour, with a best finish of tied 17th and a second-round loss in the WGC-Accenture Match Play Championship.

When the Masters rolled around, Immelman had just two heavyweight international career victories under his belt – the 2004 Deutsche Bank-SAP Open and the 2006 Western Open where, tellingly, he beat Tiger Woods by two shots. His five other career wins had all occurred in South Africa.

The weekend before the Masters, he missed the cut at his main curtain-raiser, the Houston Open. On the second day, "a savage storm without lightning" rolled through the area, leaving most of the golfers competing in virtually unplayable conditions. "I wasn't too worried about my game, and there were some encouraging signs in Houston," Immelman said.

When he reported for duty at Augusta, there was an air of familiarity about the place. After all, it was his sixth visit – the first was as an amateur in 1999. While he'd finished tied fifth at his second appearance at the tournament (as a professional in 2005), he failed to make a charge in 2006 or 2007.

Immelman describes the whole Magnolia Lane experience as "surreal", and says no golfer will ever tire of it. "It's the pride of our sport, it's the happiest you'll ever see a professional golfer anywhere... it puts a bounce in your step."

Most golf lovers around the world will never get near the town, and their impressions of the place are created by carefully stage-managed television coverage that determines the entire production and highlights the strict adherence to tradition. Case in point: the caddies' uniforms are standard: white jumpsuits, Masters hats and white shoes.

The city of Augusta, for the most part, is not for the faint-hearted. It's hot, humid, dirty and bland, and, despite its excellent colleges and hospitals, has been labelled "Disgusta" by many a visitor. Used-car dealerships compete with fast-food joints, and the local strip clubs have been known to host "Miss Green Jacket" pageants during the annual tournament. While the second largest city and metro area in Georgia surrounds one of the world's great golf courses, all is not as it seems on those hallowed greens, inch-perfect fairways and ponds (which are dyed blue for the week of the Masters).

In his book, *The Masters*, Curt Sampson notes that "a cold heart beats behind the warm antebellum facade of the famous Augusta course". And that heart belongs to the elusive and reclusive founder (and New York stockbroker) Clifford Roberts, who shot himself on the course in 1986.

And the same applies to the official broadcaster. CBS, which has the television rights to the Masters (and many other tournaments), took its stage-management too far in the 1990s when it used canned bird sounds during its coverage of an event. This after birdwatchers raised concerns that they were hearing the dulcet tones of canyon wrens at the Buick Open in Michigan when every birder worth his or her weight in seed knows that these feathered friends never venture east of Texas.

And yet Augusta will always be considered the Mecca of global golf. Fuzzy Zoeller, who won the Masters at his first appearance in 1979, spoke for many when he observed: "I've never been to heaven, and thinkin' back on my life, I probably won't get a chance to go. I guess the Masters is as close as I'm going to get."

The course is almost always in prime condition during Masters Week, when the spring air is soft and the azaleas are in full bloom. The course was formerly a plant nursery, and each hole is named after the tree or shrub with which it has become associated (i.e. Tea Olive, Pink Dogwood, Flowering Peach and Carolina Cherry).

But just a month after the annual tournament – the only Major that is played at the same course every year – the club is closed until mid-October because of the brutal heat and humidity.

On the opening day of the tournament, the heavyweights are spread out to prevent the crowds from becoming too dense in parts of the course and too sparse in others. The leaders go out last from the Friday (unlike the other Majors, where a random draw decides the order of play), which means the late starters can be affected by the inevitable spike marks from earlier traffic, as well as stronger winds.

On the Monday of that week, Immelman played nine holes with two-time Masters champion Ben Crenshaw, who put his mind at ease about the most vulnerable stroke in his game – putting. Crenshaw advised the South African to ignore the so-called "putting gurus" and "stick with the stroke that works for you". The advice stuck throughout the week.

Immelman stayed calmly focused in the days building up to the tournament and made a point of removing himself from distractions like ESPN and the Golf Channel. And he spent many hours deep in thought. He knew that 30 years had passed since the last South African, Gary Player, had won the coveted green jacket. CBS made a big deal of the fact with a one-hour documentary recalling the Black Knight's 1978 victory (which turned out to be his ninth and final Major).

Although Player's triumph happened a year before he was born, Immelman had grown up, with his brother, watching the Masters into the early hours of the morning (because of the time difference in South Africa). And, over the years, he had witnessed – either on television or in person – countless thrilling campaigns by South Africa's finest golfer and, most would agree, sportsman.

Sadly, the two giants who had followed in Player's footprints – Ernie Els and Retief Goosen – had both experienced spluttering performances in the build-up to Augusta 2008. While Els remained in the top 10 in the world rankings, he was still smarting from his crushing defeat to Phil Mickelson at Augusta two years earlier, and he wasn't seen as a serious threat. Goosen, meanwhile, had plummeted to 43rd position in the world rankings.

Immelman's brother Mark, a golf coach at Columbus State University in Georgia, believed something was brewing. The day before the tournament, he gave a "lucky" 1942 penny to his father and predicted that Trevor would win. Thursday dawned and the contingent of South Africans set forth to tackle Augusta (or the National, as its select group of members refer to it).

The gates open at 7.30 a.m., giving the crowds 30 minutes to get to the first tee for the opening ceremony. As usual, Player was there as the godfather of South African golf and the global statesman of the game.

Jack Stevens, the starter, got the field away: "Fore please, now driving, Trevor Immelman…"

The young man from the shores of southern Africa teed off in front of a hushed gallery, knowing that he was carrying the hopes of an entire nation, which had experienced so many near misses at Augusta (since 2000, there had been six South African runners-up).

The opening hole, a 365-metre par four, had been lengthened ahead of the 2003 Masters. The fairway breaks to the right and a cavernous bunker on the right-hand side guards the green, which is about 90 metres further on.

Armed with a Nike Sumo 5000 driver, Immelman's drive razored through a blanket of gentle fog that cloaked the course. He found his rhythm from the start. Driving an average of 260 metres on the spongy fairways, he was well positioned to attack the flags. He opened with a pair of 68s, to share the lead with Justin Rose.

And then, with the rest of the pack chasing, he eased ever so slightly into the lead. Brandt Snedeker, Immelman's playing partner over the final two rounds, closely observed the South African and knew then that he had the head — and heart — to see it through. Nevertheless, Immelman was still the underdog, with four-time Masters champion Woods remaining menacingly close.

"Moving day" — Major terminology for Saturday — saw light drizzle in the morning and then heavier rains in the afternoon. The first telling moment that the gods of Augusta may be smiling on Immelman came at the par-five 15th, when his sand-wedge approach sucked back, caught the slope and, for a heart-stopping will-it-won't-it moment, began gaining momentum and dribbling down the slope towards the pond. But the rain had softened the ground and the ball found what the CBS commentator described as "a tiny flat spot" on the bank and came to a rest.

Immelman then chipped to two metres and saved par. After a rain-delayed round, he finished in near darkness with a 69, to hold a two-shot lead over Snedeker, who was playing his first Masters as a professional. The South African had fogged the field, and the list of potential winners was thinning.

There are two locker rooms in the Augusta National Clubhouse – one for the players, and the other, which serves as a shrine for the previous champions. The lockers bear the nameplates of the select group of winners and memorabilia from past tournaments.

Immelman, who showered and changed in the former, knew that his place in history was within reach. "I realised that I was one good round from winning this thing."

Before leaving the clubhouse at 9.30 p.m. that evening, he checked his cell phone messages. Ernie Els, who had failed to make the cut, said he had been watching him closely that week and "you've got it in you... you've got to believe it". And moments before he jetted off to the Far East for a business engagement, Gary Player left a powerful message of encouragement. "He told me that he believed in me and that I needed to believe in myself."

Player warned him that he would face adversity during the final round, but he was equipped to deal with it. Oh, and one other thing; the little giant advised Immelman to keep his head a little "quieter" when he putted, because he was "peeking" too soon after the ball began tracking the hole.

Decades earlier, countryman Bobby Locke had offered anyone who would listen similar putting advice: "If your head moves, everything is for naught."

Thirty years may have passed since Player had secured his final Masters victory, but these two South Africans could have been a father-son duo: dynamic, dark-haired and similar in stature (Immelman is a couple of centimetres taller than Player in his youth and about 10 kilograms heavier).

Day four of the 2007 Masters dawned, and the boy wonder had slept soundly, with his family, at a rented Augusta home. When he peered through the curtains, he saw the trees billowing in the breeze and knew it was going to be a long and colourful day. The strong winds had swept the rain clouds away. The greens, soft from the previous day's rain, were inviting for anyone who could find a landing area. Immelman said he wasn't particularly worried about the raw weather conditions. "It had been building up all week; we knew something was coming. With my background, playing in the Cape, wind was never an issue."

And what about the Tiger factor? Immelman said that he took comfort from the fact that he had beaten the multiple-Major winner at the Western Open the previous year.

No doubt that message from Player had worked its magic and, in a powerful symbolic gesture, Immelman wore a black shirt – Player's favourite colour – for the final round. Player believed that the colour absorbed and stored the energy of the sun and released it whenever necessary. And with the weather playing all sorts of tricks that day, Immelman would need every ounce of energy at his disposal.

With his brother (and mentor) Mark, his parents, June and Johan, his wife, Carminita, and one-year-old son, Jacob, watching, Immelman teed off with a two-shot lead over Snedeker. And they both bogeyed the first hole. The American then eagled the second hole when his 10-metre putt tumbled into the hole, while Immelman botched his short birdie putt. But it was all square for a moment when the Tennessee resident then bogeyed the next and the sixth.

As the crowd grew to 40 000, heaving towards the final pairing, Immelman began easing away with a four-shot lead after seven holes.

Ahead lay the pressure-filled cauldron of Amen Corner, the most valuable and treacherous real estate in all of golf. It comprises the second shot at the par-four downhill 11th, all of the par-three 12th, and the tee shot at the 13th, a 470-metre dogleg par five.

The term "Amen Corner" was first used by author Herbert Warren Wind in a 1958 *Sports Illustrated* article to describe how Arnold Palmer had blitzed that section, and it reportedly came from the title of an album by the Mezz Mezzrow jazz group (*Shouting in that Amen Corner*).

Exactly 50 years later, Immelman entered the tight and twisty Amen Corner with a two-shot lead over American Steve Flesch and with danger lurking. Named "White Dogwood", this par four has decided most Masters sudden-death play-offs, including Larry Mize's breathtaking 1987 triumph.

Immelman's approach to the 11th green missed by 18 metres, and his chip snagged in the fringe. He holed a slippery five-metre putt to save par. He then faced what is surely the most photographed green in golf, the so-called "Golden Bell", which is protected by Rae's Creek, a bunker at the front and two at the back. He bogeyed it, but followed this with a clinical birdie at the par-five 13th.

Snedeker, meanwhile, had bogeyed the 13th after finding the water at Rae's Creek, which allowed the South African a five-stroke lead. At the gorgeous par-three 16th, Immelman knew he was home and dry barring a mishap. And what a mishap it was. Deep in the wind-tossed crucible of the back nine, he tanked his 7-iron shot. The ball soared towards the densely populated gallery but, whipped around by the gusts at its apex, found a watery grave in the pond, which is set hard against the green. He made double-bogey, which cut his lead to three shots over Woods.

Woods, who had never won a Major when trailing after 54 holes, was now at Augusta's handsome clubhouse, sniffing the scoreboard and monitoring any signs of a potential meltdown. But it was not to be. The final two holes – both par fours – proved to be a coronation for the South African, the end for the American.

Despite finding the greenside bunker at the 17th, Immelman salvaged par again and effectively slammed the door on any late challenge.

"At that stage, I knew I was leading, but I didn't know by how much."

Showing a maturity beyond his years, he whipped his 45.9-gram guided missile up the fairway at the 18th and it came to a rest in a great big, ugly divot the size of a dollar bill. Of course, he had to play it as it lay (many tour pros believe this is the least fair rule in the game, and that divots should be treated as ground under repair). Raymond Floyd, who had won the Masters 32 years earlier, once noted that the first step in dealing with a ball in a divot is mentally overcoming the unfairness of it.

If the lie rattled Immelman, it never showed, but he now concedes that "it wasn't an ideal situation. I had tried to remain as even-tempered as possible that week, and I tried to downplay the adversity."

He stripped an 8 iron to land in the middle of the stage in one of sport's greatest theatres. Game over, and Snedeker joined in the generous applause. "I've played with very few golfers who can manage their emotions, manage their swings and manage that golf course as well," the American noted.

For one brief, shining moment, Immelman had ripped the cloak of invincibility off Tiger Woods's vast shoulders. And his life would never be the same again.

"Here I am, after missing the cut last week, the Masters champion. It's the craziest thing I've ever heard of," he said after being presented with his green jacket by the previous champion, American Zach Johnson.

The South African had finished at eight-under 280 – three shots ahead of Woods and nine shots lower than the previous year's winning total. Tellingly, *The New York Times* noted that Woods never got close enough to plant any "negative swing thoughts" in the South African's head.

Five years later, Woods's former swing coach Butch Harmon would say that Sergio García had made a crucial mistake at the 2013 Players'

Championship when he dunked two shots into the water by attacking the pin at the par-three 17th instead of playing for par, which may have secured a play-off. "Tiger was in his head," Harmon said.

Immelman's final-round tally of 75 (the highest since 1962) followed previous rounds of 68, 68 and 69, and it's fair to assume that on a calmer day, he would have been the first player in Masters history to shoot four rounds in the 60s.

Immelman also ranked fourth in the field in driving distance and hit more fairways than anyone else (48 out of 56). He came second in finding the green in regulation and was the fourth best putter that week (coming into the tournament, he was ranked 202nd out of 204 players in putts per greens in regulation on the PGA Tour). He had also become the youngest Masters champion since Woods had won his second Masters in 2001 at the age of 25.

This was no fluke. Immelman had been the most consistent player that year, which was why he was able to recover from his wobbly at the 16th. After all, he led the field in driving accuracy (87 per cent), which helped him break Woods's record for under-par play by a champion on the par fours. He tied for second in greens in regulation, tied for fourth in putts per round (112 putts for the tournament, compared to the 120 from Woods), and was 17th in driving distance. His final score of 10 under was also two shots better than Woods when he won in 2001. Just 12 months earlier, Immelman had hit 31 out of the 72 greens in regulation, but had upped that to 51 during the 2008 edition of the tournament.

Interestingly, the youngest South African competing that weekend was Richard Sterne, who made his Masters debut with 15 birdies (as many as Immelman), but 19 bogeys wrecked his chances. The rest of the South African contingent failed to fire: Ernie Els, with two 74s, missed the cut; Retief Goosen, who shot a 76 on the Sunday, finished tied-17th; while

Rory Sabbatini, who tied for second the year before, scored a 75 and 74 and also missed the cut.

Els said that Immelman had spent so much time asking him and Player for advice on how to win a Major, "and now I can ask for advice on how to win the Masters".

"We've all tried to win it for so long. Me, Tim Clark, Retief Goosen and Rory Sabbatini have all finished second, but never gone one step further like [Immelman] has," Els added.

Across the Atlantic Ocean, my old friend Joe Myers had watched Immelman's flag-hunting final round while slumped in the armchair of his Wimbledon home. For years, this South African–born UK businessman had offered anyone who would listen the following investment advice: "A hundred quid on Immelman to win the Masters." For once, he had failed to put his money where his mouth was, and he witnessed the bitter-sweet spectacle as the 100–1 outsider romped home.

So much had happened in Immelman's life – medically and otherwise – since his Nedbank triumph at Sun City five months earlier, but, by winning the Masters, he had become only the third person after Bernhard Langer and Seve Ballesteros to have held both titles at the same time.

Woods, who had earlier in the week suggested that a Grand Slam was within his reach that season, was forced to backtrack. "I learnt my lesson with the press. I'm not going to say anything."

The American had been chasing his 14th Major, and he now knew that his dream of matching, and passing, Jack Nicklaus's 18 Major victories would get harder and harder as the new generation of young golfers continued to rise through the ranks.

Over the next few days, South Africa's Tiger-tamer rode the crest of a giant wave of public admiration. Apart from securing himself a permanent place in the champions' locker room, there was an appearance on the *David Letterman Show*, where he got to read out the 10 ways his life had changed since winning the Masters: "I've been elevated from unknown to obscure; thanks to the prize money, I no longer have to buy generic root beer; suddenly I don't look so foolish for trade-marking 'Immelmania'; I'm BFFs with Lauren and Heidi from *The Hills*; President Bush called to congratulate me on winning Wimbledon; when my caddie recommends a club, I can say, 'Excuse me, how many Masters have you won?'; [I've been] invited to Masters Winners Week on *Jeopardy*; I get a lifetime supply of them little pencils; guess who's playing 36 holes with the Pope this weekend? And I get to put my arm around Tiger Woods and say, 'Maybe next year.'"

This was followed by a trip to the top of the Empire State Building, and a guest appearance at Madison Square Gardens to watch the NBA basketball game between the New York Knicks and the Boston Celtics. When he was introduced to the crowd during one of the breaks, the *Caddyshack* theme was played. Then there were publicity shoots in China and Hawaii and a break with his parents in Charlotte, North Carolina, where they are now living (father Johan helps to run the Sbonelo Foundation, which provides scholarships for South African students).

Ironically, just like Immelman's Masters triumph had signalled his medical recovery, it coincided with the start of further physical problems that would impact his game. A few months after Augusta, he began experiencing chronic tendonitis in his left wrist and elbow. He had first noticed a muscular twitch in his left wrist towards the end of 2008, and it got so bad the following year that he had to withdraw from the US Open, the British Open and the PGA Championship. His attempts to juggle rest time with competition backfired, because his game was abysmal (even when he made the cut, he was nowhere on day four).

Within a year he had dropped to 269 in the world rankings. And rubbing salt in the wound was the fact that all the Major champions over the past five years were still in the top 60 in the world.

Because of the wrist injury, Immelman played in only 13 events in 2009. At one tournament in Las Vegas, the pain in his wrist was so unbearable that he withdrew from the tournament and flew to New York for keyhole surgery.

Afterwards, Immelman wore a cast for three weeks, and it took a further three months before he had enough strength to even hold a putter.

Although he played in 19 tournaments in 2010, he finished 163rd on the money list. By 2011, his wrist had recovered completely, and the birdies and eagles slowly began returning, and following countryman Ernie Els's searing victory at the 2012 Open, Immelman used Els's swing coach Claude Harmon to try to get his swing – and game – back on track.

In 2012, he was almost back to his best at the PGA Championship in South Carolina.

After shooting a two-under 70 in the rain-delayed third round, he found himself in the penultimate group alongside Adam Scott and Steve Stricker. If not for a missed par putt on the 18th, he would have been in the final pairing with leader Rory McIlroy.

Irrespective of where Immelman's career takes him, he will always be "humbled" by his Augusta glory, which followed, so closely, his brush with death.

9

Shrek

"He has that moment forever." — **Dave Feherty**

Picture the scene (you'll have to, as no footage exists). The shadows are lengthening late in the day in the compelling theatre of a misty Augusta Sunday, and one of the giants of the game is in the twilight of a superb career. Since turning pro at the age of 16, he has won two US Opens, three PGA titles and an Open Championship. The Masters will complete his Grand Slam but, with just four holes remaining, Gene Sarazen trails defending champion Craig Wood by three shots.

His drive has come to a rest near the centre of the par-five 15th fairway, about 215 metres from the pin and behind a small divot.

The Squire, as he is nicknamed because of his penchant for wearing designer suits, consults with his caddie on whether to use a 3 or a 4 wood. Because the grass is cut so short, he opts for the 4 (a "spoon"), figuring he needs the extra loft.

He later recalled: "I rode into the shot with every ounce of strength and timing I could muster."

The result is exquisite. The ball soars no more than 10 metres above the fairway and arrows through the fog towards the green and a 12-metre-wide pond that guards it. It bounces and bounces and rolls and rolls, closer and closer to the cup. And, after what seems like an eternity, it dives in. All hell breaks loose.

It is 1935, and a global war[*] is the furthest thing on the minds of Sarazen or the millions of people who have experienced the breathless excitement of "the shot heard around the world".

Radio, it is said, is the theatre of the mind and, from Augusta to Zeerust, there is disbelief as crackling commentary about the albatross – or double-eagle – is relayed, over and over. Through the hiss and the warble, it is evident that history has been made. Indeed, that single shot propelled the fledgling Masters tournament – which was only in its second year and was still known as the Augusta National Invitation Tournament – to new heights and secured its status as the "fourth Major".

"That double-eagle wouldn't have meant a thing if I hadn't won the play-off the next day. The aspect I cherish most is that both Walter Hagen and Bobby Jones witnessed the shot," Sarazen said. While he described the shot as "lucky", truth be told, it was the crowning moment of his glorious career. As a monument to this feat, the famous Sarazen Bridge, made from a stone and sporting a plaque, was constructed in 1955 to straddle the pond that separates the fairway from the green at 15.

Sarazen drew level at the top of the leader board with that single shot and, when a messenger delivered the news to Wood, who was on the 18th green and celebrating his 282 total (the winner's cheque for $1 500 had already been written in his name), everyone was astonished.

Sarazen parred the final three holes to force the 36-hole play-off the following day, which he won by five shots to secure his final Major and complete the first Grand Slam in history. Spare a thought for Wood, who made history by becoming the first player to lose play-offs in all four Majors.[†] There was some consolation when he finally won the Masters in 1941.

---

[*] During World War II, the Augusta course was closed and was used to graze cattle. After they had caused extensive damage, it was converted to a turkey farm. It was restored as a golf course in 1946.

[†] 1933 Open, 1934 PGA, 1935 Masters and 1939 US Open.

The game of golf had come of age.

Fast-forward 77 years to 2012. Again it's a magnificent Masters Sunday, the stakes are sky high and there's magic in the air. South Africa's Louis Oosthuizen is in a similar mould to Sarazen – of medium height (1.78 metres), light (77 kilograms) and oozing confidence. He's three shots off the lead and has hit a tidy drive at the 525-metre dogleg left.

The green is a lush, billowing carpet of bent grass 231 metres away, downhill with the pin tucked away to the far right, behind two cavernous bunkers filled with Augusta's magnificent premium sea-foam white SP 55 sand.*

Oosthuizen selects a 4 iron. There's the confident glance, steady stance, eyes narrowed on the target, that compact but quick backswing and release. The solid click of the strike follows and, a moment later, the club twirls in his hands. It's the telltale sign that the architect of this effort is satisfied. Oosthuizen steps back and wills the ball towards the green. Fate takes over. The ball reaches its apex and dips towards the target. Its first bounce, just on the green and between the guarding bunkers, indicates that it's safe. Oosthuizen's swing – fading left to right – complements the roll. And what a roll it is.

This is how CBS commentator Dave Feherty captured the moment:

> The young South African, Louis Oosthuizen, trying to use those slopes. This could be nice … could be very nice. Oh, come to Papa. Oosthuizen with a double-eagle and a share of the lead. This just changed everything. This just changed the whole tournament.
> The first double-eagle in tournament history on the second hole … the first ever at the second. He has that moment forever.

---

* Originally, it was guarded by a single bunker on the front right, and the front left bunker was added in 1946.

It was the shot that was seen around the world. For CBS, which has televised the tournament every year since 1956, it was one of the most extraordinary Masters' moments captured on film. Apart from Sarazen and Oosthuizen, only two other players – Australian Bruce Devlin (1967) and American Jeff Maggert (1994) – have recorded an albatross at the Masters.

Augusta and the Mossel Bay Golf Club, where Oosthuizen cut his teeth (and a few balls), are a world apart.

Lodewicus "Louis" Oosthuizen was born on 19 October 1982, six weeks after he and his family had survived a head-on collision. Farmer John van Rensburg recalls that he was on his farm on the banks of the Gouritz River one dank and dark spring afternoon when storm clouds were building and the deathly silence was broken by the shrieking of a vehicle out of control. There was a bang, the sound of grinding metal and breaking glass, and then more silence.

Van Rensburg ran to his canoe and rowed 150 metres across the water, scrambled up the bank, through the bush and onto the old road that ran to the mouth of the river. On the one side of the road, "at a tight bend", he found the shaken driver of a white pick-up truck; on the other, the heavily pregnant Mien Oosthuizen and her family. Van Rensburg said although nobody was seriously injured, he comforted Mien before an ambulance arrived and ferried her to hospital.

Reliving the ordeal decades later, Oosthuizen's father, Piet, who was driving the family's Toyota Cressida, told me that it was "a very lucky escape".

"We went over a blind rise and there was a vehicle in the other lane and there was nothing we could do to avoid it." He added that Mien was particularly fortunate, as she was not wearing a safety belt because of the pregnancy.

The Oosthuizens lived in Albertinia, a small town in the Overberg, where Piet was a dairy farmer and his children spent much of their childhood living the African dream. There was boating on the river, breathtaking beaches nearby and the bush, where they hunted Egyptian geese and buck.

At the age of nine, young Louis had his second near-death experience when he was playing on his father's tractor in the garage and inadvertently hit the start button. The vehicle roared into life, but a wooden barrel got caught under the chassis and probably stopped it from destroying the building and the legend-in-waiting.

Like his childhood hero Ernie Els, Oosthuizen was a natural sportsman and spent most of his spare time playing rugby, cricket and tennis. His father, a former provincial tennis player, also introduced him to the nine-hole Albertinia golf course with its oil-sand greens (because of the heat and lack of water) and cynodon-grass fairways. The boy was hooked and, a decade after his pregnant mother had her brush with death, he was introduced to Vaughn Tucker, the brother-in-law of John van Rensburg, who had assisted her at the scene of the crash all those years before.

Tucker was the head professional at the George Golf Club. He remembers the day when Dave Pirrie, who launched the Southern Cape Junior Golf Foundation, suggested that he travel to Albertinia to coach a group of seven boys, including the Oosthuizen brothers, Louis and Rikus: "I recall Louis being very small and the clubs seemed way too long for him, but he was very determined to hit the ball and to hit it correctly."

He suggested that Louis – and Rikus – should attend weekly clinics in George, 90 kilometres away. Their father agreed.

When Rikus started high school, he gave up golf for rugby and Louis, who had a deep sense of self-belief, began to chart his own destiny.

"*Dit is die grootste gholfspeler wat die wêreld nog ooit gesien het*" ("This is the greatest golfer the world has ever seen") read his handwritten note in Afrikaans, which was stuck to the wall above his bed throughout his adolescence.

At the age of 13, Oosthuizen was selected to play for the Southern Cape's under-18 division, and he never looked back.

"Louis idolised Ernie Els, and I remember he had Lynx Parralax irons, the same that Ernie had used to win the US Open in 1994," Tucker recalls.

There was the not-so-small matter of financing Oosthuizen's dream. It was beyond the means of his father, but a lifeline came in the form of the Ernie Els & Fancourt Foundation, which recognised his talent and, from the age of 17, footed the bill for his development.

For the next three years, he learnt the game he loved on the breathtaking Garden Route, South Africa's golfing Mecca. His course of choice was the Mossel Bay Golf Club, an 18-hole links with views of the Indian Ocean from every tee, large undulating greens and roaming springbok.[*]

Oosthuizen spent much of that time in his life chasing a dream of becoming a professional golfer and, with the purest of swings and temperament to match, he won numerous amateur titles.

Childhood friend Wynand Stander said that Oosthuizen was different from the other golfers. Even then, there was talk that the squeaky-clean, absurdly talented South African possessed the qualities to make it "big time" on the world stage.

"He was the special one," Stander recalls, adding that he was so laid-back that if golf had not been his calling, he probably would have been a surfer. "He's mentally perfect and golf isn't everything – he's got many

---

[*] Mossel Bay's Pinnacle Point Golf Club, where Oosthuizen also played, was recently declared a valuable archeological site. Cliffside caves below the course contain a record of human occupation over a period of about 170 000 years – from the time when modern human behaviour first emerged in the pre-colonial period. The site is expected to rank alongside the Cradle of Humankind and Olduvai Gorge as one of Africa's most sought-after evo-tourism destinations.

other interests, which keep him balanced. Also, he's got his act together off the course – he's not interested in chasing girls and stuff like that, so when he's playing, his head is clear."

Harry Vardon, who won the Open six times, would have approved: "For this game you need, above all things, to be in a tranquil frame of mind."

Despite his many obscene achievements on the world stage, none makes Oosthuizen prouder than the 57 he shot in a social "skins" game in Mossel Bay with Stander and Odendaal Koen in September 2001. To put that score in perspective, only a handful of golfers have broken 60 in official tournaments. They include Ryo Ishikawa (58) on the Japan Golf Tour in 2010, Annika Sörenstam (59) on the LPGA Tour in 2001, Gary Player (59) at the Brazil Open in 1974, and Phil Mickelson (59) on the PGA Tour in 2004.

There is, of course, no such thing as a "perfect" round of golf, but the term generally defines a round where all holes are played at one under par (birdie on every hole), resulting in a score of 54 on a par-72 course, 53 on a par-71 course, and 52 on a par-70 course. This has remained the standard and has never been achieved by a professional golfer in a professional event.

As Bobby Jones, the greatest amateur of them all, once observed: "No round will ever be so good that it could not have been better." But Oosthuizen, on 12 December 2002, near the southern tip of Africa, came pretty damn close.

Stander said Oosthuizen carved his approach to within 30 centimetres of the pin at the par-four 1st and, when his playing partners conceded the putt, insisted on playing out (a "gimme" is usually an agreement between two golfers, neither of whom can putt very well, but not when a player is of the calibre of young Oosthuizen).

Said Stander: "We knew something was up."

At the 2nd, Oosthuizen bombed his drive way left into the rough, but the ball landed on a tractor path and he was able to fire straight at the pin. The ball landed beyond the flag but sucked back towards the hole to set up another birdie. Oosthuizen birdied the next hole as well, along with the 5th, 6th, 7th and 8th, to craft a 29 on the front nine. On the back nine, he scored three birdies and an eagle. Nobody in Mossel Bay (or anywhere else, for that matter) had made the game of golf look so easy.

That number will always be associated with Oosthuizen Inc. It's emblazoned (oosthuizen57) on the back of his golf shirts and caps, it's in the URL of his official website (www.louis57.co.za), his mobile application (Louis 57) and it's incorporated into the name of his Mossel Bay restaurant (Route57), where the scorecard is displayed. Oh, and when he nailed that albatross at Augusta, Ping produced 57 replicas of his 4 iron to be auctioned off around the world.

Oosthuizen stopped short of copyrighting the score, unlike Al "Mr 59" Geiberger. When the American fired a 59 in the second round of the 1977 Memphis Classic, he became the first golfer to break the 60 barrier, which was golf's equivalent of the four-minute mile.

Within a week of Oosthuizen's 57, he nearly did it again. Another childhood friend, Bertu Nel, told me that Oosthuizen was firing on all cylinders at the same course. It was during a Wednesday competition, "and word got out that Louis was going low again". With one hole to play, an eagle would see him break 60. By the time he reached the 18th – an uphill par four – a large crowd had gathered. "He drove the ball to the fringe, just short of the green, and was about five metres away from the front pin position. He gave the putt a long, hard stare and stroked it in for a two and a 59," Nel recalled.

The teenager's first international breakthrough came at the World Junior Golf Championships in Jamaica in 2000, where he secured a three-shot victory over Finland's Erik Stenman.

The following year, he teamed up with Charl Schwartzel, Christian Ries and Albert Kruger to win his first title at the World Junior Team Championships.

Affectionately nicknamed "Shrek" – because of the gap between his front teeth and his large ears – Oosthuizen rarely took himself too seriously and fitted the role of golf's soul surfer. He used to have a club cover featuring the animated Disney character until caddie Zack Rasego complained bitterly that he was having difficulty taking his club-carrying job seriously with the green swamp monster smiling back at him. Nevertheless, like the loveable ogre, Oosthuizen's life was fast becoming a Disneyesque tale. He would clinch six amateur titles, including the Irish Amateur Open Stroke Play title in 2002, before turning professional at the age of 19 that same year.

He secured his European Tour card in 2003, and won the 2004 Vodacom Origins of Golf Tour event on South Africa's Sunshine Tour. His first real heartache came in 2005, when he failed to qualify for his first Open at St Andrews. He ended the season 139th on the money list and was required to return to qualifying school to regain his European Tour card. However, he bounced back quickly and, in 2007, won three titles on South Africa's Sunshine Tour, including the Telkom PGA Championship.

The following year, Oosthuizen shot the lights out at the South African PGA Championship at the Johannesburg Country Club, with a 28 under par 260. It was the biggest 72-hole winning margin in the history of the Sunshine Tour.

After missing the cuts for the Masters, The Open and the PGA Championship in 2009, Oosthuizen redeemed himself by winning his first European Tour event at the Open de Andalucía de Golf in Portugal in March 2010.

This was followed by the "jinxed" victory – his first in the US – when he won the Par Three Contest on the eve of the 2010 Masters; jinxed because nobody who has won that event has gone on to win the tournament proper. In Oosthuizen's case, he missed the cut altogether.

He also missed the weekend action in the US Open at Pebble Beach and, the week before St Andrews, played at Gleneagles in Scotland, where he missed the cut by one stroke.

Oosthuizen entered the 2010 Open Championship at St Andrews – the 139th edition of the tournament – ranked 54th in the Official World Golf Rankings. Like the US Open, any professional (or amateur with a handicap of two or better) can enter (at a cost of £80).

At that stage, Oosthuizen had only made the cut once in eight Major championship appearances (and he had missed the cut at The Open in 2004, 2006 and 2009). Nevertheless, the fact that he had reserved his hotel room in St Andrews until the Sunday night was the first indication that he wasn't planning an early trip home.

In the days leading up to the tournament, Oosthuizen spent a great deal of time working with Karl Morris, a Manchester-based sports psychologist, to try to improve his concentration levels. One of the measures Morris recommended was marking his gloves with a red spot as a reminder that he must stick to his pre-shot routine.

The Old Course, where the game took shape all those years ago, was created on the most forbidding stretch of shore on the east coast of Scotland. It squats, as it has for the past 400 years, between the ocean and a medieval town that was once the hub of the Scotland's religious and academic culture.

For a newcomer, it is a place like no other. When American Sam Snead first set eyes on the place from his train window in 1946 (en route to his thrilling scrap with South Africa's Bobby Locke), he thought it was a derelict, abandoned course. No, St Andrews is as a links should be, moulded by the sea, the wind, the rain and the gods.

Oosthuizen may have been a 200–1 outsider when he addressed his ball at the 1st that day, but his homeland was flying high, having successfully hosted the 2010 FIFA World Cup, which had ended in Johannesburg four days earlier. The droning of vuvuzelas may have been replaced with the wailing of bagpipes, but never again would South Africa be an underdog, and never again would its sporting prowess be underestimated.

There was a rich South African history at the home of golf, stretching back to 1957, when Locke won his fourth (and final) Open title there. And, as an interesting aside, "Shrek" could take comfort from the fact that three bunkers on the 9th hole are named Cronjé (after the Boer War general Piet Cronjé) and Kruger and Mrs Kruger (after former South African president Paul Kruger and his wife).

The 1899-to-1902 Boer War had claimed thousands of casualties, not least one of Scotland's finest golfers. Frederick Tait, a two-time British Amateur champion (1896 and 1898), had finished third in The Open Championship on two occasions (1896 and 1897) before he was recruited for the war campaign. On 4 February 1900, the 30-year-old lieutenant was shot by a sniper while undertaking a reconnaissance operation at Koedoesberg Drift in the Northern Cape. "I do not think I have ever seen any other golfer so adored by the crowd – no, not Harry Vardon or Bobby Jones in their primes," wrote golf reporter Bernard Darwin after Tait's passing.

Just over 110 years after that war, Oosthuizen, with Zack Rasego on the bag, set off under the gaze of the gods of links golf to make history. His partnership with Rasego had begun way back in 2004 at the International Final Qualifier for The Open Championship at Atlantic Beach near Cape Town. Gary Player had first recognised Rasego's potential in 1979, when the youngster was just 16. Player introduced a caddie programme at Sun City, and Rasego was selected as Caddie of the Year in 1980.

From the outset, Oosthuizen's presence was electrifying, and he announced his arrival on the greatest stage of them all with an impressive seven-under 65 on the first day. Nevertheless, there was still little interest in him. When the leaders filed into the massive media centre, all eyes were on pacesetter and crowd favourite Rory McIlroy, whose 63 was the joint lowest round in Open Championship history.

Thursday's balmy weather gave way to a raw, roiling Scottish cold front – high winds and lashing rain – that left most of the field fighting for survival. The many moods of the ocean and the wind buffeted the course and impacted every player differently. For Oosthuizen, schooled at the wet and windy Mossel Bay Golf Club, day two presented an opportunity to do some real damage. He was fortunate to get his round underway early in the morning before the cold front saw winds gusting to more than 65 km/h.

For the most part, he toyed with and teased the weather and went on a twisting, turning birdie run – nailing seven of them to shoot a 67 and the lowest round of the day. With a gritty determination and sublime ball-striking, he rampaged o'er the wee burn, bunkers (he only found one the entire week) and hillocks and through the Valley of Sin and the entire field. On that memorable Friday, Oosthuizen hit all 16 fairways to secure a five-stroke lead and a day-two total of 132 (which tied the record for the lowest 36-hole score in an Open Championship at St Andrews). It was man versus nature at its very best.

McIlroy's precocious talent had abandoned him and, tortured by the elements, he saw his challenge flounder as he limped home with an eight-over-par 80. The rain-soaked 1989 Open Champion, Mark Calcavecchia, found himself alone in second place on seven under.

As day turned into night, Tom Watson waved an emotional goodbye to The Open Championships from the 700-year-old Swilcan Bridge,[*] and

---

[*] Originally built at least 700 years ago to help shepherds get livestock across the Swilcan Burn, the bridge – which is in the style of a Roman arch – is located between the 1st and 18th fairways on the old course, and is a famous symbol of the sport.

the spotlight shifted to the gap-toothed youngster who had learnt his trade on the wild and windy fairways near the southern tip of Africa.

"Louis who?" was the common refrain as commentators, fans and foes tried to pronounce his Afrikaans surname (Oohst-hay-zin). Indeed, at the end of day two, when he strode into the swarm of jaded journalists in the media centre, the Scottish media conference moderator introduced him as "Peter Oosterhausen". Nevertheless, the boy from Mossel Bay was standing head and shoulders above the greatest golfers on the planet.

But surely the youngster's challenge would unravel on the Saturday? After all, as the journalists kept reminding themselves, he had only won once on the European Tour and had missed the cut in all but one of his Major championship appearances.

Following Oosthuizen's stellar opening rounds, it certainly looked like his campaign might be derailed at the very first hole on day three, when he three-putted for bogey. At the same time, American Paul Casey began his charge. Playing with Lee Westwood, Casey shot an outward nine of five-under-par 31, followed by nine straight pars on the more challenging inward half for an 11-under-par total.

But Oosthuizen shook off his sputtering start, poured in putts from everywhere, and recorded 13 pars and four birdies. With the course playing soft and long after the previous day's downpour, he carded a glittering 69 to prove that the opening two rounds were no fluke. By ending the day four shots clear of Casey, Oosthuizen had announced himself to the world.

Day four dawned, and "Shrek" came of age. Short, ripped and oozing confidence, he drove from the practice range to the first tee at the Old Course, when five-time Open champion Tom Watson stopped the courtesy car, opened the door and said: "Good luck, kid. I'm rooting for you."

Ahead of the biggest challenge of his life, the young South African strode to the first tee comfortable in his mind and body.

A three on the par-four 6th for Casey and a four on the par-three 8th for Oosthuizen closed the gap to three, but a searing 14-metre eagle putt by the South African at the 9th effectively killed off any late challenge.

Casey could only counter with a birdie at the same hole, effectively ending the contest. A triple-bogey by the Englishman at the 12th saw Oosthuizen strolling home with an eight-shot lead with six holes to play (while Lee Westwood was able to sneak in for a forgettable runner-up place).

At that point, television analyst Curtis Strange observed that the contest is like "a nail versus a hammer – not much of a battle".

Despite a bogey at 17, the pride of Mossel Bay sealed his maiden Major championship victory by seven shots. A lone bagpiper saluted the moment from a distance.

For four glorious rounds, South Africa's newest ambassador had demonstrated that St Andrews was ripe for a ravaging. By toying and teasing every hump, lump and bump (and there are many), he had turned the sacred links into his personal playground and unlocked all its secrets.

Years earlier, English amateur champion Gerald Micklem had observed that winning at St Andrews sets the champions apart: "It lifts the truly great golfers from the rest. There are Opens. And then there are Opens at St Andrews. Therein lies the difference."

After embracing his wife Nel-Mare and seven-month-old daughter Jana, he quickly paid homage to world statesman Nelson Mandela, who was celebrating his 92nd birthday back in South Africa. When the dust had settled, he told me that Mandela was a role model for every South African who wanted the country to unite: "Being in prison for so long and then coming out to rule in the way he did was amazing. We were all inspired to be better people."

He also acknowledged the role that Zack Rasego had played that weekend, saying that his caddie knew that you play the course by feel and not the yardage book. "He gave me room when I needed it and he knew when to get involved," he said.

Oosthuizen's 71 gave him a 16-under-par 272 – the second lowest in St Andrews history. The seven-stroke victory was the largest since Tiger Woods had made his first Open charge a decade earlier. And, for the record, Woods ended the day tied for 23rd. It was no contest. Oosthuizen had become the fourth South African after Bobby Locke, Gary Player and Ernie Els to win the coveted trophy – and he had done it on the 150th anniversary of the tournament that has no equal.

Said Els: "He is a quiet and unassuming guy, but he has shown everyone what a great champion he is."

Golf scribe James Corrigan noted that Oosthuizen did not merely defeat his rivals as much as crush them deep into the sand beneath the ground: "Yes, so much about Oosthuizen's week with the immortals insists he will be anything but the one-time golfing wonder in this all-time golfing wonderland."

Indeed, Oosthuizen had wowed the world with his own brand of simplicity. Where Woods had spent years micro-analysing his swing and attempting to fix and adjust it to compensate for the numerous injuries that refused to go away, Oosthuizen kept it simple. Perfectly simple. When his game is on song – like it was that week – he feels the shot, addresses the ball and hits it.

Former world number one and two-time Open champion Greg Norman called the young South African to tell him that, thanks to the quality of his performance, he had just watched 18 holes of golf on television for the first time in many years.

Oosthuizen retired to his farm at Gouritzmond and, I suspect, made history by becoming the first Open champion to use part of his winnings to purchase a gleaming new John Deere Series 6000 tractor (the following year, the Moline, Illinois, company invited him to tour its tractor factory and compete in the John Deere Classic).

Vaughn Tucker, who had first noticed Oosthuizen's talent and then coached him throughout his formative years, says he was "incredibly proud" of the St Andrews success.

"I know that his God-given talent was already there, but I had the honour of bringing it out. I am fortunate to have coached an Open champion."

The Open win was followed by a hangover of sorts. A series of niggling injuries held Oosthuizen back, and it seemed that when one injury healed, another flared up.

In January 2011, he claimed his third European Tour title, and his sixth in South Africa, winning the Africa Open in a play-off.

A year later, he successfully defended his title at the Africa Open with a two-stroke victory over Tjaart van der Walt. He had regained his form and, on the weekend before the 2012 Masters, secured a third-place finish at the Houston Open.

There was a distinctly South African flavour permeating Masters weekend when the players drove up Magnolia Lane. Gary Player, the first international winner of the tournament in 1961, had been selected to become the first non-American to serve as an honorary starter, along with Jack Nicklaus and Arnold Palmer.

South Africa's Charl Schwartzel had been saluted for the manner in which he had emerged victorious among a large group of contenders the year before, and for the gracious manner in which he had handled his triumph.

When Schwartzel returned to Augusta to defend his crown, he told reporters that he hoped his 2011 triumph had not changed him as a person. One scribe noted that the humility of South Africa's golfers continued to shine through, "and I'm waiting to meet a South African I don't like".

Schwartzel, a lifelong friend of Oosthuizen, was determined to make the most of the festivities, and had the honour of hosting the champion's dinner and selecting the menu (and footing the bill), a tradition that had been introduced by Ben Hogan in 1952. In 2010, champion Phil Mickelson had selected Spanish paella (as a tribute to fallen hero Seve Ballesteros),* while Ángel Cabrera had settled for the finest Argentinian steak the year before. Other notable dishes included haggis in 1989 (Sandy Lyle), and elk and wild boar in 2004 (Mike Weir).

In 2009, defending champion Trevor Immelman presented Augusta's finest with a feast of Cape bobotie (spiced minced meat baked with an egg-based topping). Wines from Fleur de Cap and Vergelegen estates near his Somerset West home were the beverages of choice, and the dessert was milk tart, another South African favourite.

But this was the first time a full-blown South African braai had competed with the scents of Augusta in the spring. As one UK scribe noted, it was akin to turning up in the Lord's Pavilion in a pair of slippers. And Billy Payne, Augusta's chairman, sought guidance on the matter before agreeing to the request.

At the time, a spoof email, attributed to a former Masters champion and addressed to Payne, did the rounds, raising "concerns" at the South African influence:

> Not looking forward to the meal, as per normal. What's a *braai*, Billy? Never heard of it. Saw the menu. What are *gebraaide skilpadjies op kapokaartappels* as a starter? Just pronouncing it gives me indigestion. *Vetkoek en koeksusters* also sounds hideous, like a pair of overweight tarts. I am also not touching the monkey-gland sauce. These South Africans are savages, Billy. Time to change the tradition and go with

---

* Ballesteros lost a 30-month battle with brain cancer in May 2011.

the safe option. A buffet never hurt anyone, and you can go back as many times as you like. There's a bunch of South Africans that have won the Masters now, Billy, and they said they all want to sit together in a laager? I thought that was a type of beer, Billy. Weird people. I drew the short straw again last year and ended up next to Gary Player. I am not sitting next to him again, Billy. He is going to be impossible this year, especially after you have made him an honorary starter. I will tell him where to put his *vetkoek*.

Kind Regards
Billy Casper (1970 champion, winning score 279, 9 under)

Nevertheless, sliced biltong and boerewors, seafood and crudités, marinated and grilled filet mignon, lamb chops, chicken breasts, monkey-gland sauce and the finest Cape Chardonnays were the order of the day.

For all of South Africa, this tournament was steeped in irony. The country's much-loved Ernie Els had spent weeks scrambling to secure his spot after dropping below the top 50 places in the world rankings. For the past 17 years, Els had carried the hopes of a nation at Augusta and had come desperately close to winning it on a couple of occasions.

Despite his failure to qualify, Els was represented, in a sense, by the shining graduate of his foundation. Louis Martin, former CEO of South Africa's Sunshine Tour, said that shortly after Charl Schwartzel had turned professional, Els took him aside and predicted that Oosthuizen, still a relatively unknown product of his Garden Route foundation, would one day match Schwartzel "stroke for stroke".

Els, who watched the tournament from his Florida home, texted Oosthuizen, urging him to carry the country's flag with honour. And when Oosthuizen opened his locker on the morning of the Masters, there was a handwritten note from Augusta legend Gary Player, wishing him well.

The fact that Oosthuizen had missed the cut at the three previous Masters tournaments was banished to history as he opened with a blistering 68, followed by a 72 and a 69.

But by the dawn's early light on day four, two-time Masters champion Phil Mickelson (74, 68 and 66) was the hot favourite.

That all changed at the par-three 4th, where he sliced his tee shot into the trees. Instead of going back to the tee and playing his third, "Lefty" hit two right-handed shots in a row to record his second triple-bogey of the tournament. That, along with Oosthuizen's sensational two at the par-five 2nd, threw the tournament wide open.

The term "albatross" originated in Scotland (where else?) and takes its name from the large and rare seabirds that fly in the Southern Ocean and the North Pacific. Their wingspan can be more than two metres long, and they use slope-soaring to cover vast distances with precious little exertion. Of the 21 species recognised by the International Union for Conservation of Nature, 19 are threatened with extinction.

To put the golfing feat into perspective, the PGA reckons a two on a par five is 10 times rarer than a hole-in-one, an achievement that most casual golfers can only dream about.

The first albatross was scored by Tom Morris in the 1870 Open Championship at the Prestwick Golf Club. Two players – professional Andy Bean and amateur Brett Stowkowy – share the record for the longest double-eagle at the par-five, 606-metre 18th hole at the Kapalua Plantation Course, Maui (in 1991 and 2010 respectively). Johnny Miller holds the record (535 metres) for a double-eagle at a Major (the 1972 Open Championship at Muirfield), while Jeff Maggert is the only golfer to score a double-eagle twice in Majors (the 1994 Masters and the 2001 Open Championship).

Dean Knuth, inventor of the USGA's slope-rating system for golf courses and handicaps, says the odds of securing an albatross are around

1 000 000–1. In the 20-year period between 1983 and 2003 in the US, for example, there were 631 aces on the PGA Tour, but just 56 albatrosses.

So, to do it on a Major Sunday, in contention for the title, is unspeakably rare.

When I relived that Masters moment with Oosthuizen's caddie, Wynand Stander, over a beer or two, it's immediately evident that the moment is forever entombed in his being.

"Louis asked for the 3 iron, but I gave him the 4."

As I scribbled this down, the former policeman blocked my hand and added: "Just joking."

Oosthuizen prepared for what will surely be remembered as the finest shot of his life. The front of the green was 210 metres away – the pin 231 – and he knew he needed to pitch it five or six paces onto the surface "to give it a chance". He wrapped his fingers around the Ping S56 4 iron – a club noted for the weight cartridge tucked behind the face, which absorbs vibrations – and steadied himself. Two years earlier, Manchester sports psychologist Karl Morris had noted that Oosthuizen's pre-shot routine "was all over the place", but the South African had subsequently become a picture of steadiness and serenity.

Grip – check – stance – check – posture – check – rhythm – check – balance – check.

The crowd settled down and Oosthuizen swept his body through the ball, twirled his sceptre like a king, and stepped back to see whether it would clear the front bunkers and feed towards the hole.

"On television, you don't get a sense of the undulations at the 2nd. There's a hectic drop down to the green – about 25 metres – so an approach from 200 metres is only playing to 175," Stander said.

A half a century earlier, Augusta's architect Bobby Jones had this to say about the 2nd hole, the longest on the course: "A well-hit tee shot will take a good run down the fairway as it slopes over the hill. It was one of our guiding principles in building the Augusta National that even our par fives should be reachable by two excellent shots."

At around 2.54 p.m. (EST) on 11 April 2012, Oosthuizen had just hit his second excellent shot.

Stander said his eyes switched from his boss to the ball, and then to the gallery on the left-hand side of the green, where the missile was tracking. It began banking right towards the green, landed, and then rolled for 25 metres towards the pin.

"We knew that if it cleared the bunkers, it would release. The gallery on the left gave the first indication that it was on track. The ball had disappeared from our view behind a slope, but when we saw the spectators on the left rising together, we knew that it was good. Then the spectators in the middle, and then the right, all rose up together – it was like a Mexican wave. And then there was this explosion. The noise was unbelievable."

Legendary South African golfer Dale Hayes, who was commentating at Augusta that day, backs this up: "I have never heard noise like that on a golf course."

The caddie and the king looked at each other in awe.

At that moment, the young South African – following in the footsteps of countryman, friend and incumbent Masters champion Charl Schwartzel – had turned the championship race on its head. Game on.

Oosthuizen strode onto the green, removed the treasured trophy from the cup and, unbelievably, tossed it into the crowd.

New Zealand–born, Pennsylvania resident Wayne Mitchell, who found himself behind the second green with his wife, Joss, had earlier told a friend that it would be "kind of neat" to witness an eagle in that breathtaking setting. For good measure, the South African had doubled that. As the vice-president of an Allentown (yes, from the Billy Joel song) engineering company joined hundreds of millions around the world in celebrating

Oosthuizen's achievement, the ball, a Titleist ProV1, soft-centred, tiled with 328 dimples and marked with a red "No. 4", landed in his hands.

When I tracked Mitchell down – he was on holiday in Rotorua, New Zealand – he said that "frozen-in-time" moment had changed his life significantly, "starting with the fact that I became front-page news around the world".

"I went there anonymously, but I don't feel as though I'm anonymous any more," he added.

As the final pairing, Phil Mickelson and Peter Hanson, walked past, Mitchell said he was showing the ball to curious spectators (or as the suits at Augusta prefer, "the patrons") when reporters arrived and began interviewing him.

"And then a marshal placed his hand on my shoulder and said: 'Sir, you are not in trouble, but we need to talk.'"

The couple was then "escorted" in a cart to the former plantation homestead that now serves as the clubhouse. Inside and away from the carnage of the thrilling duel that was shaping up between Oosthuizen and Watson, they were introduced to club officials, who suggested that Oosthuizen might regret having thrown the ball away.

Although this historic memento was already being valued at around $20 000, Mitchell said, "It was never about the money or what I could get in return. At the end of the day, I just wanted to do the right thing, and I believe I did."

The ball was handed over, and Oosthuizen later signed it. It is now part of Augusta's fabled history – housed in a trophy cabinet alongside Sarazen's prized ball from 1935 (a Wilson No. 3 multilayered ball consisting of a solid core wound with a layer of rubber thread and a thin outer shell).

A family friend arranged for the Open champion to sign a photo of Mitchell holding the famous ball ("To Wayne and Joss – great catch", the inscription reads).

Mitchell said the returns he received from his gesture were "priceless", and it has given his wife, three daughters and friends a great deal of happiness. It also established a bond between him and Augusta, and he was subsequently invited to play a round at the course, a gesture that is about as rare as – yes, you guessed it – an albatross.

Accompanied by a club caddie, Mitchell and a couple of friends ("it was on the bucket list, for one") had the round of their lives. An "average to below average" golfer, Mitchell said his drives found most of the fairways about 165 metres from the green, "which is very problematic ... not where you want to be".

"The greens are deadly, almost impossible," he added.

Following in the footsteps of Oosthuizen at the 2nd, he recorded a double-bogey, but of course it didn't really matter. "Walking onto the green there was a hum, not from the crowds, but from a fleet of mowers sculpturing the course. Then there was an eerie calm as they silenced their machines. We were now the centre of attention as we played out the hole, and there were high-fives all around."

Although Mitchell never had the pleasure of meeting Oosthuizen, he learnt that they had more in common than their southern hemisphere roots: "As a Kiwi living in the USA for the last two decades, I was amused to see that Louis has a base in Cheshire, England, not far from where my wife and I lived and bought up our children in the 1980s."

As impressive as Oosthuizen's effort was, it is still not the most famous televised golf shot of all time – that feat surely belongs to Alan Shepard, who made one small swing for mankind (with a collapsible 6 iron) on the moon in 1971.[*]

---

[*] The head of the club was a normal 6 iron, but the shaft was made up of three separate aluminium sections, fitted with Teflon joints and weighing 453 grams. It is displayed at the US Golf Association Museum in Far Hills, New Jersey.

About 400 000 kilometres from the nearest golf course, the 15-handicap *Apollo 14* astronaut had to hit one-handed because of his bulky spacesuit. Nevertheless, with precious little gravity, the ball, which would have travelled about 30 metres on earth, flew for an additional 150 metres. When Shepard returned to earth, he received a telegram from the Royal and Ancient Golf Club of St Andrews congratulating him on the extraordinary feat and issuing a (tongue-in-cheek) warning: "Please refer to Rules of Golf section on etiquette, paragraph 6 – before leaving a bunker, a player should carefully fill up all holes made by him therein."

And, for the record, an albatross is not the rarest shot in golf. There is, after all, the condor (an ace on a par five). It takes its name from the largest flying land bird in the western hemisphere, and it has only happened four times in history – and just once on a straight path of 472 metres. This achievement is usually associated with strong tailwinds, thin air and an extraordinary bounce, and it's never been recorded in a professional tournament.

There are also a handful of par-six holes around the world and, in the event of a golfer ever achieving a virtually impossible ace on one of these, the term "ostrich" has been reserved.

But I digress. With Oosthuizen's awesome feat at Augusta, it seemed that a fairy-tale ending was on the cards. Despite his height – or lack of it – the South African found himself towering above the greatest golfers on the planet. His childhood friend Charl Schwartzel, who had faded towards the end on day four, was the holder of the green jacket and was gearing for the most emotional of handovers.

But, as we have seen time and again, this is the most fickle of all sports, and while news of Oosthuizen's extraordinary feat was reverberating around the world, he was tasked with composing himself for the 16 holes of regulation golf that remained.

The single biggest moment of his life had occurred on the single biggest day of his life – Masters Sunday with a serious crack at the title. When he stepped onto the third tee, that shot that was still reverberating around the world was knocking around in his head as well, and he momentarily lost his composure.

"Our heads were buzzing, and he nearly shanked his drive at the 3rd," Stander recalls. Oosthuizen dropped a shot on that hole and did not make another birdie until the 13th.

Oosthuizen concurs: "It was tough over the next five holes to get my head around it … just to get my head right," he said in the post-tournament press conference.

While he managed to keep his composure on the run-in, Bubba Watson – with his homemade swing – was firing on all cylinders, with four birdies providing the colour on the back nine. Two months after Oosthuizen's runaway victory at the 2010 Open, Watson (his birth name is Gerry) had lost a play-off for the PGA title to Martin Kaymer, so he had been in the cauldron before. Also, he had spent his college years at the University of Georgia nearby, so he was the overwhelming crowd favourite.

After four days of beautiful golf and a thrilling final round that had a little bit of everything, Oosthuizen and the idiosyncratic left-hander were all square at the 18th.

The tension was palpable when the American clattered an errant drive into the trees on the second hole of the play-off. "Fore right!" Oosthuizen seemed poised to strike, but he also failed to produce the goods, even though the end result – light rough – wasn't as drastic. The grass tugged at the bottom of Oosthuizen's approach, which was safe but short of the green. He then stepped back to get a first-hand account of Bubba golf.

As the sun dipped behind the Georgia pines, Watson stepped up to make history. The weapon was loaded, the safety was off and, with one wild, curling, magnificent swing, the 33-year-old from Florida's panhandle changed the way pundits, gurus and swing coaches would ever view the game again.

Not since the late Seve Ballesteros had the world witnessed such wondrous talent. Like Ballesteros, Watson had a simple swing, but an incredible imagination that enabled both of them to manufacture match winners from next to nothing. Trick-shot artist Ballesteros, who had cut his teeth on a discarded 6 iron (with potatoes as balls), is well remembered for the 2-iron shot he hit from a car park at the 1979 Open.*

And the left-handed Watson, whose only golfing instructions had come from his father, matched that with a bone-crushing, soul-destroying left hook. The banana shot seared and soared 37 metres through the narrow tunnel, banked sharply right and, with freakish precision, came to a rest some three metres from the pin.

Acclaimed swing coach Butch Harmon would later say that Watson, Ballesteros and Phil Mickelson were the only golfers in history who could have pulled that shot off. Two putts from there and the devout Christian gave thanks and broke down in the arms of his caddie, Ted Scott. He had become the eighth consecutive first-time Major winner at the Masters and the fifth left-handed winner in the last 10 years. As he embraced his wife, Angie (they have an adopted son named Caleb), he wept openly.

"I hit a crazy shot that I saw in my head, and somehow I'm here in a green jacket talking to you," he told journalists afterwards.

Four players finished tied for third – the overnight leaders Phil Mickelson (72) and Peter Hanson (73), Matt Kuchar (69) and Lee Westwood (68). Ahead of the 2013 edition of the tournament, the emotional defending champion broke down when he recalled how he had wrapped young

---

* The Spaniard had a right arm slightly longer than the left, a curiosity that made it seem like he had the perfect stance.

Caleb in the green jacket when he returned home. "That's the only thing I did with it – out of respect, out of honour."

In the fog of defeat, Oosthuizen was left to lament on whether that superb deuce may have ended up around his neck. Stander, who carried Oosthuizen and his bag on that roller-coaster Sunday, said they had both been thrown off "by that moment".*

"In a perfect world, Louis would have got the albatross on the back nine – nothing would have stopped us then," he suggested.

Giddy with glee, the pair had celebrated that double-eagle with a high-five, but their flaying hands missed and the moment was captured in slow motion and relayed to a global television audience of many millions.

With the noise having died down at last, Oosthuizen and Stander found themselves back in South Africa, surrounded by family and friends. The occasion was the christening of Oosthuizen's second daughter, Sophia. The setting was the family farm at Gouritzmond, where his journey had begun nearly three decades earlier. That Sunday morning's festivities were centred around the champion's back-yard bunker and putting green. During the course of the day, the guests took turns playing a wide variety of shots. And, as Stander recalls, "Whenever anyone did anything, they would celebrate with missed high-fives in slow motion."

It was one of those unique, "only in South Africa" moments.

---

* A year after their thrilling play-off duel, Oosthuizen failed to make the cut while Watson limped home at seven over par.

10

The Machine

"A curiosity of a champion he might have been, but do not dismiss him lightly." — **Oliver Brown**

There was a telling moment at the 15th hole on the final day of the 2011 Masters when Tiger Woods fired his second shot at the pin and threatened to turn the tournament on its head. There was the telltale fist-pump, that menacing tear-your-heart-out glare as he strode towards the green under the towering loblolly pines. The ball landed majestically, 1.5 metres from the hole on the flattest green on the course. Perfect.

More than a year had passed since the world's first billion-dollar sportsman (and the second-richest "African American" in the US after mother confessor Oprah Winfrey) had won a single golf tournament. It had been a roller-coaster journey for the 14-time Major winner as his world came tumbling down following a car accident, rumours (then confirmation) of marital infidelity, therapy and, of course, the inevitable comeback. Like Muhammad Ali after being stripped of his title (for refusing to serve in the military), the sporting world waited with bated breath to see whether he would rise again, whether he could match the genius of his hapless youth.

The world's most famous sportsman, who started the day seven shots behind leader Rory McIlroy, had fired a five-under-par 31 on the front nine (highlighted by four birdies and an eagle) to taste blood and stake a challenge for the tournament. McIlroy subsequently endured a complete meltdown and the American, as he strode towards the flag with that get-in-the-hole determination, was now just a single shot behind.

The man who had come the closest to taming Augusta's pure but deadly greens (he once went 113 holes at the course without three-putting) was on the prowl, circling his prey and full of threat. On that bright spring day, he was centimetres away from a breathtaking eagle and sole possession of the lead with three more holes waiting to be assaulted. But the putt stayed out, and Woods recoiled in horror. His 2011 campaign had reached its nadir[*] and, for the first time, the greatest golfer of his generation seemed to be frightened of his own shadow.

For most front-runners, the Masters only really begins on the back nine on the Sunday, but for Woods that year, that's where it ended.

As the tiger slinked away, the cameras panned to Charl Schwartzel, an unlikely hero who was in the vibrant milieu of that final day and more than ready to meet the moment. Over the next hour or so, the boy from Vereeniging was all class, leaving many of the top golfers in the world in his wake.

Schwartzel was born on 31 August 1984 in Johannesburg and, at the age of two, was given his first golf clubs – a plastic baby set. When he was four, the family moved to Pietersburg, a small mining community in what is now North West Province, where his father, George, worked at a quantity surveying firm.

A talented amateur before turning professional in the late 1970s, Schwartzel Snr had a chequered career and is often remembered for his temper on the course. There was the self-inflicted injury (a broken toe) when he hit the sole of his shoe with a putter after missing a sitter, chasing

---

[*] It marked a career-long run of 11 Majors without a title.

his caddie up the 9th fairway at Zwartkop after losing a ball, and, exasperated by the slow pace of play during a tournament at Milnerton (a seaside links in Cape Town), removing his clothes and wading into the ocean (he signed out for a 78 and never played as a professional again).

Speaking for millions of golfers around the world, Schwartzel admitted that his frustrations with the sport had "made a monster out of me".

Like fellow competitor Dale Hayes, Schwartzel Snr probably realised that he didn't have a Major in him and, unlike Hayes, he took up chicken farming in Vereeniging.

In 1988, George, Lizette, Charl, brother Attie and sister Lindi moved to the Kruisenentfontein chicken farm in Deneysville, where Lizette had grown up. It's located on the Free State side of the Vaal River, where the jackals howl and the sky is huge. And that's where our future champion cut his teeth. He earned the nickname "The Machine" because of his reputation for rolling up his sleeves and getting the farm work done. He spent 20 years in the same bedroom in the family home (the room was subsequently converted into a study for Lindi) and, despite his busy travelling schedule today, he still frequently returns to the homestead.

Schwartzel spent much of his childhood following his father around the nearby Maccauvlei Golf Club,[*] either helping to read the putts or hitting a few balls himself. The course is named after the *wilde makoue* or spur-winged geese that used to nest and breed in the area. Within a year of its construction in 1926, it was chosen to stage the South African championships. It is located adjacent to the Vaal River (on the Free State side) and is essentially parkland in style but, because of the undulations and the proliferation of bunkers, it also passes as an inland links. In total, it hosted four South African Open championships – the last in 1949.

---

[*] George, Charl and Attie Schwartzel have all been crowned club champions.

This was a region known more for its culture of braaing and rugby than producing champion golfers. But George Schwartzel told me that his son was different.

"I saw it when he was very small – he had the talent. I had spent years playing with Dale Hayes at Swartkops [Golf Club in Pretoria], and he reminded me of Dale. There were times when I wondered how he had been able to produce a particular shot ... it was very special," he said.

And Hayes, who has always been quick to identify a champion, said that from the age of 14, it was evident that the young Schwartzel "had everything" and would go all the way. What he lacked in star power, he made up for with one of the straightest shots in the game.

The teenager, who played with his father most Fridays (and caddied for him on Wednesdays and Saturdays), was fast to learn.

From an early age, Schwartzel was consumed by the game. "As a youngster, I would chip around my garden and pretend I was playing the Masters. I would have four balls, one for me, one for Ernie, one for Retief Goosen and one for Nick Price. I would chip around the garden all day, playing the Masters and the British Open," he said.

One bit of advice his father handed down was to "let the clubs do the talking", which is exactly what he has done for most of his career. "He taught me my golf swing and made it simple," the son recalls. So simple that it consists of maintaining the right grip, stance, posture, rhythm and balance.

The young boy also spent hours studying videotapes of Ernie Els's magnificently simple swing. His father also had lead tape wrapped around the head of an old wooden driver to build his son's core muscles, and it became an invaluable aid.

George Schwartzel recalls how his son's game came together "nicely" at the age of 13. The young teenager beat junior Springbok Etienne Bond, who was in matric at the time, by shooting a 69.

THE MACHINE

Schwartzel Snr asked his old friend and competitor Gavan Levenson to take the boy under his wing,* and Levenson, a former SA Open and PGA champion, was immediately taken by the wiry teenager's determination – "and he asked all the right questions".

"He was slightly built, but he made up for it with a magnificent short game and he was very straight." Levenson said that by the time Schwartzel (just) made it into tour school, "he had a classic swing, one of the best in the game".

Levenson said he also had the mental strength and extremely high concentration levels. "He wasn't scared to shoot a low score. If he shot a 65, he would go for the 64 ... it's that kind of drive that can make all the difference at that level."

PGA professional and CEO of the SA Golf Development Board Grant Hepburn has witnessed Schwartzel's swing evolve over the years into the finished product. I asked him to take us through it:

> When he addresses the ball, his arms hang outwards from
> his shoulders, giving him room to swing freely through impact.
> At this moment, his eye line looks directly at the ball, which helps
> his shoulders to move on the correct plane. The ball is positioned
> a couple of inches inside the left heel, which enables him to set
> up with square shoulders and hips.
>
> When the hands get to waist height in the take-away, the shaft
> is parallel to the line of his feet ... it's textbook good. His hips begin
> to coil, which helps his shoulders turn. As the club reaches the top
> of the swing, his spine angle is the same as it was at the address.
> He has simply coiled around it, allowing him to retain his original
> posture. At the same time, his left knee has moved across to the

---

* As a teenager, he was also coached by Pete Cowen and Martin Whitcher.

right, which facilitates the coiling of his hips and turning of his shoulders.

The club sits in a perfect position over his right shoulder as he finishes his back swing. The club-face is perfectly square as a result of his excellent grip and wrist action. His body has worked well to support the swinging of the club to the top – he has a full shoulder and hip coil and his chest is turned over his right knee.

As he begins the downswing, his plane is ideal. His left arm is still across his chest, while his right elbow is on the side of his body. He leads the downswing with his legs and moves his weight laterally towards the target, but his head remains behind the ball. He pulls the grip end of the club down, which results in a late whipping action through the ball, creating a great deal of club-head speed.

At the point of impact, his elbow is still tucked in close to his right side while the club is swinging on the ideal path – marginally from the inside and then down the line towards the target. As the ball leaves the club-face, his eye line remains the same as it was at address, while the shoulders are turning on the same plane as they did in the back swing. The extension and crossover of his arms give an indication that he has completely released the club.

His swing ends as it began – perfectly balanced. The body is slightly arched, with the weight balanced on the outside of his left foot and the tip of his right toe.

Easier said than done. The real challenge, as Alistair Cooke once noted, is to carry out a continuous and subtle series of highly unnatural movements, involving about 64 muscles, that results in a seemingly natural swing, taking all of two seconds to begin and end.

In 2000, Schwartzel may have been a few years away from attaining this near-perfect swing, but he was good enough to win the South African High Schools Provincial, the Harry Oppenheimer Trophy, the International Teams Championship and the Riviera Resort Junior Championship. The following year, he won nine tournaments, including the Mpumalanga Open, the South African Schools Provincial Championships and the World Junior Golf Team Championships in Japan (with Louis Oosthuizen, Albert Kruger and Christian Ries).

He was also selected as the South African Junior Golfer of the Year and was firmly established as the leading amateur in the country. The only setback was that his prized Scotty Cameroon "Catalina" putter was stolen at a junior tournament in England and it took years to find a suitable replacement.

In 2001, Schwartzel and his good friend Louis Oosthuizen met an agent who would change the course of their careers. A former UK postman, Chubby Chandler had made the European Tour decades ago. His first tournament coincided with Seve Ballesteros's first tournament, and that's about the only thing they had in common. While Ballesteros went on to win 91 times (including seven Majors) as a professional, Chandler had one solitary win (in São Paulo in 1985). As his playing days drew to a close and he reflected on the hits and (mostly) misses of a somewhat unremarkable career, he realised that his chances would have been greatly enhanced if he had had a manager or agent in his corner.

Two years after his retirement, he set up International Sports Management (ISM) with one heavyweight, the charismatic Darren Clarke, on board. They were soon joined by Lee Westwood, and Chandler earned a reputation for being honest and reliable. At the Nedbank Challenge at Sun City in 2001, he bumped into George Schwartzel, an old tour friend from the 1970s. Schwartzel said his son, Charl, was making waves as an amateur and needed an agent. Overnight Schwartzel and his close friend

Oosthuizen were in Chandler's camp and winging their way to Europe to begin the most extraordinary chapter of their lives.

Schwartzel set up camp in Manchester with Oosthuizen and Richard Sterne, another hugely talented young South African.

With the guidance of Yorkshire swing coach Pete Cowen, Schwartzel won some amateur events in other countries, including the 2002 Indian Amateur and English Open Stroke Play Championships. He also represented South Africa in the 2002 Eisenhower Trophy.

He turned professional at 18 and qualified for the European Tour (the second-youngest South African golfer to do so after Dale Hayes) within months. In 2003 and 2004, he earned enough appearance money to retain his European Tour card. During the 2004/05 season, he won the Alfred Dunhill Championship at Leopard Creek, a leading tournament in South Africa that is co-sanctioned by the European Tour.

It was a big break for the young professional. "There is nothing like your first win – it will always be the one you remember. It's a big milestone, and the longer it takes, the harder it is to get," he said.

A second-place finish at the SAA Open a week later and four other top-20 finishes saw him finishing the season in 52nd place on the money list.

Victory at the 2005 Vodacom Tour Championship took Schwartzel into the top 100 in the Official World Golf Rankings for the first time, and within a year he was ranked 55 in the world.

In 2006, he lost narrowly at the Barclays Scottish Open after Swede Johan Edfors shot the lights out with a final-round 63. Similarly, at the Deutsche Bank Players' Championship of Europe he also finished second, despite posting a magnificent 21 under par.

At the PGA Championship at Medinah, he was on the right side of the cut after shooting opening rounds of 72 and 73 before countryman Trevor Immelman holed a 7.5-metre putt at the 18th that ended Schwartzel's debut campaign.

In April 2007, Schwartzel's victory at the Open de España, where he beat Jyoti Randhawa by one stroke, took him into the top 40 in the world rankings.

The following year he won the Madrid Masters. Schwartzel finished in 28th position in the 2008 Order of Merit, which gained him a place in the 2009 Open Championship at Turnberry.

But Schwartzel felt that he was starting to lose his way on the golf course. A quiet individual, he prefers golfing with low-key partners and is most content when he is in the bush or at the controls of an aircraft. He's been a licensed pilot since 2007 and, in 2009, purchased a six-seater Cessna 206 Turboprop – with the monogrammed tail number ZS-SCH.* It's a far cry from Tiger Woods's $60-million Gulfstream G550, but then the fuel bill is significantly lower.

Towards the end of the decade, Schwartzel began drawing inspiration from Angus Buchan, a former Zambian farmer who had moved to Greytown in South Africa and begun to preach in his local community. Buchan set up the so-called Mighty Men Conference, which grew from 40 people to 400 000 followers. Schwartzel described him as "a farmer who gave his life to God".

At this stage of his life and career, Schwartzel felt he needed time alone. He travelled through the Namib, a coastal desert that stretches for more than 2 000 kilometres along the Atlantic coasts of Angola, Namibia and South Africa, extending southward from the Carunjamba River in Angola through Namibia to the Olifants River in the Western Cape.

His destination was a small agricultural town in northern Namibia. Otjiwarongo, which means "beautiful place" in the local dialect, is located

---

* He uses the aircraft's serial number ZS-SCH as the identifying mark on his Nike One Star Tour D golf balls.

in the Otjozondjupa region between Windhoek to the south and the Etosha National Park to the north. There are around 19 000 residents, including a family friend of the Schwartzels.

In the area's solitude and breathtaking beauty, the young sportsman felt a stirring in his soul. After a couple of weeks, he went to a local hardware store and purchased a carpet mat to hit golf balls off. And as he powered his drives into the desert, he found his form again and the sense of inner calm that is such an important ingredient of the game.

Despite a winless 2009 season, Schwartzel began 2010 with a bang, winning two consecutive tournaments on the European Tour and making the cut in all four Majors.

At the WGC-CA Championship on the Blue Monster in Doral, Florida, he also reined in his childhood idol – South Africa's greatest post-apartheid golfer. With a third-round 67, Schwartzel took a share of the lead with Ernie Els, who is 15 years his senior.

Twenty-two years earlier, Schwartzel's father George, then a pro player in South Africa, had played against the up-and-coming Els.

As an affiliate member of the golf programme supported by Els's foundation and a guest at Els's home in Jupiter that week, Schwartzel was magnificent. Els was coming off a season in which he had failed to win anywhere in the world for the first time since he turned professional.

The following day, Schwartzel put up a brave fight on the front nine, responding to Els's early trio of birdies with two of his own to haul himself back to within a shot of the lead. However, bogeys at the 11th, 15th and 17th saw Schwartzel's challenge fall away as he carded a two-under 70 to take second place. The Big Easy shot a six-under 66 to take the title with a score of 18 under.

At the beginning of 2011, Schwartzel based himself with Louis Oosthuizen at the Old Palm Golf Club near West Palm Beach in Florida.

The 2011 Masters marked the 50th anniversary of Gary Player's historic performance when he became the first international Masters champion.

Schwartzel felt he was well prepared for the 75th playing of the year's first Major championship, particularly as he had spent several weeks practising on hard, greasy greens to adjust to the terrifying undulations Augusta offers. The pristine parkland fairways, framed with little rough, are balanced out by the lightning-fast greens. The South African also spent many hours seeking counsel from experienced Augusta golfers and studying every break and roll on the greens, which can make the different between an eagle and a double-bogey (or worse).

Three-time Major winner Nick Price had advised him to find the fastest putt on every green at every course in the build-up to the Masters to get the feel and to learn how to strike the ball that softly. The speed on these greens can never be underestimated. Just ask Tom Watson, a two-time Masters champion, whose 6-iron approach ended 18 metres from the hole on the 16th green in 1996. Five putts later (a career first), his ball dropped. "I went from 60 feet below to six above, to 40 below, to four above, to two below, then I made that one," he recalled. And Seve Ballesteros, who four-putted the same hole a few years earlier, offered this succinct explanation: "I miss. I miss. I miss. I make."

A private audience with Augusta's favourite son, Jack Nicklaus, also proved to be invaluable. They were introduced by mutual friend Johann Rupert at the fundraising pro-am golf tournament for the Els for Autism Foundation in Florida a few weeks before the Masters. When Rupert asked Nicklaus to give the rookie a couple of tips on how to tackle Bobby Jones's masterpiece, neither was expecting a blow-by-blow analysis of each and every hole from the Golden Bear.

Nicklaus, who had won six of his 18 Majors there, explained that there are three different areas that come into play: green zones that you aim for, red zones you avoid and orange zones that are the bailout area. And, of course, he emphasised the importance of positioning a drive on the fairway so that you are best situated to attack the relevant quadrant.

Horton Smith, the first man to win the Masters, in 1936, noted that Augusta was one of the few courses that really presents two games on each hole – a game to reach the greens and another to figure out the ever-challenging contours of the green.

Much of Nicklaus's tutorial went over the head of the awestruck Schwartzel, but Rupert listened intently, scribbled down some notes and later emailed them to Schwartzel.

Three weeks before the tournament, there was another telling experience, this one involving cow dung.

Before his departure for the US, Schwartzel spent a weekend in the bush with close friends Richard Maree, Gerrie and Divan van Zyl, and their wives. With the fire crackling and the alcohol flowing (coffee liqueur was the drink of choice), there were toasts to his recent victory at the Johannesburg Open and, of course, the upcoming Augusta campaign. Although Schwartzel is a very moderate drinker, the liqueur softened his inhibitions and he announced that he would win the tournament. With Georgia on their minds, the celebration ended late that night with them jumping into the nearby cow pool and, ankle-deep in dung, saluting the Masters.

When Schwartzel pulled up at Gate Two at the old cathedral (by invitation only, of course) and drove through the archway of magnolia trees to Fountain Circle, 230 metres away, the lanky lad from Vereeniging was in a good space. And Johann Rupert, who was there, had been advising the American reporters to learn to spell the name S-c-h-w-a-r-t-z-e-l.

An opening round of 69, followed by a 72, saw him tied in 12th place. A 68 on the Saturday put the 26-year-old just four shots off the lead, which is where, Justin Rose told him, "you want to be. You've got nothing to lose and everything to gain."

Like countryman Trevor Immelman three years earlier, Schwartzel received a message of support from Gary Player, who advised him to believe in himself and to remain calm.*

That final day, which was full of sunshine, would turn out to have one of the most dramatic endings to any Major, with eight different golfers at some point or another having at least a share of the lead. And there was a real international flavour to the proceedings. Apart from Africa, North America (Tiger Woods), Australia (Jason Day, Geoff Ogilvy and Adam Scott), Europe (Rory McIlroy), South America (Ángel Cabrera) and Asia (K.J. Choi) were all in the mix. In fact, the only continent that wasn't represented was Antarctica.

Schwartzel, playing in only his second Masters, was fast out of the blocks. On the 1st hole – a 406-metre slight dogleg right – a long, languid 3 wood found the centre of the fairway. With a light westerly wind, he then pushed his 6-iron approach into no-man's land, a gulley to the right of the green, 32 metres from the pin. Normally, he would have used a lob wedge to attack the flag, but the ground was "rock hard" because it had been trampled by spectators.

Former Masters champion Nick Faldo, who was commentating, suggested that the Augusta novice would do well to keep his third shot on the green and escape with a bogey.

Schwartzel selected the 6 iron – again – and punched a jaw-droppingly magnificent pitch-and-run, which tracked the pin from the moment of impact. When it rolled in for a birdie, Faldo said: "Oh my word."

The South African was within three shots of the lead.

His former coach Gavan Levenson told me it was at that astonishing moment that Schwartzel's tournament really kicked in. "That approach took huge skill, just to get the ball on the green from there," he said.

---

* Ahead of the Masters every year, Player hosts a braai for all the South African participants and their families at the Gary Player Group's rented home in Augusta.

At the 3rd, a short par four, Schwartzel served notice that he was spoiling for the fight of his life. Although the heart-shaped green (guarded by one large bunker) was out of sight, he hit another perfect drive, setting himself up for a wedge-in from 104 metres "with the wind in my favour". The approach funnelled towards the fat of the green, landing about 27 metres from the pin. But, aided with enormous spin, it squirted towards the hole and dived in (following in the Masters tradition, he would later donate that club, a 54-degree wedge, to Augusta).

It's been said, time and again, that the Masters doesn't begin until the back nine on a Sunday. And so it was on this Sunday as all hell broke loose.

At the 10th, McIlroy, who had started the day with a four-shot lead, began his infamous near-collapse. With the lead down to one at the 10th, the Ulsterman butchered his drive and the ball ended up between two cabins, deep in the rough and embarrassingly close to neighbouring South Carolina (stunned commentator Nick Faldo said he had never seen a drive end up so far left). Three shots later, the Irishman, now patently off-colour, hit a tree and went on to score a triple-bogey. He followed this with a double-bogey on the 12th, and his torrid campaign ended with a score of 80. "This golf course can bait you into being too aggressive, and that's what happened to Rory out there," Tiger Woods later observed.

It was the biggest Augusta unravelling since Greg Norman had lost a five-shot lead in 1993. By the time the Irishman signed off his card, the focus was firmly on an unknown South African who was taking ownership of only his second Masters.

After shooting a bogey at the 4th hole, Schwartzel and his caddie Greg Hearmon steadied their ship, maintaining par for the next 10 holes to keep in contention for the lead.

And yet, as Schwartzel would later recall, "I wasn't losing, but I wasn't gaining."

But the plot changed dramatically at the 15th. Schwartzel's 6-iron approach at the 485-metre par five narrowly missed the cup and ended 2.5 metres from the hole, just off the green. "I knew if I could relax my hands, I could hit a proper stroke." The ball disappeared down the hole, "and that birdie putt got me out of the par mentality". The elastic South African now had the clubhouse in sight. Nevertheless, there was still a five-way tussle for the lead. Scott, who was paired with countryman Jason Day, briefly broke away with a birdie at the 14th for a two-shot lead at 12 under.

When Gary Player won his first Masters, he was overcome with a sense of tranquillity, a state of optimism, an "in-zone" state of being where the mind and body are perfectly in sync and in harmony. As he marched through the back nine with the throbbing tempo rising by the minute, Schwartzel experienced a similar state of being. He was as balanced as a newborn baby, quietly confident, safely in his zone and experiencing an overwhelming sense of calm. It was much the same as he had felt throughout most of the first three rounds.

Day, who was playing in his first Masters, later said that it was probably the most excited he had ever been in a golf tournament: "You're out there in the middle of the fairway, and there are roars around you and you don't know what's going on. And then all you see is that little number pop up on the leader boards and everyone [is] screaming. And it's an amazing feeling to be out there in the thick of things."

Schwartzel, playing behind the two Australians, went for broke and made his play for history and one of the biggest heists in golf. Armed with a deadly putter (a Nike 004 prototype with a Ping grip), and every aspect of his game in perfect sync, he began to elbow his way through the pack.

Thanks to clutch-putts at the 16th (4.5 metres) and 17th (3.6 metres), he scored three birdies in a row to take a one-shot lead going into the final hole. The South African was in the driving seat and looking cool and comfortable. A par at the last would give him the championship (and his first tournament win in the United States).

On the Thursday, Friday and Saturday, Schwartzel had played it safe on the 18th tee-box, using a 3 wood and leaving a comfortable approach and two putts for par. This was the most important shot of his life, at one of the most demanding finishing holes in championship golf. The 388-metre uphill dogleg right is protected at the elbow by two deep bunkers on the left-hand side of the fairway. As Schwartzel peered through the enormous tunnel – created by trees and thousands of spectators flanking the tee-box and fairway – he had a change of heart.

He would later remark on how narrow that tunnel becomes on Masters Sunday – particularly with a slender one-shot lead. He selected his driver, stepped back, peered into the light and delivered every ounce of his 79-kilogram frame to the ball, flushing a nerveless drive. The result was sumptuous, even by Schwartzel's Herculean standards. The ball exploded off the club-face, arched between the pines and landed in the middle of the fairway, with just 118 metres left to the pin. Displaying unshakeable calm, South Africa's latest sporting icon was left with a straightforward wedge to the pin.

When that approach kissed the green – and danced for a moment – settling two metres from the hole, the tournament was over. Like the previous three holes, it required but a single putt to turn Schwartzel into the master of the universe. After all, he had become the first champion in tournament history to score birdies on the last four holes (he later recalled that he had no idea that he had birdied the last four because he was so focused on the shots he needed to play).*

In his wake were Scott and Day in joint second place, with another Australian, Geoff Ogilvy, tied for fourth, with Woods and England's Luke

---

* American Art Wall birdied five of the six final holes to win the 1959 Masters.

Donald. The result may have left the Masters as the only major golf prize never won by an Australian, but the international contingent had filled seven of the top 10 places.* Ogilvy summed it up with the following offering: "They're going to write a book about this Masters."

The final-day drama had been a harrowing experience for father and mentor George, whose own frustrations with the game had fuelled his anxiety levels whenever Charl or brother Attie played.

When the stakes were high, he preferred to turn away from the tension. At Leopard Creek, when Charl won his first European Tour event in 2004, he reportedly spent much of the final round lying under a tree, well away from the cauldron. And in 2010, when Charl played in the final group in the WGC-CA Championship in Florida with Ernie Els, George took a sleeping pill and tried to take a nap.

And that was the plan for day four of the Masters – afternoon in Augusta and evening at the family farm in Vereeniging – until father saw son hammer home that breathtaking pitch-and-run at the 1st for a birdie. He never swallowed the pill and managed to sit/stand glued to the television set for the longest five hours of his life. During the last half an hour of the tournament, his only daughter Lindi began crying, and when that last putt dropped at 5.48 p.m. (12.48 a.m. in South Africa), he allowed himself a tear.

Filled with enormous gratitude and respect, he witnessed the biggest underdog in recent Masters history stride past a bruised Woods and climb into a golf cart for the short ride to Butler's Cabin for the prize-giving ceremony. En route, the phone rang.

"Yes, there's a famous picture of him sitting in a golf cart and grinning on the phone – it meant so much connecting with him so soon after the

---

* Adam Scott would put an end to more than 50 years of Australian misfortune at the Masters with his play-off victory in 2013.

win," George told me. And he acknowledges that the chaotic finish, which saw the lead change so many times, had made it "a win to remember".

"All we were hoping for was that he would do well enough at the tournament to secure his [playing] card. It was all so unexpected. It was only at the 17th [when he snatched his third birdie in a row], that I realised he could do it."

At the cabin, Phil Mickelson, the all-American boy-next-door, handed him the jacket (a long-standing Augusta tradition), which signalled the fact that, for the first time in history, the US held none of the four Majors nor the Ryder Cup.

Writing in the *Daily Telegraph*, Kevin Gartside noted how the tide had turned in favour of golf's *laaities:* "This has been a tournament at which the New Generation has come of age. And what a generation. Charl Schwartzel, the exceptional champion, is just 26. Behind him on the leader board was Jason Day, who at 23 is only two years McIlroy's senior. Also on the course was Japanese supernova Ryo Ishikawa, a global star at 19, and poster boy Ricky Fowler, at 23 already a force in the game. Nick Watney, Dustin Johnson, Martin Laird, Alvaro Quiros and Gary Woodland were just some of the twentysomethings launching rockets off the tee that day."

The young South African conceded that the experience had been overwhelming: "There [are] so many roars that go on around Augusta – especially the back nine. It echoes through those trees. There's always a roar. Every single hole you walk down, someone has done something, and I'd be lying if I said I wasn't looking at the leader board."

He said Louis Oosthuizen's seven-shot victory at the Open the previous year had given him the belief that he could be a contender.

"He inspired me so much, seeing him do it. We grew up together. And he made me think it was possible to win a Major like this."

No doubt, Schwartzel had also drawn strength from his caddie Greg Hearmon, who had been on Retief Goosen's bag when he won the 2001 US Open at Southern Hills. Schwartzel saluted his final-day playing partner K.J. Choi, who finished tied eighth, by saying that the Korean's calmness and standard of play on the day had complemented his own game: "We fed off each other."

If there was any downside to the celebrations, it was the fact that Schwartzel had beaten his idol and mentor Ernie Els to that coveted green jacket.

Asked about the impressive global contribution to the 2011 edition, Schwartzel noted that "America is big, but the world is bigger". And he told reporters in his post-tournament press conference that he hoped his status as a Masters champion "will help me find a way to get biltong into America".

UK journalist Oliver Brown, who witnessed Schwartzel's charge on day four, said the pilot had slipped under the radar magnificently: "He was not the accidental hero who happened to profit from Rory McIlroy's unravelling or the tortured Tiger Woods's error-strewn back nine, but a champion who grasped the prize with a feat never before accomplished."

The *Wall Street Journal* said that while Schwartzel had the restrained mien of a substitute librarian, he also produced "a tenacious game that never wilted on a sticky, furious Sunday at the Masters".

Within hours, golf's new phenomenon found himself on the same aircraft as McIlroy, winging his way to another tournament, in Malaysia. Ironically, both of them were using the same manager – Chubby Chandler – whose emotions couldn't have been more mixed. In his one camp, the gutted Irishman; in the other, the unlikeliest of golfing superstars... Chandler had waited 21 years for a Major, but with Schwartzel and Oosthuizen in his camp, he had secured two Majors within a year. They had become a remarkable double-act.

McIlroy was quick to pay tribute to Schwartzel, commenting that "at least the green jacket is on the plane" (only the current champion is allowed to remove the jacket from the club).

The victory saw Schwartzel rise from 29th to 11th in the Official World Golf Rankings.

Alongside his win at the Masters, Schwartzel finished tied for ninth at the US Open and had a solid run at the Open Championship before a third-round 75 wrecked his challenge. He ended the season ranked fourth on the Race to Dubai.

Not to be outdone by close friend Louis Oosthuizen, who had purchased a John Deere tractor with his Major winnings, Schwartzel bought a Bell 206 Jet Ranger helicopter, even though he didn't have a licence yet and was 4.5 kilograms shy of the minimum weight requirement (he strapped jugs filled with sand to the aircraft to make up the difference).

Schwartzel's dream year culminated in his marriage to Rosalind Jacobs – a cousin of PGA star Justin Rose and the niece of his former coach Gavan Levenson – at Muldersdrift outside Johannesburg in September. Among the celebrity guests were Thomas Aiken, Richard Sterne and, of course, Louis Oosthuizen. Charl's younger brother Attie (a pro on the South African circuit) was the best man.

The newlyweds moved into their home at Blair Atholl, Gary Player's family estate on the outskirts of Johannesburg. This keeps the young professional near both the bush and the city, from where he can make quick getaways to destinations around the world. Schwartzel also contributed to the construction of a thatched-roof home on his grandfather's 2 500-acre bushveld farm near Thabazimbi (which has two giraffes named Charl and Ros).

So how did the Masters victory change Schwartzel's life? For starters, his star fell so far in the months that followed that it was hard to fathom that he had managed to crush his Augusta rivals with such cold-blooded precision. Indeed, the Major win launched the longest drought of his career. For the rest of 2011 and 2012, he failed to secure a single victory or top-three finish. His performances in the 2012 Majors were forgettable. His best was tied 38th in the US Open, while he missed the cut at The Open championship.

Throughout, his putting let him down badly, and he began to experiment with a number of different grips. But putting is all a state of mind – as every golfer knows.

Puerto Rican legend Chi Chi Rodriguez disputed claims that the craft of golf is 50 per cent technique and 50 per cent mental: "I really believe it is 50 per cent technique and 90 per cent positive thinking, but that adds up to 140 per cent, which is why nobody is 100 per cent sure how to putt."

During that hangover period, the man who had conquered Augusta's slippery greens sometimes looked like he would have trouble buying a putt. Case in point: during the 2012 Deutsche Bank Championship at TPC Boston, he was in contention for the lead before his putter turned on him. On the 18th green, he attempted to power home a 90-centimetre putt for birdie. The ball lipped the back of the cup and squiggled out. Then came the par putt. Another miss.

In a pique of frustration, he tried to bury the ball with the back of his putter – despite the pleas of the television commentator ("No, don't do that") – and he watched it defy gravity again. The fourth dropped, but the reality is the man who had made history by nailing four breathtaking birdie putts on the last four holes at the Masters needed four putts from under a metre, and it sealed his fate in Boston. That eight-over 79 killed his challenge, cost him $19 000 and left him out of the top 70 in the FedEx Cup standings.

To be fair, an abdominal injury had affected his swing, and instead of giving it time to heal, he continued to compete. It also resulted in minor, enforced swing adjustments that affected his rhythm and results. A busy travelling schedule also took its toll.

So, is it fair to imply that he could be a one-hit wonder when it comes to the Majors? "Never," is the retort from Wynand Stander, Schwartzel's former caddie, who says he was simply going through a slump. "He has the complete game and, even though his putting is off, he will work through it. He is incredibly determined," Stander added.

When I finally got to meet Schwartzel at the Nedbank Challenge at Sun City at the end of 2012, he was in no mood to exchange pleasantries or to offer insight into the state of his game. The man who has been known to snap his clubs and present his middle finger to the hole after missing a putt also refused to be drawn into the benefits of that spiritual journey to Otjiwarongo and, with regards to his Augusta triumph, simply offered that "everything came together at the right time".

Nevertheless, our brief encounter coincided with a remarkable return to form. That weekend he was beaten to the post by Germany's Martin Kramer for the Nedbank Challenge title but, a week later, he snapped his 20-month drought when he cantered home at the Thailand Golf Challenge to win by 11 shots – the biggest margin at any significant international tournament that year (second place went to Bubba Watson, the golfer who had succeeded him as the Masters winner and who had pipped Louis Oosthuizen in the play-off).

Pain-free and with a return to his best, Schwartzel jetted back to South Africa and, a week later, romped home at the Alfred Dunhill Championship at Leopard Creek. With a final round of 69, he scored the lowest-ever tournament total at 24 under par and, fittingly, it occurred at the same course where he had produced his first career win back in 2004.

11

A South African Tiger?

"If it wasn't for golf, who knows what I would have done. Golf changed my life, and now I'm in a very good place. I wanted to give that dream to other people. I'd like to go find that Tiger Woods of South Africa, because he's out there." — **Ernie Els**

Our journey ends where it began all those years ago.
Cape Town is surely the most beautiful city of them all. Its 1087-metre-high sandstone and granite mountain – flanked by Devil's Peak to the east and Lion's Head to the west – squats above the city and Table Bay. Depending on the season, and the weather patterns, this World Heritage Site reflects the mood of the moment.

On a clear day, its impossibly flat top is visible for many kilometres and, for centuries, has served as a beacon for sailors. When the weather is fair, no scene is more beautiful. But when the wind is blowing from the southeast, warm air rushes up the slopes and jagged cliffs and into colder air, where the moisture condenses to form a breathtaking "tablecloth" of cloud.

When the cold fronts move in during the winter months, the shadow of the mountain looms ominously through the fog and mist. "Moody bitch, isn't she?" an Australian visitor once remarked to me.

The slopes of Table Mountain feed down to pristine beaches, ripe vineyards and fertile gardens. While these slopes are home to the most valuable real estate in South Africa, as the land levels, so, too, does the quality of its soil deteriorate. On the so-called Cape Flats, where the mountain sits afar, a ramshackle collection of thousands of dilapidated buildings and shacks rest uneasily on the shifting sea sands, providing a home for the poorest of the poor.

Like its social tapestry, which is woven of so many strands, Cape Town has a chequered past. At first the home of the indigenous Khoikhoi, from 1652 it also hosted Jan van Riebeeck and other employees of the Dutch East India Company. Whether they ever played golf in their homeland is unclear, but a version of the game was played in Loenen aan de Vecht in the Netherlands way back in 1297. By the time Van Riebeeck set sail, some of his countrymen had modified the sport by using clubs to stroke leather balls into holes in the ground.

The Dutch settlers were followed by the British, who captured Cape Town in 1795.

In 1910, Britain established the Union of South Africa and the Mother City became the legislative capital of the Union, and later of the Republic of South Africa. During the first half of the 20th century, the port city welcomed sailors from around the world, most notably during the two world wars, when it served as an important base for troops travelling from Europe to Burma and the Pacific Islands (my Scottish grandfather, who was injured in the Great War in Kenya, was transferred to Cape Town, where he married my grandmother after she had nursed him back to health).

When the National Party swept into power on its platform of racial segregation in 1948, the Cape's multiracial franchise began to erode. In addition, its District Six became one of the cornerstones of the Group Areas Act, which classified all areas according to race. When this multicultural melting pot on the slopes of Table Mountain was declared a whites-only region in 1965, District Six was completely demolished and over 60 000 residents were forcibly removed.

Across the bay, the prison on the desolate Robben Island detained many of the country's future leaders, including Nelson Mandela. And when he was released in 1990, he was escorted to Cape Town City Hall, where he addressed all of South Africa: "I stand here before you not as a prophet but as a humble servant of you, the people. Your tireless and heroic sacrifices have made it possible for me to be here today. I therefore place the remaining years of my life in your hands."

Those were the first words he had spoken in public[*] since his statement from the dock at the end of the Treason Trial in Pretoria nearly three decades earlier, when he had faced the death penalty: "I have cherished the ideal of a democratic and free society in which all persons live together in harmony and with equal opportunities. It is an ideal which I hope to live for and to achieve. But if needs be, it is an ideal for which I am prepared to die."

The country would never be the same again.

When the weather is clear, the view from the 18th tee-box at Cape Town's Mowbray Golf Club is one of the finest in the world. The fairway of this 424-metre, stroke-three, par-four hole is a blanket of lush kikuyu grass framed by rows of pine blue-gum trees on both sides. A large pond on the left and three large bunkers frame the green. Squatting behind this setting is the recently rebuilt clubhouse (the previous one was destroyed in a fire in 1998). And, towering above it all, is Devil's Peak, rising 1000 metres into the sky.

---

[*] On 10 February 1985, Mandela asked his daughter, Zindzi, to address the nation from the Jabulani Stadium in Soweto. At the time, he was incarcerated in Pollsmoor Prison. President P.W. Botha had offered to release him if he publicly renounced violent struggle. Mandela declined, saying: "I am not prepared to sell the birthright of the people to be free."

Mowbray is descendant from the Cape Golf Club, which was founded in 1885,* making it older than any course in the United States. It has hosted the South African Open seven times, the Bell's Cup on three occasions and all major amateur championships. Many of the world's biggest names in golf have played here, including all the South African Major champions.

The parklands course is divided by a railway line and, like just about everything in this land of racial divisions, it has a chequered past.

Sitting on the veranda of the clubhouse, Martin Galant, president of the Western Cape Development Academy, recalls how this setting was the preserve of white South Africans throughout his youth. "But there were exceptions. On Christmas Day, Mowbray and some of the other clubs in the city opened their doors to other races while white members took a break from golf. But they didn't even leave the flags in for us," he said. "So, whoever got to the green first in our four-ball would find the hole and place a stick in it for the others."

But the end of apartheid and the dawn of democracy have seen South Africans of all races coming together. What has made the achievements of

---

* In 1910, the Royal Cape Golf Club was founded. The mother club in South Africa, it was originally situated at the Wynberg Military Camp, Waterloo Green, from 1885 to 1891, before it moved to the Rondebosch Common in 1891 and, finally, to Ottery in Wynberg in 1905. That course was opened in 1906. There is almost certainly a course or courses in the US older than the Royal Cape, but certainly no club, as the first club in the US was started only in 1886. When the Cape Golf Club moved to Ottery Road, some members stayed behind, continuing to play golf on Rondebosch Common, and in 1911 they formed the Rondebosch Golf Club. A few of them, not happy with the playing conditions on the common, decided to move elsewhere. They identified land on the farm Raapenberg, now Pinelands, built a course and started the Mowbray Golf Club there in 1911.

Although there are several competing claims to being the oldest club in the US, it was only in 1894 that delegates from the Newport Country Club, Saint Andrew's Golf Club, Yonkers, New York, The Country Club, Chicago Golf Club and Shinnecock Hills Golf Club met in New York City to form what was to become the United States Golf Association (USGA).

most of South Africa's post-apartheid Major winners even more special is that their career peaks coincided with that of probably the finest golfer of all time.

The young cub Eldrick Tont Woods (he was nicknamed Tiger in honour of his father's military friend, Colonel Vuong Dang Phong) exploded onto the scene long before he turned professional. As a two-year-old child prodigy, he appeared on *The Mike Douglas Show* with Bob Hope and, at age five, in *Golf Digest* and on ABC's *That's Incredible*.

As a teenager, it was clear for all to see that a leap to Major-winner status was inevitable. When Tiger announced that he was turning professional (in a hard-hitting *Wall Street Journal* Nike advertisement), he declared: "Hello World. There are still courses in the United States I cannot play because of the colour of my skin. Are you ready for me?"

By the time Woods won his first Major (the Masters in 1997), at the tender age of 21, he was a global superstar. Apart from winning the tournament by 12 strokes, he became the first African-American and Asian-American to wear the famous green jacket. Never before – and never again – would Augusta seem so vulnerable. Overnight, Woods had single-handedly transformed the sport, with golf's television viewership breaking the 50 million barrier for the first time.

And, overnight, golf's image as a pastime for the predominantly white, country-club elite had been shattered. The strength of Woods's driving saw many courses in the PGA Tour rotation (including Major Championship sites like Augusta National) lengthen their holes in an effort to reduce the advantage enjoyed by long hitters like him, a strategy that became known as "Tiger-proofing". He had single-handedly raised the game to levels never seen before.

Certainly, in the decade that followed, there was a dramatic increase in the sport's popularity, largely thanks to Woods's contribution. He must be given credit for drawing the largest spectator – and television – audiences in the history of the sport.

When he was in contention for the lead on Major Sundays, this man-turned-myth was responsible for increases of up to 50 per cent in television viewership.

Almost overnight, he had taken the game out of the waspy country clubs and into the ghettos of America, the townships of Africa and the rice paddies of Asia.

Nevertheless, there were concerns that Woods could drive the spirit of competition out of the sport – much the same as Michael Schumacher throttled the competitiveness in Formula One motor racing during his championship reign. Some of the Tour players, only half-jokingly, referred to the PGA as the TGA (Tiger Golf Association).

When asked by *Sports Illustrated* (in the mid-1990s) whether his son would have a greater impact on the world than Nelson Mandela, Mahatma Gandhi or Buddha, Earl Woods said: "Yes, because he has a larger forum than any of them." He went on to describe his son as "the Chosen One", adding that he would have the power "to impact nations".

And when Tiger first met Nelson Mandela in Johannesburg in 1998, his father suggested that "it was the first time that Tiger [has] met a human being equal to him".

Nevertheless, the champion had become a global phenomenon partly because he was not white (he refers to his ethnic make-up as "Cablinasian", a syllabic abbreviation he coined from Caucasian, Black, American Indian and Asian).

During George W. Bush's ill-advised invasion of Iraq in 2004, the following joke did the rounds: "You know you are living in strange times when the world's leading golfer is black, the leading rapper [Eminem] is white and the Germans don't want to go to war."

A SOUTH AFRICAN TIGER?

Famously difficult to read, there was always an air of mystery surrounding Woods, and he carried an aura of invincibility. And yet, there was also a sourness about him. The Open's famous television commentator Peter Alliss said, "He gives nothing back and looks like he hates every minute of it."

Throughout the early 2000s, the untouchable giant was the dominant force in golf, spending 264 weeks from August 1999 to September 2004 and 281 weeks from June 2005 to October 2010 as world number one. He became the youngest player to achieve a career Grand Slam and only the second golfer, after Jack Nicklaus, to achieve a career Grand Slam three times. The list goes on: He was the first athlete to gross $1 billion in earnings and endorsements and, with 14 Majors, was closing in on golf's record of 18, held by Jack Nicklaus.

His red shirts on a Major Sunday became one of the defining images in sport. Muhammad Ali spent much of his glorious career telling everyone who would listen that he was "the Greatest". And few doubted him. But, unlike Ali, it was often difficult to love Woods, the world's greatest golfer. Even at the peak of his powers, with the so-called "Tiger-slam" behind him, he was intensely private, and often surly and aloof.

The highest-paid athlete of all time was always an enigma, a trait he frequently used to his advantage as he steamrolled his opponents.

As South African Major winner Trevor Immelman once observed: "I don't think it's ever easy to win a Major in any era. But you know, I'm playing in Tiger Woods's era. The guy boggles my mind."

Immelman said that he and the rest of the South African contingent, in particular Els and Goosen, have had to deal with the greatest golfer the world has ever seen. "There [is] something surreal about being in the vicinity of him, ahead or behind him … The crowds let you know what is happening. The atmosphere is always charged and, when we played with him, he hit shots that left us scratching our heads."

Els concurs, saying that it was "extremely difficult" competing as a foreigner in the US when Woods was on top of his game and had home support.

And it wasn't just a South African issue. American Davis Love III found himself in a play-off with Woods in Las Vegas in 1996, where Woods secured his first professional victory and then went on to obliterate virtually every golfer (and course) in sight.

Love notes that Woods won about one third of the tournaments he competed in and left many talented golfers in his wake. "Without him, there would have been 75 more wins to be divided up. Think of where that would have left Mickelson, Els and Love," he told *Golf Digest*.

During the 2001 Open Championship, *Sunday Times* columnist Hugh McIlvanney observed that Woods had become as pervasive as the weather in the lives of all other tournament professionals: "His form governs the climate of their existence."

University of California academic Jennifer Brown discovered that other golfers played worse when competing against Woods than when he was not competing in tournaments. Their scores were nearly one stroke higher when playing against Woods. However, this disappeared during his well-publicised slump between 2003 and 2004.

The dramatic turning point in Woods's career occurred late in 2009. Millions of eyebrows around the world raised in unison as news began filtering through that Woods had been involved in a car accident – he had driven his Cadillac Escalade into a fire hydrant, a tree and a couple of hedges – outside his luxury Florida home in the early-morning hours after Thanksgiving. His Swedish wife, Elin Nordegren, had delivered the *coup de grâce* by shattering the rear-view window with a golf club. The world's most influential sports personality was deep in the rough.

Incidentally, for better or worse, the couple had got engaged at South Africa's Shamwari game reserve after the 2003 President's Cup at Fancourt.

There was so much media interest in the visit that a public-relations satellite office was set up to field the calls. The only guest who was permitted to meet Woods was acclaimed conservationist Ian Player (Gary's brother). About 300 staff members at Shamwari celebrated the news of the engagement, but when Woods learnt that it had made the papers, he was furious.

When reports of his extramarital affairs began filtering through, it sent shockwaves around the world. Two days before the accident, on 25 November, the *National Enquirer* had published a report claiming that Woods had had an extramarital affair with New York City nightclub manager Rachel Uchitel, a claim she initially denied.

As the layers began peeling away, Woods, who admitted only to "transgressions", was exposed as a deeply flawed individual, more of a super-freak than a superhero.

Not surprisingly, once his blood was spilt and he was in free fall, his form dipped alarmingly. By November 2011, he had dropped to a career low of 58th in the world.

When Woods chose the eve of the World Match Play Championship in Arizona to make a live, televised apology – in Florida – for his transgressions, Els took a swipe at him.

"It's selfish," he told a reporter from American magazine *Golf Week*. "Mondays are a good day to make statements, not Friday. This takes a lot away from the golf tournament."

And when Woods committed a glaring rules violation during the second round of the 2013 Masters and lived to play another day, Els joined others in claiming that he should have withdrawn from the tournament. "I'm a pro now, since 1989. I've never seen a guy sign for a scorecard and then come back and play the next day after a rules infringement. It's as simple as that."

Woods's decline had coincided remarkably with that of other American heavyweight golfers. For the first time in history, in 2010 there would not be an American winner in any of the four Majors, the Ryder Cup, the Players' Championship or, for that matter, the World Match Play title. The last time all four Majors were held by Americans was way back in 1982.

As the former colossus eventually started emerging from his tabloid hell and began a harrowing journey of self-discovery and a career resurgence, he found himself looking over his shoulder at a growing pool of young and talented golfers who had begun strutting their stuff on the world stage, aware of Woods's ravaged reputation and uninhibited by the precocious talent and the mania that had surrounded him for so long.

As youngsters like Rory McIlroy and Ricky Fowler begin staking their claim, so, too, did a group of hugely talented South Africans. Brandon Grace, Richard Sterne, James Kingston, Anton Haig, Justin Harding, Jake Roos, George Coetzee and Thomas Aiken have all made their mark both locally and abroad. At the 2012 Open at Royal Lytham and St Annes, where Els won his fourth Major, the South African contingent had doubled (from seven to 14) since the tournament was last played at that course 11 years previously. And on the European Tour in 2012, South African golfers won nine times (that's a 20 per cent hit rate).

Despite the fact that there are only 180 000 registered golfers in South Africa, the rude health of the game is underlined by the filtering system from juniors through to the professional divisions, where the weakest are discarded.

And yet there is a troubling trend. Without exception, every Major winner this land has produced has been white. The jury will always be out on whether Papwa Sewgolum would have won a Major, had circumstances been different, and I hope this study has contributed to that debate. Others have demonstrated enormous potential, but have failed to reach the pinnacle of the sport for various reasons.

Ironically, the first black African to play in the US Open was raised in Zambia. Madalitso Muthiya, who was born in Lusaka in 1983, began playing golf at the age of six. As in most African countries, golf takes a back seat to football, and there are only 17 courses located around the country. Muthiya started off with a set of ladies' clubs (with pink grips) and taught himself by watching Nick Faldo instruction videos. As the owner of an insurance company, his father, Peter, was able to support his efforts and, as a teenager, Muthiya caught the eye of Frederick Chiluba. The Zambian president helped arrange for him to play in the 1999 Nolan Henke/Patty Berg Junior Masters in Fort Myers, Florida.

Muthiya won in the 16- to 18-year-old age group and went on to play college golf at the University of New Mexico before turning professional in 2005. He finished second in the 2006 Zambian Open and came through qualifying to become the first Zambian and black African to play in a US Open at the breathtaking Winged Foot Golf Club in New York, a world away from the rough-and-ready courses of Zambia. He may have missed the cut (along with Tiger Woods), but he had become a household name in Zambia and an inspiration for millions of Africans.

Like Papwa Sewgolum, Johannesburg-born Vincent Tshabalala's career was affected by South Africa's race laws. And, like Sewgolum, he used a cross-handed grip to good effect. He tied the SA Non-European Open with Sewgolum in 1965, and won the title in 1971, 1977 and 1983. In May 1976, two months before the Soweto riots, he won the French Open. Later that year, he was selected for South Africa's World Cup team, but refused to take part.

However, there was a reprieve of sorts. Despite a series of injuries, he made a comeback in the over-50 ranks, finishing in the top 20 on the European Seniors Tour Order of Merit four times in the 1990s, despite not winning any tournaments. He also played on the Southern Africa Tour after racial restrictions were abolished in the early 1990s, but by then he was almost 50 and he didn't win any official money events. However, he did win the Nelson Mandela Invitational in both 2004 and 2005, playing with Ernie Els and Tim Clark respectively.

Theo Manyama was regarded as the third member of this trio, the so-called "three giants". Manyama, who was only permitted to play on the Sunshine Tour "at the ripe old age of 30", recalls the visit that changed the landscape for black golfers in South Africa. In 1971, Gary Player received government permission to invite black American golfer Lee Elser to play in the country. Four local golfers – including Manyama – were invited to play against Elders in the PGA at Johannesburg's Huddle Park, but Manyama declined.

Then there is James Kamte. During the 2008 Dimension Data Pro-Am at Sun City, Kamte would refer to his notes whenever the chips were down ("They put their trust in God and were never disappointed" – Psalm 22, Verse 5). The former Eastern Cape caddie went on to win the tournament and, the following year, found himself striding down the fairway at the US Open at Bethpage with none other than Tiger Woods. It may have been only a practice round, but the sight of two black men teamed together at a Major tournament turned many a head.

Kamte, the son of a St Francis Bay labourer, only took up the game at the age of 14. Like Louis Oosthuizen, he is a product of the Ernie Els Foundation. Els described Kamte's qualification for the 109th US Open as "one of the proudest moments of my life".

These are some of the near (and far) misses, underlying the fact that South Africa, with all its depth and diversity, has yet to harvest its own Tiger Woods – a young, talented black golfer who has what it takes to go all the way.

Johan Immelman, the former commissioner of the South Africa Tour and father of Masters champion Trevor, has a different take on the matter: "It's a global problem." After all, apart from a handful of giants like

Woods and Vijay Singh, very few countries have produced top non-white golfers.

Nevertheless, numerous programmes are now in place to ensure that South Africa capitalises on the gains that have been made by the Major winners, and that any so-called "black diamonds" are being identified and nurtured.

Since its formation in 1999, the South African Golf Development Board (SAGDB), a non-profit organisation, has established a network of coaches and officials who work across the country to develop the game in the cities and the most remote areas. With a mission to identify and develop talented players from underprivileged communities, the board has coached over 17 000 youngsters, while several of its most talented players have been invited to join prestigious and recognised high-performance centres.

One of the shining stars of the board is Riaan Grootboom, who has used golf as therapy to help address some of his problems. These include losing his mother in a shack fire in the Borchards Township on the outskirts of George in 2008.

Grootboom and his sister were taken in by their elderly grandmother, but with no counselling available to him, he began rebelling and found himself in trouble with the authorities. At the age of 10, he hit a golf ball for the first time, and the experience changed his life.

SAGDB coach Joseph Booyens recalls the boy's grace and power as he fired golf balls across a rugby field at the Parkdene Primary School.

Within months, Grootboom had mastered the nearby mashie course and was beginning to turn heads at the George Golf Club. And within three years he was playing off a five handicap. As one of the top five in the SAGDB Southern Cape Regional squad, he was selected for specialised coaching at the KeNako Academy in George. "Golf has given me a reason to live," Grootboom says, adding that he aims to win a Major.

Former SAGDB student Musiwalo Nethunzwi is another rising star.

He grew up in Soweto and made history in 2012 by being selected (on merit) to compete in the Africa Zone VI Golf Championships in Malawi. Two other Soweto golfers are also making a charge. Sipho Bujela and Musi Nethunzwi start their day at 4.30 a.m. in Primrose, Soweto. An hour and a half later, they find themselves in the leafy northern suburbs of Johannesburg, where the Gary Player School of Champions is based.

Bujela and Nethunzwi begin their day in earnest with a gym session at the World of Golf from 6 to 8.30 a.m. After a breakfast break, the rest of the morning is spent "learning the technical stuff" with a team of highly trained coaches. After lunch, it's hands-on practising until 3 p.m., and they then spend the rest of the afternoon back at gym or working on their individual game. Both men – they are in their early twenties, are in a similar mould: tall, elastic and lithe. And both are hoping to turn professional "soonest".

There are similar stories throughout the land. Johannes Kutumane, for example, is a long-time member of Mowbray Golf Club and caddied for Cobie le Grange in the 1970s and 1980s (Le Grange, incidentally, beat Jack Nicklaus head-to-head to win the Australian Masters, and he also won the British and South African Masters).

Kutumane's four sons, Jack, Gary, Nicklaus and Arnold (named after you know who), share his love of golf. Of the four, Jack has made the biggest gains (so far). By the age of 13, he was a scratch handicap who had a string of junior titles and a small green jacket to show for winning the South African Mini Masters in 2002. He subsequently received an annual invitation to compete for the Enchede Golf Club in the Netherlands and, in 2005, was crowned the club champion.

By 2013, there were nearly 50 non-white players on the Sunshine Tour, the gateway to the global tours. One of the more promising youngsters on the tour is Teboho Sefatsa, who won the feeder Big Easy Tour of Merit and the BMG Classic in 2012.

A SOUTH AFRICAN TIGER?

Hannes van Niekerk, CEO of the Ernie Els & Fancourt Foundation, concedes that "every effort" is being made to identify talented non-white golfers.

At any given time, 24 members of the foundation make up the so-called Ernie's Army, which was established in 1999. Most of the students live on site and attend a local school in George. Members have access to hands-on training, practice facilities and some of the most magnificent courses in the world, including the Gary Player–designed Links Course, which hosted the 2003 President's Cup.

Van Niekerk says about 85 per cent of their members are underprivileged, and the only Major winner it has produced – Oosthuizen – is white. Another pale-male graduate of this foundation is Brandon Grace, whose four victories on the European Tour in 2012 propelled him into the top 50 in the world.

In 1986, Ernie Els broke Bobby Locke's 51-year-old record by becoming the youngest South African Amateur Champion. Since then, there have been three 16-year-old Amateur champions. The most recent is Thriston Lawrence, who was crowned 2013 champion at the Johannesburg Country Club at the age of 16 years and 88 days.

When Els secured his title, his father Neels was at his side. Twenty-seven years later, Neels caddied for his grandson – Ernie's nephew – at the same tournament. Jovan Rebula, South Africa's under-15 stroke-play champion, is turning heads everywhere and is threatening to follow in the giant footsteps of his famous uncle.

Jovan is the son of Els's sister Carina and her Serbian husband, Dragan. A scratch-handicap golfer from the age of 14 (just like his uncle), he has been one of the country's standout junior players. And another Els nephew is also making waves. Dirk (Ernie's brother) and Sunette Els's son, Reece, was playing off a 13-handicap at the age of 11 and has a bright future.

One of the most exciting prospects at the Els Foundation is Prinavin Nelson, like Papwa Sewgolum "a Durban-born Indian". "He is one of the members I'm most proud of. He's dedicated, a very focused youngster and one of the best amateurs in South Africa right now," Van Niekerk said.

I asked Ernie Els for his take on why a non-white global champion has yet to come through the ranks. "I am really not sure why it hasn't happened. The programmes are in place for everyone. I'm sure it's inevitable."

Time will tell.

References

BOOKS

Alliss, Peter. *The Open*. London: William Collins Sons & Co., 1984
Anderson, Dave. *The Story of Golf*. New York: Beech Tree, 1998
Bishop, John, and Tiki Dickson. *Talking Balls*. Cape Town: Zebra Press, 2009
Canale, Norman. *Snakes in the Garden of Eden*. Cape Town: Don Nelson Publishers, 2013
Canfield, Jack. *Chicken Soup for the Golfer's Soul*. Florida: Health Communications, 1999
Cooper, Michael, and Tim Goodenough. *In The Zone*. Cape Town: Zebra Press, 2009
Dabell, Norman. *One Hand on the Claret Jug*. Edinburgh: Mainstream Publishing Company, 2006
Feinstein, John. *A Good Walk Spoiled*. Toronto: Little, Brown and Company, 1995
———. *The Majors*. London: Little, Brown and Company, 1999
Johnston, Barry. *The Wit of Golf*. London: Hodder & Stoughton, 2010
Joyce, Peter. *100 Memorable Sporting Moments*. Cape Town: Zebra Press, 2012
Heney, Hank. *The Big Miss*. New York: Crown Archetype, 2012
Keohane, Mark, and Gary Lemke. *Business Day (50 Great Reads)*. Cape Town: Highbury Safika, 2010
Locke, Bobby. *Bobby Locke on Golf*. London: Country Life Limited, 1953
Lusetic, Robert. *Unplayable – An Inside Account of Tiger's Most Tumultuous Season*. London: Simon & Shuster, 2010
McCormack, Mark. *The World of Professional Golf 1995*. Henley-on-Thames: Watchword Books, 1995
Murray, Francis. *The Open – A Twentieth Century History*. London: Pavilion Books Limited, 2000
Newell, Steve. *A Round with the Tour Pros*. London: Collins Willow, 2002
Nicholson, Chris. *Papwa Sewgolum: From Pariah to Legend*. Johannesburg: Wits University Press, 2005

O'Donnell, Paddy. *South Africa's Wonderful World of Golf.* Cape Town: Don Nelson Publishers, 1973
Pinner, John. *The History of Golf.* London: New Burlington Books, 1988
Player, Gary. *Grand Slam Golf.* London: Cassell & Company, 1966
Player, Gary, and Michael McDonnel. *To Be the Best.* London: Pan Books, 1992
Rhoodie, Eschel. *The Real Information Scandal.* Pretoria: Orbis SA, 1983
Rice, Jonathan. *Curiosities of Golf.* London: Pavilion Books Limited, 2003
Rotella, Rob. *Golf Is Not a Game of Perfect.* New York: Simon & Schuster, 1995
Vlismas, Michael. *Extraordinary Book of South African Golf.* Johannesburg: Penguin Books, 2012
Vlismas, Michael, and Gary Player. *Don't Choke.* Cape Town: Zebra Press, 2010
Ward, Andrew. *Golf's Strangest Rounds.* London: Robson Books, 2007
Williams, Michael. *Grand Slam.* London: Hamlyn Publishing Group, 1989
Worrall, Frank. *Rory McIlroy – The Biography.* London: John Blake Publishing, 2012
Zingg, Paul. *An Emerald Odyssey.* Cork: The Collins Press, 2008
Zullo, Allan, and Chris Rodell. *When Bad Things Happen to Good Golfers.* Kansas City: Andrews McMeel Publishing, 1998

NEWSPAPERS AND MAGAZINES
Business Day
CompleatGolfer
Golf Digest
Golf World
Sports Illustrated
The Leader
The New York Times
The Telegraph
Washington Post

WEBSITES
www.masters.com
www.theopen.com

Index

Aaron, Tommy 45
Achenbach, Jim 132
Ackerman, Raymond 28
African Cup of Nations
   (1996) 10
African National Congress
   (ANC) 9, 167–168
Agg, Frank 24
albatrosses 260–261
   Oosthuizen, Masters,
     Augusta 2012 1,
     244–245, 261–266
   Gene Sarazen, Masters,
     Augusta 1935
     242-243
Albertinia 246
alcohol 15, 27, 34, 52, 53,
   115, 116, 118, 159, 165,
   185, 280
Allem, Fulton 55

Allenby, Robert 216
Alliss Peter 18, 20, 22, 80,
   175, 297
Amen Corner, Augusta
   235–236
American courses and
   playing style 74, 128
American Golf Hall of
   Fame 52
American Golfer, The 158
Anglo-Boer War 123, 252
apartheid 6, 9, 30, 55–56,
   90–91
   and anti-apartheid
     movement 54, 81–83,
     90, 119, 135
   District Six 292

Group Areas Act 106, 107
   and 'open' tournaments 98
   and Player 81–83, 87–88,
     90–92
   and SA sport 87–88,
     119–120
   and Sewgolum 104,
     106–111, 112–115
   Soweto uprising 122
Appleby, Stuart 176
Aronimink, Philadelphia 76
Augusta 230–231
   albatrosses at 1, 243,
     244–245, 261–266
   Amen Corner 235–236
   Magnolia Lane 64, 230
   menu selection 258–259
   race and gender politics 91

Baiocchi, Hugh 13
Ballesteros, Seve 76, 95,
   145, 148–149, 166, 239,
   258, 267, 275, 279
Barclays Bank 59, 103
Barkow, Al 23
Barnard, Chris 88
Beachwood Golf Club 94,
   95, 96, 97
belly putters 182–183,
   196–197
Beuthin, Gary 56–57
Big Five 179, 217
Big Three 77–78
black golfers, SA 13, 300
   development of 302–306
   Ishmael Chowglay 12, 110
   Jack Kutumane 304
   James Kamte, 302

Johannes Kutumane 304
Lawrence Buthelezi 4
Madalitso Muthiya
   300–301
Musi Nethunzwi 303, 304
Prinavin Nelson 306
Ramnath "Bambata"
   Boodham 12
Riaan Grootboom 303
Sipho Bujela 304
Teboho Sefatsa 304
Theo Manyama 302
Vincent Tshabalala 12, 95,
   301–302
see also Sewgolum,
   Sewsunker Papwa
Black Panthers 83
Blalock, Jane 132–133
Bland, John 55
Blumberg, George 64
Bobby Locke Place, Yeoville
   41, 55, 56, 60–61
Bodmer, Bobby 27
Bodmer, Maurice 27–28,
   48–50
Boers 15–16, 202
   Anglo-Boer War 123, 252
Boodham, Ramnath
   "Bambata" 12
Boon, Ron 57
Booyens, Joseph 303
"born free" golfers 9–10
Botha, P.W. 167, 205
Bradshaw, Harry 36–38
Braid, James 43
Brews, Sid 12, 25, 28, 104
Brooks, Mark 208–209,
   211–213

309

Brown, Deon 223
Brown, Eric 44
Brown, Oliver 269, 287
Brutus, Dennis 106
Bruyns, Dennis 20
Buchan, Angus 277
Budd, Zola 120
Bujela, Sipho 304
Bullock, Fred 72, 73
Buthelezi, Lawrence 4
Buthelezi, Mangosuthu 4

Cabrera, Ángel 258, 281
caddies
   importance of 151
   origins of 3
   see also specific caddies
Caddyshack movie 201, 240
Calcavecchia, Mark 253
Calder, Sherylle 185–188, 193
Canale, Norman 24, 68, 115
Cape Golf Club 294
Caponi Young, Donna 132
Carner, JoAnne 132
Carnoustie 79–80
Casey, Paul 254, 255
Casper, Billy 80, 127
Catherine of Aragon 3
Champions Tour 10–11
Chandler, Chubby 275, 287
Chitengwa, Lewis 228
choking 209–210
chole 2
Chowglay, Ishmael 12, 110
Churchill, Winston 5
Cink, Stewart 208–209
Clampett, Bobby 146
Claret Jug 146, 147, 156, 177
Clark, Tim 2, 13, 302
Clarke, Darren 35, 196, 207, 275
Clovelly Country Club 28, 49, 61–63
Cohen, Barry 61–63
Cole, Bobby 12
Committee for Fairness in Sport 87–88

condor 265
Cotton, Henry 25, 28, 131
Cowen, Pete 273, 276
Cradle of Humankind 15–16
Crampton, Bruce 44
Crawley, Leonard 24
Crenshaw, Ben 231–232
cross-handed grip 95, 142, 301

Dabell, Norman 146
Daily Mail 40
Daily News 105, 109
Daily Mirror 109
Daily Telegraph 286
Daly, Fred 40, 42–43
Daly, John 145, 159, 214
Darnley, Lord 3
Dart, Professor Raymond 16
Darwin, Bernard 35, 252
Davies, David 211
Davies, Laura 136
Day, Jason 281, 283, 284, 286
De Klerk, F.W. 107, 167, 205
Demaret, Jimmy 32, 45
Deneysville 271
De Vicenzo, Roberto 40, 45–46
De Villiers, Dawie 119
De Wit, Gerard 104
Dibnah, Corinne 136
District Six 292
divots 83, 237
Dobereiner, Peter 7–8
D'Oliveira, Basil 119
Donald, Luke 184, 221, 284–285
Durban Country Club 107–110, 121
Durban Indian Golf Club 94, 100
Dyer, Alfred "Rabbit" 84, 85, 86, 91

Edgar, J. Douglas 33
Elkington, Steve 172, 176
Els, Ben 177, 183–184, 196

Els, Ernie
1984 Junior World Golf Championship, San Diego 167
1989 Open, Royal Troon 167
1994 US Open, Oakmont Country Club, Pittsburgh 152, 157, 169–172
1994 World Match Play tournament 165–166
1995 PGA Championship, Riviera Country Club, Los Angeles 172–173
1997 US Open, Congressional, Washington, D.C. 173
2000 US Open, Pebble Beach 162–164
2002 Open Championship, Muirfield 175–177
2004 Open, Royal Troon 178
2004 wins 177
2010 US Open, Pebble Beach 181
2012 British Open, Royal Lytham & St Annes 188–196
2012 US Open, Olympic Club, San Francisco 188
and alcohol 185
and the belly putter 182–183, 196
birth and childhood 165–167
early achievements 166–167
early professional achievements 169
Els for Autism Foundation 184–185
Els for Autism Pro Am 184
Ernie Els & Fancourt Foundation 247, 305

INDEX

Ernie Els Foundation 1, 302
  and Goosen 212, 213, 214
  injury 2005 179
  later achievements 195–196
  and Leadbetter 180
  legacy 197
  and Locke 167, 169
  and Montgomerie 170, 171, 173–174, 175
  motor car accident 168–169
  and Nelson Mandela 10, 172
  and Norman 197
  and Oosthuizen 246, 247, 256, 259
  Oubaai links course, Garden Route 117
  and Player 166, 167, 169
  putting 180, 182–183, 186, 187–188
  slump, 2000 & 2001 175
  slump, 2005–2012 179–182
  son's autism 183–185
  turns professional 167
  and Vanstiphout 180–181
  wins triple-crown 169
  and Woods 162–164, 175, 189–191, 197–199, 299
Els, Liezl 177, 183, 184
Els, Neels 165, 166
Els, Reece 305
emerging SA golfers 303–306
Erleigh, Norbert 24
Evans, Doug 71
Eye-Gym computer program 187–188

Faldo, Nick 148–149, 152, 157, 281, 282
Faxon, Brad 153
fear 65
Feherty, David 177, 182, 244

Feinstein, John 12
female champions, South Africa 13
Fenton, Mary 33–34, 48, 55, 57
FIFA World Cup, 2010 124
Finsterwald, Dow 64
Flesch, Steve 236
Floyd, Ray 45, 82
Formula One racing 120
Fotheringham, George 36
Fraser, Sally 100, 101
Frost, David 13
Furyk, Jim 188

Galant, Martin 294
Gallwey, Tim 207
Gandhi, Mahatma 5, 96
García, Sergio 195, 207, 226, 237–238
Gary Player School of Champions 304
Geiberger, Al 249
gender 91, 127–128, 138
George Golf Club 246, 303
Germiston golf course 17, 18
Gibb, Maud 13
Gibson, Perla 140
Goalby, Bob 45, 76
gold 16–17
golf
  Bobby Jones on 36, 65, 248
  early history 2–4
  equipment, changes to 158
  Hale Irwin on 65
  Mark Twain on 164
  on the moon 264–465
  origins 2
  Pat Ruddy on 66
  "perfect" round of 248
  rules 36–37, 44–47
golf course design 28–29, 76
  Augusta 261–262
  "Tiger-proofing" 295
Golf Digest 46, 67, 95, 224, 295, 298

Golf magazine 82
Golf World 131, 203
Goosen, Francois 202
Goosen, Retief 5, 10, 177, 178
  2001 US Open, Southern Hills Country Club, Oklahoma 208–213
  2002-2003 results 214–215
  2004 US Open, Shinnecock Hills 177, 215–217
  2005 US Open, Pinehurst 217
  achievements 2005 217
  and the Big Five 179, 217
  birth and childhood 202–203
  demeanour 204
  early professional successes 206–207
  and Els 212, 213, 214
  injuries 217, 218, 219
  and the Masters 2
  military service 205
  mixed results 1990s 206–207
  mixed results 2006–2012 217–218
  putting 209, 211, 216
  Retief Goosen Charitable Foundation 219
  steady head 205
  struck by lightning 202–205
  and Tracy Retief 206, 208
  turns professional 206
  and Vanstiphout 201, 205, 207–208, 212, 213
  and Woods 217
Goosen, Theo 202, 203, 210
Grace, Brandon 300, 305
Graham, David 172
Grand Slam 79, 201, 243, 297
Granger, Dale 224
Green, Butch 20, 50

311

Green, Hubert 89–90, 166
Grootboom, Riaan 303

Hackett, Bob 34, 53
Hagen, Walter 19, 40, 44, 157, 210, 243
Hain, Peter 114
Halt All Racist Tours (HART) 114
Hamilton, Todd 178
Hammond, Clark 23
Hansen, Soren 175
Harmon, Butch 35, 180, 199, 237–238, 267
Harmon, Claude 35, 241
Havers, Arthur 39
Hawkes, Jeff 120
Hayes, Dale 12, 24, 125, 262, 271, 272, 276
Hayes, Otway 24
Hearmon, Greg 282, 287
Henderson, Judy 132
Heney, Hank 198, 199
Henning, Allan 109, 111
Henning, Harold 12, 62, 71, 73, 109, 111
Hepburn, Grant 273–274
Hogan, Ben 21, 31, 69, 79, 83, 186, 258
   1951 US Open 41–42
   and Locke 21, 32, 35
   motor accident 50–51
Hope, Bob 32
Hutchinson, Denis 35, 55, 77, 106, 108

Immelman, Carminita 235
Immelman, Johan 221–222, 302–303
Immelman, Mark 222, 229, 232
Immelman, Trevor 183, 297
   2001 & 2004 South African Open 225
   2007 Nedbank Golf Challenge, Sun City 226–227
   2007 Nedbank Golf Challenge, Sun City 221
   2008 Masters, Augusta 229–230, 231–240
   birth and childhood 221–223
   career as a teenager 223
   coached by Mark Immelman 229
   and David Leadbetter 223, 226
   description of 225
   early professional career 225–226
   and Els 225, 232, 234, 239
   illnesses and injuries 227–229, 240–241
   marries Carminita 225
   menu selection, Augusta 258
   on-course etiquette 223–224
   and Player 221, 232, 234, 235, 239
   putting 231–232, 234, 238
   rehabilitation after surgery 229–230
   swing 221
   tumour in diaphragm 221, 227–229
   turns professional 225
   and Woods 226, 229, 233, 235, 236, 237, 239, 297
Indians in South Africa
   as indentured labourers 94
   discrimination against 96–97, 107–108
Information Scandal 88–89
International Sports Management (ISM) 275
Irwin, Hale 65, 151
Ishikawa, Ryo 181, 248, 286

Jiménez, Ángel 163, 164
Johnstone, Tony 12
Jones, Angela 205
Jones, Bobby 148, 192, 201, 243, 248, 252, 261
   and Locke 18, 19, 31, 32, 39, 40
   on golf 36, 65, 248

Kamte, James 302
KeNako Academy, George 303
Kerzner, Sol 226
Killarney Golf Club 70
King Edward VII High School 7, 68
Kingston, James 228 ,300
Korsen, Tracy 60–61
Kutumane, Jack 304
Kutumane, Johannes 304

ladies' professional golf 127–128, 129
Ladies' Professional Golf Association (LPGA) 127, 128
Langer, Bernhard 146, 239
Lawrence, Thriston 305
Lawton, James 64
Leadbetter, David
   and Els 180
   and Immelman 223, 226
   and Price 145
Lees, Arthur 40
Le Grange, Cobie 108, 304
Lehman, Tom 26, 173–174, 189, 190
Levenson, Gavan 13, 273, 281, 288
Levet, Thomas 176
lightning 201–204
links 28–29
Little, Lawson 23
Little, Percy 124
Little, Sally 2, 13, 122–123
   1978 Colgate Women's

INDEX

PGA European
  Championship 131–132
1978 US Open 132
1980 LPGA
  Championship, Mason,
  Ohio 132–133
1982 Nabisco Dinah
  Shore 134
1986–1988 136
1988 du Maurier Ltd
  Classic 136–137
1989 Ben Hogan
  Award 137
and the American
  game 128
and anti-apartheid
  activists 122, 135
birth and youth 124–125
descriptions of 123, 127
diagnosed with
  endometriosis 135
early achievements
  125–126
early professional titles
  129–131
knee injury 125, 128
motorcycle accident at 15
  125, 134
overweight 129
and Player 125, 135
return to SA 2005 137
Sally Little Charitable
  Trust 138
Southern Africa Golf
  Hall of Fame 138
three wins, 1981 133
US citizenship 135
Women's International,
  Moss Creek Plantation
  129–131
Locke, Bobby 1, 7, 15
  1939 Dutch Open,
    The Hague 104
  1946 Open, St Andrews
    28–29
  1947–49, PGA Tour, US
    31–35, 38–39

1949 Open, Royal
  St George's 35–38
1950 Open, Troon 39–41
1951 US Open, Oakland
  Hills 41–42
1952 Open, Royal Lytham
  & St Annes 42–43
1957 Open, St Andrews
  43–45, 47
and alcohol 15, 34, 52, 53
birth of 15, 17
Bobby Locke on Golf
  18, 26
and Bob Hackett 34
childhood 17–19
conflict with US PGA
  35, 38–39
death and funeral of
  54–55
demeanour 19
dress 24
drive and approach 19–20
early career 24–25
hook ball flight 20
and Lilian Locke 28, 43
at Maccauvlei club 25
and Mary Fenton
  33–34, 48
and Maurice Bodmer
  27–28, 48–50
and money 33
motor car accident 48–52
and Observatory Golf
  Club 54
and Parkview golf
  course 54
and Player 8–9, 15, 23, 43
putters of 18, 21, 50,
  57–59
putting 15, 18, 20–24, 32,
  36, 62
R&A Golf Club honorary
  member 53
record of titles 48
and Rob Rotella 22, 34–35
and Sam Snead 11, 29,
  31, 59

shooting of Ndlovu 53
short game 20
stance 20, 21
temper of 18–19
"trusty rusty" putter 18
ukulele of 15, 42, 63
World Golf Hall of
  Fame 53
WW II, South African
  Air Force 25–27
Locke, Carolyn 48, 55–57,
  58, 59, 60, 61
Locke, Lilian 28, 43
Locke, Mary 33–34, 48, 55,
  58, 59, 60
Longhurst, Henry 31
Lopez, Nancy 128, 131, 132
Love, Davis III 141
Lowe, Jack 97, 99
Luyt, Louis 87–88
Lyle, Sandy 146, 149, 258

Maccauvlei Golf Club 25,
  271
MacKenzie, Alister 29
Madame Tussauds 43
Maggert, Jeff 151, 173–174,
  245, 260
Magnolia Lane, Augusta
  64, 230
Majors, the 2, 4, 12, 179, 197
Mandela, Nelson 1, 5, 8,
  9–10, 30, 123, 167–168,
  169, 293
  and Ernie Els 10, 172, 196
  and Oosthuizen 255
  and Player 91, 92
  and Woods 296
Mangrum, Lloyd 23
Manyama, Theo 302
Marting, Harold 37
Mary Queen of Scots 3
Mbeki, Thabo 121
McCauley, pastor Ray 56–57
McCormack, Mark 77
McDonnell, Michael 85
McDowell, Graeme 181, 188

313

McIlroy, Rory 241, 269–270, 300
   and Oosthuizen 253
   and Schwartzel 281, 282, 287–288
McKenzie, Jimmy 59
Medlin, Jeff "Squeaky" 151, 152, 155, 159–160
Metropolitan golf course, Cape Town 123–124
Metz, Richard 59–60
Mickelson, Phil 156, 167, 177, 178, 179, 191, 198, 199, 208, 215–216, 217, 222, 232, 248, 258, 260, 267, 286
Miller, Johnny 211, 260
Million Dollar Challenge, Sun City 6–7, 226
Mitchell, Wayne 262–264
Montgomerie, Colin 156, 170, 171, 173, 174, 175, 212
Moriarty, Jim 195
Morris, Karl 251, 261
Morris, Tom 260
Mossel Bay Golf Club 245, 247
Mowbray Golf Club 293
Mozambique 100
Mugabe, Robert 9, 139
Muirfield 72
Muthiya, Madalitso 300–301
Myers, Joe 239

Nagle, Ken 78–79
Nasser, Colonel 43
Nel, Bertu 249
Nelson, Byron 31, 32
Nelson, Louis 105
Nelson, Prinavin 306
Nethunzwi, Musi 303–304
New York Times 11, 33, 152, 224
New Zealand and apartheid 112, 119–120

Nicholas, Alison 136
Nicholson, Chris. *From Pariah to Legend* 107
Nicklaus, Jack 4, 7, 79, 146–147, 148, 153, 156, 164, 209–210, 297
   and Gary Player 7, 10–11, 76, 77–78, 80–81, 82, 85
   and Schwartzel 279–280
Nipper, Ernest 83, 91
Norman, Greg 92, 151, 152–153, 155–157, 197, 256, 282
Norval, Ronald 23

Oakmont Country Club, Pittsburgh 169–170
Obama, Barack 91
Observatory Golf Club 54
Ogilvy, Geoff 195, 281, 284, 285
Oil of Olay 98
Olander, Clarence 24
Olazábal, José María 157, 169
Olympic Games 9
O'Meara, Mark 157
Oosterhuis, Peter 85, 86
Oosthuizen, Louis
   2010 Open Championship, St Andrews 1, 251–257
   2012 Masters, Augusta 257–268
   albatross, Masters' Sunday, Augusta, 2012 1, 244–245, 261–266
   amateur career 247–250
   birth 245
   car accident before birth 245
   childhood 246–247
   description of 244
   early professional career 250–251
   and Els 246, 247, 256, 259
   injuries 257
   and Karl Morris 251
   and Mandela 255

   and McIlroy 253
   and Mickelson 260
   near-death experience age 9 246
   nicknamed "Shrek" 250
   and Schwartzel 259, 278, 286
   scores of 57 and 59 248–249
   temperament 247–248, 250
   and Vaughn Tucker 246, 247, 257
   and Wynand Stander 247, 248, 261–262, 268
   and Zack Rasego 250, 252, 255
Oosthuizen, Nel-Mare 255
Oosthuizen, Piet 245, 246
Oubaai links course, Garden Route 117

Palmer, Arnold 4, 64, 66, 170
   and Player 23, 75, 76, 77–78
Papwa Sewgolum Golf Course 121
Parkview golf course 54, 55
Parnevik, Jesper 153–156
Paul, Fred 110, 112
Payne, Billy 258
Pienaar, Francois 168
Pietersburg (later Polokwane) 5, 202, 270
Pignon, Fred 40
Pinnacle Point Golf Club 247
Player, Gary 1–2, 7–8, 45
   1959 Open, Muirfield 72–74
   1961 Masters, Augusta 75–76
   1962 Masters, Augusta 64–65, 66
   1965 US Open, Bellerive Country Club in Missouri 73–79

INDEX

1968 Open, Carnoustie 79–81
1969 PGA Championship, NCR Country Club in Dayton 81–82
1972 PGA Championship, Oakland Hills Country Club 83–84
1974 Open at Royal Lytham & St Annes 84–87
2009 Masters, Augusta 90
on American courses and playing style 74
and anti-apartheid protests 81–83
and apartheid 81–83, 87–88, 90–92
birth and childhood 66–69, 95
and black 235
bunkers 70
career achievements 92
cheating allegations 86–87
and the Committee for Fairness in Sport 87–88
death of mother 67–68
early career 70–71
and Els 166, 167, 169, 179
father of 66–67
Grand Slam 79
Grand Slam Golf 67
and Hogan 69
and Immelman 221, 232, 234, 235, 239
and the Information Scandal 88–89
Karoo farm 89
later career 115–116
and Locke 8–9, 15, 23, 43, 62
and luck 70
and Mandela 92
marriage and children 71
and the mind 65, 78

and Nicklaus 7, 10–11, 76, 77–78, 80–81, 82, 85
nutrition 77, 78
on Palmer 23
self-hypnosis 65, 78
and Sewgolum 103, 111, 112, 115
short stature 66, 68
swing of 70
and "The Big Three" 77–78
and "the Black Knight" 69
To Be the Best 82, 83
training and exercise 65, 77, 78, 92
and travel 11
and Virginia Park golf course 69, 70
and Vivienne Verwey 69, 70, 71
Player, Ian 66, 67
Plummer, Jack 59
Potgieter, Henri 203
Potter, Stephen 151
Pottick, Tracy 206, 208
Pratt, Alfred 26, 27, 51–52
Price, Nick 9, 13, 77
  1982 Major Championship, Troon 145–148
  1983 joins PGA full time 148
  1983 World Series of Golf 148
  1988 Open, Royal Lytham & St Annes 148–150
  1992 PGA Championship, Bellerive Country Club in St Louis 151–152
  1994 Open Championship at Turnberry 152–156
  1994 PGA Championship, Southern Hills, Tulsa 156–157
  achievements 1992–1994 152, 157
  as an amateur 143

background and birth 140–141
career wins 160
childhood 142–143
coached by David Leadbetter 145
decline of career 158–160
description of 141
early professional career, 1978 144–145
and Medlin 151, 152, 159
putting 145, 154–155, 158
and Rotella 145, 150–151
swing 145, 158
and tobacco 142–143
turning point 1991 151
and Woods 158, 160
World Golf Hall of Fame 160
and Zimbabwe liberation war 143–144
Price, Sue 155, 159, 161
Price, Wendy 156
Purves, William Laidlaw 35
putting 186–187, 209–210
  belly putters 182–183, 196–197
  choking 209–210
  past and present 24
  see also under individual golfers
Pyles, Steve 58

racial discrimination
  Augusta 91
  New Zealand Maoris 112
  SA golf clubs 107–108, 294
Rafferty, Ronan 153
Rand Daily Mail 109
Rasego, Zack 250, 252, 255
Ray, Ted 78
Rebula, Jovan 305
Rees, Dai 4, 40
Reeves, Jill 56–57
Retief, Dan 23
Reverse grip 95, 142, 301
Rhoodie, Eschel 88

315

Rice, Condoleezza 39
Robben Island 123, 293
Roberts, Clifford 91, 129, 231
Roberts, Loren 170–172
Roberts, Ricci 166, 171, 181, 189, 195
Robert the Bruce 146
Robson, Ivor 190, 195
Rodríguez, Chi Chi 95, 289
Rodriguez, Sixto 6
Rose, Justin 2, 233, 280, 288
Ross, Donald 76
Rotella, Rob 11–12
   on Augusta 66
   Golf Is Not a Game of Perfect 66, 186–187
   and Locke 22, 34–35
   and Price 145, 150–151
   on putting 186–187
Royal and Ancient (R&A) Golf Club of St Andrews 3, 47–48
Royal Cape Golf Club 294
Royal Lytham & St Annes golf course 84, 190, 191, 193–194
Royal St George's golf course 35
Royal Troon golf course 39, 145, 146
Ruddy, Pat 65–66
rugby 10, 114, 119–120, 168
   Rugby World Cup (1995 and 2007) 10, 168
rules 36–37, 44–47
Rupert, Johann 185, 279–280

Sabbatini, Rory 2, 12, 224, 225, 239
SABC 69, 109
Sanders, Doug 209–210
Sarazen Bridge 243
Sarazen, Gene 28, 79, 244, 245
   albatross, 1935 Masters, Augusta 242–243

Sarazen World Open 159
Sauerman, Peter 25
Sauers, Gene 151
Sbonelo Foundation 240
Schieffer, Bob 149–150
Schreiner, Olive 6
Schwartzel, Attie 271, 285, 288
Schwartzel, Charl 2, 5
   2010 Championship, Blue Monster, Florida 278
   2011 Masters, Augusta 279–288
   and Angus Buchan 277
   birth and childhood 257, 270–273
   and Chubby Chandler 275, 287
   and Dale Hayes 271, 272, 276
   early amateur achievements 272, 275, 276
   early professional games 276–277, 278
   and Els 272, 278, 287
   and Gavan Levenson 273, 281, 288
   and Greg Hearmon 282, 287
   marries Rosalind Jacobs 288
   and McIlroy 282, 287–288
   menu selection, Augusta 258–259
   and Nicklaus 279–280
   nickname "The Machine" 271
   and Oosthuizen 259, 278, 286
   as a pilot 277, 288
   and Player 281
   and Price 279
   slump after 2011 Masters 288–290
   swing 272, 273–274
   temperament 277, 290

   time out, Namibia 277–278
   turns professional 276
   and Woods 270
Schwartzel, George 270–271, 272, 273, 275, 278, 285–286
Schwartzel, Rosalind 2
Scotland and early history of golf 2–3
Scott, Adam 190–196, 221, 281, 283, 284, 285
Sefatsa, Teboho 304
Sewgolum, Nisharlan 117–118
Sewgolum, Rajen 97, 117–118
Sewgolum, Sewsunker Papwa 9, 13
   1959 Dutch Open 103–104
   1959 European Open Championship 99, 103
   1960 Dutch Open 106
   1961 South African Open 106–107
   1963 Natal Open 107–110
   1964 South African Open 110–111
   1965 Natal Open 111–112
   1965 South African Open 112
   1966 Natal Open 112
   1967 Open Championship, Royal Liverpool 114
   1970 Open, St Andrews 115
   1977 Natal Open for "non-whites" 115
   albatross 96
   and alcohol 115, 118
   and apartheid 104, 106–111, 112–115
   awarded the Order of Ikhamanga 120–121
   birth 94

INDEX

in Calcutta 114
childhood 93–96
death 116
decline of 116, 118
early successes 97–98
flight to Europe, 1959 99–102
funding of 105
funeral 116–117
and Graham Wulff 97–103, 116
grip 95
marriage and children 97
Natal Non-European tournament 107
Papwa Sewgolum Golf Course 121
Papwa – The Lost Dream of a South African Golfing Legend 104
From Pariah to Legend. Chris Nicholson 107
and Player 103, 111, 112, 115
prize-giving, 1963 Natal Open 9, 108–110, 118–119, 120–121
raid by security police 112 and Security Branch 112
spirituality 96
Western Province Open 112–113
Shah of Iran 4
Sheard, Alison 13, 126
Shepard, Alan 264–465
Simon, Ashleigh 137
Simpson, Sir Walter. *The Art of Golf* 209
Simpson, Webb 188, 196
Singh, Vijay 46, 115, 145, 169, 179, 217, 303
Smith, Ian 139
smoking 76, 116, 142–143, 159
Smuts, General Jan 96
Smyth, Des 146
Snead, Sam 30–31, 65, 73, 95
and Bobby Locke 11, 23, 29, 31, 32–33, 59, 251

Snedeker, Brandt 191, 233, 234, 235, 236, 237
soccer 119
2010 FIFA World Cup 124, 252
Somerset West Golf Club 222, 223
South Africa 5–8
barred from Olympics 9
emerging golfers 303–306
female champions 13
first democratic elections 169
great golfers not winning Majors 12–13
negotiated settlement 167–168
see also apartheid
South African Golf Development Board (SAGDB) 303
South African Golf Union (SAGU) 106
Southern Africa Golf Hall of Fame 59, 126, 138, 197
Soweto uprising 122
sports boycotts 109, 112, 114, 119, 120
sports psychologists 11–12, 66
Morris, Karl 251, 261
Vanstiphout, Jos 180–181, 205, 207–208, 219–220
see also Rotella, Rob
Sports Science Institute, Cape Town 185
Stacy, Hollis 130, 134
Stander, Wynand 247, 248, 261–262, 268, 290
St Andrews golf course 1, 28–29, 251, 252, 255
St Andrews Golfing Society 3
Stellenbosch Academy of Sport 185
Stephenson, Jan 130
Sterne, Richard 238, 276, 288, 300
Stewart, Payne 162–163, 216

Sun City 6–7
Sunshine Tour 221, 250, 259, 304
Sutton, Norman 36
Suzman, Helen 110
Swaelens, Donald 114

Table Mountain 291–292
Tait, Frederick 252
Taitz, Colin 58
Tebbutt, Gillian 126
Telegraph, The 68, 205
television 32, 45, 69, 166, 181, 231, 295–296
tennis, women's 131
Thomson, Peter 42–43, 44, 45, 48, 194
"Tiger-proofing" golf courses 295
Time magazine 33
Trevino, Lee 7, 20, 153, 196, 202
Troon golf course 39, 145, 146
Truth and Reconciliation Commission 5
Tshabalala, Vincent 12, 95, 301–302
Tucker, Vaughn 246, 247, 257
Turner, Greg 153
Tutu, Desmond 5, 54, 69
Twain, Mark 164

UN General Assembly 96, 97, 114
United Nations Centre Against Apartheid 120
Urquhart, Craig 203
and death of Payne Stewart 162
and Locke 7
meeting Schwartzel 290
and Player 8
and Rajen and Nisharlan Sewgolum 117–119
reporting on crime 56
on South Africa 5

317

USGA Golf Journal 23

Van de Velde, Jean 210–211
Van Niekerk, Hannes 305
Van Rensburg, John 245, 246
Van Rensburg, Nico 168
Vanstiphout, Jos 180–181, 205, 207–208, 219–220
Vardon, Harry 24, 43, 78, 86, 248, 252
Vereeniging Country Club 28
Verwey, Bobby 108
Verwey, Jock 69, 70
Verwey, Vivienne 69, 70, 71
Verwoerd, Hendrik 6, 104, 107, 112, 113, 166
Virginia Park golf course 69, 70
Von Donck, Flory 73
Voortrekkers 15–16
Vorster, Balthazar Johannes 88, 113

Wall Street Journal 287, 295
Waltman, Retief 112
Washington Post 11, 33, 308
Watson, Bubba 1, 266–268, 290
Watson, Denis 46
Watson, Tom 4, 84–85, 87, 89, 146, 150, 153, 198, 253, 254

Webber, Teddy 55
Weir, Mike 258
Westwood, Lee 254, 255, 267, 275
Wilkes, Brian 71
Williams, Steve 190–191, 194
Wind, Herbert Warren 93, 236
Windsor Castle 3
woman champions, South Africa 13
Women's Professional Golf Association 127
women's tennis 131
Wood, Craig 242, 243
Woods, Earl 79–80, 295, 296
Woods, Tiger 79, 158, 179, 281
 2000 US Open at Pebble Beach 162–164
 and 2010 Open Championship, St Andrews 1
 2011 Masters, Augusta 269–270
 childhood 295
 early achievements 164–165
 and Elin Nordegren 298
 and Els 162–164, 173, 175, 189–191, 197–199, 299
 extramarital affairs 299
 and Goosen 208

 and Immelman 226, 229, 233, 235, 236, 237, 239, 297
 and James Kamte 302
 and Mandela 296
 other golfers on 297–298
 and Price 158, 160
 and Schwartzel 270
 slump from 2009 298
 swing of 256
 temperament 297
 transformation of golf 295–296
 violation of Rule 26 47, 299
World Cross-Handed Tournament 95
World Golf Hall of Fame 53, 92, 160, 197
World of Golf 304
Wright, Mickey 129–131
Wulff, Graham 97–103, 116

Yalta Court, Yeoville 41, 53, 55

Zimbabwe 9
 liberation 139
 liberation war 141, 143–144
Zingg, Paul 23
Zoeller, Fuzzy 153, 231

Do you have any comments, suggestions or
feedback about this book or any other Zebra Press titles?
Contact us at **talkback@zebrapress.co.za**

*

Visit **www.randomstruik.co.za** and subscribe
to our newsletter for monthly updates and news